One

A lice Castle left the factory gates at two o'clock but instead of going straight home she walked through the town. She was restless and unhappy without being able to understand exactly why. It was April 1944 and the war showed no sign of ending, the routine of factory work throughout the gloomy winter months had perhaps taken its toll, and the seaside town of St David's Well was certainly dull and weary after almost five years of war. There were plenty of reasons to be lacking in joy. But the unhappiness, the restlessness, was from inside her. A dread feeling that nothing would change except for the worse.

The two rooms which she had furnished simply, almost sparsely, where she waited for her soldier husband, Eynon Castle, to come home, were uninviting on this Saturday afternoon, and although the holiday crowds hadn't begun to fill the town with their excitement, she headed for the beach. She wanted to lose herself among people, strangers who expected nothing from her.

She felt in her pocket for the letter she had received the previous day. Perhaps she would take it to show Eynon's parents. Marged and Huw were always grateful for news. Letters were all they had to convince themselves that the war would eventually come to an end and Eynon would come home safely. But she wouldn't go today. Today she wouldn't be capable of supporting Marged and Huw – she was too miserable to be any help to them.

The town was so drab on that Saturday. It was dark for an April afternoon with a drizzly rain adding to Alice's mood of despair. Exhaustion showed on the faces of the people passing by: the war had gone on so long and little by little the everyday fabric of life was being lost.

1

A laugh rang out and she turned to see two women exchanging parcels. 'I don't like parsnips but I bought some anyway,' one was saying. 'I know your lot enjoy them.'

'And I've got a few new potatoes from Alfie's allotment for you.' Still laughing, the two women walked on and disappeared into one of the cafes. Alice's mood lifted. She was wrong: people were a long way from despair and she was the only one feeling miserable that day. Summer was coming and the beach would be the same as always. Even with the lack of fathers, the sands would be filled with children having fun, while mothers and grandparents looked proudly on.

Posters advertising forthcoming events were already displayed in shop windows and on notice boards throughout the town. The summer entertainments attracted great numbers and there were groups peering at the list of promised attractions. Inter-school cricket, fancy-dress parades, best-dressed dolls, gardens competitions, cheap days on the seaside fairground rides. The list went on with something for everyone. Concerts were planned for fund-raising and an auction of unwanted items was advertised with the proceeds going to the charity that sent parcels to prisoners of war. Alice smiled as she remembered the many happy events organized by her friend Eirlys Ward in previous summers. Eirlys's enthusiasm showed no sign of flagging.

The beach was sombre, yet even on such a day as this, with rain clouds low, obliterating the distant sea and the far-off coast of Somerset, there was a hint of the magical days to come. Hidden behind the dark curtains of intermittent rain there was a feeling of hope, the promise of better things to come. Even in her mood of melancholy she could feel it, a certain something in the air.

Soaked but as always soothed by the constancy of the sea, she began to walk towards the bus stop. There was no one else waiting and restlessly she turned again to look at the sea.

A few of the gift shops and cafes were open, evidence that St David's Well Bay was slowly wakening after its winter slumbers. The season was barely begun though people were trickling in as the days grew longer and the sun strengthened, but today, with the drizzle and the overcast sky there were

2

only a few braving the weather to sit on the sheltered seat on the promenade and no one was dancing about at the edge of the icily cold waves.

She looked around her to find something to tell Eynon in her next letter. He loved hearing about the beach. Leaning on the stout sea wall and staring across to where the tide was washing the edges of the rocks around the headland, she forced the remnants of her melancholic mood from her and tried to imagine Eynon down there on the sand, chivying the holidaymakers and day trippers to pay for a ride.

She walked along the prom and, finding a sheltered corner, she took out the most recent letter she had received from her soldier husband and reread it. Eynon had always loved the beach. From a small child he had worked with his parents and his Uncle Bleddyn: serving on the stalls, helping with the helter-skelter and the swingboats, his cheerful patter enticing the visitors to enjoy the fun.

Alice glanced up to where his parents would be serving customers with snacks. Tomorrow she would go and help, but today was a day to wallow in self-pity and dream of Eynon's return. A bus appeared, turning the corner at the other side of the bay, and she ran and jumped on.

The shops were crowded with shoppers, even on such a dismal day. Water dripped from hat brims, umbrellas caused irritation and little comfort, water underfoot chilled weary feet. Most women carried empty baskets, searching for something to satisfy their families' appetites and provide an interesting meal. The entrance to the town's market, where it was at least dry, was crowded with those trying to get in and others reluctant to leave its shelter.

There was a queue at the fish stall, where fresh fish had arrived. At the fruit and vegetable stalls in the market people crowded around, hands waving, hoping to buy some of the green stuff and potatoes before even that meagre supply ran out.

Her brother-in-law, Eynon's brother Ronnie, ran the stall and, seeing her, he waved and pointed to a brown paper bag near the till. 'Hang about, Alice, I've got some tiddly carrot thinnings. Mr Gregory sent them.'

3

'Where's ours then?' a woman demanded, and others echoed her complaint.

Ronnie spread his hands and apologized. 'Sorry I am, Mrs, but these are nothing more than scraps, honest, not enough to share. But soon there'll be fresh carrots and lettuce and tomatoes and you'll be able to eat your fill.'

'Eat our fill? That'll be the day, Ronnie.'

Alice waited until the customers had been served, then thanked Ronnie and accepted the gift. Small they might be, but fresh vegetables were welcome.

'Good news about our Beth, eh?' Ronnie said with a wide smile. 'Imagine her with a baby boy.' He was referring to his sister Beth who, until the birth of her son, had run the busy market cafe.

Their words were overheard and the busy shoppers all added their good wishes with demands that Beth get back as soon as possible to her cafe. 'This new girl doesn't make a cup of tea like your Beth,' was the general opinion. Ronnie promised to hurry her up. 'I'll get the little chap into school as quick as I can,' he joked.

Alice stayed to share news of the family with him for a while, then left the busy market and the patient customers searching for something tasty that wasn't on ration, and headed for home.

Aware of a deep, bone-aching tiredness, she went home to write to Eynon and then sleep. Tomorrow was Sunday and a welcome day off from the noise and smells of the factory. She listed in her head all the tasks she would do. She wanted everything perfect for when Eynon came home and with talk of the Second Front and an invasion of Europe, it had to be soon. She skipped the last few steps in a sudden surge of excitement, imagining Eynon appearing at the door, calling her name. Closing the door behind her, the silence once more surrounded her and the room locked her into its loneliness.

One Sunday morning a few weeks later, she awoke early to the sound of rain. There wouldn't be much business on the beach today. Perhaps Eynon's parents wouldn't need her to help in their cafe and she could use her day off catching up with some routine housework and write a long loving letter

4

to Eynon. And to daydream about his return. Daydreams that were becoming harder to create. She could picture Eynon in her mind's eye, but wondered if the man who came home to her would be the same one who went away.

She looked at the front page of the morning newspaper and sighed. Fighting was still continuing in Italy, North Africa and Burma. The rumours of a Second Front to take the battle into Europe had grown into an imminent certainty but now, in May 1944, there was no news of the invasion. Eynon would not be home for a long time yet. She wasn't even sure where he was. The last time he had written he was in North Africa but waiting for a new posting.

Alice had married Eynon in September 1942 and after only two days together, he had gone back to his unit and she'd had only letters to reassure her that he still loved her and was longing for their reunion. What if he had changed? Until he had joined the Army, all his life had been spent here, in St David's Well, a small seaside town on the coast of South Wales. To have experienced so much, how could he return and be the same person?

And what about herself? Would he find her changed from the woman he had married? She was no longer the timid Alice Potter who had looked after her sick father, a man whose mood could change from amiability to wild rage in moments and who needed all her understanding. Colin Potter had been a boxer and had suffered brain-damage during his last fight. She lay there, looking out of the bedroom window, the gloomy view of the houses opposite blurred by the falling rain, and remembered.

With her mentally ill father she had lived in a derelict property that had once been a shop. The only rooms that were at all safe to use were two bedrooms and a tiny kitchen. The living room, with its two chairs and a wireless, where they occasionally sat, had been damp, the plaster falling from the walls exposing the old stone, and an ill-fitting window threatening to fall out at any moment. Her attempts to keep the awful place clean had been futile but she hadn't complained, believing they had no money for anything better. Then Colin had died and she found his savings. Enough for her to have made his last years comfortable. But he had been determined to leave the money to her, his last, loving gesture and one that even now made tears form in her eyes.

She would have remained that timid person her father had known if she hadn't met and married Eynon Castle and become a member of his busy family. She had been so lacking in confidence she had found it impossible to offer an opinion that differed from others and she had dressed in what his sister Beth had once called, 'Pretend I'm not here' clothes. Dull, unobtrusive, that was how she would have stayed. Even when she helped on the beach during the busy summer season she had found herself a place in the kitchen away from the lively crowds. But being forced to work in a factory with girls from every walk of life had changed her as nothing else could.

She quickly realized that she needed to cope with their teasing, her nicknames, their sometimes ribald remarks about her naivety or be completely defeated. She dealt with them by laughing with them, exaggerating her own failings and adding to their conviction of her unworldliness and innocence. Now she was no longer apart from the rest, she gave witty answers as swiftly as the best of them. But, she wondered, would Eynon still love her, now she had changed?

It was too early to worry about getting up and she took out all the letters she had received and picked a few at random to read through. A couple of hours later, putting the letters carefully away in the box she kept on her bedside table, she dressed and caught a bus to the beach. Whatever the weather, the Castles' cafes and stalls and rides on the sands would be open for business to anyone who wanted to come. If Eynon's parents needed her assistance she would willingly use her only day off doing what she could. It brought Eynon closer to be with his family, knowing herself to be a part of it. Or, she amended, if not truly accepted as one of them, at least able to share a little in their busy day and surely find something interesting to include in Eynon's letters.

The Castle family was well known in St David's Well. Marged Castle's grandparents, called Piper, had started the business by opening the cafe high above the sands which could be reached from the footpath around the cliff top or by using metal steps that led up from the beach. They owned several beach stalls, selling the usual seaside requirements for a day on the sands, as well as the helter-skelter, a children's roundabout and the popular swingboats, all of which stayed on the sand all summer and were stored away throughout the winter. There was also a fish and chip cafe in the town, run by her father-in-law and Huw's brother, Bleddyn.

As it was Sunday and the town cafe was closed, Alice expected both brothers to be manning the beach stalls and rides but there was no sign of them. Huddled in the doubtful shelter of the deckchair store were eight donkeys and beside them mournfully puffing on his pipe sat their owner, the donkey man, Bernard Gregory. When Alice made her way across the raindrop-pitted sand of the beach, she saw that Huw and Bleddyn were with him.

'Not many customers today, then,' she called as she struggled with her umbrella against gusts of wind that threatened to make her airborne. 'I've called to see if you wanted any help, but I don't see a queue of customers.'

'More sense than us, young Alice,' Bernard replied. 'Gone back to bed the whole bang lot of 'em, I reckon.'

'I'll be glad when we get them weather forecasts again,' Huw grunted. 'Then we could stay in bed too.'

'Ridiculous precaution if you ask me.' Bleddyn's bearded face split to show strong even teeth as he laughed. 'I can't see how it would help Hitler by knowing the rain is going to soak us and the donkeys, can you?'

On being told that Marged was in the cafe serving the few stalwarts who had braved the downpour, Alice left them and, as the tide was out, made her way up the metal steps to the cafe above.

'Alice, love, there's good of you to come.' Marged smiled a greeting as her daughter-in-law stepped inside and hooked her umbrella on the top of the steps. 'Not rushed off our feet, but Bernard says it will stop soon and we'll have a dry afternoon.'

Alice looked out of the window where rain streamed down the glass, distorting the view of the beach. She pulled a face showing her doubt.

'He's usually right, mind,' Marged said, 'even if he does go by cows and birds and clouds and things. Country-man our Bernard is, and they know how to read the signs.'

Taking off her coat, Alice washed her hands, accepted an apron and began mixing the ingredients for Welsh-cakes, the flat, tasty cakes that were cooked on a heavy metal plate locally called a bakestone. Not as much fruit as there used to be, and the proportions of fat to flour had changed dramatically, but freshly cooked and served warm, they were still a popular item with the visitors.

'Have you heard from either of the boys?' Alice asked.

'Bleddyn had a letter from his Johnny, but nothing from our Eynon.' She looked hopefully at her daughter-in-law. 'Have you had a letter?'

Alice fingered her most recent letter from Eynon and hesitantly handed it to Marged. 'You can read this one if you like.'

Letters within the family were shared but were usually read out so the personal, loving words could be held back, savoured by the recipient alone. But news had been scarce over recent weeks and Marged's hopeful enquiry was something she couldn't ignore. She went on with the cake mixture as Marged read the short note. There was little in this one to mull over, few clues to help them work out where he was and what he was doing. Assurances of his love were brief too.

'I suppose he didn't have time to write more,' Alice said, tucking the precious letter back in her pocket. 'Sometimes they have to move with hardly any time to pack let alone write to us.'

'As long as we keep writing to them,' Marged said softly. 'And at least we can share. Bleddyn reads Johnny's letters to Hannah and the girls as well as his own, and I get to share yours.' Impulsively she hugged Alice. 'I'm so lucky that our Eynon married you, Alice. You've been such a comfort and us Castles are so glad to have you in the family.'

Alice couldn't return the hug without covering Marged

with flour, so she kissed her on the cheek instead, warmed by the show of affection.

'Right then,' Huw announced from the doorway. 'Where's our cup of tea, our Marged? Three thirsty men you've got waiting here.' He watched as Alice placed the first of the Welsh-cakes on the bakestone and added, 'And a couple of them wouldn't be a bad idea either.'

Their conversation, between serving the straggling line of soggy customers, was about the birth of Beth's baby. 'It's funny to think that I'm an Auntie,' Alice mused. 'It makes me feel older somehow.' She told them about the demands of the market customers for Beth to return to the cafe as soon as possible.

'I hope she'll stay home for a while,' Marged said. 'Enjoy the early years with the little boy, but I can't suggest it. Nothing kept me away from the beach for long, even having four children didn't persuade me to stay home.'

Bleddyn explained that his daughter-in-law, Hannah, had promised to look after the little boy as soon as Beth felt ready to leave him.

'That's all right now,' Marged said. 'But when the war's over and your Johnny comes home, she might want to stay at home.'

'The girls will work something out. Capable they are, your Beth and our Hannah.'

At three o'clock, when the rain had stopped but the day was still reluctant to brighten, Alice left. A couple of local boys had arrived willing to work on the stalls and with their help, Marged, Huw and Bleddyn would cope for the couple of hours left of the miserable day. Bernard Gregory admitted he had been wrong and led his string of donkeys off the beach and headed for home to Peter and Beth and his new grandson.

As she approached Holby Street, where she had two rooms and the use of the kitchen, Alice turned away. Instead of going home she went to see Marged's sister, Audrey. She needed to talk to someone and Marged, although loving and kind, was too close to Eynon to enable her to be honest. The restlessness had been revived by talk about Beth's baby and she recognized it as a slow growing fear. How would she react to Eynon's return? Would they greet each other as lovers or strangers? Would their reunion be awkward and end in failure? These problems were not subjects to discuss with Eynon's mother.

In the flat above the cafe she owned, Audrey invited her to stay and have tea with them. Audrey's recently acquired second husband, Keith, and the two orphaned girls Maude and Myrtle, to whom Audrey had given a home, sensed Alice's need to talk. Audrey made an excuse for Alice to go with her for a walk while the girls prepared their meal. Maude and Myrtle offered to make pancakes with a couple of precious eggs and a sprinkling of diluted vinegar as a pretence of lemon.

The weather was still dull and with the day approaching its end, the prospect of a walk was hardly enticing but they shrugged themselves into coats, hats and scarves and set off through the gloomy wet streets.

'There's nothing wrong, is there?' Audrey enquired. 'Have you heard from Eynon? Is he all right? So worrying, this talk of the Second Front. I sometimes think people forget that it's our young men and women they're sending out there, cheerfully waving them off to risk their lives. Victory at any price sounds noble but they won't all come back to enjoy it, will they? That aspect of war seems to be ignored by the people who write slogans on walls demanding a "Second Front Now". If only there was another way of defeating the enemy instead of sending people to be—' She stopped as she realized that Alice was struggling to hold back tears. 'Oh, Alice, how thoughtless of me. You haven't heard for a while, is that it? You're worried about our Eynon and there's me prattling on in my stupid way.' She hugged the girl and Alice allowed tears to fall. 'You'll get a letter soon, dear, you know how the post piles up and you don't hear, then it comes when you've almost given up hope. Remember that time when you had five letters on the same day? How lovely that was.'

'I have heard and Eynon is all right – so far as I know,' Alice assured her in a voice muffled by her handkerchief.

'I just wish this war would end and he could come home. I miss him, Auntie Audrey and – and I don't feel certain that he's missing me.'

'What a lot of rot, dear. I can't think what's got into you, thinking such nonsense. I hear from Eynon too, remember, he's that good at writing to us all, and all he thinks about is coming back to you.'

'We were married for two days and he went away. I won't know how to act towards him, he'll be a stranger,' Alice whispered, turning away to hide her blushes as she thought about sleeping with a man she hardly knew.

Audrey guessed what she was thinking and busied herself by unnecessarily adjusting her scarf and refastening her coat buttons, avoiding Alice's eyes. Then she said, 'Can you imagine how difficult it was for me when I married Keith? I'd known your Uncle Wilf all my life, there had never been anyone else, and then at my age to start again with another man, well, I was very anxious. In fact I was afraid I would fail and make us both very unhappy.'

'And was it as difficult as you expected, allowing another man to become a part of your life?'

'Alice, love, it wasn't difficult at all. I love him you see. Oh, I know people of my age aren't supposed to have such feelings but I love him and he loves me. Yet he had doubts similar to mine and they almost ended it before it had begun. Once we were honest with each other, reassured each other, everything was perfect. So you see, dear, you aren't alone. In fact, look at the houses on this street alone. Each one hides at least one person with anxieties about the end of the war. Concentrate on making Eynon happy and it will happen just like in your dreams, just like it did for Keith and me.'

Alice felt better for having spoken her fears aloud and when they returned to Keith and the two girls, apart from a voice that sounded as though it came through her nose, she had recovered. Audrey had made some soup with some oddments of vegetables and thickened with split peas which they ate with some freshly baked bread, followed by the luxury 'afters' of pancakes. Alice went home feeling better than she had for weeks. Although she still hadn't admitted the other half of her fear, that she might not feel the same towards Eynon. Her recurring melancholic mood returned.

She tried to visualize him and when she couldn't she panicked and took out the few photographs they had taken and stared at his face. She stared and stared – and saw a stranger.

Keith had said that the war news was hopeful, Italy would soon be free of German troops and once the Second Front opened and the Allied forces were back in France they would advance rapidly towards Berlin. 'You mark my words, we'll be in Berlin for Christmas,' he had predicted, offering up a silent prayer.

Alice had a surprise visitor almost a week later. Audrey called on Friday morning before Alice left to start her afternoon shift at the factory.

'A bit worried I was, dear. You were feeling a bit low on Sunday and I wanted to reassure myself you were all right. I couldn't get away before today.'

'Thank you, Auntie Audrey. I'm all right now. I get a bit miserable sometimes, like most of us, the weeks turn into months and years and still there's no sign of an end to this war. I want Eynon home so we can start our life together. I don't have much hope of him coming home before September and then we'll have been married for two years. Two years. There's nothing to show for it apart from letters, and it sometimes feels unreal, as though it never really happened.'

While Alice busied herself making tea, Audrey looked around the sparsely furnished room. The curtains were thin, and the tea towels and hand towels draped across the line close to the fireplace were worn ragged. Alice's clothes were old and ill-fitting. She knew it wasn't money or even rationing that had caused the rooms to be so poorly furnished and lacking in comfort. It was because Alice was saving all the best, all the wedding presents they had received, for when Eynon came home.

'Have you heard about Davies's shop selling damaged stock?' she asked as Alice handed her a cup of tea. 'Cassie Davies who has the drapers on Crown Street has been promised some damaged, off-ration linen. The sale is tomorrow –

shall we go? You could do with a few replacements and I know you want to save the best for when Eynon is home.'

'I'm working at two o'clock,' Alice said doubtfully.

'She opens at nine. I bet if we're there at half eight we'll get in first and find a few bargains. Is that too early for you after working till ten tonight? I desperately need some tea towels for the cafe and there might be a few other things.'

'I'll meet you there at half eight.' Alice looked quite excited. 'I wonder what she'll have? I'd love to get a couple of cushions, this room doesn't look like a home, does it?'

'To me, it looks like a lady-in-waiting – for her husband to come back and her life to begin.' Audrey sipped her tea. 'Come on, dear, drink up and I'll walk you to the factory gates.'

'On the way we can stop at the shop and see what she's advertising,' Alice said as she gathered her coat and handbag.

Cassie Davies closed the shop that evening, cursing the continuing need for blackout. Even with the lighter evenings, the windows had to be covered in case she needed to come back for some reason, like the time she had a break-in and the police had to go inside. She shuddered at the memory, and leaned against the door to make sure it was firmly locked. After dropping the bank bag with the day's takings into the night safe, she hurried home. It was Friday and Joseph would be home.

She had the accounts books under her arm. Just returned from the accountants, they showed a very healthy profit. Joseph would be pleased. Taking advantage of the many marriages in the town, with couples being given dockets to spend on their new homes, Cassie had made sure she had a good selection and offered prices that persuaded them to spend their money with her rather than go further afield. With her plans to open a second shop selling mostly damaged stock, and sub-standard oddments, tomorrow's sale was a try-out, to see how the idea of imperfect items was received. Then there was the off-ration cotton knitting yarn. Nothing more than dishcloth yarn really but it would sell if she called it 'fabric strands' suitable for modern attire. It was much harder to knit, stiff and unwieldy, lacking the softness of wool, and sometimes, even with the most expert knitters, it resulted in shapeless garments, but after years of shortages, people were only too glad to give it a try. Pity about the peculiar colours, and the unreliable dyes.

Before finding herself something to eat, she sat and went through the details of the second shop. When Joseph came home at ten o'clock she would have all the facts to set before him. There was even a young woman ready to take over the running of the place. All it needed was Joseph's signature on a few forms and they could open the shop in a couple of weeks, just in time to interest the day trippers and summer visitors that would soon fill the town, people with a few extra shillings to spare and an eagerness to take home a bargain.

This war had certainly brought her and Joseph wealth. With no sons or daughters to worry about, and only a cat to feed, theirs had been a moderately trouble-free war. Joseph had been too old to serve and they had no relations to give them concern. No friends either, she thought with a wave of disappointment. All their efforts had gone into building the business.

She did regret not having children, although, she thought with a sigh of relief, if they had had them they would have been at the age to be called into the Army with all the accompanying worries that would have brought. She had wanted children but Joseph kept on telling her there was plenty of time. Next year, or the year after that, they would make that important decision. Always, when she tried to discuss it, 'today' was not the right time; the business had to come first so they had a sound financial base, something to offer a child. And now she was sixty and it was too late. Loneliness was something she pretended to ignore. Instead she concentrated on plans for their retirement to that cottage they had dreamed of in one of the beautiful villages in the Vale of Glamorgan.

With Joseph away all through the week and even some weekends, on secret war work, she had filled her time over the past five and a half years working at ways of increasing their income. All day in the shop and most evenings she pored over books and considered offers and deals. It had paid off and this latest plan would increase their wealth even more.

At ten o'clock she turned off the wireless and sat sewing, waiting to hear his key in the lock. She had looked through the fire-damaged stock she had bought ready for tomorrow's sale and was considering the best way to display it. Most of the towels, tea towels and pillow cases had been folded and the damage was on the folds. One or two of the towels she had cut into four, removing the damage to make face flannels.

Several dozen tea towels had been burned along the top and bottom edge and she was cutting the singed strips and hemming them neatly. If she repaired a few to show the customers what could be done it might increase sales, not that she envisaged any difficulty selling what she had bought. People were so desperate to replenish the basics, they wouldn't even examine them before handing over the money. Perhaps if she sewed some ribbon over the scorch marks across the folds of pillow cases she might sell those as well. Engrossed in her tasks, she was startled when eleven o'clock struck. Where was Joseph? Perhaps the trains had been delayed again.

She set aside her work and slowly her eyes closed. When she woke again, she was stiff, cold and her sewing had fallen to the floor. A glance at the clock told her it was 6 a.m. It looked as though she would have to manage the sale on her own. Joseph must have been unable to get away. It happened sometimes, more frequently over recent weeks. It was probably to do with this Second Front. Army vehicles and men were gradually crowding into the coastal areas, or so she'd been told: it must be imminent and needing his expertise. Although exactly what that expertise was, she had no idea.

The secrecy surrounding his work included wives and families. He didn't discuss what he did. Careless talk costs lives, the posters warned them, and she was proud of his integrity, although at times like this she wished they had a telephone so he could at least warn her not to expect him.

She gathered up the work, and put it ready to take to the shop, made herself a hot drink and tried to settle to sleep for the two hours she had left. Irritation that she was having to

15

deal with the sale without help soon passed. It would be more to tell Joseph and she smiled as she imagined his delight at the way she was managing their business. The politicians were always reminding the women about doing their bit. Well, Joseph would have nothing to criticize when he finally came back to a business that had more than doubled in size since he had been called away to do important war work.

News of the sale of damaged stock had spread around the town and when Alice went to meet Audrey she had difficulty in finding her at first. Although they were early, a queue of hopefuls had already curled around the corner, up a side street and along the lane at the back of the premises. Inside the shop, Cassie was moving chairs and a couple of tables so she could control the people coming in and going out. At nine o'clock she took a deep breath and opened the door.

'Only three people in the shop at a time,' she ordered and obediently they patiently waited until the first three had been served before a second group entered. Audrey was about twenty behind the first trio.

When Alice eventually entered the shop, the queue of people was becoming less orderly. Three at a time meant a long wait before the queue moved, and once inside the shop, customers took their time examining all that was on offer. Cassie began to worry. If only Joseph were here to help he would have bustled this lot out ages ago.

'Please hurry, ladies,' she asked briskly. 'Remember all those busy ladies waiting outside in the cold.'

There were a few who pushed in before their turn, others shouted that they had to get to work, those who were less tolerant complained that it was draughty on the corner and the less polite shouted for her to 'Shift yer arse.' Alice could see that the woman serving was getting in a state. Impulsively she said, 'Mrs Davies, can I come round and help? Everything is marked and I can stay for a couple of hours if you like.'

Cassie looked at Alice, recognized her as one of the Castles, and in desperation agreed. 'Thanks, I think they'll invade the place and help themselves if I don't serve them quicker than this.' She briefly explained about the limit she put on individual purchases so everyone waiting had a chance of something, and Alice began to help her attend to the now thoroughly irritable crowd.

Between serving customers now moving more quickly through the shop, Cassie told Alice that her husband had been detained and hadn't come home to help her. 'Important war work, see,' she said. 'Some weekends he can't get home. I know he'd be here if he could, but there you are, we all have to make sacrifices until the battle's won.' Alice said nothing, thinking how fortunate the woman was to have her husband home most weekends.

Audrey called back at one o'clock when the shop was closing for lunch and invited Alice to go to the cafe for a snack before going to work. 'We've got some chips and a bit of spam and some bread and butter,' she promised.

Alice gratefully agreed it would be better than going back to her cold room for a slice of bread and marmite. 'I only have an hour, mind,' she said doubtfully.

Audrey assured her there was plenty of time to eat and get back to the factory by two o'clock. 'That was kind of you to help Cassie Davies like that. I could see she was in a bit of a state. Fancy not getting some extra help. Too mean to pay for an assistant she is. Skin a flea for a ha'penny she would. I bet she didn't give you anything either.'

Alice smiled. 'I was offered a few pillowcases that were so singed across the folds that they cracked when I tried to open them out. I thanked her and declined.'

'Stingy old devil!'

'But she did let me have six tea towels, Auntie Audrey, and I want you to have them. I can manage and when Eynon comes home and I unpack my wedding presents, I'll have plenty. With the cafe you need them more than me.'

Audrey protested but Alice insisted and they found that apart from needing a wash the huckaback towels were perfect.

'Oh well, she isn't so bad after all,' Audrey said. Alice didn't tell her that Cassie had made her pay for them and her only thanks for helping that morning had been a promise to find Alice a couple of cushion covers when she next went to the warehouse.

17

Working the 2 p.m. to 10 p.m. shift meant a late night for Alice. Getting home after eight hours in the factory she couldn't go straight to bed and sleep. She needed a few hours to unwind from the thumping and wailing of the machines and the chemical smells that clung to her skin and that even a wash and fresh clothes failed to disperse. She lit the electric fire that stood in the grate, made herself a snack and sat with the tray nearby and wrote to Eynon.

Writing regularly was easier than the occasional notes she wrote to Eynon's cousin Johnny. The trivia of each day gave her a thread to follow and details in which he wouldn't normally be interested filled the pages in her small writing. Telling him about how she ended up behind the counter of Cassie Davies's shop became an amusing incident, and having lunch with his Auntie Audrey filled a page too.

She ate the toast and jam and drank the tea and dreamed of the day she would no longer have to fill her writing pad with unnecessary words, and instead could hold him and whisper all he needed to know.

She rose late the following morning to a bright day, with the rain clouds of the last few days driven from the sky and everywhere glistening in the spring sunshine. She had a few hours before starting work at two o'clock and once again, the beach beckoned. She would see Eynon's parents. Perhaps they would have had a letter.

A sulky-looking girl was serving a trickle of customers with teas and coffees and, walking past her with a brief nod, Alice found Huw and Marged in the cafe kitchen.

'Useless she is,' Marged was saying in a harsh whisper. 'Miserable face she got, worse than rain to drive the customers away that face is.'

'We have to keep her until we get someone else,' Huw muttered.

'No use nor ornament our Mam would have said.' She sighed. 'If only our Lilly would help.'

'Don't go down that path, Marged. It's a waste of time. You know if she doesn't want to do something, our Lilly's face would be worse than a thunderstorm.' Huw saw Alice then and smiled a welcome.

'Where is everyone?' Alice asked, going to the sink and beginning to wash dishes.

'You can well ask. Young Stanley is still at the shop where he's worked all winter, hanging on one more week he is, working out his notice. Maude and Myrtle are helping Auntie Audrey in her cafe, as you know. And girls like her –' she pointed to where the assistant was laboriously wiping the counter – 'worse than useless, she gets in the way of those of us who do work! More lazy than our Lilly would be – if that's possible.'

'I have a week off starting Friday. Holidays I saved in case Eynon managed some leave, but I have to take it, so I'll come and give you a hand, shall I?'

Relief softened Marged's rather severe expression and she hugged the girl. 'Thanks, you're a dear girl.'

'The boys will soon be home now the invasion is about to begin.'

'Hush!' Huw warned. 'Careless talk costs lives, remember!'

Alice clapped her hands over her mouth, leaving soapy suds on her face. Huw tilted his head on one side and teased, 'No, our Alice, a beard wouldn't suit you.'

Alice smiled as she wiped her face. 'Our' Alice. She loved being reminded that she belonged to the Castle family.

Marged and Huw had four children. Ronnie was married to Olive and they had a little girl. Ronnie had been invalided out of the Army and now ran a fruit and vegetable stall in the town's market. Beth was married to Peter Gregory, the donkey man's son, and she too worked in the market, running the small, busy cafe for shoppers and stall-holders. Or had done until her son had arrived.

Their daughter Lilly had produced a daughter while unmarried and had then married a man much older than herself after first becoming friends with the man's soldier son. Lilly was a lazy girl and had never willingly worked in the family business on the sands, and now, knowing the difficulties Marged and Huw faced getting suitable staff, she insisted she was too busy looking after her daughter and husband.

Then there was their youngest, Alice's husband, Eynon.

Eynon had never wanted anything other than a life working on the sands, helping visitors to enjoy their stay in St David's Well. In a mood of bravado he had followed his friend Freddy Clements into the recruiting office and signed up as a regular. Bullying had led to him absconding, and during the time he was being hunted by the Military Police, Alice had helped him and love had grown. They had married and spent a brief few days together before he'd had to return to his unit.

She stayed in the cafe until twelve thirty, then caught the bus back to change and get ready for work. Marged gave her a couple of pasties and some Welsh-cakes and she carried them with her through the gates at five minutes to two. She would eat them during her break. Another piece of useless information to tell Eynon in tonight's letter, she thought with a sad smile.

When she went out the following morning, a young woman was walking past the house with a little boy on reins struggling to run ahead and a younger child in her arms. The boy's reins were made of leather with straps leading back from the shoulders and others fastened at his waist. On the ornate leather front, bells were fastened and the little boy was jigging up and down to make them jingle. The mother pulled impatiently as she struggled with the obviously heavy child in her arms and tried to make the boy walk properly. Alice wondered why the mother didn't have a pushchair.

'Come here, Walter,' the young mother called sharply and the boy turned to stare at Alice.

The boy walked towards Alice and asked, 'Are you her mother, then?' He gestured with a thumb to the child in his mother's arms.

Alice laughed. 'No, I'm not anyone's mother.' She looked at the young woman to share her smile but the woman had turned away and was hurrying back down the road, the boy crying as he was now dragged along, his feet tripping over each other as he tried to catch up.

Another fatherless family she surmised, the little boy perhaps getting muddled between mother and missing father. Then she saw the telegram boy turning the corner on his red bike and held her breath. 'Please don't let it be Eynon,' she whispered and only released her breath when the boy passed her door, rode around another corner and out of sight.

She looked again at the woman with the two children, hurrying down the road. Had she been one of the unlucky ones? Had the red bike and its rider stopped at her door? She shivered as she turned and went up the road to the shops to buy her week's grocery ration. At least, with no news to the contrary, for that moment he was safe. Another day had passed and Eynon was still alive.

Two

I n the house in Sidney Street, Marged woke and, although it was very early, she slid out of bed without disturbing Huw and crept down the stairs. There was so much to do these days. However early she rose, there was never enough time to fit in all she had to do. Once the summer season began bringing the crowds to the town, her days were long. She made a cup of tea, then set up the iron and began dealing with the gingham tablecloths for the cafe on the beach.

It had been so much easier when her mam had been there to help with the many routine tasks, and when her sister, Audrey, had dealt with the housekeeping and much of the cooking. They had worked well together, cogs in the machinery of a St David's Well summer. They'd all had a part to play and the routine rarely faltered. Yet even in those days there had been a rush to get everything done. Now, with Granny Molly Piper dead and Audrey having left them to run a cafe of her own, everything seems to land on my back, she thought with a sigh.

Nursing a second cup of tea, she sat, her eyes looking around the shabby, familiar room in which her children had grown up, ears listening in the silence for echoes of those long-lost days, her nose aware of the fresh smell of the newly ironed linen piled ready to take over the beach. The empty grate needed cleaning and resetting ready for the evening, although she and Huw rarely had time to sit and enjoy it.

The months of May and June were what her mother had referred to as a rehearsal; a slowly increasing introduction to the busy months of July and August, when the town and the beach would be filled with holidaymakers and day trippers. These early months were a time to adjust to the long days and to remind the members of the Castle family of their tasks. May was almost out and the difficulties of finding staff had not been solved.

Knowing it was futile self-indulgence, she sat back and wallowed in her memories. From the end of March, Huw and his brother had always worked on maintenance until the day the beach was open for business. Everything was cleaned, repainted where necessary and repairs dealt with until the stalls were as bright as new and the cafes shone with their efforts.

Before the Army had stolen them away, their four children and Bleddyn's two were as full of enthusiasm as the holidaymakers who came bent on having fun. Now Bleddyn's Taff was dead and Johnny was far away.

She knew she had been more fortunate than some, with only Eynon out there in the fighting. Ronnie was now running his stall though her hopes of him giving it up once summer came had been dashed. Olive had never liked working on the sands but the stall in the town's market was different. She enjoyed selling fruit and vegetables to their regular customers, so Ronnie had stayed on the stall. Beth had also left the beach. Although now, with her new baby, Beth couldn't help, even if she wanted to. If only she could persuade Beth to come back to the beach instead of returning to the cafe, she mused. Beth was so reliable. She had managed to work when her own four were small and between them they could look after this darling little boy. That is, if the will was there – but it wasn't. The war had disrupted families in other ways besides robbing them of their sons. Beth would go back to the cafe as soon as she was able to leave the baby.

She felt irritation rise as she thought of her firstborn, their Lilly. For Lilly, life was a constant game to avoid work. She had never taken to the family business and had become adept at finding excuses to stay away from the stalls and cafes, even when the family was desperately needed, like now. Lilly, she thought with increasing anger, had succeeded in finding the perfect life, married to a man as old as her father, who demanded little and had the money to indulge her.

She reminded herself that the situation was only temporary,

that one day soon, their Eynon and Bleddyn's Johnny would come home and everything would be as it should be. Even as the thought leapt into her mind, a protective false confidence, she knew she was kidding herself no longer. How could anything be the same as before?

It was almost seven thirty and time to wake Huw. She cleaned out the grate and set the paper sticks and cinders ready to light when they returned that evening, then made a fresh pot of tea and went to call him. Her footsteps sounded loud as she walked along the passage to the stairs. In her mind she heard the running footsteps and shouts of long ago as they all tried to get into the bathroom first.

In the house next door, her mam and Audrey would be waking at the same time and they would knock on the wall to reassure each other that all was well. Ronnie and Olive now lived there in rooms upstairs, and with Audrey and Maude and Myrtle now living above Audrey's cafe in the town, the rest of the house next door was as empty as this one.

Carrying the cup of tea, she went in to wake Huw, wondering why everything had to change; why couldn't life stay at the time when everything was perfect? Unaware of her melancholy thoughts, Huw nevertheless answered her.

'Thank goodness we're past the stage of small babies,' he said, taking the cup of tea and drinking gratefully. 'Can you imagine waking up several times each night to pacify a demanding child?'

'I loved it,' Marged said sadly.

'Course you did, Marged, and so did I. But I've loved all the other stages of our life too. Thankful I am that things change and we're still together and can enjoy it all.'

Over several days, Alice saw the young woman watching her. Curious, she tried to approach her and ask what she wanted, but each time the woman turned and hurried away. She saw her twice in the vicinity of her home in Holby Street and several times near the factory gates.

'She seems to be noting my movements,' she told Auntie Audrey, after a week of these odd occurrences.

'Don't let it worry you, dear,' Audrey said. 'She's probably bored, living in a couple of rooms with two small children and she's just filling her time watching others.' Although she reassured Alice that there was nothing to worry about, she mentioned it to Keith, and asked him to look out for the young woman and, if possible, find out something about her. Keith was a builder and he worked in and around the town on building-repair work. It was likely that some time their paths would cross.

Then a week went by without Alice seeing her and the incidents were forgotten in the rising activity in the town as the summer season got underway. Alice had taken the holiday due to her and, relieved to be free from the factory, was helping in the Castles' cafe high above the sands on St David's Well Bay.

'Perhaps she's lost sight of me with the change in my routine,' Alice said when Audrey asked towards the end of the week.

'Or perhaps she's found someone else to be curious about.'

Alice was sorry to finish the week at the beach and have to face returning to the factory. Besides preferring to work out of doors among the cheerful day trippers and holidaymakers, she knew that Marged and Huw were finding it hard managing without sufficient help. They had to depend on seasonal help from strangers, which was anathema to the family-orientated Marged.

Stanley Love, who had come to the town as an evacuee with his two brothers in 1939 and had stayed, was an enthusiastic member of the team. Huw often said that with a couple more like Stanley he could put his feet up. The fifteen-year-old encouraged the hesitant ones, pleaded with the children to ask their mothers to pay for a ride on the helter-skelter or the swingboats, cajoled others to have a second ride and gave cheeky comments that shocked some and amused many. As Huw and Bleddyn often remarked, 'Stanley Love is a natural.'

Like many others who worked on the sands, Stanley had found a job for the winter months and now he had given his notice and looked forward to spending the season helping Huw and Marged, Bleddyn and his wife Hetty with the stalls and rides set up on the sandy beach.

With his brothers, Harold and Percival, Stanley Love lived with Eirlys and Ken Ward, their small son Anthony and Eirlys's father Morgan Price. It was a full and busy household but Eirlys ran it efficiently as she did everything else. She had a very difficult and hectic job organizing the summer entertainments programme in the town. Working out of the council offices, she managed to deal with the various aspects of a complicated schedule, besides running the household efficiently and feeding them all. Her husband, Ken, was also involved with show business, arranging tours and concerts to entertain the forces and factory workers or, to raise money for one of the many war charities. Although their work was similar in nature, they rarely worked together. Ken was often away from home and Eirlys managed the household and her job without apparent regrets at his absences.

As a typically busy person, Eirlys also managed to make items to sell in the gift shop run by friends of hers. Hannah Castle, married to Johnny, was a dressmaker and she did most of her work in the shop. Her father-in-law, Bleddyn, had bought her a second sewing machine to make this possible. Eynon's sister Beth also worked for the shop whenever she could, although, at present she was fully occupied dealing with her cafe and her baby.

For the gift shop there were no fixed hours, the three girls all did what they could and worked together in relaxed harmony. When Eirlys returned to work, Hannah and Alice between them also looked after baby Anthony. Life was complicated but they managed to do what was necessary to enable those who worked to feel confident their children were cared for.

Involving themselves in so many activities was not unusual. Most women in the town did one, two or even three jobs, many of them also sharing child-minding with friends to enable them to work. There was little spare time between work, child-minding, the necessary household chores and the endless search for food, as well as the voluntary work for which most women found at least a few odd moments. The only escape from the frantic hours, and the frustration of trying to feed and clothe their families, was the cinema, giving a glimpse of a pretend life where women were beautiful, lived in palatial houses with teams of servants, dressed in smart clothes and ate wonderful food.

When Hannah and Alice took Hannah's children to the Saturday-morning cinema as a special treat, they saw Lilly strolling through the shops with her daughter, three-year-old Phyllis. They watched as she went into a cafe and, through the window, saw her join a young woman who was trying to control two children who seemed set on destroying the place. They were running around, in and out of the tables, threatening to knock dishes to the floor.

The boy, who looked to be about four years old, was chased and dumped on to a chair and a wagging finger warned him to stay put. Then the little girl of about two years, who, in her excited determination to defy her mother, was unsteady on her feet, was grabbed and pushed, wailing and struggling, into a high chair provided for customers' use. It was a tight squeeze but the mother was determined and the little girl, pouting and red faced, glared and continued her struggles to be free.

'I bet Auntie Audrey's glad they haven't chosen her cafe for their morning coffee,' Alice said with a laugh. 'They look like hard work and I bet young Phyllis won't need much coaxing to join in.' She watched for a moment as the young woman fastened Phyllis's walking reins around the back of a high chair and then gasped and turned to Hannah. 'That's the young woman who seemed to be following me a while back.'

'I wouldn't worry about her. She looks harmless enough.' They were words Alice would remember.

Lilly sat talking to her friend and ignoring the behaviour of the children. Phyllis was usually a placid child, but seeing the little boy getting down from his chair and running around the crowded cafe and the little girl freeing herself from her mother's half-hearted attempts to restrain her and climbing down from the high chair, she was keen to join in the fun. The little girl followed her brother, dragging her reins, which were getting caught in various obstacles, and it was so much like a party, the temptation was too much for her. Down she got and ran with them to the annoyance of other customers.

27

Lilly laughed as Phyllis helped herself to a cake from someone's plate. When the manageress was called, Lilly drew herself up to her full height and complained loudly when she suggested they left.

No one supported her and she huffily dragged her daughter away from where she was attempting to enter the kitchen with her friend's little boy. They were escorted to the door and her surly attempt to pay their bill was waived. 'I'm never coming in here again,' she remarked and the manageress, with great self-control, declined to make the obvious reply.

'Where shall we go?' Lilly asked. 'My sister Beth has a cafe in the market, we could go there. If I tell the temporary assistant who I am we'll probably get a free lunch.'

'The market caff? That's a bit of a comedown after being thrown out of that posh place, isn't it?' They both laughed.

'The beach it is, then. Quick, here's the bus!' They scrambled on and took the back seat, where the three children could look out of the window and Lilly said, 'Like the beach, do you? My family own the rides and stalls on the sand.'

'You aren't related to the Castles, are you?'

'I am. And if they had their way they'd have me slaving away from May till September selling teas and snacks, washing endless dishes, scrubbing floors. Huh, I soon gave that up!'

'But fancy, having all those stalls and things. They must be rich.'

'Not short of a penny,' Lilly agreed. 'And neither am I since I married Sam Edwards.' She turned to her companion. 'What does your husband do?'

'In the Army, I think. He left me before little Dolly was born.'

'Oh, there's sorry I am. My stepson is in the fighting. He's Sam too. His dad worries about him so much.' She laughed at the question forming in her friend's mind. 'Yes, a stepson the same age as me, strange, eh?'

The two women hadn't known each other long. They had met in the small park in the centre of town where they went regularly to allow the children to play. They began to talk, politely at first then they began to share confidences in the fascinating beginnings of friendship. They began to look out for each other and keep a place on a seat, and had recently taken a further step and ended their afternoons by finding a cafe and sitting for a while over coffee, which Lilly hated but considered smart. They had exchanged names, Lilly learning that the girl was nineteen and called Netta Mills.

The age of the little boy, whose name was Walter, made her realize that Netta Mills must have been barely out of school when he was born, but she avoided the topic of dates and ages. After all, her wedding to Sam had taken place long after she had given birth to Phyllis.

Netta lived some distance from the park and said how pleased she was that she had called there one day after visiting the library and had met Lilly.

'I'm pleased too. It's nice to have a friend to talk to. It's lonely sometimes, even with my Sam. Him being so much older than me we run out of things to say.'

At home, Sam was preparing their meal and while the potatoes were cooking ready to mash for the cottage pie, he was finishing ironing Phyllis's little dresses. On the table was a letter from his son. He had opened it and read it and excitement glowed in his eyes. Sam Junior was coming home on leave. Seven days, then he would be sent back. He wondered whether the leave was before Sam was transferred to the army preparing for the invasion of Europe which government officials denied and everyone knew would happen.

He finished the dresses and placed them across a chair. Tomorrow he and Lilly would scour the shops for what food they could find ready to welcome his son home. Perhaps Lilly would help him air the bed and get everything ready, although he doubted it. He had spoilt her and enjoyed doing so, but sometimes lately, when he felt particularly tired, he would have been glad if she would offer to do something other than take Phyllis out, read magazines and listen to the wireless.

The following morning, when Phyllis was ready to go out and Sam was waiting for Lilly, the post came with another letter. This time it was for Lilly and she read it without showing her husband. Sam Senior had recognized the writing and knew it was from his son. He thought perhaps some surprise was being planned. He had a birthday on the thirtieth of June and his son often surprised him by pretending to forget then presenting him with a parcel. He had probably written to ask Lilly to arrange something.

He was smiling as they set off. Many thought his decision to marry a woman half his age was asking for trouble, but he was fond of Lilly and enjoyed spoiling her. And he thought little Phyllis, named after her dead father, Phillip Denver, was a darling.

Marged placed the freshly laundered table cloths on the cafe tables and looked around her. Everything looked perfect. The floor was clean, the windows looking out across the beach were shining. Through them she could see that the sea looked troubled, a gusting wind blowing the waves on to the beach, throwing them about with foamy splendour. Although foamy splendour was not what the visitors wanted. They wanted calm and sunshine and an atmosphere in which to forget worries, not to look out over an angry sea and wonder about the fate of their loved ones.

It was still early, not yet half past eight in the morning but already, Bernard Gregory was below with his donkeys, sheltering near the store of deckchairs. He had told her the wind would go out with the tide. She hoped he was right. It was due to turn within the hour.

A boy she didn't know arrived on a bicycle and handed her a written message. She read it and groaned. Hetty was unable to come in. Huw then told her that Stanley Love had sent a message too. He was unable to leave his job as a shop assistant until the following week.

In desperation, Marged decided to try to persuade Lilly to help. Surely she would spare them an hour or two during the afternoon when she understood how desperate they were?

Sam invited her into the neat terraced house but shook his head when Marged explained the reason for her visit.

'She's out, I'm afraid,' he said. 'She'll be that sorry to have missed you.'

'I'm sure,' Marged said cynically. 'Will you tell her Auntie Hetty is ill and Stanley can't start until next week and we're desperate? If she could help out for a couple of hours around lunchtime and early afternoon, it would be a life-saver.'

'I'll tell her, Marged. Although, I don't expect her back for hours yet. She's meeting a friend and they'll be looking at the shops and you must remember how easy it is to forget the time when you're young.'

'I understand,' Marged sighed, remembering no such thing. She had worked in the family business from a small child and had loved it. 'Tell her, though, will you? Desperate we are, mind.'

As the door closed behind her mother, Lilly came down the stairs hand in hand with Phyllis. 'Sam, dear, you're a wonder. D'you think she suspected? You sounded real convincing to me.'

Smiling happily, Sam said, 'Come on, get your best dresses on. I'm going to take my two beautiful girls out for lunch.'

Cassie Davies's shop had been very busy that day. Another consignment of damaged goods had reached her and the sale had been even more successful than the first. She had even dared to increase the prices a little and the bank bag was satisfyingly full. She hid it in her shopping basket under an apron which she was taking home to wash and locked the shop door.

She was late leaving the premises. Joseph was not coming home and there was no rush, so she had stayed to enter the day's transactions into the accounts book before going home. After the past four and a half years she ought to be used to going back to an empty house but she still found it difficult. Cold, silent and unwelcoming, her first action was always to switch on the electric fire, the second to fill the kettle for a cup of tea. One plate, one cup, one saucer. It was depressing and it was hardly surprising that she wasn't in a rush to get home.

On impulse she didn't go straight to the bank. Audrey Castle, now Mrs Keith Kent, kept her cafe open until nine o'clock. Perhaps she would go there and have something to eat. Only chips, she supposed, but at least there would be other people around, and walking into her hollow-sounding rooms could be delayed for a while at least.

Audrey greeted her politely. As business people they knew each other but had never been more than what Cassie called nodding acquaintances. She gave her order and sat looking around the cafe. Cheerful groups, mostly young people, sat talking and laughing as they ate the simple food. She recognized several shop assistants and a couple from the library, besides the neatly dressed office girls, and factory hands with their overalls and turban headdresses. They were obviously meeting their friends between work and the pictures or before going home or to start the late shift at one of the small factories. It was obviously a popular rendezvous. She smiled at the flirting glances between boys and girls, and felt old.

In the mirrors on the walls she saw herself. She *looked* old. Grey coat, grey hair and tired face. She had never worn make-up and she looked at the young people around her and wondered if she had ever been as beautiful. She thought not. Thank goodness Joseph wasn't interested in beauty. A partner to help him run his business, and make a home for him, that was what Joseph had seen in her and he hadn't been disappointed. She touched the bag hidden in her shopping basket and smiled. Wait till she told him about this week's takings. He would be so proud of her.

Two girls were helping Audrey that evening. Maude and Myrtle lived with Audrey and Keith in the flat above and, when they weren't helping Audrey in the cafe, Cassie knew they were at the beach filling in a few hours at the Castles' beach stalls and rides. Now, when there was no one demanding their attention they sat with their friends while keeping an eye on the tables in case they were needed, joining in the conversations and the laughter.

With everyone so busy these days, it was nice to think young people had time for some fun. She enjoyed the meal Audrey had provided, and sat, relaxing over a second cup of tea, enjoying the buzz of conversation around her, the laughter and the comings and goings of the customers, most of whom greeted Audrey by name.

By comparison, her own life was dull – like I am, she

thought, with another glance at her sombre self in the mirror. She patted the bank bag again but the excitement of the successful week seemed less of a joy. It was nine o'clock when Audrey and the two girls were joined by Audrey's husband to close the place, but still Cassie didn't leave.

She began a conversation and pretended to be unaware of Audrey's reluctance to participate. She didn't want to go home and face another lonely night. Tomorrow was Sunday and the hours stretched out empty and long. When she could delay the woman no longer, even with the promise of some more tea towels, she left through the door where the blackout curtaining was in place although it was hardly dark, only the dull day making it appear later than it was.

She was unaccountably tired and she thought she might forget the bank and take the bank bag home. She could always pop it into the night-safe tomorrow. Sunday was a dull day with only the accounts book for company – it would be an excuse to go out. Searching in her shopping bag, she found her torch and headed for the railway arch.

Sam pulled up his coat collar. Rain had ended the day early and the streets were gloomy and chill. It was hard to remember that in a few days' time they would be into the month of June. He paused near the beach and glanced across the cold water, wondering when the armies of liberation would set off on their dangerous mission.

Experience of the previous war brought pictures to his mind of men, vehicles and animals bogged down, drowning in deep, foul-smelling mud and he hoped today's men would fare better. Thank goodness that in two more days Sam junior would be home. War made you very selfish, he thought. He offered sympathy to the bereaved but in his heart were grateful thanks that the victim was not his son.

It was surprisingly cold and he moved faster. Perhaps he would take a short cut through the alleyway that went under the railway line. He took out a torch, pulled his collar even higher and hunched himself into his coat and, head bent low, entered the darker shadows of the arch.

*   *   *

33

Cassie hesitated at the railway arch as she approached it from the opposite direction. It was so dark it was like walking into a cupboard and she almost turned back. She held her torch out in front of her, its thin beam worse than useless. The eerie shadows pressed in on her and when she heard light footsteps behind her she turned with relief, thankful not to be alone. There wasn't even a momentary thought of danger. Not until the weapon hit her head and a leg was placed in front of her and tripped her up.

She didn't even scream. She was stunned by disbelief. Instinct made her search for the bag in her basket and grip it with the tenacity of a maniac. As she lay on the ground with the man leaning on top of her, hitting her, hurting her with his knee digging into her stomach, it was then she began to shout, and scream, still clinging to the bag, determined not to let the thief succeed.

Having found her voice, she felt hope, but only for a brief moment as a train then lumbered overhead and drowned her cries. Still she clung to the bag and still she screamed and shouted for help, her voice startlingly loud once the train had passed by.

Then there were other footsteps, and shouts and the man pulled even more desperately on her bag and she felt her fingers slipping. The man was pulled from her and as her other hand was freed she grasped the bag to her chest and began to sob.

The man ran off; soft footfalls receding, he was invisible in the darkness. Then a voice close by murmured that everything was all right. The newcomer began to help her up and unbelievably the first man returned on silent feet, knocked her rescuer down and pulled the precious basket from her grasp.

To her alarm the second man didn't move and she crawled towards him and spoke to him. 'Get up. Please get up, whoever you are.' She looked back in the direction the thief had run, blinded by darkness and fear, and briefly grieved for her money, then tried to lift the man's head. 'Please get up, I can't leave you here to get help. We have to go to the nearest house. Please!' The word came out as a scream as sobs overwhelmed her.

The man groaned and began to sit up. 'He kicked me in the head and it stunned me for a moment. Sorry if I frightened you.' He struggled to his feet and offered her his hand, feeling blindly for her in the darkness. 'I didn't lose consciousness so I don't think I need a doctor, I was just confused. I thought he'd gone, you see.'

'So did I.'

'Did he hurt you? Or take anything?'

'Money. I suppose we were lucky. Although it was quite a lot of money. I went to the cafe instead of taking it to the bank first. My husband will be furious with me. I'm Mrs Joseph Davies, we have the linen emporium in Crown Street,' she explained.

'Oh yes. My first wife used to buy all her requirements from you. Well, Mrs Davies, I think our first stop should be the police station, don't you?'

'Joseph will be so angry. Why didn't I go to the bank as I usually do?' she wailed.

Sam thought it likely that whatever she had done, the man would have attacked her. He had probably been watching her for weeks to learn her routine and decide on the best place to steal the bank bag. He didn't say anything. To imagine being watched by someone planning to rob her would only unnerve the woman even more.

It was late when he reached home and Lilly was dozing on the couch, the kettle simmering on the gas stove ready for their nightly cocoa.

'Sorry Lilly, dear. But I didn't get to meet the others. A woman was attacked under the railway arch and I stopped to help her and we ended up at the police station.'

'Sam! You could have been hurt!' She rose from the couch, her eyes filled with alarm and threw her arms around him.

'I was, the evil man hit her and when I tried to intervene I was knocked to the ground and kicked.'

'Oh Sam. We have to call the doctor now this minute.'

'No, dear. I'm not badly hurt.'

'Then first thing tomorrow.'

'I might go to the surgery on Monday. There'll be some

bruising and I don't want Sam Junior to be alarmed when he sees me.'

'Oh Sam. I've been trying to tell you, thinking of a way to soften the blow. The letter I had from your son was to tell me that leave had been cancelled. He won't be coming home after all. I'm so sorry.'

'What a disappointment. I was looking forward to seeing him so much.'

'That does it,' Lilly said firmly. 'It's the doctor for you and we want a note telling those in charge that you've been attacked and injured and need to see your son.'

When Lilly wanted something she made a fuss and when Lilly made a fuss everyone knew about it. The doctor examined Sam's bruises then promised to do what he could to put a case for compassionate leave for Sam's son.

News of the Normandy landings spread through the town after the sixth of June and the relief that at last the Germans were being attacked by ground forces as well as by air filled the population with hope. Those who suspected their sons and husbands and brothers were among the early invaders smiled with the rest and told themselves it was almost over, that fate wouldn't be cruel enough to take them after surviving for so long.

In the factory there was great excitement as the girls working on the benches planned how they would spend their time once they were no longer needed to make armaments. For those first few days everyone imagined that the end of the war was no more than a walk to Berlin. A matter of weeks and it would be over.

Alice heard about the attack on Cassie Davies at work that day amid the jubilation about the landings. At her first opportunity she called on the woman.

'Joseph should have been home,' Cassie said, still distressed as she explained what had happened. 'Women managing alone, it isn't right.'

News of the invasion of Normandy had just broken and Alice asked, 'Involved in the fighting, is he? I thought he'd be a bit too old.'

'Secret work, he can't even tell me all of what he's doing.'

'I suppose the fact that he hasn't been home so often these past weeks is something to do with the Normandy landings?'

To Alice's alarm Cassie's eyes filled with tears and her mouth quivered like a child about to howl.

'I have the feeling that work isn't the reason he doesn't come home. I don't think he wants to. I'm not worth the effort and perhaps someone else is!'

'Nonsense,' Alice said soothingly. 'Everyone is doing more than they're asked to do and he's probably working extra hours. These are desperate times, Mrs Davies.' Alice glanced at the screwed-up face of the unhappy woman and found it strange to imagine her being so concerned. Surely she wasn't thinking of Mr Davies finding another woman? Not at their age? The idea seemed ludicrous. Then she thought of Auntie Audrey and her new husband, Keith Kent. They had fallen in love and they weren't that much younger than Cassie Davies. It was easy to sympathize and be understanding to those you know and love; strangers seemed to come in a different category altogether. Disapproval and derision came more easily.

It was almost closing time and there were no customers needing attention. Alice offered to walk Cassie home. 'I know you aren't nervous and I don't want you to feel the need of support,' she explained. 'But being lonely is something I understand. So, come on, we'll go and have a cup of tea with Auntie Audrey and it isn't far out of my way to keep you company back home.'

'You're very kind, young Alice.'

'Not really.' Alice smiled and added, 'I know what it's like to want your husband back home. We have to be patient a little while longer. It's sure to end soon.'

'"Over by Christmas", eh? They've been saying that since 1939 and it has to be true sometime,' Cassie agreed, but with little conviction.

Alice was afraid to look at the newspapers during the days following the invasion of Normandy. There had been no news from Eynon or Johnny and she didn't want to keep asking

Marged and Huw or Bleddyn if they had heard, it only made the waiting seem worse.

Through the town there was a lifting of spirits but the external joy was hiding the fears that grew daily with the reports of losses.

'And we aren't being told the half of it,' Cassie told Alice when she called in one day. 'You can take it from me.'

Alice looked at the woman curiously. 'Do you think so?' Was Cassie privy to information that was concealed from the general public?

Cassie guessed what Alice had taken her words to mean and she didn't disabuse her. It was a small deception and allowing people to think she knew more than most, made her seem more interesting. The truth was that when Joseph had come home after being told about the attack he had hardly spoken a word and had certainly not discussed the war. He was only a clerk and the only secret he held was the destination of the food and materials he requisitioned for the camps in certain areas. Although that was sufficiently revealing for it to be a top secret during the weeks leading to the Allied invasion of Northern France.

Marged and Huw were very busy on the beach during the month of June 1944. It was as though wives and mothers flocked to the beach to be as close as they could to their loved ones. Marged noticed many women pointing out to sea and, ignoring the fact that Somerset was visible, insisted to their children that the land they could see was where their father was. She mentioned the mild deception to Alice and Hannah one day as the cafe was about to close, and they stood at the window of the cafe and pretended, just like the rest, that Eynon and Johnny were almost within sight.

Below them, the donkeys were gathering to leave the beach. Impatient, knowing their supper awaited them, they pushed each other and Bernard Gregory, who was in charge of them, shouted with equal impatience but with no malice. He pulled the leader, Charlie, out from the mêlée and as he led him towards the slope leading up to the promenade, the others automatically arranged themselves in their usual pattern for the walk home to Sally Gough's field.

The children had all left the beach and there would be no more rides wanted that day. He looked up to the cafe and, seeing the faces near the window, he waved and pointed the whip, which he had never used, in the direction of home.

Since the birth of his grandchild, going home had an even greater pull. He increased his speed with the donkeys as he approached the corner from where he would have his first sight of the smallholding where he lived with his daughter-in-law, Beth. There were a couple of people at the gate and at first he thought it was customers calling to place an order for vegetables from his smallholding, but then he recognized his son. He waved and as though picking up on his excitement, the donkeys moved even faster, running when they passed the gate, heading for rest and food.

'Peter, what a surprise,' Bernard called as he passed the beautiful sight of Peter and Beth with their baby. 'I'll be back as soon as I've sorted this lot.'

Handing the child to Beth, Peter called, 'I'll come with you.'

Bernard looked at his son and inwardly groaned. He was even thinner than the last time he was home. He had been in France in advance of the invasion of Normandy, living rough and helping to support the invasion by sabotaging strategic targets alongside the brave resistance fighters.

'Home for good this time, I hope,' Bernard said, looking at the thin and weary face of his son. For Peter it had been a hard war.

'Soon, Dad. But I'm too useful for the moment. I've spent a lot of time there and my contacts, my knowledge and my language skills, make it difficult to find a substitute.'

Peter was home for a week, and with Beth and the baby he spent a lot of time on the beach, running alongside the donkeys with their excited riders. The happy children, the sun, and the rest and peace of being among loved ones and friends performed their magic. At the end of the week he looked less strained and his face boasted a light tan and had even filled out just a little.

During the night before he was to leave, Beth woke and stretched out her arms, expecting to feel his warm body beside her but the bed was empty. She rose and slipped quietly into the baby's room. Peter was sitting nursing the sleeping child and staring out into the night.

'Sorry, my darling. I didn't mean to disturb you.'

'Are you all right?' Beth whispered.

'I'm fine. I'm just storing up a few memories like a picture gallery or a snapshot album, or a wonderful film complete with sound and scent. They keep me going until I'm home again.'

Arms around each other and their baby, they sat for a long time, silently watching dawn break. A fox barked in the distance, a cart rumbled past, then they heard Bernard shuffling downstairs and the sound of the kettle being filled and they knew it was time to face yet another parting.

Peter went to Sally Gough's field with his father to gather the donkeys and fit them with their saddles, then watched as they set off to the beach. He and Beth stood on the corner of the lane until the sight then the sound of their trotting feet faded. Then he kissed his wife and child and got into the lorry that would take him back to his other world.

Although neither Beth nor Bernard spoke the words aloud that evening, when they discussed Peter's brief and happy leave, they each wondered fearfully how much longer Peter could survive. Expertise and courage were there, but when it came to it, survival in wartime was basically a matter of luck.

Twice during that week, Huw came home from a shift at the fish and chip restaurant to find Marged asleep. He was worried, but reminded himself that they were getting older after all, and the business was a strenuous one. He woke her gently and tried insisting they found extra help as soon as possible so she could rest more. She refused.

'What's the point in paying people who don't know what they're about? They only get in the way. Never any use taking casuals – you know that, Huw. We just have to get on with it. If only we had more help from the family, things wouldn't have got to this state.'

'If you're talking about our Lilly then forget it.'

'Our Lilly isn't the only one not pulling her weight,' she said between yawns as she went up to bed.

Huw sat near the dying fire for a while, staring into its grey heart. He was worried about Marged. She was doing too much, but if she refused to advertise for assistants there didn't seem much he could do. He couldn't fit in any more than he already did. Out at the beach all day, collecting stores, dealing with problems on the stalls and rides, helping a couple of nights at the chip shop. If only the boys were back. Perhaps he could persuade Ronnie to give up the stall and come back to the sands? He shook his head in answer to his own, unspoken question. No, that wouldn't happen. They would have to struggle on and hope to survive the hectic summer once again.

Lilly's letter enclosing the note from Sam senior's doctor bore fruit in that Sam junior was given leave. No date was given, but Sam was so pleased, he gave Lilly a few shillings with which to treat one of her friends to tea in a cafe, something he knew she enjoyed.

'What about that new friend of yours, Netta Mills, is she called? Why don't you invite her to the cafe near the park?'

'I'd love to, Sam, dear. But I don't know where she lives. I think she manages on very little and maybe she's a bit too embarrassed to invite me to visit. But I see her quite often and I'm sure she'll be thrilled to have a nice tea with me and our little Phyllis.' She amused Sam by telling him again about the chaos Netta's children caused in the cafe from which they were requested to leave. Sam chuckled. He loved hearing about Lilly's daily trips to the shops. She exaggerated for his amusement and made even ordinary incidents sound like great fun. She was so young; she made him very happy.

Lilly met Netta the following day and was told that it was Dolly's second birthday.

'Right then, we need a real celebration. Come on, we'll go to the cafe over near the lake.' They placed the three children at a table and ordered the best of the available cakes with drinks of lemonade for them.

'I'll pay as it's my daughter's birthday,' Netta offered,

taking out her purse, but Lilly would have none of it.

'This is my treat. My darling Sam gave me some money for Phyllis and me to have tea in a cafe and it's much more fun to share it with you.'

The day was warm and they sat looking through the open door of the cafe watching mothers passing, leading children with sailing boats under their arms, planning to create sea battles on the safe, calm water of the lake. Behind them their three children made an unbelievable mess as they shared out the cakes until they were little more than crumbs. At the counter the waitress stood with a hand brush at the ready, willing them to leave and not come back.

Lilly enjoyed playing lady bountiful, and boasting about the Castle family and their successful business, a subject about which Netta couldn't have enough.

'When did you say Alice married your Eynon?' she asked as Lilly ordered more tea and cakes.

'September 1942. Only married for two days they were, before he had to return to his unit. Ever so romantic.'

'It was about that time Dolly's father left us,' Netta said sadly. 'No romance there though, eh?'

Sam Edwards junior was in Leicester waiting to be transported to France and was given a weekend pass on compassionate grounds to see his father. He arrived on their doorstep one Friday evening towards the end of June, when his father was out with the little girl and Lilly was alone, sitting in the garden reading the *Radio Times* to decide on her evening's entertainment.

Sam had been a friend of Lilly's before introducing her to his father and now there was a shyness between them that had not been apparent before. Since Lilly had become his stepmother they had only met in the company of his father.

When he saw her he opened his arms then allowed them to drop to his side. He took a few hurried steps then stopped. How should he greet her? Lilly jumped up and stood hesitatingly: she too was wondering how to react to his arrival. Then she threw down the magazine and walked up to him and kissed him. She was aware of a sharp, almost painful starburst of desire and his arms wrapped themselves around her, pressing her body against his, leaving her in no doubt that he felt the same.

Their kiss became passionate, a crazy, urgent prelude to a hasty, staggering climb up the stairs and into the bedroom in which he slept on his rare visits home.

Their love-making was fierce, demanding, greedy and desperate. The coming together a longed-for, long-awaited hunger. Half undressed, clothes abandoned in their wild need for each other, they lay on the bed and didn't hear the door opening, or the footsteps climbing the stairs, a more sedate progress than their own had been. They failed to see the figure standing at the door, his eyes filled with pain and disappointment.

Shirley Downs, the stepdaughter of Bleddyn Castle, was a singer. She gave her time to perform in concerts to entertain the forces and factory workers, and to raise funds for the various wartime charities. She had been to see Eirlys Ward, who organized the town's Holidays at Home plans, to finalize arrangements for an open-air concert on the promenade. A few acts were booked to appear, a comedian and juggler and a few acrobats, but the main purpose of the evening was a sing-song, something that most people enjoyed.

Stanley, the oldest of the evacuees, came in while she was with Eirlys and said he would have to go back to the beach, even though it was officially his afternoon off. 'Marged isn't well,' he explained.

'Mrs Castle,' Eirlys automatically corrected.

'What's wrong?' Shirley asked at once.

'Don't know.' He shrugged. 'Just tired according to Huw – er – Mr Castle.' He turned to Eirlys and demanded, 'How the heck are you going to know which of them I'm talking about? Bleddyn's Mr Castle too. And Hetty's Mrs Castle ain't she? Blimey, Eirlys, you don't 'alf make life complicated!'

'I'll go and see if I can help,' Shirley said, hiding a smile.

'She – Marged,' he said defiantly, 'Marged said to let her Audrey know. That's Mrs Kent to you,' he added cheekily.

The two women wrote down the order of the performances and Eirlys promised to let Shirley have a typed programme the following day; then Shirley went to catch a bus that would take her to the beach. Stanley grabbed a slice of cake, and went with her.

That evening, while Marged rested in bed under doctor's orders to do nothing for a few days, the rest of the Castle family had a conference. It was after nine o'clock when Audrey and Keith, Maude and Myrtle arrived. Until the previous summer, Audrey and the two sisters had worked on the sands and it was the opening of Audrey's cafe, taking the two girls with her, that had made life so much more difficult for Marged to staff the cafe and stalls and rides.

Feeling guilty at the exhaustion of her sister, aware that it was partly due to herself, Audrey said at once, 'We've discussed this and Maude will go back to working on the beach.'

'Best for her too,' Huw growled. 'We got her out of working in that factory on condition she worked out of doors, remember. If she's seen in your cafe they could make her go back. Right?'

'Sorry, Uncle Huw,' Maude said. 'I intended to come back once the season started, but I didn't know whether you still wanted me, after going with Auntie Audrey. You weren't too pleased with us at the time.'

'Let's forget all that,' Bleddyn said quickly. 'If Audrey can spare you and you want to come back to the sands, you can start as soon as you like. Right, Huw?' Still disgruntled, Huw nodded.

He was frightened by Marged's illness. Marged was never ill. She had the strength of two and nothing ever distracted her from doing what was needed to run the business. What would they do if Marged wasn't there to organize everything? Since her collapse and the doctor's visit he was even more aware of how much they all depended on her. They didn't know just how much she did until there was the possibility she wouldn't be able to do it!

'I'll be there to open the cafe tomorrow morning,' Maude promised.

Upstairs, standing on the landing, bending low so she could hear what was being said, Marged smiled. 'Me ill indeed,' she muttered. 'Never been ill in my life. But I had to make that sister of mine see sense and let me have Maude back.'

Three

Shirley Downs was developing a career as a singer that augured well for the future. Starting with local competitions and small venues, she had become well known and was increasingly in demand. Her work often took her out of town and necessitated an overnight stay.

Travelling was often difficult and she remembered arriving at one venue on a horse. Another time she had been stranded far from a town in a country lane after accepting a lift from the wrong person. On both these occasions she had been helped by a man called Andy. Vaguely she wondered where he was and what had happened to him.

People regularly came into her life and were then left behind. Although she accepted the brief encounters that would always be a part of her life as she toured the country, Andy remained a strong memory, one that hovered and wouldn't go away. Perhaps he would appear again one day unexpectedly, when she again needed help.

Many of the concerts were to raise money for the war charities. The Red Cross parcels for prisoners of war was considered an important scheme in the town, where many families waited anxiously for news of their loved ones held in enemy hands.

From a little local girl coaxed on by family and friends, she had now risen to the point where her name was often the only one displayed on tickets and posters. 'Shirley Downs and supporting artistes' was the usual encouragement for people to buy tickets. She rarely sang to an audience where there were empty seats; the tickets sold as soon as they were issued. Pride in the local girl added to the pleasure of listening to her voice.

When she wrote to Freddy Clements she said nothing of this. The impression she gave him was that of an enthusiastic amateur, singing at out-of-the-way places in small community rooms and church halls with people sitting on uncomfortable chairs and draughts whistling through ill-fitting windows and doors. Making light of her talent was something she couldn't explain: she didn't really understand her motives herself. Perhaps she didn't want to frighten him off by thinking she wasn't the same person he had left behind.

Freddy's parents had died and the house he had called home was now rented by Maldwyn Perkins, who worked at Chapel's flower shop. He and his wife had moved there when they had married and now Freddy had nowhere to come back to.

In her letter, Shirley mentioned this, asking Freddy if he wanted her to investigate the possibility of his renting a place when the Army had finally finished with him. She suggested that rooms, with a landlady providing food and other services, might be best and she filled a page or two asking for his thoughts on where he would like to live. Then she tore it up.

She threw the scraps of paper on to the fire and stared into space. She and Freddy had spent a lot of time together, firstly out of devilment during the time he had been engaged to Beth Castle. Their affair had been exciting and spasmodic, and had ended without much regret on either side. She had begun to write to him because there were few who would bother and she understood how important it was for serving soldiers to have contact with home. That was all it was, a correspondence linking him with St David's Well, until the war ended and he came home.

She started to write again, this time only telling him about the small incidents happening in and around the town now the day trippers and holidaymakers were filling the place. Because her mother and stepfather were involved with the beach, much of what she told him was about the Castle family.

Then her pen started following her brain as she again began to wonder where he would go and what he would do when he came home. Surely she could offer to find him a place to live? Briefly she asked whether he needed her to look out for a couple of rooms. 'If you need any help to find a place to come home to when this war is finally over, write and tell me what you want me to do and I will find somewhere for you to stay while you decide on long-term plans.' That was vague enough. There was no intrusion, no suggestion she might presume to be included. She was confused about whether or not she wanted to be a part of his future. She ended by signing with the usual 'love from your friend, Shirley' and put it in the post-box with a feeling of almost tearful dissatisfaction.

Alice was writing to Eynon and for her there were not the difficulties faced by Shirley. The Castle family and their activities were enough to fill the pages without having to put down her thoughts. Her doubts and fears about their meeting again were easily kept from Eynon's letters. She mentioned what she suspected was a trick on his mother's part to persuade Audrey to let Maude go back to the beach and hoped he would laugh. She loved to imagine him laughing: Eynon had always been a happy person.

Not for her any worries about what Eynon would do or where he would live when he came home. She smiled as she imagined him getting up on his first morning home and going straight to the beach to resume the summer delights of encouraging others to have fun.

They would look for a house and she knew it would have to be close to his family and within easy reach of the beach. Her father had left her enough money for them to be able to choose where they wanted to live and she daydreamed of them selecting their own home, the thoughts warming her – until the fears returned and she wondered if he would still feel the same about her. Until he had joined the Army in 1939 with his friend Freddy Clements, he hadn't left the town. It was unlikely that after all he had experienced since he would come back unchanged.

Hannah Castle had anxious moments too. She was older than her husband and although Bleddyn and Hetty did every-thing they could to make her feel loved and a part of their family, she occasionally had doubts. She had been married before, and had two girls. It hadn't seemed possible someone like Johnny Castle could love her. But he had gathered them up and taken them to live with Bleddyn and Hetty and hadn't given the smallest hint of regret.

She was writing to Johnny a long letter to which Josie and Marie would add a postscript and, like Alice's, hers was full of the activities in and around St David's Well.

Johnny and his cousin Eynon had never imagined doing anything other than work on the stalls and rides on the sands. She hoped Johnny would have no doubts about returning to them, or to her.

When the letter was finished she set off with the girls to the gift shop, intending to post it on the way. It was Sunday and although the shop was shut she offended a few of the righteous by working in the shop, her sewing machine busily completing her present work, which was a trousseau of night wear and underclothes made from barrage balloon silk, acquired in ways mysterious about which she didn't ask. There might be a little over and shyly, unable to share her idea with anyone, she had planned to make herself a set for herself, for when Johnny came home. Blushing at her private thoughts she popped the letter into the post-box and hurried to the shop. She carried milk and the makings of tea, beside a few cakes. Perhaps one of the others would be there and she hurried in anticipation of friendly chatter.

Alice went to the gift shop that Sunday morning and before she had opened the door the sound of laughter told her there were children inside. Dropping to her knees, she pushed open the door and crawled in, to be at once surrounded by Josie and Marie and Eirlys's almost-two-year-old Anthony. A chase ensued with Anthony and the girls hiding and Alice, still on her knees searching for the half-hidden, noisy threesome, pretending to be unable to see a fat knee here and a plump bottom there.

'Hello, Alice,' Hannah said in mock severity. 'It's "good-bye peace" when you turn up!' Alice busied herself making tea and when they had eaten their fill of cakes she began sewing up the dolls Eirlys had knitted in her few spare moments.

The young women worked well together, each capable of finishing something started by one of the others, except that Hannah had a real talent for dress-making and her toys were of an exceptionally high quality. The best work was always left for Hannah.

Someone had given her an old fur coat and with this she was making teddy bears. With leather paws and feet and glass eyes found in a junk shop, the teddies were of a very high standard and most appealing. They took a lot of time in the making and there was a list of customers waiting for them. That morning she sat with a needle, patiently easing the fur out around the seams so the joins would be as invisible as possible. 'Goodbye, Teddy,' Anthony said with a sigh. He had been told the wonderful toy was not for him.

'Any news?' Alice asked and took out her much read last letter from Eynon for the others to read. Hannah took out two letters from Johnny and proceeded to read parts of them, being gently teased about the parts she didn't share with them.

'My Ken is in Kent,' Eirlys told them. 'I don't expect him home for a couple of weeks. He and his performers are touring the camps, and the hospitals. There are a lot of wounded arriving back from France since the sixth of June.' This was a subject neither Alice nor Hannah wanted to consider. Alice jumped up and asked brightly, 'Anyone fancy another cup of tea?'

The news from France was mixed, with rumours making it impossible for the public to understand the truth. Pockets of resistance held the armies back and a lack of fuel delayed repeated attempts to move on. Wounded victims of the invasion of France and the other theatres of the cruel war continued to return home: strangers, who were sometimes scarred and many having lost a limb. Some young men had white hair and sunken eyes, almost unrecognizable to those who loved them. Equally worrying were those who looked the same but were so changed inside their heads they would remain strangers for always. In spite of it all, hope remained high and in every town plans were being made to celebrate victory when it was finally declared. Alice, Beth, Hannah and Shirley and the rest watched them and offered silent prayers for their own loves' safe return.

The activities on and around the beach reached their peak during August. Eirlys worked very long hours, thankful sometimes to relax and do very little when Sunday gave a brief respite from the whirl of arrangements she augmented. Most of the entertainments were repeats of the past few years, with giant chess, dancing by moonlight and the concerts and varied competitions. She always made sure she involved all ages and that evening there was an open-air concert given by school children in aid of the victims of the latest horror raid in London.

Since June, the pilotless 'buzz bombs' had terrorized Londoners with their menacingly deadly approach, the almost unnoticed low groan of their engines suddenly stopping and the flying bombs falling to earth at terrifying speed.

A momentary easing of her busy schedule made Eirlys grateful for her friends and the little shop they had made into a meeting place as well as a growing business. They planned to leave for the concert directly from the shop and Hannah's two girls, Josie (eight) and Marie (seven), were vainly preening themselves in the dresses their mother had made out of other garments, ready for them to perform.

Lilly had found a way to write to Sam junior and it was her new friend, Netta, who had given her the idea. Throughout July and August, she and Sam exchanged letters filled with loving words, by using Netta's address.

Lilly would hand the letter to Netta, who would privately add her own address on the back of the envelope and post it. Netta was still reticent about where she lived – something that amused Lilly, who believed that with her comfortable home and her being one of the famous Castle family, she made her friend ashamed of her poor home. Sam junior's replies were given to Lilly when she met Netta for tea in one of their favourite cafes. Sam senior would never know and she felt no guilt, telling herself and Netta that if he didn't know and wasn't hurt, she was doing no wrong. In fact, she told herself, she was helping Sam junior to cope with the horrors of war. It was easy to find justification even for something so blatantly wrong. Besides the letters secretly conveyed, she had always added a note at the end of Sam's letters to his son, trivial words about things that were happening in the town, and remarks about his father's health. One day, she daringly added a PS that was far from the innocuous comments she normally made. Knowing Sam was in the room while she wrote it was so exciting. She scribbled words of love, assured him that her feelings hadn't changed, confident her trusting husband wouldn't read them.

It wasn't all that daring, she mused, he never did read her postscript, even though she had previously left the envelope unsealed in case he wanted to see what she had written. Her words were brief, just a reminder of their wicked and wonderful time together and telling him how she longed for him to come home. Then she sealed the envelope and smilingly left it on the hall table for her husband to post. He liked the weekly ritual of a walk to the post office with his son's letter and had never shown any curiosity about her brief dutiful additions.

When she went out for a walk with Phyllis, Sam declined to go with her and, with the aid of a steaming kettle, carefully unsealed the letter. He read Lilly's postscript and resealed the envelope with equal care with Gloy paste. His expression showed no dismay. He appeared calm as he went on with the morning chores, peeling vegetables for their lunch, putting the small piece of bacon to boil.

Plans formed in his mind and were rejected as he considered his response to her betrayal. Ideas tumbled over themselves in his desperation to do something. He couldn't ignore it, not now: his pain forced him to do something to pay her back. Then the tenseness left him as he made up his mind. He relaxed as further refinements to his plan evolved. He still half hoped that Lilly would confess, plead forgiveness and promise it would never happen again, that everything would miraculously be all right. But the words she had written on his letter to his son gave no credence to that foolish dream.

And could he ever forget the sight of his son and his wife on that bed? He knew he could not.

Now wasn't the time to deal with this situation but he'd better not leave it too long in case he had an accident, or Sam failed to return. He didn't want there to be any mistakes. First he had to get all the information he needed.

Lilly was in her Auntie Audrey's cafe chatting with Netta, whose interest in the Castle family was unabated. Amid flattery to put Lilly off guard, Netta asked question after question, sometimes suggesting something which she knew was incorrect so Lilly would put her right and add more to her knowledge. She learned a great deal about each member of the family, storing the information, knowing the day was coming soon when she would make use of it, to her advantage.

Leaving the bacon simmering, locking the door as a precaution against Lilly returning sooner than he expected, Sam searched their bedroom. There was anxiety clearly showing in his eyes as he opened the first drawer. He hoped against hope he wouldn't find anything. He had been so happy until his son's visit had ruined everything.

In a drawer containing underwear, a place he would never normally touch, he found the letters tucked under the lining paper right at the back. They were from his son, and he almost put them back unread, so badly did he want to pretend all was well. But his memory of that awful day when he had seen them together wouldn't go away. Now he had found them it was impossible for him not to read them.

They were passionate letters, reminders of Sam junior's brief compassionate leave and promises for future times. Sam put them back with infinite care, then went out to make an appointment with his solicitor.

When Lilly returned, he was standing in the kitchen putting the finishing touches to the meal. He put down the jug of parsley sauce and went to hug Phyllis.

'Don't I get a hug as well?' Lilly said with a playful pout.

'See to the table, will you, Lilly? I've been out and I'm a little behind with things.'

A brief frown crossed her features but curiosity quickly faded and she picked up a magazine she had bought and sat to read it. 'There's no hurry,' she said. 'I had a bite to eat in Auntie Audrey's cafe. Nice it is. You'll have to come next time I go.'

'Thank you,' he said, but his sarcasm was wasted on his wife.

The welcome of the townspeople toward visitors didn't lessen as the season came to an end. The enthusiastic determination to ensure every visitor enjoyed their stay was as genuine at the end of the busy months as it had been at the beginning. Supplies were beginning to run out: the stalls selling requirements for a day on the sands were decorated with extra bunting and small flags to hide the gaps; the paint on the rides touched up when necessary so the sight that greeted them was as appealing as the banter was lively.

There wasn't much spare time for those involved in the holiday activities but whenever a chance offered, many went out into the woods to collect wood for the winter fires. Bernard Gregory began sawing lengths of wood and filled sacks ready to sell once autumn came. The brightness of the beach and the enthusiasm of the late summer crowds couldn't hide the fact that winter was approaching with its shortages of fuel and no let-up on the limits of food rationing.

Audrey saw Cassie Davies in her cafe often as the summer of 1944 faded and autumn began to hint of cold dark days to come. One day when Cassie called in to buy a cup of tea after closing the shop, Alice and Hannah were there. Alice was behind the counter helping to serve a group of young people who were on their way to the pictures after work. The sudden bustle with only Audrey serving had threatened to make the customers impatient. A brief offer of assistance and Audrey had accepted her niece's help with relief.

When the lively crowd had settled at their tables, Alice sat with Cassie and could tell at once that the woman had news to impart.

'I'm going to open another shop,' Cassie said. 'I've been looking around with the plan half made, and when I saw the premises that used to be a sweet shop, I decided.'

'What will you sell?

'Flags, bunting, anything red, white and blue that people will need when the war is over and the celebrations start.'

'But there's a long time to go yet,' Alice said, then she looked at Cassie and wondered once again whether she had information others hadn't been told. 'Hitler isn't dead, is he?'

'No, but the Allies have kicked them Germans out of the Channel Islands and now the armies are in Paris and that will make them give up. The Germans must know they're beaten now they've been kicked out of Paris.'

'Berlin's a long way from Paris,' Alice said gloomily. 'And heaven alone knows where Eynon is. His letters tell me very little these days.'

'D'you know they're talking about ending the blackout next month? If that doesn't tell you Hitler is beaten nothing will. Imagine it, the streets lit up again. And soon the shop windows able to show what they have to sell.'

Alice's eyes glowed. Perhaps it was true and the end of the war really was in sight.

'We've as good as won,' Cassie said with conviction, 'and as soon as the announcement comes I want to be ready with all the needs for the street parties and decorations. Marvellous it'll be.'

Cassie went home almost as excited as if the announcement had already been made. It had to be soon. Joseph would come home and they would work together just as they always had. A few more years and they would sell up and move into the Vale, where they planned to spend their retirement.

She took the long step-ladder from under the stairs and carried it up to the landing. Pushing the loft door open she climbed up and with the aid of a torch began to look through the collection of boxes. The Union flags in various sizes were a bit dusty but still sound after waiting all these years and she noticed some of the bunting had been nibbled by mice. Apart from those few problems the rest of the stored materials were as good as new.

One of her suppliers had told her about a firm in Cardiff where more of the celebratory red, white and blue items might be for sale. As soon as the end was imminent she would go there and buy what she could. She didn't want to miss anything but there was no sense buying too soon: money lying idle was not good business sense. She would ask Joseph to make enquiries when he next came home. She sighed. He hadn't taken a weekend off for three weeks. She told herself he was helping the war effort and earning extra money and how could she complain about that? It wouldn't be for much longer. She stifled the persistent niggle of doubt.

Audrey was closing the cafe that evening and Keith was helping her. She told him about Cassie's regular visits and explained that it was probably loneliness, her husband working in Cardiff and only occasionally able to get home.

'War work, she says, and she implies his work is secret, but between you and me I think she's exaggerating his importance. Boring little man he was as I remember and I doubt the war has changed him.'

'If you're talking about Joseph Davies the draper, then I saw him recently. Remember I did some work in Cardiff a few weeks ago? Painting a shop front I was, and he was pointed out to me as a shopkeeper from St David's Well, so I introduced myself. He didn't seem very keen to talk, though. He hurried away like I had the plague and later I saw him again and he walked past pretending not to see me. Perhaps he *didn't* see me. Overalls and a tin of paint and no one gives me a second look and he had other things on his mind. It wasn't far from the station and he stood there obviously waiting for someone. I watched him as he greeted a young woman. Laughing and hugging they were, far from boring each other, believe me. I thought they looked like – well – you know, lovers on a date.'

'You must have been mistaken, Keith. It doesn't sound like his wife.'

Keith smiled at her. 'I know love when I see it,' he whispered softly.

'Poor woman.'

'Lucky man! I wish everyone could be as happy as you've made me, Audrey Kent.'

*　　*　　*

55

With the last of the entertainments finished and the trickle of visitors slowly dying out, the stalls on St David's Well Bay were dismantled. They were transported to a warehouse to be stored until the new season began. The sands looked naked without them. The store where the deckchairs were stacked during the summer was also taken away, a loss to lovers and the occasional stray dog. The remaining prizes left over from the hoopla and other games were carefully wrapped, the chalk figures stored in the loft of Marged and Huw's house in Sidney Street, rag dolls offered to Alice and Hannah to sell in their shop, the sad little goldfish given to some of the local children.

News on the progress of the war was mixed, with battles for the bridges over the Rhine at Arnhem, Nijmegen and Grave being less successful than hoped, but the push towards Germany went on. A landing of the Free French Army back on their own soil back in August had been cheered by many, but for Beth the news had brought added fears. The resistance fighters were out in the open at last and Peter was surely there fighting with them in the streets with the confusion of snipers and booby-trapped buildings adding to the dangers.

Optimism grew throughout the last weeks of the year and when the lights went on in September, the children roamed the streets in wonder, some of them hardly remembering the freedom given by the lighting each evening of the gas lamps. The lamp-lighter went around with his long pole at dusk turning them on one by one, and a small band of children accompanied him, cheering as each flickering flame grew in strength. Adults too were unable to resist watching the progress of the lamp-lighter and they stood in groups on doorways and discussed the news and silently cheered at the small victory of lights being lit, without the wardens shouting, 'Put that ****** light out.'

The border town of Aachen fell in October and in November the Home Guard was disbanded. The headlines told the public that the Germans were on the run. But the V2 rockets devastated the places where they landed and fear encouraged more families to send their children away from the capital to safer places.

Grieving for the strangers who were suffering the new and deadly attacks on their home, hiding their increasing fear for their loved ones, Alice, Hannah, Beth and Shirley cheered with the rest when encouraging news was announced. Their letters to Eynon, Johnny, Peter and Freddy, were filled with descriptions of the excitement the town displayed, and, as always, their increasing longing for the day they came home.

In the weeks before Christmas no letters arrived from Johnny, Eynon or Freddy Clements. Three weeks without a word was the longest they had known without a letter from one or the other and they were afraid. Lilly didn't hear from Sam junior either but whereas the others wrote more letters and tried to reassure each other, Lilly sulked and didn't write to Sam junior at all. 'If he can't be bothered to write to me then I'm not wasting time writing to him,' she told Netta with one of her famous pouts.

'Aren't you afraid he's hurt?' Netta asked.

'You don't think he is, do you?' She forced a tear from her eyes, then said, 'No, we'd have been told. No, he's just forgotten all about me and two can play that game! And to think of all I risked for him!'

Planning for Christmas was more difficult than previous years. Besides the difficulty of finding food, and the anxiety of not hearing from the men making any celebration a half-hearted affair, no one wanted to use what luxuries they they still had in their stores. Some tinned stuff had been kept for years and in lofts, apples rotted, while the owners waited for the excuse to use them. Jars of preserves darkened in colour while they stood in pantries waiting. Everything that was at all special was hidden away for the promised street parties when Germany was finally beaten.

Lilly invited Phyllis's grandmother, Mrs Denver, to share their Christmas dinner. Three-and-a half-year-old Phyllis was Phil Denver's child and although he and Lilly had never married, Lilly was happy to include the dead man's mother in her life to enjoy watching her granddaughter grow up.

'You're such a kind and understanding man, Sam, dear,' she said when he agreed to her suggestion. 'You bear no malice towards Mrs Denver, or to little Phyllis, knowing she was another man's child. A heart of gold you've got and I love you very much.'

'I love Phyllis. And Mrs Denver is her grandmother even though you and Phillip never married. We'll have to find a little gift for Mrs Denver to put under the tree with the rest, won't we?'

They discussed what to buy and Lilly's mind drifted to thoughts of Sam junior. Would she be as happy with him? Would he care for her as much as his father did? She still hadn't heard from Sam junior and she looked across at Sam senior and thought that life with him was pretty good. Enough money, freedom to come and go as she pleased and there were very few demands on her as Sam had continued to manage the house and the cooking as he had done since his first wife had died. She hoped Sam junior was all right. With him for some illicit fun, life would be perfect.

Convinced that Sam junior was safe, but too lazy to write to her, she wondered what would happen when he came home. Would he live with her and his father? If so, would they be able to keep their attraction for each other a secret? Thoughts of the secret and forbidden love that had filled her letters to Sam now overflowed into her dreams.

Christmas was a duller than usual affair. Little more than a brief respite in the day-to-day routine. Church services apart, everyone seemed to be poised, waiting, looking beyond the celebration towards the news of victory.

Marged and Huw invited Bleddyn, Hetty and Shirley to share their Christmas dinner, and Audrey, Keith and the girls came too. Ronnie, Olive and their daughter came from their rooms upstairs and tables were joined together to accommodate them all.

A huge log fire burned in the grate, and an impressive array of drinks were on offer. At closer inspection these consisted mostly of soft drinks for the children: dandelion and burdock, sasparella, orangeade. A bottle of port and one of sherry plus a few flagons of beer were festooned with garlands to make them seem special.

The parcels under the tree were opened and admired. Socks and handkerchiefs, perfume and hair slides wrapped to make them exciting. Sweets for the children. Three parcels stood there unopened bearing the names of Lilly, Sam and Phyllis.

Marged had hoped to see Lilly but apart from a card there had been no contact.

'Tomorrow we'll go and see our Lilly and her Sam and little Phyllis,' she announced. 'Who's coming?' Hands were politely raised and all hoped a reason could be found for changing their mind. A visit to Lilly was not an exciting event.

In a lull in the fighting, Freddy Clements sat writing to Shirley. He was exhausted. They had been moving almost continuously and he hadn't had even his greatcoat off for several days. He looked down at his feet and gave a grim smile. Boots, which no longer kept his feet dry, were covered in slimy mud which rose up over his ankles and stained his sodden trousers. He daren't imagine the state of his feet when the boots finally came off. He could never have believed he could allow himself to get into this state.

No thought of such discomfort or filthy clothes had entered his head on the day he and Eynon Castle had joined up. Everything was neat and clean; polish had been an important part of their training – something that strongly appealed to him. He had always been fussy about his clothes, his appearance a priority above everything else. Fastidious was how people had described him in civvy street. How had he learned to accept all this?

He thought of the times he had refused to wear a freshly laundered shirt because the collar didn't sit precisely, or there was some imagined imperfection in the way the button fastened when it had been replaced. His poor mother had taken such a pride in his appearance, and taken so much trouble to please him. What would she have thought of him now?

'I am fine,' he wrote to Shirley. 'The food is okay but I'll be glad to have some decent fish and chips from Castle's cafe. That's a date. You and me eating our fill at Castle's fish and chip cafe.' He allowed the pencil to drop. Writing cheerful letters was getting harder to do. He was so tired. Gunfire in the distance went on continuously day and night and the explosive sounds seemed to beat into his brain.

A voice called and he rose to his feet. They were off again. Hastily adding a scrawled signature below the word 'love', he pushed the unfinished letter into its envelope, ready to hand to the corporal. Perhaps Shirley would get it and perhaps, he thought with a grimace, I might never know.

Eynon was writing to Alice, a loving letter full of plans for when he came home. In answer to one of her questions, he wrote down a few of the streets where they might look for a house. 'But,' he added, 'wherever you want to live is fine by me. Short of the Antarctic or the equator, so long as you and I are together I'll be happy.' He handed it in and hoped it wouldn't be blown up, like rumour told him had happened to the last ones.

Johnny's letter to Hannah was similar to Eynon's, filled with plans for his return. He hadn't changed, the beach was still what he wanted. Summers on the sands and winters doing whatever work he could find. He did a cartoon drawing of the two girls at the end and added a note to each of them before signing it with love.

Almost oblivious to the progress of the war, Sam senior went on with the usual routine of his life and writing once each week to his son. He always looked at the brief PS's at the end of his letters, written by Lilly, but there was never anything amiss. No need, he thought sadly when she can write to him care of her friend.

He had taken advice given by his solicitor, who had at first tried to persuade him to change his mind about what he planned to do. When he realized Sam was determined, he carefully, albeit reluctantly, set out the details.

Sam's first action was to put his neat little house on the market. The estate agent was given firm instructions not to bring a prospective buyer around until Sam had agreed the time. Viewers came when Lilly was out with Netta.

The days were dark; winter had the country in its cruel grip. Day after day, the ground was either slippery with solid unrelenting ice, or dismally cold and wet. On occasions there were a few days when snow covered the ground and Sam knew it was not the best time to sell a property. So, when anyone called, he made sure the house was shining and clean and warm; and with a roaring wood fire, he made the place as welcoming as he could, and the place was sold within two weeks. Lilly knew nothing.

Lilly's friendship with Netta and her children had grown, so they met almost every day. They met at Auntie Audrey's cafe, as the weather discouraged walking any further.

One afternoon in February when they called to escape the cold wind and the rain that threatened to turn to snow, Audrey's cafe was so full they failed to find a seat. Lilly waved to attract her aunt's attention but Audrey shrugged expressively and went on serving.

'Come on, Netta, I'm not standing here for ever,' Lilly said with one of her famous pouts. 'Auntie Audrey knows we're here and she hasn't made any effort to find us a place to sit.'

'Where can we go?' Netta asked as they struggled to hustle the three children back out into the wind and rain. 'I can't afford to eat anywhere else – we'd have to pay.'

'Mam and Dad will be home, we'll get a cup of tea there.'

Netta tried to hide her delight. This was what she had been hoping for since she had first approached Lilly and offered friendship.

Marged and Huw were both at home, sitting close to the fire and with blankets across their knees. Marged stood up when she heard her daughter call. Lilly came through the back door and put Phyllis down to run to her grandparents.

'There's a lovely surprise!' Marged hugged the little girl and smiled a welcome. Then Lilly pushed Netta's two children forward and Huw turned and beamed in delight as he asked who they were. That he and Marged were pleased to see them was in no doubt. Children were always welcome. Introductions were made, food offered and Marged and Huw began to get to know Lilly's new friend.

Lilly telephoned a corner shop and asked the owner to tell Sam she was at her mother's and would be late, and she and Netta stayed for the rest of the day. Sam stared around the house where he had lived for so many years and was overcome with guilt. What he was doing was cruel. Yet he knew he wouldn't change his mind. If cruelty was the consideration, Lilly's behaviour was far worse than this. He spent the time that Lilly was out, up in the loft, packing unused china his wife had collected and rarely used. Tomorrow he would talk to one of the dealers about selling all the surplus. Lilly was out so much, he wouldn't find it difficult to do all he planned.

At the Castles' house in Sidney Street, they were joined during the evening by Alice, and Hannah with her daughters. With five lively children there was a party mood which only Alice failed to enjoy. This was the girl she had seen watching her and she was suspicious of her presence there. Although Netta joined in the conversation, Alice noticed she gave very little information about herself, neatly twisting each query around to become a question of her own. She made comments about the members of the family as though they were all friends and her knowledge of them all was puzzling. She must have been very curious about them to have gleaned so much information. With a shiver of apprehension she wondered why.

When Alice was leaving, Marged brought out the family photograph albums and Lilly groaned. 'No, our Mam, please don't! Dad, don't let her show Netta the one of me at seven when I had no front teeth!'

Curious, Alice stayed a while longer and was alarmed when Netta showed a strong reaction when Marged proudly held up a snap of Eynon in Army uniform.

'What is it, Netta? You don't know my son, do you?' Marged asked.

'No, Mrs Castle, he just reminds me of someone I once met, that's all.' She glanced at Alice and quickly turned away.

Alice told Audrey about the visit, which she considered an intrusion, the following day. 'She knows so much about us all, it's uncanny. Ages, birthday and anniversaries, everything. Why is she so interested?'

'Eynon worked on the sands every summer, Alice. There must be plenty of people who would half-recognize his face and not remember exactly where they'd seen him.' She looked at Alice and added, 'You could ask Eynon when you write. He might remember her from somewhere.'

Audrey tried to reassure her, but she too found it puzzling. What motive could there be? What could Netta gain from studying the Castle family so thoroughly? Was it nothing more than loneliness? A desire to belong even if it were only a pretence? Or something more sinister? Keith laughed at her fears when she mentioned it and told her she'd read too many Agatha Christie mysteries.

Alice wrote to Eynon when she got home but didn't mention Netta Mills in her report of her visit to his parents' house. He wouldn't be interested in hearing about a stranger when there was always plenty to tell him about the family.

Cassie opened her second shop in March. All the items she had bought ready for the victory celebrations were packed in a back room ready to bring out as soon as Germany's surrender was announced. Beside those things she had little to sell. She had found some faded lisle stockings in a warehouse sale, patchily coloured by having been left in the sun some years before. There were a few dozen extra-large knickers and some unattractive material, plus more hanks of knitting yarn. She had also found more of the damaged stock. To fill the window while she waited for the real sale, she did a display of the royal family, photographs of them walking through the ruins of the blitz and Princess Elizabeth repairing Army lorries. She didn't display any flags. The town, like the rest of the country, was waiting.

Joseph had come home and his help was valuable. Once he had signed the lease, he helped her to clean the shop and while she arranged the stock in convenient rows, he painted the visible areas to smarten it up. It augured well for the future, Cassie thought: starting on a new project, widening their business and strengthening their partnership; although she wished he would tell her so occasionally, instead of accepting it all without a mention of her hard work and imaginative marketing.

'Aren't you proud of me, Joseph?' she asked as he packed to return to Cardiff on that Sunday evening.

'Very proud, Cassie dear. I'll always be grateful to you for what you've done during the last few years. Because of you, I can plan a really good future.'

'*We* can, you mean,' she said teasingly. She stepped forward for a hug but he moved around her and picked up his case to leave, holding it in front of himself. In her disappointment she felt that he used the case as a shield to keep her away and the rejection was hurtful.

She tried to make excuses for his lack of affection. Joseph had never been very demonstrative and perhaps he hated leaving her and the apparent coolness was his way of hiding his regret. Or perhaps his mind was already racing ahead to what faced him when he got back to his responsibilities in Cardiff? Whatever, he had been delighted with the way the business had grown. 'Proud,' he'd said, she remembered. 'Very proud.' Even if she'd had to put the words into his mouth, he had said them. 'Very proud.' She smiled as she washed their dishes later and prepared to go to bed. A really good future: that was all she wanted. That was praise enough.

Four

'Seen the window of Cassie Davies's new shop?' Alice asked Marged one afternoon when she had called to deliver some khaki gloves she had made for the on-going collection for the forces. 'There seems to be some off-ration towels and pillow-cases and even a few sheets. Where d'you think she got them from?'

'Who cares? If we can get there the minute she opens the shop I won't ask any questions, will you?'

She lifted up a small piece of towelling that had started life as a towel large enough for the bathroom and which now had been stitched around, using the best parts, discarding the shredded areas, leaving it no larger than a face flannel. She let her hands fall in despair. 'Oh, Alice love, when will we ever get back to how things were? I started the war with a good stock of household linen but with curtains and the rest going on ration, then in October 1942 having to use precious coupons for towels, I think most of us gave up hope of ever restocking.' She pulled at the tender fabric she had tried to save and it came adrift like the rag it was and she threw it down in disgust. 'What makes it worse is that people think that with us having extra allocation because of the cafes, we've got plenty. The truth is we were too honest. I should have hidden what I had in store and pleaded for more than we were entitled to. I'm sure there were many who did just that.'

'I had a bottom drawer when Eynon and I married as you know, and I've tried hard not to use any of it. I begged and pleaded for some of the muslin that covers the lamb carcasses in the butcher's shop and they've been used for many of my needs, so I still have a few brand-new towels and tea towels ready for when Eynon comes home.'

Marged looked around her, at the oddments of china on the shelves, the minimal foodstuff in the open cupboard and the threadbare tablecloth on which she had placed crocheted doilies to hide the wear. The war and the accompanying shortages had gone on so long everyone was struggling to keep their homes looking welcoming.

Weekends saw families going for walks and returning with anything they could use: sticks for the fire, logs to replenish their coal ration, or a walk could result in a feast of blackberries or nuts, flowers to add cheer to a dark corner, or even a few stolen apples.

Store cupboards were almost bare, even dogs and cats were vegetarian, she thought with a weak smile, living on a share of whatever the family meal consisted of. She looked at her daughter-in-law and, as though she were the one needing encouragement, she said, 'Don't worry Alice, love. The end is in sight, and soon we'll be using the dregs of our precious store cupboards and planning the street parties, giving the children something to remember all their lives.'

The words were cheerful but when Alice looked at her, Marged looked so weary that her impulse was to offer her all she had. 'You can have my towels and tea towels, Mam,' she said. 'I've got some clothing coupons left and I don't need much until the spring. There's sure to be an end to rationing once the war is over. Imagine,' she added, her face aglow with the image, '– imagine the shop windows full of everything and the assistants begging us to buy. Linen stacked outside the shop doorways, all the food we want. Wonderful it'll be. I'll be able to find everything I need in plenty of time for when Eynon comes home. I know how difficult it is for you, with the cafes and shops. Take what I have, Mam, you're welcome.'

'Thank you, lovely girl. But no, you keep your precious bottom drawer. We'll go early and try to get some of Cassie Davies's off-ration bargains. With a bit of luck and if she's in a generous mood we might be able to buy enough to justify throwing the worst of our tea towels away. Not enough for a real fresh start, but it will help.'

'Right then. I'll meet you tomorrow at half past eight.'

A drizzly rain was falling when the light came on in the rather shabby shop. A crowd had gathered and organized themselves into an orderly queue. Some women had children with them and these climbed on to the window sill and tried to look between the blinds into the shop, where Cassie was busy piling up the items she had for sale.

Finding the chance of a peep irresistible, Alice pressed her face to the glass and peered inside. To her surprise, she saw Cassie rubbing some of the piles of pillowcases on the dusty wooden floor of the shop. Surely the damaged goods would be dirty enough without adding to the mess? She nudged Marged and encouraged her to look but by the time Marged managed to find a gap in the still closed curtaining and peer inside, Cassie was innocently putting the extra grubby pillow cases next to the towels and pillow cases on the counter.

'What am I looking at?' Marged asked.

'Oh, nothing. I'll tell you later,' Alice replied with a frown.

There was some consternation as someone pushed through the crowd and knocked on the door. Protests about queue-jumping – a heinous crime – resulted in their being told she was Cassie's assistant. Kathy Richards had been employed to help during the sale, and would run the shop once the sale had finished and business had simmered down from the chaos of the bargain-hunters to the calmer business of a regular linen store.

When the town-hall clock had struck nine o'clock, the queue began to get restless and several women knocked on the window and shouted for Cassie to hurry. At five minutes past the hour the shop door opened and Cassie announced that she would allow the first three customers into the shop.

As the first three customers each had several children, Cassie was knocked back against the door in the rush of impatient people.

'Only three I said,' she protested. Ignoring her, telling their children to 'be'ave', the three women grabbed their requirements from the piles on the wooden counter and a rather anxious assistant totalled the purchases and took their money.

When it was Marged and Alice's turn they asked how many of the grubby-looking towels they were allowed and trying not to be heard by the others, Cassie promised Marged a dozen, plus a few face flannels, and two dozen tea towels for Alice.

Behind an open hand she whispered that she had put some aside for Audrey, as she wasn't able to come to the shop. Sharp ears overheard and an argument ensued which was quashed by Cassie's explanation of the special circumstances, the order being for the cafes and not a household. That didn't discourage the protesters so she raised her voice, her jaw belligerently thrust forward, threatening to send them away with nothing if they didn't shut up.

As Alice and Marged were paying for their purchases, another three customers were allowed to enter. One of them picked up one of the hand towels and said suspiciously, 'Not damaged at all, just a bit of dirt. I wonder where she got this lot from?'

'Stolen for sure,' her friend replied in a hoarse whisper. 'Probably bought from one of them spivs we keep hearing about.'

One-handedly the first woman looked through the piled up merchandise. 'You're right, Ethel. Damaged stock my eye! There's not a brack in them, only a bit of dust that'll come off in the wash.'

'If you don't want them, please don't mess up the counter display,' Cassie said sharply and Alice glanced at her and saw her grimace, giving the impression that the women's comments had been heard and the accusation had worried her. The goods certainly looked undamaged. What was Cassie doing rubbing the pillowcases on the floor to get them dirty if she wasn't hiding the fact?

Alice didn't have to be at the factory until two so they walked through the streets to Audrey's cafe. It was not yet ten o'clock and the cafe was closed. Marged knocked on the side door which was opened by her sister.

'We've been to that sale at Cassie Davies's new shop and she's put some things aside for you,' Marged said, as they went inside.

They opened out their purchases and examined them. Dirt along the folds, a few pulled loops on the towels and some loose stitches on the corners of the tea towels. Nothing that couldn't be easily repaired. They told Audrey what Alice had seen and Cassie's reaction to the suspicions of the shoppers, and decided the items were suspect.

'What are you going to do?' Audrey asked.

'Get them home and washed as quickly as we can!'

Alice laughed. 'Once they're in our cupboards we won't worry about the whys and wherefors. Glad to have them we are, and if we hadn't bought them someone else would.'

'That's an excuse that's been used for years to justify dishonesty,' Audrey said. Then she smiled as she added, 'Damned if I won't be doing the same, mind!'

Cassie had begun to have doubts about the stock Joseph delivered late at night to the newly opened shop, as soon as she unpacked the first parcel. There were certainly plenty of the right lines to sell to an eager, commodity-starved public, but they showed no evidence of being rescued from fire or flood or bombed buildings. She wished Joseph were there. She shouldn't have been left to deal with it alone. What if the police had called?

Joseph had left so much to her over the past years and during the recent months she had hardly seen him. These boxes, suspiciously un-crushed, the contents pristine, had arrived late one evening after the shop had closed, with three men in khaki overalls and carrying official-looking clipboards to carry the consignment inside and with no message for her, except for a previous letter telling her to assess the prices and sell everything as quickly as she could so the supplier could be paid.

If only she could reach him by telephone, hear him reassure her that everything was legal. She had a growing fear that was something he couldn't do. She sat down after the shop was closed and the assistant had gone, and wrote to him, telling him about the success of the day's trading and asking for his reassurance that she needn't fear a visit from the police.

Most of the goods had been sold. All that was left were a few items she had put aside for herself and the pile of tea towels for Audrey, and all of a sudden she wanted them out of the place. Bundling them into a couple of paper carriers, she went out and locked up the shop. She still remembered the experience of being robbed of her day's takings and she nervously followed a group of people as she made her way to the bank with the day's takings, aware of the danger of walking alone, thinking with unusual irritation that Joseph should have been there to do the dangerous errands. She thankfully dropped the bag into the night-safe and hurried to Audrey's cafe.

Both of the girls Audrey had taken in after being found homeless and ill were there: Myrtle helping clear tables and Maude behind the counter. Myrtle was now sixteen and had grown into a beautiful young woman. She spent most of her spare time with the oldest of the three evacuees, Stanley, and her growing love for him showed in her eyes.

Maude was now nineteen and had been allowed to leave the factory, where she had been sent on war work, because of her weak chest, and allowed to work on the beach with the Castles who had become their family.

While Cassie waited for Myrtle to bring her tea and a piece of toast, she looked through her bank book. She and Joseph had become surprisingly wealthy over the war years. The profit from the second shop would bring more and she worked out that once the shops and the house they lived in had been sold, they would be able to buy a small cottage in the beautiful Vale of Glamorgan and enjoy a comfortable retirement.

She smiled inwardly. Most of their success was down to her. Joseph would be so pleased when she told him how well placed they were. He probably didn't know how wealthy they had become. He never bothered with the day-to-day running of the business, he confidently left all that to her. When the war ended – and that seemed likely to happen in months now rather than years – they would celebrate not with street parties and welcome home banners, but by looking for their dream house. For the rest of their life they would be together every day. Life would be 'perfect'.

She was unaware she had said the word aloud until Myrtle, who had arrived with her order, smiled and said, 'Perfect? An ol' bit of toast? You must be a happy person, Mrs Davies, to enjoy such simple pleasures.'

'I am, Myrtle. I am.'

'Me too, Mrs Davies. Life is great, isn't it? And once this war's over it'll be even better.'

'You still seeing that Stanley Love? Nice boy he is, even if he is a bit cheeky.'

'At least he didn't have to go away. There's my poor sister living for the postman's visits in the hope of a letter from that boy-friend of hers. You remember Reggie, who helped Mr Gregory when he extended his smallholding? Soft on him she is, our Maude.'

Cassie remembered how she had felt about Joseph all those years ago. She was soft on him and still was, even though Myrtle would consider her past such feelings, she thought with a happy smile.

Happiness was not apparent in the home of Lilly and Sam Edwards.

'What?' Lilly gasped. 'You're telling me we have to move from this house and go and live in two rooms? Sam, dear, what's got into you? The house is yours, it's your home and mine and Phyllis's. How can you tell me we have to leave it?' Lilly stared at her husband in utter disbelief. 'Sam, dear, what's happened? Are we short of money? I can work. I'd hate leaving you every day but I can get a job with our Mam and Dad, we'll manage.'

'Too late, Lilly. The house is sold and we have to be out of it at the end of May.'

'But, where will we go?' Using his love for her daughter, she pleaded her case. 'How will Phyllis cope with such an upheaval? She's so happy here, so close to the beach and the park and all her friends. She loves her own little bedroom. I'm so happy here. I thought you were too. Just tell me what's happened and we can sort it out. Please, Sam, tell me what's gone wrong.'

Sam looked away from her, afraid she would see the sadness, his dislike of her, reflected in his eyes. 'I had to sell the house, we don't have enough money to live on.'

'Why didn't you tell me? Why wait until it's too late? Mam and Dad would have helped us. There are plenty of things we could have done. Please, Sam, don't do this. Go and see the estate agent, tell him you've changed you mind.'

'It's too late, the deed is done.' The deed he was thinking of was the sight of his young wife in bed with his son. 'There's no going back.'

'Where are they, these two room you're taking us to?'

'They're a few doors away from your Auntie Audrey's cafe.'

'What?' She began to sob then. 'You're going to embarrass me by taking me to two rooms in that awful street where Auntie Audrey can see me every day?'

'Perhaps she'll find you a job, so we can save up and perhaps buy a house again.'

'What about your Sam? Where's he supposed to go when he comes on leave? He won't have a home any more.'

'He's old enough to find a place of his own. After his – varied – experiences he's mature enough to cope, wouldn't you say? Being adult is more than making love to a woman, it brings responsibilities as well as fun.'

Something in the slow way he said the words made her nervous. Surely he didn't know about her and Sam? She lowered her head sorrowfully and asked, 'When are you taking me to see this place, these two rooms that will be our home?'

He didn't answer. Instead he said, 'The rooms, particularly the kitchen which we'll be sharing with other people, will need a bit of cleaning. I thought you could make a start on that while I take little Phyllis to deal with the final arrangements. I have to sell a lot of the furniture, and I have to discuss times with the removal firm.'

'And we have to be out of here in a matter of weeks?'

'I'm afraid so, yes.'

'But it's impossible. Why didn't you tell me before?'

Ignoring her remarks he said, 'So if you'll start cleaning the rooms, I'll attend to the rest.'

'Sam, this is crazy. I have to go and tell Mam and Dad, now this minute.'

'Tomorrow. Today you must go to look at the rooms and decide on what we need to take to make them into a home for me and yourself and little Phyllis.'

Although he spoke in his usual soft voice there was a steeliness in his tone of which she had been previously unaware. He must know. He no longer called her 'my dear', a small thing in itself but it made her afraid. He must have found out about her affair with Sam junior. But how? And why would that make him sell the house, his home as well as hers? She began to cry and this time it wasn't affectation. She was afraid and deeply ashamed of the way she had cheated on him.

He handed her a piece of paper on which he had written the address. 'Someone will be there to open the door for you, and I suggest you take all you need to start on the cleaning.'

As the tears fell she forgot her shame and regrets and turned the whole sorry mess around to blame Sam junior. He must have said something, he must have been careless, let the odd word slip. In her deep misery she convinced herself he had been the one who had started the affair. He who had taken advantage of her. She relived the scene and saw herself backing away from his advances, protesting until he weakened her resistance. Yes, this was all Sam junior's fault. She had been seduced. The word both frightened and thrilled her.

In the gift shop Hannah was finishing the last of the teddy bears she had made from the old fur coat, when Beth came in with her small son, Peter. Eirlys's two-and-a-half-year-old Anthony at once ran to greet the newcomer.

Eirlys Ward was working and Hannah and Alice between them looked after Anthony for her. Hannah put down her sewing and held out her arms for the baby.

'Have you heard from Peter?' she asked as Beth reached for the kettle to make the inevitable cup of tea.

'Not yet, but it's so confused over there at present. It seems likely the war will end within days, then they'll all come home.' To Hannah's alarm she began to cry, and Hannah's first thought was that her friend had received bad news. The end of the war might be imminent but the dying went on.

The baby was put in the cot they had bought to accommodate their children while they worked and she went to hug her friend. She said nothing. It was so easy to say the wrong thing.

'I'm being silly, Hannah. I haven't had bad news, or heard any rumours but I haven't heard for ages. I do know that the underground fighters – the people he's worked with for six years – are now out in the open. Peter will be with them, standing beside the partisans and street fighters, and in the confusion not knowing friend from foe.

'He'll be careful, you have to believe that and trust him.'

'This is something the Maquis have waited for for years, a chance to come out in the open and fight. The battle will be furious, the heroes and the foolhardy, risking their lives, there'll be no chance of being cautious.'

'Confusion or not, you'd have heard if Peter was injured.' She deliberately didn't say killed. There were plenty of nightmare scenarios racing through Beth's head without adding to them. She reached into her handbag and offered Beth a letter. 'It's from Johnny, but news of a cousin is better than none.'

The letter gave no news, it was no more than a few words written in haste, assuring Hannah of his love and signed with kisses. Handing it back, Beth managed a smile.

'You're right, Hannah. Peter and Johnny and our Eynon will soon be home, clambering to get back to the beach, pretending none of the last six years have happened.' Briskly she asked, 'Right then, what d'you want me to do?'

'Sew up those wedding-dress dolls' clothes if you would. Eirlys is running a best-dressed doll competition next week and there are customers waiting for them. We make dresses and the children are supposed to decorate them.'

'I don't know how Eirlys keeps up the enthusiasm for the Holidays at Home scheme, do you? She must be weary of competitions, chess games, competitions, races, concerts, dances. Yet she enthuses and makes everyone feel the excitement of yet another summer at the beach and in the town.'

'She wasn't going to work another year but her bosses persuaded her. Now Anthony is settled into the routine of coming here or being looked after by Alice, she's decided to stay on and work full time throughout the year.'

'Brave. It's hard work running a house and looking after Ken and her father and the three evacuees.'

'I suppose she's looking ahead, to when the need for Ken to organize concert parties for the forces is no longer needed and he'll have to find a career for himself. Her wages will give him the chance to start again.'

'We both know it's more than that,' Alice said sadly. 'Ken's affair has left her less than confident in the future. She needs to know she can earn enough to survive if he leaves them.'

The rooms which Sam Edwards had taken, a few doors away from Audrey's cafe, were not as filthy as Lilly expected, but nevertheless, dark walls and dark linoleum, forty-watt light bulbs and dirty windows gave a depressing first impression. As she was coming out after making a list of necessary jobs to be done and listing the furniture they would need to bring, Audrey called from across the street. With her were Myrtle and Maude. Coming towards them was Sam with Phyllis holding his hand.

'What are you doing here, visiting?' Maude asked. 'Who do you know in this street?'

Lilly tightened her lips and was clearly not going to reply, so Sam said, 'This will be our new home. We're moving in at the end of May. You must be our first visitors, mustn't they, Lilly?'

'You've bought Mrs Summers's house?' Audrey said in surprise.

'No, we'll have just two rooms. They'll be plenty for us, won't they, Lilly?'

'Plenty,' Lilly said, avoiding her aunt's eye.

'If you need any help—' Audrey offered.

As Lilly brightened up, ready to accept, Sam interrupted

and assured Audrey firmly that Lilly would manage, 'Just fine.'

Audrey quickly guessed that the planned move had not been the idea of her niece and when the few questions fell into a silence she hugged the child, smiled politely at Sam and left them. She was frowning, wondering what had gone wrong. They wouldn't be moving from a house to two rooms unless they had met with a problem. It was also clear that at present, Lilly didn't want to talk about it.

Lilly saw Netta the following day as she was on her way to the park, and as soon as Netta greeted her she burst into noisy tears. After walking a little way to allow Lilly time to calm herself, Netta led her to a cafe where Lilly told her what had happened.

'He must know,' she said, drying her red eyes with a sodden handkerchief. 'Somehow that stupid Sam let him find out about our affair and now my life is ruined. Why did I let myself be persuaded? Seduced I was, mind,' she added, glancing at Netta to see the effect of the emotive word. 'I tried to stop him but he seduced me and now my life is ruined and poor little Phyllis hasn't got a proper home.'

'She would have if you went back home to Sidney Street,' Netta suggested.

'What? And have to be grateful to Mam and Dad? It's the month of May, remember. The holiday season has started. Go back home and have to slave away on the beach all summer? No thanks!'

Marged and Huw were concerned abut Lilly's change of circumstances and Marged wondered if Sam might be ill. 'Perhaps he's preparing Lilly for widowhood,' she suggested. 'Heaven knows she's never been a capable person and maybe he's trying to make her face up to looking after herself and Phyllis.'

'She's never mentioned him seeing a doctor, except when he was attacked in the railway arch the night Cassie Davies was robbed. It couldn't be anything to do with that, could it?'

'Best we go and see him,' Marged said emphatically.

When the cafe was closed and cleaned ready for the next

day, instead of going straight home, Marged and Huw went to see Lilly and Sam. Sending a reluctant Lilly out to make them a cup of tea, Huw asked Sam if he was well. 'We wondered, Marged and me, if you were ill and that was the reason for you moving to somewhere cheaper.'

'I am in the best of health and the reasons for the move are nothing more than financial,' Sam said. He slapped his knees as he stood up and followed Lilly into the kitchen to help with the tray, making it clear he had no intention of saying anything more on the matter.

When Marged and Huw left, he went on sorting out the unwanted items from the house. He didn't ask Lilly to help – that would have been too cruel. Besides, every discarded piece brought back memories of the years he had been married to his first wife and the sadness was almost pleasurable.

Sam had grieved when his wife Marjorie had died even though she had been ill for years and had needed so much care. He had spent so many hours of each day caring for her that her death had left an enormous void. He had been desolate when she died but that suffering was nothing compared with this. Then, as now, he had felt suicidal but for different reasons. Then it was because he had wanted to join Marjorie, now it was because he wanted to get away from Lilly; she was a reminder of his failure and stupidity. Only Phyllis, the innocent one in all this, held him back.

A young man stopped and looked at the assortment of jumble he had piled at the gate.

'Excuse me, sir, but if that lot's to be thrown out, can I have it?'

'If it's any use to you, yes. Take it and welcome,' Sam replied.

'Thanks. Er . . .' The young man grinned cheekily and asked, 'D'you think I could borrow your wheelbarrow to take it away?'

'Take the wheelbarrow too. I have no further use for it.'

The man made two trips with the barrow piled high, to an empty house at the edge of the wood. He was delighted with his good fortune. Prepared to offer payment, he hadn't even had to pay a penny. After a small charge to hire a market stall for a day he would be able to make a few pounds with this lot. When he was leaving with the second load, Sam called to him and gave him half-a-crown for his kindness. Whistling cheerfully, he hurried away to begin the pleasurable task of pricing everything ready for his sale. What a bit of luck. It showed that the gods were still smiling on him.

'Our Mam and Dad tried to find out why we have to move,' Lilly told Netta the following afternoon. They were sitting in a cafe, the three children tucking into a mock chocolate cake. In a corner a wireless murmured, unheeded by them.

Most people in the country followed the news throughout every day with great excitement. The death of Hitler and the shooting of Mussolini at the end of April had brought cheers to everyone's lips. Every item of information was repeated, dissected and analysed.

Everyone knew that the announcement about the end of the war in Europe was imminent but for Lilly there was nothing to think about other than her stupidity. Unaware of the excitement she sat and stared glumly into her coffee cup. Around her people talked and laughed and even Netta seemed unaware of her misery. Then suddenly, at three o'clock, everything went quiet. The manager turned up the volume on the wireless but Lilly remained unaware. All she could think of was the devastation of leaving the neat little house kept spotless and comfortable by Sam.

She didn't hear the owner of the cafe make an announce-ment. So when the huge shout and roar of several dozen voices rose and filled the room, she was terrified. She stood up and grabbed her daughter preparing to run, from what, she didn't know. Looking outside they saw crowds of people running, shouting and climbing the steps of the town hall. At the top of the steps a group of men appeared and one was shouting something through a megaphone.

The words were repeated, shouted, one to another and it took only a few moments more for the realization to reach them. The war in Europe was over. Germany had surrendered.

The news spread like magic, neighbours knocking on doors and calling everyone out. Shopkeepers stood on doorways and shook hands with everyone that passed. One woman set fire to her ration books and knew she would spend ages queuing for replacements and didn't care. Within hours everyone was out on the streets. Doors were left open as the occupiers ran joyfully out. Some waving Union flags; some with the Welsh dragon. Others ran with flags wrapped around their shoulders. The instinct of the population was to gather where they could stand together, and share their joy. People leaned out of office windows, boys climbed lamp posts and waved their hands. Whistles were blown together with mouth organs and Boys Brigade bugles and people sang. Sammy Richards, carpenter and handyman, walked along the street playing 'God Save the King' on his accordion. Dogs ran through the hastening feet, tripping people up, barking and joining in the new game, and cats ran for shelter, tails twitching in anxiety.

At the cafe on the beach, Marged and Huw looked down to see people running among the picnicking few, shouting. Opening the door and stepping out, Marged turned to stare disbelievingly at Huw and Maude and said, 'It's over,' and promptly burst into tears.

In Audrey's cafe, someone ran in to tell them and Audrey put the remaining sandwiches and cakes on the counter and told people to help themselves, then she closed the cafe and with Keith and Myrtle, hurried towards the beach.

The streets were packed with the celebrating population of St David's Well. Everyone was on the move, some heading for members of their family, others to share the wonderful moment with friends. Many, by pre-planning or telepathy, made for the square outside the town hall and hugged ecstatically when they met. Near the main shops, a long gaggle of women and children were dancing the conga, their voices clear above the general hubbub. Children were crying and being dragged along with the rest.

Near the railway station, a house caught fire and the fire-engine couldn't get through the crush of people in time to save it. The owner had draped garlands usually saved for Christmas across his room and in the window he had lit candles. One of the garlands, insufficiently fastened, had fallen, caught fire, and the flames had quickly reached the curtains.

A few neighbours tried to dowse the flames with buckets and bowls of water but most people ran past, the victory more important than a house fire on that incredible day. The few who did stop and stare momentarily, wondered vaguely if it was a part of the celebration.

Eirlys was working in her office at the council offices and with the rest of the staff she left, and hurried to the shop to collect her small son. Buses were unable to get through the streets so she ran. The two younger evacuees Harold and Percival were there, having been collected from school by her father. Rosy-faced with the excitement, they all set off for the beach. Only young Percival looked less than thrilled.

'Isn't this wonderful?' Eirlys said as she steered Anthony's pushchair through the crowd with Percival holding the handlebar. She was puzzled by his lack of excitement, although he was always the most dour of children.

'Teacher says everyone will be going home,' he said in his low, slow voice. 'We were told once about the people in the Channel Islands being freed from the Germans, and how they could go home again. And how the soldiers will come back.'

'Yes,' she agreed, 'everyone will be back where they belong. Johnny and Eynon Castle will be back on the beach.'

'They won't need our Stanley any more, will they?'

'Our Stanley will work on the sands for as long as he likes.'

'Not when the soldiers come home though,' he insisted.

With so many distractions Eirlys didn't finish the conversation and seeing Lilly and her friend Netta, she waved and the two young women with their children pushed through the throng to walk with them. Percival's eyes were wet as he fought back tears. Eirlys wasn't telling him yet, but he knew he would be sent back to London. Everyone back where they belonged. That was what he had been told and he belonged in a barely remembered dingy room in London.

Houses left open as the occupants celebrated offered opportunities for thieves, and sadly there were a few. Some households lost rent money or milk money, left for convenience on a hall table. Books for the insurance man with the weekly payment tucked inside were pilfered with ease.

Marged and Huw kept the cafe open but there was some confusion about their customers paying and they eventually gave up trying to claim their money and just gave away the little they had left. With the door closed the family stood looking down at the sands, laughing at the crowd below, each with their own thoughts. Huw and Marged thought about the return of their son Eynon. Bleddyn and Hetty's thoughts were with both Johnny, and on Taff, lost early in the conflict. As they finally walked home through the still crowded streets, Marged summed it up. 'A time for laughter and tears,' she said. Then, 'Now we must get the street parties organized. Our street doesn't have many children, so we're going to share with the one behind. We've made a list of who will lend trestle tables and tablecloths and –'

'For Heaven's sake, Marged,' Huw interrupted with a laugh. 'Let us enjoy today before starting on next week, can't you?'

Drunks roamed the streets late that evening. Some happily celebrating, others trying to drown memories of sons and brothers and fathers who would never come home. There were still children who cried, confused by the day and unsettled by the unusual behaviour of their families. No one thought about bedtime. Everyone stayed out in the streets until long after midnight had chimed. About 3 a.m., night finally settled over a weary, shabby town that would wake to a world that had been transformed by a few words into a town filled with hope.

Cassie celebrated alone. She opened a bottle of port and set a tray with a half-full bottle of whisky, two glasses and some food, and waited for Joseph to come, convinced he would leave his desk and come home to share the moment with her. He was only in Cardiff, no more than an hour's journey. There had been a time when he would have walked it to be with her. He should have come to share this moment with her. He didn't work twenty-four hours in each day. At midnight she went up the stairs to her cold, empty bed and tried to pretend she understood.

81

Alice went back to her two rooms in Holby Street and sat for a long time in the dark, her anxious heart racing, and wondered how Eynon would greet her. Would he be disappointed in her? She was no beauty and perhaps his memory had distorted her in his mind into someone more lovely. Memory was not always truthful, and the men were sure to have exaggerated the wonders of the girl they left behind. Eynon could have made her into a person she couldn't live up to, someone clever, beautiful and – she shied away from the word 'sexy', but her imagination led her to the bed they would share. All her thoughts had been fears of Eynon not loving her and for the first time she wondered if perhaps she would find it difficult to get into those cold sheets with a man who was almost a stranger. Unable to settle, she wrapped herself in a blanket and sat in the one comfortable chair. She took out Eynon's letters and read them through until her eyes grew heavy and sleep overcame her.

Stanley came home late, having spent the evening with Myrtle and Maude and Auntie Audrey. He crept in, trying not to disturb Eirlys and Ken, and didn't see Percival sitting near the remnants of the fire, wrapped in a coat belonging to Morgan. When he heard his brother close the bedroom door, Percival pushed sticks into the dying ashes and added some logs. He tried to work out what would happen to him. Would he be taken back to London and left there? Would his brothers be with him? His mam was dead and he imagined living on his own in one of the sad little rooms in which he had spent his early years. Tears trickled down his face, he was one of the few for whom the day's news was not joyful.

Shirley walked back through the town with her mother and stepfather, singing in her sweet confident voice to the entertainment of the passers-by. Some recognized her and called. Others asked for a favourite song to be sung. She obliged them all, glad to avoid her thoughts. Like Alice she wondered what would happen on the day the men came home. She and Freddy Clements had kept up a regular correspondence throughout the almost six years of war. Freddy, who had once been engaged to Beth Castle, had joined the Army with Eynon, both signing for three years.

Any agreement about years of service had been forgotten and now they expected to be demobbed with the rest. Letters in which people told their innermost thoughts were no substitute for a courtship and, although she had a strong affection for Freddy, she didn't know whether she wanted to share the rest of her life with him. She also didn't know whether he wanted to share his life with her. They signed their letters with love, but affection written on a page to someone far away, and true love-you-for-ever love, and love-you-above-all-others love, were different. Freddy hadn't replied to her offer to find him a temporary place to stay. In a cowardly mood, she decided to go and talk to Ken Ward to see whether he could fix her up with a long tour of concerts. If she were out of town when Freddy came home, he would find somewhere to live, and get a job, without her involvement. He could wander around, reacquaint himself with his home town and plan his future. Satisfied she had at least made a decision, she slept. She woke a few hours later to the realization that she held his savings. If she ran away, he would think the worst. Whatever happened later, she would have to be there when he came home.

Beth couldn't sleep. Peter was somewhere in the chaos of France and although the surrender documents had been signed, the dangers were not over. There were certain to be pockets of resistance, German soldiers who had not heard the news. There would still be unexploded bombs, booby-traps, mines at sea. Every time she closed her eyes she saw pictures of death in its many cruel forms. She rose quietly trying to avoid waking Bernard, checked on her child, who slept soundly, unaffected by living through such a historic day, and went to the kitchen.

As the kettle boiled she sat looking out of the doorway at the dawn breaking on the first day of peace. Footsteps alerted her and she turned to see her father-in-law shuffling into the room with a greatcoat over his shoulders.

'Sorry I disturbed you,' she said as she reached for a second cup and saucer.

'You didn't. I was wide awake and wishing it was time to rise.'

They sat companionably outside the door looking at the colours changing as the day began. Deep shadows hid everything at first, shapes of familiar objects distorted and strange. Then as the light strengthened, buildings, trees, bushes, grassy banks beside the road were slowly, magically revealed. Then the flowers: late spring and early summer flowers, their colours strengthening and showing them the beauty of that May morning.

They heard footsteps approaching and Bernard said, 'It seems we aren't the only ones unable to sleep, Beth.'

A figure emerged, faint at first then as the darkness eased its grip, it grew out of the shadows to become someone familiar. 'Peter!' Beth whispered, before running, struggling with the gate and falling into his arms.

Bernard waited and after hugging his son, made excuses and disappeared into the house. He puffed on his pipe and sighed with contentment as he watched the young couple walk into the house. Peter was home, the war was done with, and in his cot a new generation was preparing to take over. Leaving them to their reunion, he went up to sit with the donkeys. Perhaps he'd knock on Sally Gough's door in case she hadn't been told about the victory. He could tell her about Peter coming home too. It was a time for talking. 'Damn me,' he said to no one at all, 'it's not yet five o'clock and already it's been a grand day.'

Five

Eirlys, as many other people that morning, woke to a feeling of disbelief. Was it true? Had they really heard the announcement that the war in Europe was over? 'Has the war really been won?' she asked Ken as she began to prepare breakfast. 'Or was yesterday's excitement nothing more than a particularly vivid dream?' She ran upstairs to call her father. He was already up and behind him, coming down the stairs was Harold.

'Stanley's already out,' Harold said. 'And Percival must have gone with him. He isn't in bed. Stanley just couldn't wait to get over to the beach. Not even any breakfast. They're mad.'

'Don't worry, Marged and Huw will feed them. It'll be such a strange day after yesterday's news. Few will get to work on time. In fact, I doubt if many will turn up for work at all. We'll need more than a night's sleep to calm us down. Marged and Huw and Bleddyn will be there to open the cafe and stalls though. Nothing will dissuade them from the beach. They'll be glad of the boys' help.'

'No school either? I doubt if Percival will be back in time.'

'We won't worry about it. Not today.'

'Does that mean I don't need to go either?' he asked hopefully.

'Just this once,' Eirlys replied. 'We'd better make sure Percival's there though. I like to know exactly where you all are.' She turned to Ken. 'Will you go and make sure Percival's with Marged and Huw, Ken? I'll be telling him off for going out without letting me know where he is.'

Ken agreed, but promptly forgot.

It was Morgan who went to see if Marged and Huw had seen Percival, and on being told he had not been there, he began to look for him. He tried the houses of all his friends and became more and more alarmed when no one had seen him. Where could he be?

Morgan went to Eirlys's office, where she was putting the finishing touches to plans for the judging of the best spring garden. She looked up anxiously when her father came in. 'Dadda? What is it? It isn't Anthony, is it?'

'Anthony's fine. No it's young Percival. No one seems to have seen him today and I wondered if you have any ideas for places to look where I haven't already tried.'

Immediately anxious, Eirlys and Morgan compared suggestions and, excusing herself, taking an early lunch, she went out with her father to try the most likely places again.

It was after two o'clock when Ken remembered his promise to check up on Percival and, setting aside the work he was doing, he left the house, and went to the beach. Morgan was in the cafe at the beach talking to Marged and instead of joining them, Ken went along the promenade and into the amusement arcade. There, in front of a slot machine, watching as youngsters tried their luck with the clacking, humming games machines was Percival. His hair was tousled, his clothes carelessly worn, and buttons incorrectly fastened, which, together with his over-long short trousers from which his two skinny legs protruded, made him look forlorn and unloved.

'Percival? What are you doing here?' Ken asked, putting an arm around the boy.

'Hello, Uncle Ken. I've been trying to get a job.'

Stifling a chuckle, afraid of offending the sober child's dignity he asked, 'Why do you need a job? Isn't your pocket money sufficient for you to manage on? We could discuss it with Eirlys and maybe get you a rise.'

Before Ken could give him a chance to answer, Morgan saw them, came over and hugged Percival.

'Where have you been, Percival? We've all been so worried about you.'

Ken interrupted Percival's reply. 'He tells me he needs a job but perhaps an increase in pocket money might suffice. Eh?'

Percival struggled to hold back a sob. Ken holding one hand and Morgan the other, they led the unhappy boy out into the sunshine. Eirlys looked at him and knew that the problem, whatever it was, had not been resolved. 'Are you hungry, Percival?' she asked, hoping that food might at least be a temporary comfort, until she could work out the reason for his unhappiness.

'Starvin',' was the reply. 'Can I have chips and spam with Auntie Marged?'

'A double helping,' Morgan promised.

'What is it?' she asked as they walked towards the cafe. 'Have I done something to upset you?' He shook his head and, when they reached the cafe and sat waiting for their food, Morgan tried another tack.

'When I'm fed up about something, I talk to someone. Just one person, a best friend who'll listen and understand. Who's your best friend, Percival?'

'You are, Uncle Morgan, but I don't want to talk.'

'Perhaps later?'

'P'raps.'

He ate with unusual enthusiasm but wouldn't be drawn on the reason for his sombre mood. Eirlys found him later that day with all his possessions laid out on his bed. 'What are you doing, Percival? Having a sort out?'

'Yeh. Seeing which of these things I've grown out of and don't need any more.'

Eirlys felt a growing concern as she studied the serious young face. Something was troubling him, but she knew this wasn't the time to try to find out. It was best to wait until he was ready to talk.

The joy following the announcement that the war in Europe was over was tinged with continuing anxiety for other people besides Percival. The horrifying war in the Far East was yet to be settled. While the families of those promised an early release celebrated, the rejoicing was only a partial relief to others. To them it was at least the beginning of the end, and they worked with the rest to arrange the V.E. – Victory in Europe – street parties that were being prepared all over the town.

For Eirlys the parties meant an easing of her plans for entertainments. Until the parties were over, there would be little demand for other activities; everyone's efforts went into making their special neighbourhood celebration a success. She and Ken decided to join in the Sidney Street plan and her main contribution, apart from providing some of the food, was to lend them some bunting and flags from the town's supplies. Shirley Downs agreed to lead the singing that would inevitably end the evening. Ken arranged for a group of clowns to come and entertain the children while they waited for the tables to be filled with food.

The intention to hold parties in the street had long been discussed and preparations were quickly made. Most houses had a few treats hidden in their pantries in anticipation. Shirley had volunteered to help prepare the food for the celebration organized by Marged and Audrey, and as she walked towards Sidney Street she thought she saw a face she knew. It made her start and she stared along the lane from which she had seen the head and shoulders of a young man appear, then dart back as though not wanting to be seen.

Surely it wasn't Andy Probert? It was uncanny to imagine seeing him so soon after she had been thinking about him. Had she dreamed up the image out of her memories? Of course it wasn't him. Just someone resembling him, nothing more. A second glance and the similarities would be hard to find. Andy, whose brother Reggie had worked for Bernard Gregory for a while, had popped into her life on several occasions but he never would again, Although she didn't quite approve of him, draft-dodger and petty criminal that he was, she had always been happy in his company. He had brightened her day and left memories that made her smile, even now, when she thought of him.

Andy had had the ability to appear unexpectedly, but now he was dead. Drowned after his ship had sunk, just as his recurring dream had foretold. It couldn't have been him. And after all, she had thought she'd seen him several times before, so it must be her imagination, her mind playing tricks. But it unsettled her and she walked quickly on, thankful to go inside Marged's house and join the team of busy neighbours with their happy chatter, amid piles of food that seemed sufficient to feed a small army.

A few tempting sandwiches of salmon, spam and eggs were mixed with large quantities of meat paste and Marmite. Large quantities of small cakes appeared and some had had their tops scooped out and filled with cold, chopped jelly, a pretty sight if a bit difficult to eat. The pieces of cake that had been removed were not wasted; these went into trifles together with a few precious tins of fruit.

Bernard and Peter came with Beth and the baby and Reggie Probert, Andy's brother, came too. Reggie looked around hoping to see Maude but it wasn't to be: he had less than an hour, and she was still at the cafe on the beach.

Shirley saw him and sighed with relief. It must have been Reggie she had seen. They weren't exactly alike, but the similarity would have been sufficient to mislead her as Andy had been in her thoughts. Thank goodness. She was wondering if her mind was playing tricks.

Everyone had a job to do. Assorted trestle tables were spread lengthways near the middle of the road and any traffic was left to find another route. Tablecloths hid the motley collection and small decorations made by Hannah, Eirlys and Beth added cheer. Chairs and stools were brought from the nearest houses. A piano was dragged into the street and someone found who could play it. Huw staggered out with a gramophone which was placed on a small table with a pile of records slithering dangerously whenever anyone went near.

The piano immediately came into use and the men and women sang as they set everything out ready for the feast. The music swelled, bottles and glasses clinked and, with the cutlery, performed an accompaniment, the percussion section of the orchestrated day. At three o'clock the clowns leaped into the street and engaged the children in games. At four, everything was ready and with a swoop the children found their seats. All except Percival.

He held back as the rest of the children found their place, half hidden in the doorway of Marged's house. It was Beth who saw him and she tried to coax him to the table with the rest.

'Is this a party so everyone can go home?' he asked in a whisper barely heard by Beth.

'Yes, Percival. All the soldiers will be coming home very soon. You'll be able to see Johnny and my brother Eynon – you remember them, don't you?'

'Everyone where they belong?'

'That's right. Now, come on or you'll miss the best of this lovely spread. This is one celebration you mustn't miss. It's one you'll never forget.'

Peter came over as Beth was seating a reluctant Percival on a corner seat. When Beth walked away to pour lemonade for some children holding up their empty glasses, he knelt down beside the twelve-year-old and asked, 'Is something wrong? Did you want to sit beside your brother, Harold?'

'No, it's all right, Uncle Peter. I'll have to get used to being on my own.'

'What d'you mean?' He looked along the table to where Harold was showing off to a couple of girls, his fourteen-year-old face covered in mock cream from which he had fashioned a beard and moustache and thick eyebrows. 'Oh, I see, Harold has his own friends and you're left to manage on your own. He'll be glad of you in between flirting with girls, believe me. And things change. Stanley still looks after you and when he realizes how grown up you are, Harold will include you in his adventures, too. Give it time, old chap.'

Percival took a bite out of a cake and pulled a face of dismay. 'These currants is boverin' me,' he said and tears filled his eyes. 'My mam used to pick 'em out for me.'

Peter presumed that thoughts of everyone coming home had reminded the boy that the reunions excluded his with his mother, who had been killed a few years previously, and his heart ached for the lonely little boy.

'Give it to me, young Percival, I'll make sure I remove every last one of them.'

Peter stayed with Percival for a while, trying to coax him to talk about his mother but Percival said very little and he eventually moved away, accepting that the boy's dead mother was not a subject for the day when many were celebrating.

The noise in the normally quiet street was deafening and as Lilly came around the corner she pulled a face. 'Sam, dear, I don't think I can cope with this. It's making my head split.'

'Phyllis will love it and look, they've already started eating. I told you we were late.'

Although they weren't officially members of the street, as Lilly's parents, Marged and Huw had made sure they were invited and Lilly was relieved to see them. A couple of chairs were found and Phyllis was seated where Sam could help her to whatever she wanted. Lilly left Phyllis with him and followed her mother around as Marged tried to attend to the demands of the excited children. 'Mam, I want to talk to you.'

'What is it, our Lilly? Can't it wait till later? You can see I'm busy. Either help or go and sit down. We can talk later.' She thrust some used plates into her daughter's hands and Lilly immediately put them back on the table. She hadn't come here to work.

The stalls on the beach and the cafes were open and it was with difficulty that Bleddyn and Hetty had managed to find staff to take over so they could join in the fun.

Alice and Shirley Downs stood beside Shirley's mother and stepfather and marvelled at the achievement of the women who had provided the food on the groaning tables. After years of rationing and shortages, they had arranged a party for about forty children that looked as good as anything in the pre-war years. Everyone had contributed something, including those without children of their own, but even so the wonderful display of food and the decorations both on the table and across the street were remarkable.

'Pity the men aren't home to join in,' Bleddyn said, thinking of Johnny, trying not to dwell on thoughts of Taff. 'Our Johnny and your Eynon would have loved it.' He smiled at Alice and added, 'Perhaps we'll have another even better one when they're safely home, what d'you think, Alice?'

'I can't imagine Eynon or Johnny saying no to that,' Alice replied. 'Specially if we hold it on the beach.'

Bleddyn turned to Shirley and asked, 'What about you and Freddy? Be celebrating together, will you?'

'I don't know, I really don't know.' Shirley look around her, half expecting to see Andy Probert waving, or blowing a kiss. But he couldn't. He was dead, drowned in a cruel sea. She saw Maude arrive and go into the house and went to tell Reggie, but it was too late, his brief, unoffical visit was over.

Hetty looked at her daughter, saw the worry displayed on her face and decided that she would coax her to talk about her feelings for Freddy, but not now. This was a time for the children.

'This celebration isn't the end of something, mind. It's the beginning. A time to reflect and decide what you want for the years ahead,' Bleddyn said. He saw that his words were not as reassuring as he'd hoped and turned to hug Eynon's quiet young wife. 'No need to ask what your future will be, young Alice. Working on the sands with you, helping the trippers to have fun, will still be Eynon's dream, sure to be.'

As the dishes were sorted into ownership and stacked to be taken home, Lilly found a moment with her mother. 'Mam, I want to come back home.'

'What are you talking about, our Lilly? Married you are and your place is with Sam. Old as he is and not our choice for you, but he's your husband and it's with him you belong.'

'But you know what he's done, sold the house we called our home and moving us into sad little rooms a few doors from Auntie Audrey's cafe. I can't live there, Mam. It's shabby and gloomy and there isn't as much money as before and worst of all, he won't tell me why.'

Marged stared at her daughter, her eyes gleaming with sudden suspicion. 'You haven't done something stupid have you, our Lilly?'

'No, Mam!' There was outrage in her voice but she looked away from her mother's searching eyes.

'Then you have to talk to him. Perhaps he's been spending his savings and they've gone. Generous he's been but he probably has a small pension and with the savings gone he has to cut back. Selling the house is better than getting into debt and having everything taken from you by the bailiffs.'

'Will you talk to him, Mam? He might tell you. He certainly won't discuss it with me. It's my life, I'm his wife and he loves Phyllis like his own, so how can he do this?'

'He must have his reasons. Perhaps he doesn't want you

worried. He's managed the money ever since you married him, so you can't expect him to suddenly change and . . .' she was about to say, 'Treat you like an adult,' but held back and instead said, 'expect you to understand the problem.'

'You think there's a problem?'

'Heavens above, girl, how do I know? You'll have to talk to him, make him explain. Now, I have to get these dishes washed and ready for the grown-ups to eat what's left. Fancy giving me a hand?' She watched her daughter move through the lively children who were leaving the now wrecked display of food, making her way back to Sam and Phyllis. 'I thought not,' she muttered.

Alice, Eirlys and Hannah had arranged some activities and they led the children through the familiar 'Ring o' roses', 'Farmer in the dell', 'What's the time, Mr Wolf?', 'Hide and seek', while the sorry remains of the food was cleared and the tables folded. Some of the children looked sleepy and several were sick but a sing-song revived them and by seven o'clock everyone had their second wind and the mood livened once again.

Shirley was helped on to a make-shift stage later in the evening, and a couple of solos were followed by communal singing; sentimental songs that brought tears and fears mingled with joy and optimism. As the applause died, Huw wound up the gramophone and announced the dancing.

The children watched as their mothers danced with the few men present, then with each other. Shirley declined several invitations to join in. A few years previously she had suffered a serious injury to her legs that had ended her career as a dancer and they still ached if she overdid things.

Moving from the music and the chattering crowd, she wandered up the road where those who hadn't been involved stood on their doorway and watched. She smiled at some, waved to others but didn't want to stop and talk. She needed to think. The street party was another step towards the day when she and Freddy would be reunited.

When Freddy's parents had died and he'd been given compassionate leave to settle their affairs, he had given her some money to look after for him. She wished he had settled for a bank account instead. It was a complication she didn't need. She had sold the contents of his parents' house and added the money to the amount he had left with her. That trust had added to the commitment she had given by writing to him, implying something greater than being his temporary partner in an illicit affair.

There was another complication too. She still had a certain illogical longing to see someone else. Her strange friendship with Andy hadn't led anywhere and she knew it never could. She had met Andy Probert only a few times and those times had been brief. She knew little about him except that he was untrustworthy. He had been evading call-up since the beginning of the war. Running, hiding, living on his wits and showing a dishonest streak that he had implied was nothing more than a bit of fun. He had kept a step or two ahead of the military police until he had finally been arrested and taken to a military prison. Twice he had escaped before being sent to his unit to begin the military service he had evaded for so long. Now he was dead, so why was she still thinking of him, imagining seeing him?

Andy's brother, Reggie, had worked for Bernard Gregory on his smallholding and, through him, Shirley had learned of Andy's fate. His death was poignant as it had happened exactly as he had foreseen in a recurring dream. The nightmare had been his excuse for not joining up when he'd been called. He had seen himself drowning in the sea with people around who were unable to help him and from the little Reggie had learned, that was exactly what had happened. His body had never been found and somewhere, deep inside her, Shirley wondered if his wily nature had triumphed again and he had used the tragedy to escape the Army once more. Inexplicably she knew she couldn't make a decision about Freddy until she had cleared her mind of thoughts of Andy Probert. But how she would achieve that, she had no idea.

Lilly left soon after the disappointing response from her mother. She had avoided listening to another lecture by keeping out of Marged's sight, which wasn't difficult with the continuing activities in the street. Telling Sam that Phyllis needed to get to bed, she left him with a glass in his hands, talking to some of the neighbours and wandered back through the streets, her spirits fading with the noises from Sidney Street as she moved further away from the partying crowd and nearer to the almost empty house that would soon no longer be her home.

Unaware of how much Sam had drunk, she looked back from time to time, hoping, expecting, to see Sam trying to catch them up. Surely he wouldn't stay at the party and let her go home alone? At the front door she fumbled for her key, unable to see into her handbag as much from the tears as the darkness.

The living room was chilly but it hardly seemed worth bothering to warm it up. Taking Phyllis into bed with her, not caring whether Sam squeezed in beside them or settled himself on the couch, she hugged her daughter and tried to sleep.

Sam recognized Eirlys's father, Morgan, and joined him. Morgan having brought a few flagons of beer in case there wasn't enough to go round, they took their glasses and sat against the wall of Marged and Huw's house.

'I have mixed feelings about this party,' Morgan said sadly. 'Celebrating makes you remember all that's happened, happy and sad and much of it, in my case at least, is very sad. I lost my wife, you know. Killed in London trying to help these evacuees of ours.'

'Was it an air raid?' Sam asked, accepting a refill of his beer glass.

'Road accident.'

'I'm very sorry.'

'Devastating it was, and I can't let it go. The guilt I mean, the guilt won't go away, you see.'

'Were you responsible then?'

'No, no. It isn't her death making me guilty. Before that dreadful accident I'd treated her bad. Real bad. Another woman, see. Another man's wife, Bleddyn's wife, and I drove the poor woman to suicide. My Annie stayed with me, even after that. And then I did a bit of burglary. I'd had some stupid idea of making it up to her. And before that I'd neglected the business my father had left me, and we'd had to move from a beautiful house to a little one and my Annie had to work. I've been a driven man, driven to ruin everything. And poor Eirlys lost her inheritance. Beautiful house we had. And a good life, until I spoilt it all.'

Sam, who was beginning to have difficulties with the letter 's', said, 'Sh'funny, we've jusht moved. It'sh my wife you see. Not my fault. She's been the one to stray. So, I shold the house and we're moving to two roomsh, and she'll hate it there, and I'm pleased she'll hate it there.'

'Too young she is, man. I made that mistake with the boys' mother. Went off proper she did, carrying on something awful. Left me with debts, then, she died too. Beautiful she was, and she died. My punishment for being such a terrible husband.'

'You think they should be punished, shtraying wives?'

'Like your Lilly? Absolutely. I take my punishment like a man and she should too.' He gulped as though about to howl, and said, 'If it wasn't for the three boys, my evacuees who stayed with me when their mam died, well, I don't know what I'd do.'

The three boys Morgan referred to were having fun in various ways. Stanley, the oldest, was dancing with Maude. Since going to the local dances they had become quite proficient and enjoyed holding each other close and moving to the music. Harold was supposed to be dancing too, less successfully, but with a great deal of laughter he fooled around, making silly, exaggerated movements partnering some of the girls he knew from school. Percival was watching, crouched in his brother's jacket which he was minding for him, and with a pout that could have been used to launch a boat.

Myrtle left the dancing and came to sit with him. 'Want to try a waltz?' she asked.

'No, I want to go 'ome. I think it's terrible to have a party when it's bad news for some of us.'

'How can the end of the war affect you, Percival? Are you thinking of your mam, knowing she'll never come back home?'

'I'll be going back to London, so what difference does it make that Mam isn't there?'

'What d'you mean?' she asked. Stanley called to her then and she began to move away, then stopped, and beckoned Stanley over to join them. 'What *do* you mean, Percival?' she asked, gesturing for Stanley not to speak.

'Everyone back where they belong, that's what they're saying. So I'll be going home.'

'You are home, you stupid boy!' Stanley said. 'What are you talking about, going back home? You belong here, in St David's Well, like I do.'

'I'm from London, ain't I? That's where I belong. It's all right for you, you've got a job, but I ain't old enough.'

'Our mother and father are both dead,' Myrtle reminded him. 'So Maude and I are in the same situation as you and Harold and Stanley. But we belong here now, with the Castle family, like you belong to the Price family. Uncle Morgan and Eirlys and Ken and little Anthony, they're your family now. They've accepted you and love you like you were their own. We're the lucky ones, you and I.'

'Is this what's been putting a face on you like a thunderstorm on Bank 'Oliday Monday?' Stanley asked, putting a hand on his brother's shoulder. 'Silly sod, why didn't you talk to me?'

Morgan came over then and overheard enough of the conversation to understand what was going on. He remembered Percival talking about everyone going back where they belonged and suddenly understood.

'Tell me what you're worried about, son,' he said. 'You aren't thinking of going away and leaving me are you? That would break my heart.'

A tear-stained face looked up at him. 'Would it, Uncle Morgan?'

'You three boys *are* where you belong, my son. Here with me and Ken and Eirlys, and what would baby Anthony do if you left him? He loves his big brothers, doesn't he?'

Eirlys saw them and came running and by now Percival was howling unrestrained.

'What's happened? Why are you crying?'

'We'll be staying?' Percival wailed.

97

'Crying because he's happy, that's all,' Morgan said, edging towards tears himself.

'I thought I'd 'ave to go back to London and live all on my own in a dark room like before,' Percival sobbed, now enjoying being centre stage. 'Sleepin' on a bed that smells of pi—'

'Percival —' Eirlys warned.

'You're staying here, with your family. For always,' Morgan said.

'Yeh, it'll take more than victory against ol' 'Itler to make me move from St David's Well,' Stanley said. Then he pointed across the street, faintly lit by lamp-light, open doors and a few candles. 'Go and talk to some of your school friends, our Percival. And for Gawd's sake, smile!' He shook his head, sharing his half amused, half worried emotions with Morgan. 'Kids, eh?'

'Stanley?' Percival said hesitantly.

'What now, you little twerp?'

'I'm hungry, d'you think Auntie Marged would let me have a bit of cake?'

Morgan watched the brothers as they went to find Percival some food and then he rejoined Sam.

Lilly's friend Netta appeared at the party at ten o'clock, explaining that a friend was staying with the children. When she couldn't find Lilly she approached Sam, who, by this time was smiling inanely and treating Morgan to his innermost confidences.

'You shee, Morgan, my friend, she let me down and I can't go on pretending, sho I've shold the house.'

'Yes, so you've said, at least six times, Sam. Come on, I think we'd better get you home.'

As the two men struggled to stand up, Netta asked, 'Is Lilly here, Mr Edwards? We planned to meet but I was delayed.'

'Lilly? I've no idea. She's probably got an ashig— ashig—'

After struggling through several attempts Morgan said the word for him. 'Assignation?'

'With my son,' Sam finished.

Both Morgan and Netta looked shocked and Morgan, suddenly sober, hastily said, 'That wasn't what it sounded like, mind, and don't you dare repeat it. He's muddled up something we were talking about with something said earlier. I'm warning you, whoever you are, that what you heard was the muddled words of a drunken old fool. Right? If I hear one wrong word I'll know where it came from. Right?'

'It's all right Mr er – I won't say a word. Honest.' She could hardly tell the man that she knew all about it, that Lilly had told her about her affair with Sam's son. But her eyes sparkled at the possibility that the truth would come out. Netta's friendship with Lilly Castle had been encouraged for a specific purpose and the time was approaching when that purpose would be revealed.

Cassie had wandered down to join the late-night revellers as they danced and sang. Gradually those with children drifted away and she sat for a while with Marged and Audrey and sang with the rest.

'Your Joseph not home this weekend?' Marged asked, and Audrey's slight shake of her head made her speak quickly to avoid the need for Cassie to reply. 'It'll be some time before the men can get back to their own lives, the reorganization won't happen overnight, will it?' she said.

'What's wrong d'you think?' Marged whispered to her sister when Cassie moved away to talk to others.

'Probably nothing, but Joseph doesn't come home very often and he's only in Cardiff, so Keith and I have wondered if there's a particular reason he neglects her.'

'Ungrateful. And her working so hard too,' Marged said, tutting in disapproval without knowing anything more.

Netta had joined Beth, Peter, Bernard and Reggie. The baby was wrapped up in his pram fast asleep and Netta looked at him, chanted a few flattering comments and sat near them.

'I'm a friend of Lilly,' she explained, then began talking to Beth about her brothers, wording her comments carefully so she gave the impression of knowing them well.

'Your Ronnie got over his injuries well, didn't he?' she began. 'And he runs that market stall as though he's done it all his life. Lovely to see him and Olive so happy, isn't it?'

Bemused, Beth only gave a brief nod in reply.

'Heard from your Eynon lately?' Netta then asked. 'Poor

99

Alice gets so worried when she doesn't hear for a while, but I'm sure he's all right.'

A bit taken aback by this stranger talking like a close family friend, Beth responded briefly and stood to move away. There was something impertinent about the girl's manner which she found off-putting.

'Is your Ronnie here tonight?' She looked around at the groups of people huddled together talking and laughing. 'When will you be going back to your market cafe, Beth, when the baby's old enough to go with you?'

Beth turned and said firmly, 'I haven't decided yet. When I do I'll be sure to let you know!' Her sarcasm was wasted.

'Great. If you need any help any time, Lilly will know where to find me,' Netta said brightly. 'I'll be glad to help the Castle family.'

Peter put an arm around Beth and together they pushed the pram, with Bernard, puffing on the inevitable pipe, following thoughtfully behind.

'Goodnight then,' Netta called, unabashed by their indifference. She looked around for someone else worth talking to, and saw Huw and Marged. Picking up a few dishes from the pavement near the lamp post, she went to join them. They were so engrossed in clearing up and discussing the way the evening had gone, she couldn't break into their conversation, so she sat on a doorstep and waited. She wasn't ready to go home just yet.

It was long after midnight before the party finally ended. Huw and Marged, Bleddyn and Hetty were among the last to go, with a few small groups sitting on doorsteps and the remaining chairs, talking in subdued voices as they dreamed about the men coming home. Alice was among them, sitting on Marged and Huw's doorstep with Ronnie and Olive, while their child slept inside.

'The release of the men will start very soon,' Olive said. 'Imagine! Your Eynon could be back here within weeks.'

Before Alice could reply, there was a crash and they jumped up to see what had happened. In seconds Netta was beside them and she went with them towards the source of the noise. Bleddyn was laughing as he tried to pull Huw from the wreckage of the temporary stage he had been dismantling.

'Anyone hurt?' Ronnie asked.

His father called back, 'Twisted my leg a bit, I think my ankle's broke.' But he was laughing as he said it and no one believed him. 'Damn me, it hurts, mind. I don't think I'll be any use at the beach tomorrow.'

'I'll help if you need an extra pair of hands, Mr Castle,' Netta said.

'No, you're all right. I'll be fine in the morning.'

'What if you aren't? Best to have cover in case you need it. Shall I come over and see if I'm needed, Mrs Castle? Just in case?'

'Sorry, Netta, but no. You've got children. You'd have to have adequate arrangements for them to be looked after properly. We need people we can rely on.'

'I'm reliable. I've got sound arrangements for someone to look after the children. Someone who loves them as much as I do.'

In the confusion of trying to extricate Huw from the boxes and planks of their half-demolished stage, and the lateness of the hour, and Netta's persistence, Marged agreed even though she thought it was unnecessary. 'Oh, all right then. Come if you want to.' Netta turned to go home, well pleased with her evening. Huw limped into the house supported by his brother, while Marged and Hetty told them how stupid they were. Keith and Audrey went to help Bleddyn make safe the remaining planks and boxes.

Shirley walked home through the silent streets with her mother and took the opportunity of telling Hetty about Andy Probert.

'He kept turning up when I needed someone and he had such a light-hearted attitude to inconveniences like a bus not arriving, that he made a disaster into a joke. A problem was transformed into a chance of adventure.'

'And you like him enough to want to see him again?' Hetty asked.

'I can't. He's dead. At least I almost believe he is. He was

101

evading the military police as he had run away from the Army because he had a recurring nightmare about being drowned. And, according to his brother that was what happened. His death occurred exactly as in his dreams.'

'So why do you expect to see him? You haven't started seeing ghosts, have you?'

'He'd run away twice previously, after being arrested. He's a survivor. And although he was declared dead, his body was never found and, Mam, I think I saw him this evening, watching us from the shadows.'

'That's understandable. When my grandfather died I kept looking out for him, convinced he wasn't dead, that a mistake had been made. Once or twice I believed I saw him.'

'It's not wishful thinking, Mam. I almost convinced myself it was Reggie and not Andy I'd seen but not quite. The truth is, I really can't believe he's dead. He was so wily. He wasn't exactly honest and I couldn't imagine ever sharing my life with him, but I still feel as though I'm waiting for him.'

'We deal with death in our own way: some close themselves off from the truth, pretend it hasn't happened; others comfort themselves by blaming someone, some vague official who had neglected to follow an order, or had given a wrong instruction. Or even the person themselves, angry with them for dying and leaving them to cope alone.'

'I don't think any of those reactions relate to me.'

They had reached their gate and Hetty hugged her and said, 'No, Shirley, love. With you it's partly unfinished business with Andy, and mostly your doubts about Freddy. You can't make up your mind whether you love Freddy or not and putting Andy in the way of a decision is your way of dealing with it – for the moment. I'm afraid you'll have to wait until you and Freddy meet, knowing he isn't going away again. Then you'll know, one way or another, and Andy will fade from your mind.'

'I hope so.'

'And so do I, love. We can't step into the future until we have laid to rest the past.'

*   *   *

An inebriated Sam, escorted by an only slightly more capable Morgan, struggled to walk in a straight line along the kerb and he kept falling off the edge.

'Damn me, Sam, I don't know what to do with you. Too heavy to carry and too useless to walk.' Morgan turned and called to Keith, who was gathering the last of the planks, making them safe until morning. 'Keith, come and help me with Sam, will you? I won't get him home till morning at this rate. Sam sat himself down on the pavement, leaned against Morgan's legs and sang softly to himself. Keith and Morgan got him to his feet and over to Marged's house.

'Best he stays with us,' Huw said. 'I can't see him getting much sympathy from our Lilly, can you?'

'I doubt she'd even answer the door,' Marged agreed. 'Bring him inside.'

'Great,' Morgan said. 'Thanks Marged. Now I can go home before Eirlys locks *me* out!'

'Wait a minute, not so fast,' Marged said, pointing to her silly, giggling son-in-law leaning on their front door. 'You can help us sort this merry old soul out first.'

They managed to get Sam on to the couch and Marged wrote a brief note explaining the absence of her husband, for Lilly. 'It's to put through the letter box if she doesn't answer your knock,' she explained to Morgan.

Lilly heard the knock and the voice calling her name but she didn't move. Uncaring of where her husband spent the night she lay there cuddling Phyllis, wrapped in misery, wondering why everything had gone wrong.

It had been such a wonderful thing to do, to marry Sam when her parents thought she was courting his son. Wonderful too to move into Sam's neat little house and have him spoil her with attention and money and all the freedom she wanted to meet with friends and with few demands on her for work around the house.

Then Sam junior had come home and reminded her of all she had been missing. With a sigh of deep melancholy she thought Sam might live for another twenty-five years and she would be trapped until she was an old woman with no chance of a different sort of life.

Her eyes opened wide then, as she felt the shame of her

thoughts. Besides not wanting to wish him dead, she knew she needed him. She and Phyllis were safe in his keeping and she didn't imagine there were many men who would give her such an easy life. No, she didn't want him to die, but perhaps she could find a way to continue seeing Sam junior without him finding out.

Perhaps moving into those awful rooms would have an advantage. Sam junior would have to find a place to live – there was no room for him there, and it could be a place for them to meet. Curiously she stepped out into the hall and peered through the window to see whether Sam was still patiently waiting. She would let him in, he'd been punished enough for her having to walk home alone. Instead she found Marged's note and she was immediately angry that he had been given a comfortable place. Tomorrow she would tell him she hadn't seen the note but had lain awake worrying about where he could be. She pushed it back out through the letter box and went back to bed.

Morgan revived the coal fire with a few sticks and sat in the quiet room, drinking a glass of water to ease the sourness of his stomach after too much alcohol and not enough food. He wished Sam hadn't confided in him. It wasn't a secret he wanted to share. It was too much a reminder of his own infidelity and those of Dolly, mother of Stanley, Harold and Percival, whom he had once hoped to marry. He decided that next time he and Sam met he would say nothing to suggest he remembered. He hoped that Sam would have forgotten telling him.

On the couch, with the embers of the fire glowing in Marged and Huw's living room, Sam lay thinking about his foolish marriage and the cruel reminder of his stupidity when he had found his son and his wife together. After a brief doze he had woken with a mind as clear as ever and he remembered telling Morgan what had happened.

Why hadn't he kept quiet? What was it about drink that obliterated the common sense of confidentiality? It gave a sense of brotherhood to people who would normally be strangers. And a need to show deep and everlasting friendship

104

by sharing secrets, displaying honesty and an openness that should never be revealed.

Although he had known Morgan for many years, they had never been close and he didn't know enough about the man to guess whether or not he would forget what he'd been told. Perhaps his intake of drink had clouded his mind sufficiently for him to have missed it completely? For a moment that hopeful thought brightened him but then doubts returned. A juicy bit of gossip like that would have revived the most drunken of men. An old fool like himself being cheated on by a too-young wife, who would be able to keep that to themselves?

Cassie was another person not able to sleep well that night. The war was over and although she didn't expect everything to revert back immediately in some magical way to pre-war conditions, she did wonder why Joseph was still unable to come home. An hour, that was all it took for him to travel home. For months he had left everything to her and she was tired and lonely. The street party, with families gathered together for celebration and lots of foolish fun, had deepened her unhappiness, reminding her of all she had missed.

A letter had come offering some fire-damaged bedding which had to be collected from a warehouse and instead of waiting for Joseph to get in touch and ask him to arrange for its collection, she decided to go there herself and at the same time call at the office where he worked. Surely now, with the war in Europe ended, there wasn't a need to stay away? The distribution of supplies to the army bases in Great Britain couldn't still be a heavily guarded secret.

She would go there and ask for him. The worst that could happen was to be told he wasn't available or unable to leave his work. Comforted by the decision, she set her alarm for two hours' time and went to sleep.

Lilly eventually slept too, having decided to plead with her parents to be allowed home.

At the time Cassie and Lilly were finally closing their eyes, Netta woke and dressed herself as smartly as she could. Today she was starting work with the Castle family and she was going to make sure they were pleased with her performance.

Six

Ken put down the magazine he was reading when he heard Eirlys coming in. He went out to greet her and took the shopping she carried and placed it on the table. Morgan was at work and the three boys were out. Now seemed to be a good time to sow a few seeds of an idea he had in mind.

'I was talking to an actor friend today. Geoffrey Casterton. I phoned him about a young actor who he might audition for a small part in a play he's touring with. Someone was taken ill and they're desperate.'

'Has he agreed to see him?' Eirlys asked, as she packed her shopping away.

'The frustrating thing is, if I lived nearer to London, I could have taken him along and introduced them. It helps to show your face. Once I'm better known they would come to me when they were searching for an actor instead of me trying to find an opening for those on my list.'

Eirlys showed no reaction and he wondered if the thought had penetrated her mind. She was so busy and with so many differing parts to her life she was sometimes lost when he tried to discuss something. London was where he wanted to be. His plans would not take root here, in the small town of St David's Well. He needed to be where the action was, in London. But how could he persuade Eirlys that it was what they should do?

She made no comment on his remark and when she did speak it was clear that her mind was on her own work and not his.

'I'll be seeing Marged and Huw later, I have to tell them about a meeting they should attend. Shall we all go? The boys won't mind a trip to the beach and Anthony will enjoy it too.'

'Lovely,' he said, hiding his disappointment. He would

106

have to try again, when she had less on her mind, although when that would be he had no idea. It would have to be soon. With the war over and everyone coming home, he knew he had to move and find his place quickly while the opportunities were still there.

Later that evening, Eirlys picked up the magazine Ken had been reading to put it on the pile with the boys' comics and the newspapers, and she noticed the page that was open advertised offices to rent. She frowned, but then shrugged. It couldn't be for Ken; he must be investigating the possibilities for a friend, she decided.

In the phone box on the corner, Ken was working his way down a list of numbers. He was checking on cost and availability of offices to let.

A meeting of the entertainments committee was called for early June to confirm arrangements for the activities for the following months. Eirlys sat on the platform near her bosses, Mr Gifford and Mr Johnston, and prepared to take notes. She had her own list prepared, together with the dates and bookings already made.

The first alteration was the inclusion of a Victory Parade, with children dressed in the uniforms of the services and national costumes, carrying banners and flags of all the nations who had fought with Britain in the conflict. There would be a concert given for the children who were taking part. This was planned for the end of June, by which time it was hoped some of the fathers and older brothers would have been demobbed and able to watch the children taking part.

Eirlys suggested a collection, with people standing on the pavements rattling tins, as the parade of children walked past, and she promised to arrange for volunteers. Yet another note on her ever growing list of things to do.

When the meeting broke up, Eirlys handed her neatly written notes to Mr Gifford, keeping a carbon copy for herself, and slipped away to talk to Huw and Bleddyn, who, as owners of the beach cafe, stalls and rides, had been invited to contribute. Bleddyn told her he and Huw were offering free rides to the children in fancy dress on the day of the parade,

107

and she went back to report this to her boss. To her surprise she saw Bernard Gregory and his son talking to them.

'Dad's offering the donkeys to join in the procession,' Peter explained. 'In Crete and other places, the donkeys helped against the enemy and Dad thinks they should be represented.'

Smiling agreement, Eirlys left them and returned to the office. She would be working late again that evening, writing letters to confirm bookings for the concert and inviting others to attend. There was a pile of collecting tins in an unused office and she went to see whether they could be relabelled and used for the collection alongside the procession. There was still a war to be won and the Red Cross needed funds.

The room which was below the ground floor was the one in which she had worked before the war. It was small, dark and it had contained three desks where three typists and a filing clerk struggled to do the work sent down from the offices above. Life was certainly better now she was able to use her talent for organization. Thank goodness she would never have to return to the boring work of those days.

In a matter of weeks after the European victory, Alice was told she was no longer needed at the factory. With relief she called on her parents-in-law and offered to work on the sands.

'Only till Eynon and Johnny come home,' she said. 'I know you won't need me then. But until they get back I can work for you in the cafe.'

Marged and Huw looked at each other.

'Pity is, we've got enough at the moment, Alice, love,' Marged said, 'with the new girl helping in the cafe, and Maude and Stanley, and me and Huw. Bleddyn and Hetty run the fish and chip shop with part-time help.' She shrugged in disappointment.

'Stanley might be glad of some help on the stalls, mind,' Huw added. 'The busiest time is to come and, good as he is, he can't run two rides and a stall during the holiday months.'

Trying to smile, Alice said, 'It seems you don't need me. That's good, I'm glad you haven't had worries like last year, when Beth and I left the business and Audrey opened her own cafe with Keith. Don't worry, I'll find something.'

'The truth is, Alice, we couldn't pay you enough. You'll

do better somewhere else, somewhere permanent, not just for the season. And this Netta's a bit of a find,' Huw confided. 'She works real hard, and doesn't seem to mind what she's asked to do.'

'Netta? That wouldn't be Lilly's friend, would it?'

'Yes, d'you know her?'

'Remember I told you about a young woman following me? That was Netta. I know you think I imagined it, but she met Lilly in the park and I have the feeling she deliberately cultivated her friendship until she was introduced to the rest of you.' She shrugged as though expecting them to laugh. 'I know. It sounds ridiculous. But Lilly told me she asks a lot of questions about the Castles. Lilly was flattered, being reminded of how famous her family is, but I am less happy. She makes me uneasy.'

'Don't worry, we'll keep an eye on her,' Huw said.

'Both eyes!' Alice joked, but although she made their faces crease in a smile, the laughter failed to reach her own. She was hurt. Why hadn't they thought of getting rid of Netta? She was family, an important member of the workforce, and now she was free, surely she had a place within the family business? But was it all a pretence? Nothing more than politeness because she was married to their son? She felt bereft, she no longer belonged. Would she feel that way with Eynon? Would he with her?

She went home and wrote to Eynon, telling him about her uneasiness regarding Netta but, unwilling to worry him with something that might after all be in her imagination, she tore it up and started again, writing a light-hearted description of the fancy dresses Hannah and Eirlys were making for their children. She ended by hoping that he would be home in time to share the fun. Letters to serving soldiers were often torn up during the war years. A chance remark that might cause worry was quickly relegated to the rubbish bin. No one wanted the men and women to worry about things they weren't able to change.

News of demobilization was now being discussed with the same enthusiasm as the war had been. The discharging of forces was due to begin in the middle of June and already families were preparing their own celebrations. Paint was found to create banners to hang over doorways and 'Welcome home, Dad' flags were made from any material that could be found.

By the time the day of the Victory Parade came, many houses had greeted their loved ones and for them, victory was complete.

Demobilization was by way of selection with age and length of service priorities for early discharge, but there were those with particular skills who were allowed to leave sooner than the rules allowed. Builders, farm workers and those concerned with industry were quickly discharged to ensure the country got back on its feet as quickly as possible. So one of the first familiar faces to be seen back in St David's Well with his discharge papers and a new suit was that of Reggie Probert, who had worked on Bernard Gregory's smallholding when the authorities had taken Sally Gough's fields and handed them to Bernard to grow more food.

He had discussed a permanent job with Bernard and it was to the smallholding he went first on arriving in St David's Well, to ask if the arrangement still stood.

Bernard agreed, aware that his son, Peter, did not intend to take on his father's business and also, that he was getting too old to continue working as hard and as long as he had over the past years. Leaving his small suitcase with Bernard, and wearing his 'demob' suit, Reggie went to find Maude.

Audrey's cafe had become *the* place where people gathered to share good news. Audrey loved the atmosphere she had created, allowing people to stay long after their coffee had been drunk and the cakes eaten, to sit and talk. As in most families, letters were shared throughout the war and now, with at least the war with Germany at an end, this sharing of news continued. Audrey stood behind the counter with Maude and listened to the lively conversations going on around her.

'Wonderful, isn't it?' she said. 'Every day there's news of someone coming home.'

'None of ours yet,' Maude said. 'Eynon and Johnny still far away, no message from Reggie since his surprise visit to the

110

street party where we missed each other. I don't know when I'll see him. And there's no sign of Shirley's Freddy.'

'Perhaps Reggie will go home to see his family first,' Audrey said. 'With his brother dead his mother will be so relieved to know Reggie's safe.'

'Of course. I'm being selfish. I wish he'd write though.'

'There'll be a letter soon, sure to be.' Audrey wondered whether Reggie was one of the young men who had encouraged girls to write, without the intention of coming back to them. They had all needed love-letters to help them believe they had a future. Now his war was over, Reggie might be content to go back to his home and his former life and loves. She said nothing of this to Maude. If Reggie failed to arrive, then the realization would come slowly, less painfully.

The subject of their conversation was at the beach. He was uneasy about meeting Maude and had been to Audrey's cafe twice and walked away. His thoughts were the opposite of Audrey's. He knew he shouldn't expect Maude to be as happy at seeing him as he was at returning to her. Everyone knew that girls wrote to soldiers out of sympathy, aware of their need for contact with home. Now he was back for good he didn't want to make the mistake of expecting her to fall into his arms and swear undying love. Although his hopes were for something along those lines.

'Reggie?' He turned as he heard his name and stared at the young woman standing near him.

'Myrtle? Gosh you've grown up. I've only been away five minutes and you've gone from a gawky school girl to a young woman.'

'Cheek! I was never gawky! Where are you going? What's with the suit?'

Reggie laughed deprecatingly and brushed an imaginary crumb from his lapel. 'Demob suit. Like it?'

'I'd better go quick and warn our Maude to take off her pinny and put on something fancy.'

'Are you going there now? I'll come with you,' he said, offering her his arm.

'I've got to go and see Stanley first,' she explained. 'Auntie

Marged wants him at the beach early in the morning because Uncle Huw is going to the warehouse for supplies.'

'All right, I'll come with you,' he said, glad of an excuse not to walk into Audrey's flat alone. Aware of the lateness of the hour and of the time he had spent wandering, he suggested they caught the bus to Conroy Street.

Eirlys was out but they were invited inside, where Stanley and Harold immediately asked Reggie how many soldiers he had killed.

'None, you gruesome lot,' he told them. 'I was in the Catering Corps.'

'Ah, I see, own goals don't count, eh?' Stanley said, ducking Reggie's blow.

Having delivered her message, Myrtle urged him to leave. 'Come on, Reggie, the cafe will be closed soon and Auntie Audrey will wonder where I am. Don't you want to see our Maude then?'

Audrey's cafe stayed open until 9 p.m., and tonight it seemed that the customers didn't want to go. A group of young girls sat crowded around three tables pushed together, sipping coffee and whispering secrets.

Shutting off the main light didn't encourage them to depart and it wasn't until Audrey went to stand by the open door that they reluctantly gathered their coats and stood to leave. Before they reached the door, a figure appeared and Audrey raised a hand and explained the cafe was closed. Then she recognized Myrtle and looked again at Reggie.

'Maude?' she called. 'Come and see to this last customer, will you?'

'Does this mean we can have another coffee?' one of the customers asked hopefully.

'Go now and you can have a free cup tomorrow. Just go.'

'One coffee or one each?'

'Go!'

Taking Myrtle's hand, Audrey led her out into the kitchen, leaving Maude and Reggie alone.

With only the light angling through from the kitchen, where Audrey and Myrtle washed dishes with unnecessary noise, Reggie and Maude sat and stared at each other.

'When did you get home?' Maude asked.

Reggie didn't reply, he just stared at her. 'I can't believe I'm here with you,' he whispered.

'Been to see your Mam?'

'I want to kiss you.'

'Reggie, stop it.'

'Stop what? Wanting to kiss you? Never.'

'I ought to be helping.' She gestured towards the kitchen, where Myrtle and Audrey were singing.

'Stop trying to make small talk. Just kiss me.'

'Reggie, someone will see us!'

He leaned across the small table, big, strong, so familiar and so loved. She murmured his name softly, closed her eyes and surrendered to his kiss. Audrey glanced in and carefully closed the kitchen door.

'Two down – Beth's Peter and Maude's Reggie – and three more to go,' she whispered to Myrtle. 'Our Eynon and Johnny, and Shirley's Freddy.'

'It won't be long, Auntie Audrey.'

When she heard that Reggie Probert was home, Shirley went to see him. Perhaps there was news about his brother? Although she was only half convinced that he was alive, she had to know for certain. With no body found and no other evidence of his death, like hundreds of other women, she couldn't quite believe it.

'Reggie,' she called when she saw him walking beside a small cart being pulled by one of the donkeys. 'Glad to see you home safe and sound. Back with Mr Gregory, are you?'

'He put me to work straight away,' he said. 'Terrible hard man he is.' Shirley was surprised to hear him criticizing his boss, until Bernard's head popped out from the other side of the cart.

'Lazy devil wanted a week off. I told him he'd skived long enough and the mustard field wanted ploughing in.'

Shirley followed them up the hill to where the field of yellow mustard flowers glowed like gold in the sun. Growing the crop and ploughing it in fed the ground with what Bernard called green manure – she remembered Andy explaining that.

While Bernard went to collect the horse, Reggie spread his coat and invited her to sit.

'You want to talk to me about Andy, I suppose.'

'I don't want to upset you, Reggie, but I think I've seen him.'

Reggie didn't show any surprise or distress. 'I don't think that's all that unusual. When someone dies in an accident and you see them and you attend their funeral, it's final and settled but when someone dies a long way from home and you don't even know where or how, it's as though the story's incomplete. So in your mind you're waiting for him to appear, denying what the facts tell you.'

'Nonsense!' Shirley retorted angrily. 'I'm not some silly girl in love with a ghost! Andy wasn't important to me and I'm certainly not daydreaming of the return of some hero! I just think he might be alive because of the kind of person he is. He was a cheat and a crook, and he avoided being sent to fight for most of the war. He was scared, Reggie. Running away in the confusion of battle was something I can believe and so can you, if you're honest.'

Reggie shook his dark head. 'If you're right, he would have contacted me. He knows I would never report him. He's my brother and I'd rather have him alive and in trouble, than dead. The nightmares he suffered where he saw himself drowning were real enough. I shared a bedroom with him and he used to wake screaming and Dad and I had to hold him until he came out of the terror he saw for himself.'

'If he's caught even after the war finally ends, he'll still go to prison, won't he?'

'I don't know. Perhaps it won't be difficult to find a new personality. There's plenty of confusion, with people missing and families dispersed. He could start again with a different name maybe.'

'But you don't think he's alive?'

'No, I don't. He'd have let me know.'

Bernard came with the horse and a collection of harness straps and buckles and Shirley left them to their work and walked back into town. She was almost convinced, but there was still a niggle of doubt. She tried to think of Freddy

114

Clements, preparing a letter in her head that she would write when she reached home. But Freddy's face slipped away from her mind and was replaced by the handsome, cheeky face of Reggie's brother with his guileless, blue eyes.

Cassie closed for the half day on Wednesday and instead of spending the time doing housework and bringing the shop's books up to date she went into Cardiff. She hadn't decided whether or not she would call at his office to try to see Joseph, but she was increasingly curious about his continued absences.

The address was in a quiet area of the town, some distance from the shops, where offices and one or two houses attracted few passers-by. Her footsteps sounded hollow on the pavement, echoing back and emphasizing the emptiness.

The buildings were large and impersonal, with many windows boarded, presumably after bomb damage, and others still criss-crossed with anti-shatter tape. Only the strong wooden door of the offices, with its polished letter boxes, showed signs of habitation. She stopped and stared at it, still wondering whether or not to knock and begin an enquiry which might lead to something she didn't want to know.

There was something off-putting about this place, where Joseph had spent the war years. She had no right to be there, it was a part of his life in which she had no part. On her one previous visit, a girl had sat typing, just inside the door and discouraged anyone from entering. That was understandable if what Joseph had told her was true and he was on secret war work, but surely everything had been relaxed from those dangerous times now Germany was defeated?

The door was a heavy one and she pondered briefly and idly on how large the key would have to be. Several brass notices were fastened to the side of it. None of them hinted at the importance of the work that had gone on inside. The firms sounded innocuous and most appeared to provide office equipment or were small printers. That was different. Before it had been connected with supplies of food. She knocked at the door loudly, trying to appear confident. Joseph was her husband, after all, and she was entitled to talk to him.

A young man opened the door and stood, his head tilted questioningly, without saying a word.

'I wish to see Mr Joseph Davies,' she said firmly.

'Sorry, madam, there's no one of that name working here.'

'What d'you mean? My husband has worked here all through the war.'

'Ah, but our area of the conflict has ended, and the Ministry of Food personnel have moved on.' He closed the door before she could formulate another question and she stood there for a long time staring at it.

'Can I help you?' a voice asked and Cassie turned to see a young woman standing beside her, obviously waiting to go inside.

'My husband works there and a young man just told me he doesn't.'

'And your husband's name is – ?'

'Joseph. Joseph Davies.'

'Oh, I know Joe. He lives in Gratton Street.'

'Has lodgings there you mean?' She was confused. 'But he worked here and had accommodation that went with the job. I don't understand. If the job has changed, why is he in lodgings with a home an hour away? He's living here!' she insisted. 'And his name is Joseph. No one calls him Joe.' Cassie was angry. She was being made to look a fool. As the young woman shrugged then reached out to knock on the door, Cassie swallowed her pride to ask, 'You don't know the number, of his lodgings, I mean?'

The young woman frowned as though trying to remember. 'We all went to a party there on V.E. night. Number seven I think it was. Yes, number seven. Green curtains. I can check for you?' she added brightly.

'No need. Thanks,' Cassie said as she turned away. The girl must be wrong. Joseph going to a party on V.E. night? He didn't even like parties. Besides, he'd have come home to her if he'd been free.

The young woman gave her directions and she walked to the end of Gratton Street and looked at the fourth house along, with its green curtains. She didn't knock. She was

116

afraid she would have to explain to another stranger that she didn't know where her husband was. Throughout the war he had lived in the same building as the offices, the staff working around the clock on a shift system. So when that was no longer necessary, why hadn't he come home? What was he doing living in Gratton Street? These were questions needing an answer but not here: she needed the security of home to ask them. She turned away and returned to the centre of the town.

Disconsolately she wandered through the market, where queues suggested the arrival of some luxury or other. She mused over what she would describe as luxuries. Things that had once been commonplace had been added to the list of items worth queuing for in the almost six years of rationing. She stretched across to see that one queue was for small, odd-shaped cucumbers, and some sad-looking pears. In the fish market people waited patiently to be allowed to buy a pound of sprats. She didn't bother. At home there was a small portion of cheese she had been saving for Joseph. She'd make a Welsh rarebit for her supper. Wherever he was, it didn't seem likely he'd be wanting supper today. His arrivals were always heralded by a letter a few days before.

At home she lit a fire and made herself a snack, then settled to concentrate on the books. She had to forget Gratton Street and other mysteries until Joseph was there. Later that night she wrote to him, making no mention of her aborted visit. Instead she told him their bank balance, and the possibility of renting yet another shop while the premises were cheap. That would please him and perhaps would persuade him to come home and discuss her proposed next stage of their business plan.

Alice came into the shop the following day and she told her that Joseph was not working for the war department any more, and of being told he had found new lodgings. Aware of the woman's anxieties that were half hidden by a cheery smile, Alice asked why she hadn't called at the address she had been given.

'I don't know. Time, partly. I wanted to get home before the crowds filled the trains. I hate not having a seat.'

To Alice the answer didn't convince. 'If you like, I'll go with you one afternoon. If you haven't heard by next Sunday, we could go in and find the place. I'll wait outside and we can come home together.'

'No need, Alice. You're needed on the beach at the weekends, I'm sure.'

'Not any more,' Alice replied. She spoke lightly, hiding her continuing hurt. 'They have plenty of willing hands these days. Casual workers they know nothing about have been taken on, so I'm not needed.'

'More fools them.'

'Yes, well, shall we go on Sunday? Or we could make it Wednesday, then we could have a cup of tea somewhere.'

'Thank you, Alice, but he'll be home before then, sure to be.'

'If you want any help, with anything, just get in touch. You know where I live.' Alice had a feeling that all was not well, but she couldn't ask questions outright and reveal her suspicions. She knew Cassie didn't find it easy to confide in someone else and a persistent offer of help might make her wary, discouraging her from further confidences. Then she wouldn't be any use at all. Suspicions were growing in Alice's mind and she guessed that one day soon, Cassie would need a friend.

The Victory Parade of children in bright fancy dress attracted crowds who lined the pavement to watch as it passed through the main road of the town. Children who hadn't joined in, tagged on the end, calling names, jeering the participants, blowing raspberries and being chased away by irate parents, then darting back to torment some more. The procession wound its way around the streets ending up at the town hall. There, transport awaited them and buses and lorries took the participants to the beach.

Every nationality who had shared the victory was represented and besides the school children walking along class by class, there were toddlers and small babies being pushed in prams or carried by proud mothers. In the middle of the line was Bernard and his donkeys.

The townspeople who watched the cavalcade pass, had been joined by repatriated soldiers wearing the hospital uniform; most were bandaged, many had lost limbs but all were enjoying the scene and cheering the children as they passed.

When they reached the beach, a concert party had gathered to reward the participants and, sitting them in rows, the teachers urged them to be quiet as the choir began to sing 'The Teddy Bear's Picnic'. At the side of the stage, Shirley waited for her signal to join in.

It was immediately apparent that something was wrong, as one section of the choir was singing in a different key. The conductor's attempts to rectify this led to another section singing at a slower tempo. Shirley began again. After several attempts to bring them to order, some choir members leaned forward and poked their tongues out at the apparently irate conductor. Some of the audience were disconcerted but others guessed it was part of the fun of that celebratory day.

Then, to convince the doubters, from within the closely packed singers clowns appeared, squirted water at everyone and ran around, falling over, tripping people up and causing mayhem. They were cheered by the audience while the conductor tried in vain to restore order.

Shirley was laughing at the antics of the intruders when one of the clowns stopped in front of her. He wore a huge painted mouth with down-turned ends and sloping lines above each eye which gave him a sad expression. He stared for a moment then gave her a slow wink. The dark eyes, which on close examination were a surprising blue, stared at her before the man ran off to rejoin the fun. Andy! It was Andy!

In vain she tried to find him amid the identically dressed, tumbling clowns but with the make-up disguising their faces it was impossible. This time she was in no doubt. It was Andy she had seen. She pushed her way through the excited children and went to where Maude and Myrtle were standing with Audrey and Keith.

'One of the clowns is Andy,' she said emphatically.

'Shirley, of course it isn't Andy. He's dead and he'll never be back.' Audrey spoke sympathetically as though to a simple child.

'I saw him. He stopped right in front of me and he winked!'

The clowns had finished their nonsense and the children were being led away to where Huw and Marged had prepared cakes for them.

'Reggie, over here,' Maude called and one of the clowns ran towards them, pausing for Maude to quickly explain.

'Did you enjoy it?' the familiar voice asked and as Shirley looked into the eyes of the clown she saw, not Andy, but his brother Reggie.

'It was you?'

'That's right, Shirley. I was forced to take part.'

'You stopped in front of me and – poked your tongue out?'

For a moment he hesitated and even with the make-up distorting his appearance, hiding any expression he might otherwise have shown, that momentary doubt alone would have convinced Shirley he was lying when he said, 'Yes. That was me.' But she had lied too and she knew for certain the man had been not Reggie but his brother, Andy.

If their intention was to convince her that it had not been Andy she'd seen, it had failed. The eyes of Reggie were not exactly like his brother's. They were similar, but Andy's were so dark they looked brown at first, until you stared and then you realized they were blue. Andy had been here, telling her he was alive.

They thought she was losing her mind, pacifying her with kind words as they would a distressed child. Angrily she turned away from them.

Leaving the others, she pushed her way to the station and caught the train back to the other end of town. She was trembling. Why was he tormenting her? Why didn't he talk to her? His quirky sense of humour was no longer a delight. She wanted to escape from the nightmare he was creating.

What should she do? What *could* she do? She wouldn't be believed if she reported his survival to the authorities and anyway she didn't want to do that. He had made his decisions and survived the war by running away from danger and the way he chose to spend the peace was up to him.

She couldn't write to Freddy that evening. Her handwriting was shaky and she couldn't think of a single thing to tell him. The fun of the afternoon had faded from her mind as soon as the clown that was Andy had stopped and winked at her.

Netta was utterly fed up with working in Castle's cafe. She hadn't been there long before the day of the Victory Parade gave them all so much extra work. Beside the usual customers coming in for trays to take down to the sand, and people demanding chips to be eaten in the cafe, the afternoon was made more chaotic serving the children wearing fancy dress, with cakes.

The children had been gathered in circles on the sand below the cafe and Netta had lost count of the number of times she had climbed down and up the metal steps to carry more cakes and drinks to the excited crowd. The offer of free cakes had been promised to those involved and wearing fancy dress, but it had been impossible to avoid sharing the treat with others who had simply followed the parade or run to the beach afterwards to join them.

'I don't blame them, do you?' was Marged's only comment when Netta complained about the interlopers holding out their grubby little hands.

Austerity meant the only way they could all be included was to make the cakes a fraction of the usual size and Netta had spent hours putting the small offerings in and then out of the oven. By six o'clock she was hot, tired and on the edge of telling Marged she wouldn't be working there any more. Then Alice came in and her resolve strengthened. It would be worth it. Very soon she would tell them, and then she wouldn't have to work any more. Like her friend Lilly, she would have an easy life just looking after Dolly and Walter, meeting friends and lazing the summer days away in the park and on the beach.

The hours she worked meant she had less time to meet Lilly but she made sure they met most days. Lilly was free and whatever time Netta suggested, Lilly was able to join her friend for an hour or so.

'Any news of your brother and your cousin coming home?'

she asked Lilly one day when they met in the cafe after closing time. True to form, Lilly had made sure the cleaning up was finished before she arrived with Phyllis, asking if there were any left-over cakes to spare.

'Eynon hopes to be home in August,' Marged answered for her. 'And no, our Lilly, I haven't any food left. I've just given what I had to Netta. She works here, remember. She's not idle like you.'

'Shut-up nagging, our Mam,' Lilly whispered for Netta to hear.

'I heard that, Lilly, and I'll have no more of your cheek! Why aren't you home getting Sam's tea for him?' Marged shouted.

'Because he doesn't want me to. He's a better cook than I am.' She tilted her head towards the door, mocking her mother's impatient tutting. 'Coming, Netta?'

Netta thankfully collected her coat and the packet of leftover food, and the two girls walked down the steps and across the sand.

'Tomorrow we're moving into those awful rooms,' Lilly told her friend. 'I've had to brush walls down and wash floors and scrub the pantry shelves. I'm worn out.'

'Poor you. Did you really have to scrub floors?'

'Well, to be honest, I didn't do much more than wet everything. I can't cope with scrubbing and all that stuff. It looked clean enough when I'd done.'

The next day, the move was done efficiently, with Sam doing most of the work while Lilly sat and sobbed. By the evening, the rooms looked as comfortable as possible even though they were over full. The bedroom was less attractive than their old one with heavy, old-fashioned wallpaper and drab curtains. To Lilly it was a place where she no longer felt at home. They slept in the same bed but were as apart as it was possible to be. No hugs, she thought. Not any more. She didn't even try, as Sam had made it clear she was no longer loved.

On her day off, Netta appeared at the cafe with her two children.

'Hello, Netta, can't you keep away?' Huw joked, reaching for a Welsh-cake to give to the children.

'Walter wanted to see where I work,' Netta explained, and, seeing a queue forming, she sat Dolly on a chair, told Walter to look after her and slipped around the counter to serve. When the rush died away, Marged came to see the children.

Walter was rather surly, but Dolly was friendly and soon enjoying the attention of the two adults.

'Walter's very quiet,' Huw commented. 'Not unhappy, is he?'

Taking him aside, Netta explained. 'Resentful he is, because he doesn't have a daddy like his friends.'

'What happened?'

'He left us,' Netta replied sadly. Alice overheard and said, 'Left you? I thought you told me he'd been killed in the war?'

'Walter's father was killed, yes, but Dolly's father left us.'

'What happened?' Huw asked, ignoring Alice's comment.

'He didn't love us, I suppose.'

Alice tried to speak, but Huw hushed her with his hand, and she turned away, anger mounting.

'Walter doesn't get letters like other children. His father went away, something he wasn't old enough to understand and all Walter was left with was knowing that Dolly's father didn't love us and doesn't want us. Poor love, he blames himself, thinks he's unlovable.'

Exasperated by the way Huw and Marged were sympathetic to a girl she mistrusted, and not believing a word she was saying, Alice went out and began to wash the counters ready to make more sandwiches.

Why wouldn't they listen to her? She had warned them about Netta; told them it had been Netta who had been following her, watching her house and walking behind her as she went to work. It must be the sympathy Netta was engendering for the children. Children in trouble was something neither Marged nor Huw could ignore.

The arrival of Netta and her two children had made Alice feel unwanted. First as Lilly's friend and now a part of the business, Netta had wormed her way into the family and at the same time, because of Alice's mistrust of the girl, Marged and Huw clearly considered her unkind. If only Eynon were home. His parents were supporting this newcomer and pushing her away. His return was going to be difficult enough without a family rift to contend with.

She glanced into the cafe where a family had just arrived and were finding themselves seats. Marged and Huw looked lost in Netta's story. Trying to shed her continuing feelings of dread, Alice smiled and went forward to serve.

Eirlys was one of the few who had no one serving. Ken had been working throughout the war organizing concert parties and he had rarely been away for more than a couple of weeks at a time. Now the need for his work was slowly ending. Fundraising went on but the promise of an early end to the fighting in the Far East made him stop and consider his future.

'I want to go to London,' he surprised her by announcing one morning. She had ignored previous hints and the bald statement, so emphatic, came as a shock. She didn't reply, just watched as he placed a page of notes and figures in front of her and began to explain. 'I intend to start an agency finding work for actors and entertainers. Once I become well known for having top performers on my books, I know it will be a success.'

'No, Ken,' Eirlys replied succinctly.

'But you haven't heard my ideas yet! Look at this list. All these people are willing for me to represent them.'

'Good. I'm really pleased for you. But you'll have to work from home; we're not moving to London. I have a job as well, remember, and it's one I'm good at and enjoy.'

'I need to be in London. That's essential. You must realize that, Eirlys. It's where I'll make the best contacts and become known. I have to be accessible.'

'And I need to be here, to look after Dadda and the boys, and, as you know, my work is here.'

Ken stared at her, the firmly closed lips, the steely eyes, the tight jaw. He grabbed the papers he intended to show her and pushed them untidily into his briefcase. 'We'll talk about it later.'

'No, Ken. I don't want to discuss it. St David's Well isn't the back of beyond. London is within reach. Five hours on the train and you're there. Forget about us moving. My job, my family and my friends are here.'

'And what about me? Aren't I classed as family? Or friend? Or am I just someone you have to suffer the presence of?'

'Don't be melodramatic, Ken. You're my husband and I love you. I just don't want you to take us away from everything else I love.'

'I should come first, above all the rest.'

'Look, I have to go. There's a meeting at ten and I need to get the papers set out and the coffee organized.' She made her escape and ran anxiously towards the bus stop. She'd been half-expecting this. Ken's conversations had been laced with the price of renting in London, and comments about the people whom he knew with places they were willing to share. The remarks were casually said, as though referring to other people, but she knew Ken's dream about working and living in London was not a trivial idea that would fade. The dream was getting stronger and he now saw it as a reality.

That evening when she went into the house after collecting Anthony from Hannah, there was an unusual silence. No wireless playing, no boys arguing and, in the living room, no sign of Ken or her father.

She played with Anthony for a while before giving him his bath and a drink of milk and settling him into his cot. When she went back downstairs Ken was standing in front of the fire. He had a sheaf of papers in his hand.

'Oh, Ken, not now,' she pleaded.

'Yes, now. I have an offer of a room in a suite of offices and it's in a good position, a good address and I want to take it. I have contracts ready for signing, and I know I can make a success of this.'

Eirlys said nothing. She just stared at him.

'If you won't come, then I'll go on my own, come home at weekends, holidays, that sort of thing. But I am going to do this, Eirlys.' Still she didn't speak and he went on, 'It won't be a profitable enterprise at first, 'specially if I have to help you here and live up there, but I'm prepared to give it a try. I think the income will be sufficient to keep me and hopefully send money home. Will you at least let me try this?'

She didn't hear the rest of his explanations. Something inside her blocked off all sound and all she could think of was her job, the position she had held on to, even when she wanted to be at home with Anthony. Thank goodness she had that. She had always feared something like this. He might be talking about weekends and holidays, but she doubted whether that would last long. No, if he wanted to leave her, try his luck in London, he would quickly disappear from her life. As he almost had once before, when he had fallen in love with Janet Copp, who had danced and sang. Her instincts had been sound. Her marriage to Ken was not.

Ken followed her around, still trying to convince her what he was doing was for their future, while she made a few sandwiches. Her father and the boys had gone to the pictures and would be hungry when they came in. What would they say? Would she tell them from the angle of an unfairly treated wife, or as a young woman who wanted to follow her husband and support his dreams, but could not? Either way, it would be untrue. Ken was leaving her and unless she threw everything away and prepared to abandon Stanley, Harold and Percival at a time when they needed stability, she would lose him.

Sadness overwhelmed her. She had begun to feel safe, secure in her marriage, but now, her pure panic reaction to Ken's proposal made her face the fact that the truth was Ken had lost her trust. She couldn't leave everything here and go with him to start a new life among strangers. She didn't have that much confidence in him.

He had failed her dreadfully when he'd had an affair and facing this situation made her realize it hadn't fully mended. She was no longer sure of him or her own feeling for him and perhaps she never would be again. Going to London, depending on Ken for everything was frightening. It was something she just couldn't do. Thank goodness I have a good job, she muttered silently. I can support myself and Anthony, thanks to my job.

*   *   *

Alice went to the beach less and less. Her in-laws had no real need of her, specially with Netta even spending the days when she wasn't working there, with Walter and Dolly enjoying the attention of Marged and Huw. They were pleased to see her when she called, but made it clear she wasn't needed.

She was lonely with only Eynon's letters for company and the two rooms began to feel like a prison. It wasn't easy to decide on a job she would enjoy, but she eventually settled for the office of a large grocery shop. It was hardly exciting and the wages were far less than the factory had paid.

She had been cautious with money and had saved quite a lot to add to the money her father had left her. She and Eynon would be able to buy the perfect house. All her thoughts were on Eynon, and his return was a regular dream both during the night and the day.

She hadn't bothered to make friends, patiently waiting until the day Eynon came home. All the time she had worked in the factory she had ignored the friendly invitations from the other girls. Now when one of the office girls invited her to go to the cinema with some friends, she agreed. The evenings were long and she looked forward to the company and the entertainment of films at the cinema and concerts and even on occasions a visit to a public house.

Whereas before, she would make duty visits to Eynon's parents she now filled her spare time with her new friends, enjoying the films they saw with the additional pleasure of being able to discuss them afterwards.

They were smartly dressed and all wore make-up and soon enticed her to wear foundation cream, a touch of lipstick and even some eyeshadow. She queued with the rest when supplies arrived in the local shops. Her hair, which had been tied up in a snood and covered with a scarf for safety for so long, when she had worked with machinery, was cut and styled and gradually life changed.

Marged and Huw both made artificially polite remarks; thinly veiled disapproval, which she ignored. She liked her new self and knew Eynon would too. Wouldn't he?

Seven

O ver the next few days, Eirlys avoided talking to Ken. Sadly, Morgan watched them both, knowing something was wrong, but he said nothing. When difficulties arose in a marriage the situation was more often worsened than helped by too many words being spoken.

On Sunday morning, Eirlys dressed Anthony, invited Harold and Percival to join her and went to the beach, where Stanley was working on the sands. She was utterly sad and even the lively activities of the children around her failed to pierce her gloom.

When they had found a place below the sea wall and unpacked their belongings, Harold undressed and helped Percival to do the same. Percival was almost twelve but still very slow and his brothers were used to helping him. As they ran down to the enticing waves Eirlys sat with Anthony, making a sandcastle and wondering how he would feel about her decision not to go with Ken to London.

He was too young to be included in the decision-making but, she wondered, was she being unfair to her son by depriving him of his father? Because that was what she might be doing. Would Ken settle for a family at weekends and holidays? Or would he find someone more willing to involve herself with his ambition?

Ken had said very little in the days following his announcement. He spent time writing letters and if they were involved in his plans to live in London she didn't know and she was afraid to ask. If he answered in the affirmative it would be one more nail in the coffin of their troubled marriage. They were pulling in different directions, both convinced they were right, and neither would give in.

Behind her on the promenade a group of children were about to perform a play depicting a beach scene of Victorian times. It had been the work of teachers in the school nearby but the suggestion had been hers. In the cricket field, some of the local teams were giving demonstrations and helping interested youngsters to learn the game. Another of her ideas. She thought of her work and for a moment doubted its validity at a time when almost the whole world had been at war. She could have been better occupied making munitions or running an office directly connected with the conflict rather than organizing fun events.

She held Anthony's hand and walked down to the edge of the tide, where children were splashing and fooling about, working hard at doing nothing, as her father often said. Anthony danced in the waves, shrieking with the rest.

On their way home they stopped to see the end of the Victorian-style drama, which had been a comedy played for every laugh they could get. The faces on those taking part and in the audience, which was made up mostly of the actors' families, showed pleasure. But Eirlys didn't share their joy. It was all a pretence. Her contribution to the war effort had been to force people to pretend to have fun when their hearts were breaking, as hers was now.

Then she saw Harold and Percival enjoying the last few minutes, pointing at the performers, sharing the laughter and knew she was wrong. There was nothing false about the audience's enjoyment. What better way of coping with the tragedies still being played out all around them than with the joy of innocent laughter? Her work was worthwhile and would continue to be. The tragedies of death and suffering would be with many families for always.

As though to add validity to her sombre thoughts, the crowd moved back to allow a blind man to pass, his solicitous companion guiding him and whispering reassurance. The young man's face was deeply scarred and she daren't imagine the experiences that had caused them. Guilt for her selfish mood overwhelmed her. The consequences of the war would never end for many citizens of St David's Well. With Ken and her father safe, she was one of the few lucky ones.

She went home, if not happy, then at least less miserable than when she had set out. Her decision had been made. She was going to stay here, where she was needed, assure Ken of her belief in him, and live for weekends and holidays when he would come home and she could demonstrate her love and trust.

When she told him her decision, Ken seemed resigned when she hoped he would be disappointed. He shrugged as though it was the answer he had expected.

'Sorry, Ken,' she said as the hurt of his reaction wrapped around her. He didn't care whether she stayed or followed.

'It's your decision, Eirlys. I thought you'd refuse to come with me. I know how low I stand on your list of importance,' he added bitterly, leaving the room without giving her a chance to respond.

'Ken,' she called, and started to follow him, but Percival gave a yell, then complained that Harold had pinched his sweets, and she went at once to deal with it. Ken was right, she thought with shame. Concern for the boys came before him. She wondered whether it would ever change.

Settling the argument between the brothers, she thought into the future, to a time when the boys were grown up and no longer in need of her. Perhaps then, she would be able to concentrate on her marriage. Her life was pulling her in too many directions and she couldn't let go.

For the rest of the evening Ken immersed himself in his books. He went out several times to use the telephone outside the house but said nothing of what he was doing. She wondered whether he was making arrangements to leave, set up his business in London and begin a life in which she had no part. The thought was frightening, but she was more worried by her lack of regret. She was capable of managing without him, wasn't she? The thought alarmed her: didn't that mean she was incapable of real, caring love? Needing no one could turn on its head, and remind people they didn't need her. Using independence as a safety net was not something of which she should be proud.

The next morning, she went into her office to find a sun-tanned stranger standing there and papers spread haphazardly across her desk.

'Can I help you?' she asked politely. Then she recognized him as a young man who had worked there until he had been called into the Army. 'Ralph? You're back! How wonderful. When did you come home? Have you seen Mr Johnston and Mr Gifford? They'll be so pleased that you're home unharmed. Will your mam be having a party?'

He laughed. 'Which question d'you want me to answer first?' He spread his arms apologizing for the untidy papers. 'Sorry about the mess, I've—'

'It's all right, I'll soon sort it out. Leave it to me and go and see the others.' She started to pick up the papers and stopped in surprise when she saw they were hers, from her desk drawer. He put a hand on them to stop her.

'No, I'm afraid that isn't how it is, Eirlys. I'm back here, to my old job arranging the entertainments. Thank you for keeping it all going for me. From what I've heard you've been doing very well. You'll be glad to relax and return to your previous position, won't you?'

She stared at him and her stomach lurched, her heart raced painfully. Had she heard correctly? She wanted to ask him to repeat his words but no sound would come out. Her face was frozen in disbelief.

'Sorry, Eirlys if it's a shock but I thought you'd know. It was promised when I was called up, me and thousands of others. You must have understood your position was only temporary, until the war ended.'

'No, I didn't know. I made this job. I started with practically nothing and made it up as I went along. Everything that came out of this office since 1939 has been mine, so how can you come back and take it and tell me it's yours? You had nothing to do with any of it. Holidays at Home. That's what it's called and I did it all.'

'Until the war, I planned the town's entertainments, and that's what I'll continue to do. I'll look through your files and see what you've been doing while I've been away and see if anything is suitable for the future.' Meeting her anger defensively, he went on, 'From what I've seen so far I'll have to make a lot of changes. Most of these ideas will go. People

131

will be less easily satisfied now. They'll demand different, more sophisticated entertainments.'

'How can you know what people want? Five minutes you've been back and I've been doing this job for almost six years!'

His attitude hardened further in response to her rising anger and he spoke in a derisory manner of her achievements. 'Processions, school choirs, amateur concerts, dances run in support of fund-raising for servicemen, all that has gone. Things will be changing, becoming more professional now I'm back. The fighting is over.'

'Stop talking about the war being over! It isn't over!' she snapped angrily. 'There are thousands of men still out in the Far East fighting the Japanese. They need our help and support. Fund-raising has to go on. The war is over for some of us but not for them. Not for this office.'

'This office is no longer yours. The decisions will be mine, Miss Price.'

'Mrs Ward,' she corrected, before fleeing from the room.

She was crying as she left the office that had been hers for so long. She didn't go to see Mr Johnston: she guessed he would be too ashamed to want to talk to her. She had done all he had asked of her and more, working hours of unpaid overtime to the detriment of her private life; and her marriage. Thinking of the dingy little office below stairs where she had once worked, she knew she couldn't go back.

The park that was high above the town and offered a view of the distant sea was empty. She sat on a seat and from her bag she took the sandwiches she had packed for her lunch. Sparrows gathered in the hope of a feast and she broke up the food and scattered it, enjoying for a moment the anxious scavenging of sparrows, starlings and a cheeky robin as they fought for every crumb.

An hour later she still hadn't decided what she would do and was still wondering whether or not to tell Ken. Unless something remarkable happened, everything had changed with the loss of her job. Her main reason for refusing to go with Ken to London had gone. She had no job. If Ken left, how would she manage? He wouldn't be able to support them: starting a new business would leave him nothing to spare; he might be able to keep himself but there would be no surplus. Everyone knew that a business needed propping up financially in the first year, even if it was successful.

He needed her there, perhaps working to subsidize him for a year or so and that was impossible. However much her father tried, it was she who ran the household, her money providing many of the extras. Dadda would never manage without her and that wasn't an excuse, it was a simple fact. Why couldn't Ken settle for a local job, a nine-to-five office job that would create a framework for a simple life?

Unwilling to go home she walked through the back streets of the town to the gift shop. Hannah was there with Beth and at lunch time, Alice joined them.

When she told them what had happened, Hannah sympathized, but Alice said, 'It's a terrible shock, and Mr Johnston should have prepared you for it. Warned you. Not wait for Ralph to walk in like that. But . . .' she added quietly, a hand on Eirlys's arm to comfort her, 'but, I think you should have guessed. Women have worked hard throughout this war but it's the man's wage that keeps a family. Men need to work and I doubt whether many women will keep their jobs if a man is in need of it.'

'It's only July and there are weeks to go before the end of the summer's entertainments. Ralph will have difficulties just walking in and throwing me out without understanding how these things are done.'

'Then help him,' Alice said. 'Go back and help him.' Unable to be idle, she took a partly made child's glove and began picking up the stitches to knit a finger.

'Absolutely not! If it had been done properly, if I'd been told and given time to adjust I'd have helped willingly but not like this. Ralph made it clear he was taking over and I'm leaving it to him. All of it. I'm not going back.' Then she cried again.

Beth sat with an arm around her while Hannah made a pot of tea.

'There's something else,' Eirlys said when she had recovered. They waited as she sipped the hot tea then she told

133

them that only hours before this bombshell, she had told Ken she wouldn't leave the town and go with him to London.

'Why?' Alice asked. 'I'd go anywhere with Eynon.'

'I want to stay here.' She glared at Alice, irritated by her attitude, her implication that she was in the wrong. 'I thought my job was permanent. It's well paid and I could look after Anthony and myself without his help.'

'Why?' Hannah asked then. 'Why are you thinking of managing alone? If you are worried about the affair he had with Janet Copp, then you shouldn't. It's over and best left in the past, not dragged along like a useless anchor. If you can't leave it behind, then surely you want to be with him, to make sure it won't happen again? And,' she added firmly, 'I'm sure it won't. Ken loves you and he adores little Anthony.'

'I don't know what to do. I can't think straight, my mind's in chaos. That isn't like me at all.'

'Talk it over with Ken. You can change your mind about going with him. He'd be delighted. We don't want you to go,' she added hastily, 'but if it means your happiness we'll understand.'

'I can't tell Ken. Not yet. For one thing he'd be second best and he'd know it. Secondly I still don't want to leave St David's Well. I won't discuss it with him until I've made a decision.'

'Wrong way round,' Beth warned. 'Making a decision before you tell Ken is insulting him, treating him as a stranger, someone of no importance.'

The three girls picked up the work her arrival had interrupted and unable to devise an alternative way to spend the rest of the day, Eirlys joined them, taking the glove put aside as the town hall clock struck two and Alice left to return to work, and continuing with its tiny fingers.

The shop was busy during the afternoon and Eirlys contented herself with attending to customers, glad not to have time to think. Anthony was home with her father and even the chance to spend extra time with him couldn't persuade her to go home.

When the shop closed at half past five, she walked a little way with Beth and her baby, then increased her pace and hurried for the last ten minutes until the house was in sight.

A man stood at the gate and from the way he was leaning on the wall he appeared to have been there a long time. 'Mr Johnston?' she said questioningly.

'Eirlys, I'm very sorry for the way you were treated today. I thought Ralph wasn't coming back. He didn't keep in touch and his mother told us he'd probably look for something else. Then he changed his mind, asked for his job back, and we couldn't do anything but agree.'

'I'm sorry for flouncing out like a prima donna,' Eirlys said with a sad smile. 'It was such a shock.'

'Will you come back, for a month at least, help him through the last weeks of your arrangements?'

'I can't. We disagreed immediately and I can't see us working together.'

'Ralph is ashamed of the way he spoke to you and, whatever you decide, he wants the chance to apologize.'

'He does?'

'He said things he didn't mean. Since looking through the record of the last years, including the scrapbook we kept of the newspaper reports, he realizes what a remarkable job you have done. But, I shouldn't be telling you this, Mrs Ward. Will you come into the office tomorrow at ten? You and Ralph can speak calmly and sort out your differences, although, once you talk properly, you'll probably realize there aren't any. You both want to do the best for St David's Well.'

She agreed because it would give her time to plan her future.

Ken opened the door as she walked down the path. 'What did Mr Johnston want?' he asked. 'He's waited over an hour to see you and wouldn't come in or tell me what he wanted. More overtime is it?'

'Something like that,' she lied.

Maude saw Reggie whenever they were both free, but with Reggie working all day at the smallholding and Maude helping in Audrey's cafe they had little time to talk.

'Can you get a few days off?' Reggie asked her one

day. 'I want you to come home with me and meet Mam and Dad.'

Maude stared at him. This invitation usually meant their friendship was reaching a new level.

'I've already asked them and they'd love to meet you. Their house is small, but there's a boxroom with a small bed and Mam will make it as comfortable as she can. Will you?'

'I'll ask Auntie Audrey.' She felt a little afraid although she knew she was falling deeper and deeper in love with Reggie. Meeting his parents was important. What if they didn't like her? How should she behave? Formal? Friendly? How would she dress? Her best frock and coat were too warm for July and she hadn't any clothing coupons left to buy something new.

'Of course you must go,' Audrey said, hugging her. 'Maude, we're all crazy, the whole Castle family including you, Myrtle and me. We work hard and never think of taking a holiday. I'll manage fine for a few days. How long would you like?'

'I thought if I could go on Saturday afternoon, when Keith is here, then take Monday off, which is half-day closing anyway, and come back Tuesday? Mr Gregory has agreed to Reggie having those days too.'

'Go on Saturday morning, that way you'll have extra time there.' She frowned when she saw Maude's anxious expression. 'Maude?'

'It might be too long. What if I hate them or they hate me?'

Audrey laughed. 'All right, If you're unhappy, phone me and I'll send a message for you to come home. Now, go and tell Reggie, book your tickets and plan a wonderful weekend.'

Shirley sat in the park in the centre of the town clutching a crumpled letter. It was from Freddy and in it, he asked if she would find him a room, so he had somewhere to come back to. He no longer had a home. His parents had died and the rented house, which Shirley had emptied, the contents given away or sold, now belonged to Maldwyn Perkins, who worked in Chapel's flower shop, and his wife, Delyth. Apart from herself, Freddy had no one. The job he had left was no longer his, he had told the owner of the gents' outfitters he would not be back. He would have to start again from nothing and rebuild a life for himself, here in the town in which he had no roots except memories.

Shirley was still unsure whether or not she wanted to be a part of it. Then, as so often recently, her thoughts turned to Andy. He had nothing and dared not go home. He was on the run, a deserter, a coward, a cheat. Like Freddy, he had nothing but he had built his own disasters.

Andy Probert was in her thoughts so strongly she looked around as though expecting to see him. If only he would get in touch, then she could send him on his way and begin to put him from her mind. She needed to talk to him, listen to his excuses for faking his own death rather than fight, then she would walk away from him and not look back.

It was the uncertainty. She was almost convinced that he was still alive but others believed he had died the death he had foreseen, in the sea with others around him unable to help him.

When Alice was asked to help at the beach one Sunday when Netta was off and Maude was helping Audrey, she was flattered and began to agree, but then something came over her and she shook her head. 'Sorry, mother-in-law, but I can't.'

'Oh?' Marged looked surprised. 'Busy are you? And on a Sunday?'

'I'm going out with some friends. We're taking a picnic and our bathers and going down the Vale. There's a bus to take us and bring us back.' Turning away to hide her unjustified guilt, she added, 'Arranged for weeks it's been.'

When Marged left, she slipped on a coat and went to see Jennifer, one of the girls she worked with. After a brief discussion Jennifer agreed to go with Alice on a picnic, just as she had told Marged.

'All except the swimming,' Jennifer said. 'Sunbathing, now that's a different kettle of fish. But the sea's too cold and too full of strange creatures for me to put a foot in it!'

Alice wasn't sure why she had refused to help Marged and Huw, but it was something to do with being taken for granted. There had been no job for her when she needed one. They had chosen Netta Mills instead, and that hurt. She wasn't sure what would happen in the future, but at the moment, she rankled under the memory of seeing Netta there, her children admired, while she had been pushed aside. Using some of her precious clothing coupons and some money intended to add to her savings, she bought a smart, stripy bathing costume. She was married, but as Jennifer constantly reminded her, that was no reason not to look her best.

There were several estate agents in the town and Shirley went to them all, asking for information about rooms to rent. They had very few. Most people, she was told, advertised small lets in newsagents' windows and she smiled. She and her mother had run a newsagent shop and had dealt with small advertisements, so why hadn't she thought of that herself?

She found three that looked possible and, walking through the streets on her way home, she found other cards in the windows of the houses themselves. She wrote the addresses down to send to Freddy, feeling strangely unkind at arranging for him to go into a house of a stranger. But there was no room for him in Bleddyn and her mother's home and she wouldn't have suggested it if there had been. She wanted to go slowly when Freddy came home, not jump into a situation from which it would be difficult to extricate herself. Ill-timed sympathy could be a pathway to disaster.

She wrote to Freddy enclosing the details of the rooms and asked if he would like her to look at them; discarding the impossible would at least save him time and frustration. Before she sealed the envelope, she re-read her letter and was horrified to see that she had addressed it not to 'Dear Freddy', but 'Dear Andy'. She tore it into as many pieces as possible and threw it away.

Her mother had also received a letter from Freddy. 'He would like to use this address for correspondence until he has a place of his own,' Hetty explained. 'Bleddyn and I have no objection, do you?'

'None. Thanks, Mam. He'll be grateful. I couldn't imagine coming home after all the years he's been away, to no home, no belongings, nothing, can you?'

'Don't let sympathy confuse your feelings for him,' Hetty warned, echoing her own thoughts. Shirley hugged her but didn't reply. It wasn't sympathy she found confusing, it was persistent thoughts about Andy Probert.

When Maude returned from her weekend with Reggie's parents, Audrey saw at once that something momentous had occurred.

'Did you have a nice time?' she asked, as she and Keith greeted her.

'Wonderful, Auntie Audrey. And Keith, you'd love their garden. Birds nesting in the hedges, rabbits in the field beyond, sheep on the hills and even a couple of badgers calling every evening for food. It's heaven.'

'And Mr and Mrs Probert, welcoming, were they?'

Maude didn't reply straight away; she looked from one to the other.

'What is it, Maude?' Audrey looked anxious.

'Oh, Auntie Audrey, Reggie wants us to be married.'

Myrtle came in as the celebratory hugs were in progress and she added her good wishes to theirs. 'When will it be, our Maude? Can I be bridesmaid?'

'Of course. And, I want Uncle Huw to give me away, if he will,' Maude said and the hugs began all over again.

'It isn't fair,' Myrtle said, thumping herself down on a chair, as she told Stanley about her sister's engagement. 'I know our Maude's two years older, but I'm the most mature and it'll be ages before I can marry.'

'Got anyone in mind, Myrtle?' he asked softly. And she looked at him and looked away, away from those soft, kindly dark eyes.

'Oh shut up, Stanley and let me sulk in peace.'

'You're eighteen but I'm only sixteen, so I expect we'll have to wait a while but remember you belong to me. You will wait for me, won't you?' he added anxiously.

'I'm saving up. I want a home, a family, like me and Harold and Percival never had until we came to live with Uncle Morgan. I can't take you to meet my family, because

I haven't got one. But I'll tell you all about Ma.'

Again she delayed replying, she didn't trust herself not to cry. She leaned towards him and they held each other tightly. There was no need for more.

The election took the place of war news on the front pages of the newspapers at the end of July, as Attlee and the Labour Party swept to victory in an election that ended the previous nine-year-long government.

Eirlys listened to the discussions going on around her but couldn't find any enthusiasm for the political wrangles. She worked hard but without joy as she guided Ralph through the intricate arrangements for the last of the summer's events.

At home she washed and ironed and mended Ken's clothes and put them ready for when he left for London. If there was regret as she completed the various tasks, none showed. For Ken it was confirmation of her indifference and for Eirlys, his casual acceptance of her preparations was more proof of his eagerness to leave her.

Morgan had been right when he thought too many words could limit the chance of an amicable end to a problem, but in this instance it was the lack of words that was so damaging.

Stanley still worked at the beach as August holidays began to swell the crowds arriving each day by bus, train, bicycle and on foot. Myrtle worked at Audrey's cafe, but on Mondays, when the cafe closed at one o'clock, he would look out along the prom for her flying figure as she ran from the bus to spend the rest of the day with him. It was the best day of the week.

'Something's wrong with Eirlys and I don't know what it is,' he greeted her as she threw off her coat and jumped on to the swingboats for a free ride. Stanley hopped up and settled himself at the other end and they began to pull themselves up, higher and higher above the sand. 'Your Auntie Audrey doesn't know anything, does she?'

'I know Ken is going to London and Eirlys isn't going with him, but I don't think it's because they're parting, just that his job will be based in London and hers is here.'

'That's the mystery,' Stanley said. 'Eirlys hasn't said

anything, but I heard that that Ralph bloke, who worked there before the war, has come home and taken his job back. In a couple more weeks Eirlys won't have the job any more. So why isn't she going to London with Ken?'

'Perhaps it's you and Harold and Percival. She's like a mother to you three.'

'We can manage. Uncle Morgan is hopeless an' helpless, but with me to sort 'im out we'll be fine.'

'Then she's silly not to go.'

'You wouldn't do that, would you, Myrtle? You wouldn't leave me, would you?'

'Never,' she said but she was smiling, and as she looked at him, she saw that he was not. More seriously, she said, 'No, Stanley. I won't ever want to leave you.'

'Nor me you, Myrtle.' He nodded contentedly as the brightly painted boat lowered them slowly back to earth.

When they locked up the rides and put the shutters in place on the stalls, they didn't want to go home. Waving to Huw, and pocketing the keys, Stanley put a possessive arm around Myrtle's shoulders and let her up to the prom. There preparations were being made for one of the early levels of the giant chess tournament. This was one of the most surprising successes of Eirlys's summer entertainments. It had not been expected to attract many people, and the advertising had been minimal, but for even the early rounds of the contest, the area around the painted flagstones, which was the board, was always crowded. This year the area had been further decorated with yards and yards of Cassie's colourful bunting, encouraging more people to investigate, and often stay to watch the game.

Few of the enthusiastic viewers played or even understood the game, but the large pieces, being pushed around under the instruction of the players, by men dressed as clowns, or jockeys riding hobby horses, or even, on one momentous occasion, men dressed as ballet dancers wearing football boots, always attracted large crowds.

Some of the players were irate at first as the movers took their time or got it wrong, or ended up fighting, but they soon realized the intention was laughter and fun and quickly settled to enjoy themselves.

Most of the shops had closed before it began and the few cafes with open doors discouraged their customers to stay. Everyone wanted to see the fun. Stanley wriggled himself into a prime spot and dragged Myrtle in beside him. They stood very close and continually whispered to each other, an excuse to be even closer.

Maude stood with Reggie, who had come in working clothes, determined not to miss it, and near them Beth and Peter with their baby, who was being held by his proud grandfather Bernard. Bernard had been a semi-finalist one year but work on the smallholding had prevented him entering again.

The whole town seemed to be there. Hands waved in the crowd as friends recognized each other. Shirley watched with her parents, who had left an assistant in charge of the fish and chip shop. She looked around, and searched the faces, wondering if Andy was among them. Or were her friends right? Was she being utterly foolish and searching for a ghost? She put thoughts of Andy aside and drank in the atmosphere, planning to describe it all to Freddy in her next letter.

Eirlys and Ken were there, with their son, and her father and Harold and Percival. The unhappy couple were pushed close together by the increasingly excited crowd, but both pulled away, as though the contact was offensive.

It was getting dark when the game finished. The winner was announced and the date of the next stage. Slowly the people drifted away. Hetty and Bleddyn hurried back to the fish and chip shop to help the assistant through the busy last hours and Shirley began to walk to the bus stop.

Several buses came, filled up and left. Shirley sat on the wall and waited, hoping the next would have room for her. Someone sat beside her and she turned to offer a pleasantry when he spoke and startled her into a shriek.

'Hello, Shirley. I'm back. Are you pleased to see me?'

'Andy!'

'Sh-sh-sh. Don't tell everyone, lovely girl, I'll really be for it if they catch me again.'

'Go away or I'll be the one to tell them,' she whispered harshly.

'Here's our bus,' he said unconcerned. 'Pay my fare will you? Broke I am.'

'Walk!' she said as she pushed her way on to the already crowded bus.

She didn't get a seat and he stood beside her and, as the conductor squeezed his way along the gangway to collect fairs, he gestured to her with a nod, implying that she would pay. With hands that trembled with confusion and anger, she did so.

He walked with her to her home and she hurried as fast as her injured leg would allow, anxious to be rid of him. He kept up with her, chatting as though nothing had happened since they had last met.

'Meet me tomorrow in the little park,' he pleaded. 'Two o'clock?'

'No, I won't. I never want to see you again. Go away.'

'I'll be there. Two o'clock in the park. Right?' With a, 'Sleep well, lovely girl,' he turned and walked away blowing a kiss.

That night she couldn't sleep and spent most of the dark hours sitting beside the dead fire, drinking tea and thinking about Andy and Freddy. The next morning she went out early and made her way to Bernard Gregory's smallholding. She found Reggie digging the beds from which the last of the small crops had been taken. He was spreading fertilizer as he dug, working it evenly into the soil, and she stood near the gate and waited until he saw her.

'Shirley? Hi,' he called. 'Looking for a job are you?'

Ignoring the teasing she said, 'I've seen Andy and if you don't believe me, be in the park in town this afternoon at two o'clock. He's asked me to meet him there.'

He walked over to her and stared, unable to decide what to say. His brother was dead. Official notice of his being missing, presumed drowned, was in his parents' house. He'd seen it and he believed it.

'Why are you doing this, Shirley? Mam's accepted it and if she hears rumours like this it'll upset her all over again.'

'Be there!' She turned and hurried away.

Reggie stared after her until she disappeared from sight,

then went back and finished his task. When he asked Bernard for an hour off he didn't have to explain, and taking a bicycle from the shed he rode to the park at half past one and stood in the trees and patiently waited.

Shirley hadn't intended to go. It was better that the brothers met unburdened by her presence. She sat in her living room, watching the clock and wondering what they would say to each other. As the minutes passed she began to listen for footsteps. Reggie would come and tell her he was sorry for not believing her and she would be able to leave any decisions about Andy to him. She would be free of him.

It was half past two when he came and he was alone. She smiled as she opened the door. 'Well?' she questioned. 'Now do you believe me?'

'Surprise, surprise, he didn't come.' There was anger in the eyes so like his brother's.

'But he asked me to meet him there. He must have been there. You just didn't see him.' She was shocked and Reggie relaxed and said, 'Look, Shirley, you must get him out of your mind. You saw someone who looked like him, and now you imagine seeing him, believing what everyone else knows isn't true. A bit of wishful thinking perhaps. But Andy's gone. He drowned just like his dreams told him he would. I'm sorry.'

For several days Shirley didn't leave the house. She pretended to have a slight cold and, being a singer, it was an acceptable excuse as she had three concerts planned for the following week. Whatever other people thought, she wasn't afraid she was losing her mind. Although she might have been mistaken about the clown, there had been no doubt about Andy travelling on that bus with her. When would he stop his foolish games and go to see his brother? Didn't his family deserve to know of his survival? What game was he playing and why was he tormenting her like this?

Huw and Bleddyn went on a voyage of nostalgia. Before the war they had employed people in a small lemonade factory and another where ice cream was made. Besides what they sold themselves, they had supplied other customers with their popular lines. With the end of the war, although with no prospect yet of an end to food rationing, they inspected the places to see how well they had survived the years of neglect.

'Your Marged is a marvel,' Bleddyn said, opening the lid of the freezing drum and admiring the spotless interior. She must have come here regularly to keep it as immaculate as this.'

'Old Granny Molly Piper always did it and when she died Marged took over.'

Satisfied that the reopening of the place was possible they locked up and left. Bleddyn led his brother to another lock-up and on opening the doors went to look at his boat.

Every summer before the war, he had taken visitors and trippers on boat rides around the bay. Like the ice-cream and lemonade equipment, the boat had been well cared for during the time it had been laid up. All it needed was fresh paint and she would be ready to resume. But Bleddyn shook his head. 'I don't think I've got the heart for it any more.'

Huw smiled grimly. 'The truth is, Bleddyn, we're six years older than when we left all this. I don't think I want to do more than we're already coping with. Even Marged, who's as strong as they come, is finding it hard to keep up with it all. And I have the feeling that when your Johnny and our Eynon come home, even they might want something different from selling ice creams and giving rides.'

'We packed everything away, convinced that one day we'd open it all up and go back to how things were, but it isn't going to happen, is it?' Sadly they closed the doors on the past.

'What about a pint to toast the old days?' Bleddyn suggested. Pocketing the keys, they went to the nearest pub.

Ken left for London at the beginning of August, and as Eirlys, Anthony and the three brothers saw him off on the train, Alice stood near them.

'Come on, Eirlys, come back to my miserable two rooms and have tea with me. I don't get many visitors and I need the place to at least feel a bit lived in when Eynon comes home.'

Tearfully, Eirlys remarked that 'Once this lot get there it'll looked lived in all right!'

'Just what the place needs,' Alice assured her as she took the handle of the pushchair and led the way.

Alice knew she had been hard on Eirlys when she had been told about the loss of her job, and her refusal to go to London with Ken. She had hoped that it might help her decide to go with her husband. That hadn't happened, so all she could do was support her while her life was rearranged.

Stanley asked if he might go now Uncle Ken had been sent on his way. 'I thought I might go to the cafe and have a cup of tea there. Okay, Alice?'

Alice smiled, knowing he was hoping for a word with Myrtle. 'Give her my love.'

The rented rooms looked smaller than ever as they all trooped in. Two-and-a-half-year-old Anthony at once began to explore, opening cupboards and grabbing everything that took his fancy. Having had the attention of adoring adults all his life, he was very active and, apart from storytelling time, was sometimes difficult to amuse.

Alice quickly sat him on a chair, a scarf tied first around his waist, then through the rungs of the chair to hold him safely but securely. He was quickly given a sheet of paper and some pencils and the boys settled to entertain him. Eirlys noted with amusement that the food was set out at one end and her lively son sat at the other.

'You've done this before,' she said with a chuckle.

Once the kettle had boiled and the tea made, they all began to eat while Alice surreptitiously watched Eirlys.

'I'm anxious about the future too, Eirlys,' she said later when Harold was reading to Anthony with Percival making the necessary farm animal noises. 'I don't know how Eynon will feel about me after all this time. He was so young when we met and like a lot of people we married in such haste too. He won't be the same person, will he? And neither will I.'

'Ken and I have changed. It's this damned war, Alice. I'm not the same person he married. I've experienced the joy of having a career, not just a job to earn a little extra money, but a responsible position, one I filled successfully. I can't go back to being a housewife and mother. It isn't enough.'

'You still love Ken, though?'

Eirlys sighed. 'We've had such a stormy relationship. First it was on, then off, then on. The affair with Janet ruined my

146

confidence in us, and the truth is, I can't escape from the resentment I felt then. That doesn't make me a very nice person, does it, Alice?'

'Ken, your marriage; aren't they worth fighting for?'

'You would? You'd fight to keep Eynon whatever happened?'

Alice stared at her for a long time then said, 'I'm thinking of offering him his freedom, if that's what he wants.'

'What? You're crazy.'

'What's happened to him these past years will have changed him. If I'm no longer what he wants I'll let him go. He might not want me, the quiet, unexciting wife, the beach and the regular routine of the summer season year after year.' She sang then: '"How'er we gonner keep them, down on the farm, now that they've seen Pareee." It makes you think, doesn't it?' she added sadly.

'Damned Hitler.'

Cassie received a large consignment of bed linen and towels and other household items on Friday evening after the shops were closed. Joseph and the van driver shared the boxes and bundles between the two premises and left her to sort out the muddle. She ran to find Alice and asked her to help her arrange the new stock to enable her to open the following morning. Although Alice worked in the office, she still helped when she could.

'No room to move if we don't put it in some kind of order,' she explained.

'More damaged stock for coupons-free sales?' Alice asked as they began pushing the boxes around to give themselves space to work. They chatted as they worked, planning where and how they would find room for it all. Cassie opened a box to check the contents and fell silent.

'What is it?' Alice asked.

'Joseph told me it was ex-army, surplus to requirements now Germany's defeated, so I expected browns and khaki, but look at this.' She pulled a cellophane-covered bed-sheet from a box. It was white and had a border of pink gingham. 'Some Army, eh?' She closed the box and pushed them all to the back of the shop. 'No, Alice, I don't like the look of this. I've had my doubts before, but Joseph assured me it was all legal, but this? I'm not selling this and risk being put in prison. Rationing and restrictions didn't end when the peace treaty was signed as well we know.'

'What will you do?'

'Tomorrow I'll close the shop and go to Cardiff. This little lot is going back where it came from. Joseph might be gullible enough to believe it's honest but I'm not. He's a fool to be taken in by someone offering this as Army surplus. Pink? For serving soldiers? Never!'

'Lucky he's got you looking after him,' Alice said as they began moving the boxes out of sight. 'I'll come with you if you like?'

'No, Alice, dear. But thanks.' She needed to go alone, her Joseph was far from gullible. He'd have known exactly what he was buying, *and* understood what he was asking when he delivered stolen goods to the shops. That house in Gratton Street would be used as a warehouse, no doubt about it. That was why she hadn't been told about it and later discouraged from visiting it. But this time she wouldn't be put off.

In Cardiff, Cassie didn't reach the house in Gratton Street. She saw Joseph at the station. He and a young woman were wrapped in each other's arms and when a train puffed its noisy way to the platform, he kissed her fondly before helping her on to the train.

She stood and waited while he waved the train out of sight and then, as he turned, she stepped in front of him and asked, 'Joseph, who was that?' She was trembling, and her voice sounded strange even to herself. Surely he was too old to be having an affair? Bed had been of little importance to him and she hadn't minded settling for cuddles instead. He was sixty, and the girl was no more than thirty. She must be a close friend. Perhaps Joseph knew the girl's husband – a business partner perhaps. All these disjointed thoughts flew through her head as she waited for Joseph to explain.

'She's called Joanna Lee Jones.'

'And who's Joanna Lee Jones when she's home?'

'A partner, someone I work with.'

'I see.'

'She's going to London to finalize a deal on blankets and eiderdowns. Very lucrative if she carries it off, and she will. She's very persuasive.'

'I see.'

'I was just on my way to see you. What are you doing here?' he asked as though just realizing where they had met.

'On my way to see you, Joseph. I can't sell the stuff you delivered yesterday. I closed the shop to come and tell you to take it away. Whoever sold it to you as Army surplus was lying. It's probably stolen. And what's more, you knew that when you brought it for me to sell.'

'Nonsense, Cassie. You do fuss so. It was taken from a shop that had been hit by a flying bomb. I discarded the worst of it and sent you the best. No coupons were needed, so you should be able to sell it with ease.'

'I can sell some to Constable Charlie Groves, can I? He's getting married and, so long as it's legal, he'd be pleased to buy some bedding edged with pink gingham. 'Specially if I tell him it's Army surplus and pink is the soldiers' favourite colour!'

'You can sell it to the Chief Constable himself, Cassie. Now for goodness' sake stop fussing and let's get home.' He pushed his way impatiently through the crowded platform, leaving her to follow in his wake. She believed him, because she wanted to, but her heart was heavy, and, she would not offer any of her new stock to Constable Charlie Groves. Joseph was not that convincing, she told herself sadly; about the stock or Joanna Lee Jones.

Eight

C assie spent the rest of that day working with Joseph but they weren't in accord. They slept in the same bed but neither moved or reached out for the other. Breakfast was as silent as the night had been. When the time came for him to leave she waited in the hope of some affection or at least thanks for all she was doing to increase their business, but he refused the cup of tea and snack she prepared, avoided kissing her and left with nothing more than a casual wave. She began to be afraid.

Eirlys was still working alongside Ralph. To make his presence felt he planned to continue the programme of entertainments for the townspeople through the autumn and winter. He seemed to have accepted her reminder that fund-raising and morale raising was still important. The idea seemed reasonable but not the things he chose to do. He seemed unable to grasp the basic principle that the intention was enjoyment. He suggested plays and concerts that were heavy in content and to which few showed interest. Eirlys watched, helped when asked, made suggestions, most of which were ignored, and fervently hoped he would grow tired of it all and leave.

She wrote to Ken regularly but still hadn't mentioned losing her job. Not telling him at once made it difficult to broach the subject now. She foolishly hoped that if Ralph found the job too much for him, he would leave, she would be reinstated and Ken need never know. When Hannah asked about her situation one lunch-hour in the gift shop, she made the excuse that Ken wouldn't understand. Alice was there, and Shirley was trying on a partly stitched dress Hannah was making for her to wear at a concert later that month.

'He doesn't understand just how much I loved my job,' Eirlys said in response to a question.

'Oh I think he does,' Shirley said with unusual sarcasm. 'Refusing to follow him where *his* career took him, that was a mighty big clue, I'd say!'

'Ralph isn't doing very well,' Eirlys said to Alice, ignoring Shirley's remark. 'I don't think they'll want me to leave just yet.'

'Leave? You won't go back to being a typist, then?'

'I can't. When Ralph decides he no longer needs me, I'll leave.'

'Have you decided what you'll do when that happens?' Hannah asked.

'I'll manage at home for a while, there's plenty of time.'

'Without money? That won't be much fun!'

A woman entered; a young woman carrying a white stick was holding on to her arm. Hannah went forward to serve while Alice placed a chair for the young woman to sit.

'My daughter needs a toy for her niece. Can you help?' the mother asked. Alice and Eirlys hesitated but Hannah said at once. 'I'll be delighted. Now, what is your favourite colour?' While a discussion took place with Hannah describing the various shades of blue in the soft toys on display and going into detail about them, the mother interspersed the conversation with the explanation that her daughter, who served in the WRAF, had been wounded when an airfield had been bombed. 'It isn't permanent,' she said although she brushed tears from her eyes and shook her head to deny her words. 'An operation in a few months' time will give her back at least some sight, and that's what we're all waiting for, eh, Marion?'

Marion chose a couple of small teddies, one blue and one pink, which Hannah assured her would be perfect for a little girl, and they watched the tearful mother help the girl out of the shop.

'Sometimes we're reminded about how trivial our worries are,' Eirlys said solemnly.

'Eynon and Ronnie were wounded but not badly; poor Taff died, but the rest of us are safe,' Hannah added, crossing her fingers so tightly they hurt. They discussed their various

151

worries about the imminent arrival and, in Eirlys's case the recent departure, of their men, sobered by the incident of the seriously injured young woman.

Something happened at the beginning of August that made people forget their small problems. Something that horrified the whole nation.

An atomic bomb was dropped on the Japanese city of Hiroshima, wiping out an area so completely that nothing recognizable remained. It was closely followed by a similar attack on Nagasaki, and the Japanese surrendered. The war had finally ended, almost exactly six years after it had begun.

When the aftermath of shock and shame had eased, and families began to prepare for more homecomings, a final end to the fears of the past six years, people once again began to make preparations to mark the occasion. Street parties were quickly arranged to mark what was known as V.J. Day, Victory over Japan Day. But for many, the pictures of the devastation took the edge off the celebrations; even the publication of the skeletal prisoners of war from many Allied nations didn't altogether ease the public conscience. But for the children, and for those awaiting the return of loved ones, it was something to celebrate.

Hannah and the others spent a lot of time in the gift shop making more bunting. The small, multi-coloured flags were made from every oddment of material they could find. 'If the townspeople look up,' Alice said with a chuckle, 'many would see flags to match their new blouse, or that nightdress you made for their daughter!'

Cassie sold the last of her collection of flags and grieved silently as the final celebration approached without Joseph making the effort to share it with her. He was always too busy to get home these days and she wondered whether Joanna Lee-Jones was the reason. Alice called to see her often and if she guessed, she said nothing, just casually promised to help her if she ever needed it. Cassie was grateful. There might come a time when just having someone to talk to would be important.

*   *   *

While amidst deafening noise the children were being fitted with home-made paper hats, tables were being spread out along the street and the food was being brought out, Freddy Clements quietly arrived at the station. He wore a demob suit and carried a small bag, and he didn't know where to go. If he didn't belong here, then where else could he go? St David's Well had been his home, but no longer; now he didn't have a destination in mind, just a hope of finding somewhere to stay, a room, somewhere he could sit and sort out what he was going to do.

He wanted to see Shirley, but didn't want to appear suddenly. After years of letter-writing, he didn't know how she would receive him. Letters from miles away, signed 'with love', were a wartime need, a lifeline, but now the war was over, they might be irrelevant.

He walked through the streets, stopping to admire the efforts of the people setting up the various parties, each trying to out-do others. He stood for a long time staring up at the house he used to call home. It looked much the same apart from brighter, more cheerful curtains. He went down the back lane and saw washing on the line, underwear and dresses like his mother would never have worn. With a regretful thought on his parents' passing he wandered on. He saw a poster advertising a concert and saw that the top of the bill was Shirley Downs. He bought a ticket, then found himself a small hotel and booked in for two nights.

Since seeing Andy and attempting to set up a meeting with his brother, Shirley hadn't seen the runaway. She doubted her sanity on occasions, and on others felt anger both with him for tormenting her and with Reggie and her mother and stepfather for not believing that she had seen him.

She was sitting in her dressing room with others getting into their costumes for the opening number, feeling restless and trying to recite words of a poem she used to calm herself and isolate herself from the frantic activity backstage. 'I wandered lonely as a cloud . . .' She saw herself lying on the couch and felt the peace of the scene invade her.

When she was prepared, she walked through the ancient corridors of the theatre and stood in the wings to watch the girls' dance routine, remembering the time before the accident when she had been able to dance. Then she peered through the curtains at the side of the stage and stared into the audience. The stage was bright but after a while she could see the faces and there, in the third row, was Andy. Angry and determined to stop his tormenting, aware that there were forty minutes yet before she needed to be ready for her act, she went around and walked along the back of the seats. She knew that Maude and Reggie were in the audience that evening. If she could find them and point Andy out to them they would have to believe her.

Minutes passed and she tried in vain to spot Reggie. He had to be there. The dress circle was closed, he had to be here, in the stalls, but where? With ten minutes before she was on stage, she gave up and went back to the wings where an anxious producer waited for her.

'Where have you been, Shirley? I thought you'd been taken ill or something.'

'No, I've been trying to trap a ghost,' she replied, and refused to add anything further.

Like the professional she was, she put aside all thoughts of Andy and his brother and sang three songs to a delighted audience. She was appearing in the finale and, assuring the producer she would be back, she went once again into the stalls.

An interval was called and it was then she saw them. Maude and Reggie with Stanley and Myrtle, coming towards her heading for the door.

'Your brother is in the middle of the third row,' she told Reggie and, without a word, Reggie left the others and pushed his way through the crowd all heading towards the door. The three rows were empty.

Hidden in a group of chattering girls, Andy watched and smiled. He would see his brother but not yet. He was having fun with Shirley and when he owned up and she forgave him . . . his thoughts drifted towards a wonderful ending in which she fell into his arms.

'As I expected, Shirley, he wasn't there,' Reggie said quietly when he rejoined her. 'Please stop this. You're making yourself ill and it isn't doing me much good, raising my hopes of finding my brother alive, then dashing them again. Just stop it. Please?'

'I know Andy's alive. He's tormenting me for some reason known only to him. One day you'll find out I'm right.'

She sang her final three numbers and an encore, then joined the rest of the cast and the audience with a few more, before standing for the National Anthem and leaving the stage. The seat on the third row remained empty.

Outside the stage door, Reggie and the others were waiting. 'Come home with us?' Maude invited, after they had all congratulated her on her performance.

'No, I have a taxi waiting and I need to be on my own to calm down or I won't be able to sleep.' She glared at Reggie before adding, 'I'll see you soon.' She stepped into the waiting taxi and waved as it moved away. Reggie shook his head and the four friends walked off to the railway station.

Not far away from where they stood, Freddy Clements also watched until the lights of the taxi faded.

The taxi only took her to the railway station and she stood on the platform, urging the train to hurry, hoping the others wouldn't catch her up. She needed to be alone. The train was full but she found a corner seat and stared unseeing out of the window. Lights of passing cars and buses were seen and occasionally a lighted house or small village. She knew the trees and fields were there but in the darkness they were invisible. Like Andy, except when he wants to be seen, she thought with growing irritation.

She loved living in South Wales among people who cared, in a small town surrounded by lovely countryside and small villages. Yet she knew that if she really wanted success, her future lay in faraway places. Once she allowed herself to be free, her voice would take her all over the country, perhaps the world, and sometimes that was what she wanted, but not always. In fact her ambition, once so strong, was becoming less and less important to her. Freddy was coming home.

If only Andy would go away she would welcome Freddy home and perhaps, just perhaps she would marry him and settle here, accept a small local career and be happy.

*   *   *

155

Freddy walked the streets of the town where Shirley had performed and couldn't break away from the sadness of his homecoming. All his dreams of a future with Shirley were shattered. He had seen her on stage that evening and marvelled at her talent. She out-classed everyone else. She was a caged bird who needed to be free. How could he expect her to think of him as anything more than a loving friend when she could fly from her cage and dazzle the whole world? She was beautiful and her voice thrilled everyone who heard her. He had such mundane dreams. Opening a shop to sell shirts and suits? He must have been mad to imagine Shirley and himself together.

He went to the hotel, where his small suitcase and a bag containing a new shirt and tie, which was all he had in the world, laughed at him. Tomorrow he would leave, but not to go to St David's Well. He would find a new town where he could begin again. A place where he could work and forget he had ever known and loved Shirley Downs.

Shirley stepped off the train and began to walk to Brook Lane. As she walked she made a decision. No matter how many times she saw Andy, and even if he spoke to her, she would say nothing to anyone else. If she pretended it wasn't happening, then others might forget she had ever thought differently.

She knew without doubt he was alive, but she wouldn't give people the opportunity to suspect she was losing her mind. The nudges, the shared, knowing looks hadn't gone unnoticed. She was fully aware of what people were saying about her. No more. Andy was dead, just like everyone thought. She felt better, more in control having made the decision.

At the end of Brook Lane she heard a voice call, 'Shirley.' It was a voice that chilled her blood, then anger overcame the shock and she carried on walking as though she hadn't heard.

'Hello, lovely girl. Marvellous you were tonight. Absolutely marvellous.' He touched her arm and gripped it, holding her back. 'I pinched a purse today so I could buy a ticket. Best seats too. Third row. Worth every penny you were.'

She slipped her key into the lock but he stopped her from turning it, his hand over hers, his breath touching her throat. 'Come for a walk, Shirley, please. Just ten minutes of your time, that's all. You can spare ten minutes, can't you?'

She turned to face him. 'Go away, Andy. I'm tired of your games.'

'Please, lovely girl. All right then, five minutes.'

'All right, I'll only talk to you on one condition. That is you promise to go and see Reggie, tell him I haven't been imagining seeing you.'

'I can't do that, lovely girl. Not yet. Not until I've sorted out what I'm going to do.'

She had turned back and was grasping the key but again he stopped it turning.

'It isn't easy, setting myself up with a new identity, a new life. Give me another week and then I'll go and see him. There, I promise. One week and I'll let everyone who needs to, know that I didn't drown. Right?'

Reggie was worried. He didn't quite believe that Shirley was suffering from delusions. Andy was such a devious character that it was just possible she was right and he had survived. He looked around him at the passengers waiting for the train. They had walked from the theatre and it was unlikely he would see Shirley. Travelling from the theatre by taxi, she'd have caught an earlier train and would be safely tucked up in bed by the time he could get to Brook Lane, but he had to go there, just in case.

On his long legs he was at the end of the lane when Andy finally talked Shirley into walking with him and listening to his story. It was curiosity that persuaded her, she wanted to know what had happened between him almost drowning and being rescued. Although, she was doubtful whether what he had to say would be the truth.

He took her arm and threaded it through his and she impatiently pulled away. They went to the park, where the railings had been taken for scrap and there were no gates to keep anyone out, and he invited her to sit beside him on a bench. She moved so they weren't touching and demanded to know what had happened.

'It was just like the dream, Shirley. The one that's haunted me all my life. I was in the water and heads bobbed all around me and there was no one to help. I couldn't breathe. My mouth and nose were covered by foul, greasy water, the surface moving up and down, covering my face one minute, choking me in thick oil and the next dropping down giving me hope of another breath. I was drowning, only this time I wasn't going to wake up in bed, with Reggie telling me it was all right. I almost gave up and accepted my fate, but a piece of wood floated near me, part of the boat I'd been in, maybe. Anyway, I grabbed it and heaved myself partly across it and, well, I was drifting for about three hours.

'Staying awake was the hardest part. I was so cold and utterly exhausted, terrified of choking on the foul-smelling oil as much as dying in the deep water beneath me. Fear can rob you of your strength – I didn't know that, but I learnt a lot of things during those three hours. It was tempting just to relax and let myself go. After all, it was what the dream had told me, that I'd meet my end in the water like that. It seemed impossible to cheat on my fate. But I kept seeing your face, and I swear that was what saved me.'

In spite of her determination to disbelieve him, sympathy flooded through her. Why should he be blamed for running away when he had been so certain he would die?

'What were you doing in a boat?' she asked.

'Running away,' he replied and she could see his grin in the darkness.

'Running away?' she repeated foolishly.

'We were boarded on to this ship, see, being taken out to France for the final push. When we were disembarking on the other side, we saw lines of men being marched up the dockside, then the drizzly rain increased to a downpour, so heavy you couldn't see a hand in front of you, so me and a couple of other lads jumped over the side and swam to a small fishing boat. We hid until they sailed and went out with the rest of the fleet and, dammit, one of them hit a mine. Our boat was smashed and over the side we went.'

'What happened to the others?'

'The other two made it and they reported me as "drowned while absconding".'

'So why did you come back here and torment me?'

'I didn't intend to torment you, lovely girl. I knew it was a risk but I had to see you and I just didn't want anyone else to know until I'd sorted myself out. There's this man, see, and he's getting me a new identity card and even a ration book. It's amazing who you meet in the Army, even if I didn't stay long. I can't give myself up. You must see that. I'm a man for the open air, the fields and the woods. I need the big sky above me. Not bars over a small window. I don't want to spend my best years in prison.'

'Sorry,' a voice said as a figure stepped from behind a bush, 'but that's exactly what you will be doing!'

'Reggie! How did you get here? I didn't know I'd be here myself until half an hour ago!'

'Tormenting Shirley was a mistake. I believed her and I've been trying to catch you. Tonight I've succeeded.'

'Not tormenting you, Shirley, believe me. I didn't want to upset you, either of you,' he added, turning to look at his brother.

'I'll hold him here while you call the police,' Reggie said, and while they were momentarily distracted, Andy suddenly darted away and headed for the open gateway of the park. Reggie followed and within seconds the two brothers were scuffling on the ground, grunts verbalizing the blows they received from each other's fists.

Both men were strong and fit but it was Reggie, fuelled by anger, who won the brief fight. He asked Shirley to phone for the police and he held Andy until they came. She did so, freed from the fascination he had for her. Ashamed that she had felt anything but distaste for someone who had cheated and stolen and evaded taking part in the war, while others fought for the freedom he enjoyed.

She went home to write to Freddy, to tell him everything that had happened, but to her surprise, on the table beside the cup set out ready for her hot drink, there were several of her letters to him, returned care of her own address. So where was he?

Every day saw more men returning from the battlefields. Many went home to children who didn't know them and who objected to the stranger who came to share their lives. Others returned to wives who no longer wanted them, some had found someone else and some admitted that the love they had once enjoyed was no longer there.

More drunks than in recent years were seen wandering the streets, thankful when the police arrested them and gave them a bed for the night. The heroes, the victims of battles already drifting into the past, wandered around the town: some sick and confused, others fit and foolish, unable to settle back into the life they had lost years before. Freddy Clements was not the only soldier to return to no one and nothing.

Reggie was told that his brother would be dealt with by the military, and he was already regretting his part in Andy's arrest. His motives had been honest. He believed that Andy needed a fresh start and the only way to achieve one was to wipe out all his previous mistakes.

Lilly wondered what would happen when Sam Junior returned. Where would he go? And how would they manage to meet? She didn't discuss it with Sam, who seemed unconcerned by the thought of his son returning to find no home. So far as she knew, he hadn't told Sam junior their new address. She had told him. In one of her letters sent via Netta she had explained fully the dreadful situation she had found herself in, living in dingy rooms and with far less money to spend.

So how could Sam call and see them? If his father hadn't explained and given his son the new address he couldn't suddenly appear. He wasn't supposed to know. There was a danger of his finding out that she and Sam junior had been in contact and the idea was both frightening and exciting.

Netta still worked in the beach cafe with Marged and Huw and Maude. She worked hard and was willing to do anything they asked of her, and only Alice was uncertain.

Netta still came to the cafe sometimes on her days off, bringing Dolly and Walter with her. Dolly continued to charm them and Walter gradually relaxed and began to accept Huw as a favourite uncle and Marged as a loving auntie. Alice watched them and her uneasiness grew. There was something in the way Netta watched her. And the ways she managed to talk to other members of the family and exclude her, putting her outside the family circle. She didn't exactly know how she achieved this, but there were many times when the group, including Marged and Huw and sometimes Audrey and Keith and even Beth and Hannah, were wrapt in something the girl was telling them, while she stood a little apart, the conversation taking place around her, isolating Alice from them.

At home, Alice considered this and wondered whether the fault was within herself. Perhaps, because she and Eynon had been together for such a short time, she hadn't really become a part of his family, and the newcomer, with her more outgoing ways, had succeeded where she had failed. The children helped: Marged and Huw loved children and patiently won the four-year-old Walter over, until he chattered away happily. Dolly, almost two, was a delight.

Alice looked around her two sparsely furnished rooms and felt renewed anxiety about Eynon's return. The fear that he had changed was always there but, looking at the rooms she had furnished, she knew she had to do something to make them more inviting. At present they were a stage set, waiting for the actors to walk in and start to bring it alive.

She talked to Hannah often about Johnny's return and her anxieties, knowing that for Hannah, the problems were less acute.

'I do worry about the first impression I give,' Hannah said, 'and whether Josie and Marie will still feel the same way about him. But I am sure of my love and I can't imagine that Johnny would have changed so much that he won't want to return to how things were. We won't have changed. That's the important thing. The thought that's kept them strong when they faced dangers and injuries is knowing we're still here, just the same as when they left, keeping a place for them to

161

slip back into without any readjustments. That's what Johnny and your Eynon will be hoping for.'

'That's one of my worries, Hannah. I'm not the same. I'm nothing like the shy girl Eynon left behind. Working with other girls, going out and having fun, these were things I didn't have confidence for. He'll look at me and see a stranger.'

Unable to contain herself any longer, Lilly asked her husband what arrangements he had made for the return of his son.

'How will he find us? Have you left a message with anyone, our ex-neighbours?' she asked. 'You say you haven't told him in your letters, so how will he find us, and more important, where will he sleep? There's no room here.'

'Not for both of us, certainly,' Sam replied and the way the words were spoken startled her. Was he implying that Lilly had a choice?

'He's your son, Sam, dear. You ought to arrange something for him. He can't sleep on the railway station, can he?' She attempted a laugh.

'Do you have any ideas? Is there anywhere you would suggest? Like in our bed?' He stared at her then and she felt his accusation chill her.

'Hardly, Sam, dear.' She tried again to laugh. 'There's only room in my life for one man, and that's you. Don't worry, there'll be a room he can rent somewhere. He's a grown man, isn't he? Old enough to help himself.' She was unaware of the irony of her remark, but Sam stared at her and said, 'Oh yes, he can certainly do that.'

Lilly went to see Netta as soon as she could leave without appearing to be in too much of a hurry. 'He knows, Netta,' she said breathlessly as she burst into her parents' beach cafe and found her friend on her own. 'I'm sure Sam knows.'

'Sh-sh-sh,' Netta warned. 'Your Mam'll be back in a minute, gone down to the beach to collect trays she has and your father's on the swingboats while Stanley takes a break.'

'Will you be free in a while? I have to talk to you. I don't know what to do.'

'I'll take a break about three o'clock. Come back and we can have a cup of tea and a chat.'

'Hello, Lilly,' her mother said as she re-entered the cafe from the metal steps from the sand. 'Where's our little Phyllis?'

'I left her with Sam. He's promised to take her to the park and around the streets to see the decorations. Getting ragged they are now, but she loved to see all the flags and banners.'

'And there are always a few fresh ones as the men continue to come home. It can't be much longer before our Eynon and Johnny are demobbed, surely,' she added with a sigh. 'Auntie Audrey and Keith have made big huge banners.'

In a terraced house in Hollis Street, a home-made banner over the door shouted its welcome home to Matthew Proudfoot. His children, a boy now seven and his daughter aged twelve, had laboriously painted flowers all over the piece of cardboard, interspersed with the words 'Welcome Home, Dad', 'Welcome Home, Matthew' and 'Welcome Home, Uncle Matt' that now hung over the front porch.

Inside the house, his wife had prepared a meal. Cakes, covered with dishes to stop them from drying up, and a tin of fruit with accompanying tinned cream stood waiting for his arrival, the tin opener ready beside them. In a frying pan, sausages sat waiting to be cooked.

Matthew hadn't been able to tell them exactly when he would be home but they had been waiting since early morning, the children unwilling to go out to play or enjoy their Saturday-morning film show.

Matthew walked slowly from the station. His wounded leg made it impossible to hurry, the scars on his body and face pulled painfully. How would they react when they saw him? He delayed longer by going into a cafe and, in a large mirror on the wall behind the counter, he saw his reflection and he stared at himself, sadness in his dark-brown eyes, the droop of his shoulders telling of weariness and almost despair.

'A cup of tea?' Audrey asked.

'Thank you,' he replied.

'Just on your way home, are you?'

'Yes,' he said as he dropped his bag and sank into a chair. 'And it isn't going to be easy, looking like this.'

'Nonsense,' she said softly. 'They'll look into your eyes and see the man they remembered. If you have children, they're bound to be curious at first, but if you can cope with their staring, within days they'll forget the scars and see only their father.' She brought him a cup of tea and added a cake, refusing payment on either. 'Welcome home,' she said softly.

Matthew sat there for a long time, looking around at the customers, mostly shoppers at this time of the afternoon, and he was pained by the way they quickly looked away, afraid to catch his eye, wanting to examine his damaged face without being seen. It was going to be like this for a long time. Perhaps for always. He waved his thanks to Audrey, who called, 'Enjoy your homecoming. I hope you'll be thoroughly spoilt.'

He smiled when he saw the childishly made banner and the Union flags that flew from the windows in his honour. A rosy-faced little boy was swinging on the gate and he realized with a start that it was his son, his six-year-old son, whom he hadn't seen for more than five years. He stopped and took a deep breath.

'Hello,' he said then.

'Hello, what happened to your face?'

'I got burnt.'

'My dad's coming home,' the boy said, looking past him, along the street, impatient for that first glimpse.

'Is your mother home? And your sister, Margaret?'

'Yeh, but they're busy gettin' ready for our dad.'

'Tell her I'm here, will you?'

'I'll try, but she's awful busy, mind.'

'Matthew!' His wife appeared in the porch to see who her son was talking to and she stared in disbelief at his face. Slowly, tearfully she approached and put her arms around his neck. She held him against her but didn't offer her face for a kiss. Matthew told himself it didn't matter; he'd been expecting it. His scarred lips were hardly tempting.

He offered an arm to his son and the child came up and

stared, a deep frown furrowing his brow. 'Margaret,' he called to his sister loudly. 'Come and see 'im. Our dad's home and he's a hero and wounded something awful.'

In many other houses welcomes were planned and, for many families, the adjustments were swiftly done. In others, children who had known only their mother were upset at being corrected by the stranger who had entered their homes. Some were cheeky to hide their anxieties, others became subdued and there were many more, the majority, who went to school and boasted about the man who was their father, who was brave, and big and home for ever.

Sam junior was demobbed and went at once to the house where he and his father had lived. Pretending not to know his father's whereabouts, he asked the neighbours where he could be found and, making sure his father was at home, he knocked on the door of the place where his father, Lilly and Phyllis now lived. He knew it would be his father who opened the door. Lilly didn't often rouse herself to do such things.

'Hello, Dad. This is a surprise. When did you move here, then?' he asked, stepping past his father and standing in the hall, not knowing which way to go.

'Sorry, son. I didn't want to worry you while you were away but we had to sell up. Financial problems. There's no room for you here, I'm afraid, but I've arranged for you to lodge with Mrs Denver, you remember her? Our little Phyllis's grandmother, in Queen Street. Will that be all right?'

'That's fine, until I get sorted. Can I see her before I go?'

'Lilly?' his father asked.

'Well yes, but I was thinking of little Phyllis. I bet she's changed since I saw her last. Eh?'

The four-year-old Phyllis was sitting at the table patiently finishing a jig-saw puzzle. She looked up, her bright-blue eyes crinkling with pleasure as she greeted him. 'I can't find the straight edge for this corner, Daddy,' she said and Sam senior went across and helped direct her fingers to the correct piece and applauded her when she completed the puzzle.

'She's beautiful, Dad,' Sam said, patting the child's fair head.

'Clever too. She does that puzzle in no time. Sociable little thing, she pretends to need help so I can become involved. She does it to me all the time.' He spoke proudly as he kissed a rosy cheek.

'Mrs Denver is expecting you for tea,' he said pointedly. 'I'll tell Lilly you're home and you can call and see her, perhaps tomorrow?'

'Fine. But I don't know when. I have to go and search for a job before they're all taken, remember.'

'We'll be here all day,' his father assured him.

Sam junior was shaking when he left his father's house. His attitude had been so formal. Nothing like the welcome he had envisaged over the past months and years. Lilly must be right, his father knew of their secret affair. He hadn't believed her when she told him in a letter what she suspected. Lilly was a bit of a drama queen, he knew that and he thought she was inventing a problem to add spice to their next meeting. But now he believed her. He had to see her, talk to her, decide how they would deal with it. But how, without his father finding out?

He went to Mrs Denver's and his welcome there was far greater than his father's had been. She had made a room as comfortable as she could and even had a fire burning in the grate.

'Not that it will be a regular thing,' she warned. 'Coal is rationed and I have to save what I have for the cooking range. This is just a welcome home.'

He thanked her and unpacked his few belongings. When he opened a wardrobe to put his greatcoat inside he was surprised to see the rest of his clothes there.

'Your dad brought them when they left the house,' Mrs Denver explained.

'I've been well and truly banished, haven't I?' His new landlady said nothing but from the expression on her kindly face he guessed that his father had confided in her. What a mess. What a stupid mistake to become involved with his stepmother – inevitable though. It sounded sordid, but he knew that when he and Lilly met, it would be impossible for them not to continue with the affair. Thoughts of her had filled his mind to the exclusion of everything else since his last visit home.

Joseph had refused to take back the suspect bedding, the pink-edged sheets and pillowcases and the only way Cassie could get rid of them was to sell them, offering them secretly – under the counter – to customers in the know. The news was spread by word of mouth and the commodity-starved people gladly risked being found out, for the treat of something new. Alice bought some for her own store and made sure both Marged and Audrey were well stocked. If the police had any suspicions, nothing was said and the piles of boxes in the back room of the shops gradually emptied. The bank balance of Cassie and Joseph rose steadily.

Shirley watched as the town's population swelled with the demobbed men and women. As with Eirlys, there were many disappointments as employees were asked to leave the jobs they had made their own, to make room for the returning men. Familiar faces reappeared and the townspeople settled down to revive their broken lives. So where was Freddy Clements?

She had written to the war office, and made enquiries at every possible office but she was told that unless they had a specific request, they couldn't divulge the whereabouts of an ex-serviceman. Cynically she wondered whether many of the requests they received were attempts to find an absconded father. Every letter she wrote to him arrived back at her own address, as he had arranged. But as for Freddy himself, there was no sign.

She had money belonging to him and that worried her. Besides the money, there were a few pieces which she thought he would like to keep, mementoes of his childhood and things his parents had loved, plus some new, carefully stored linen that she hoped they would one day share.

That glimpse of the future was in abeyance too. She couldn't know how he felt about her until they met. Letters were so unreliable. His affectionate words were perhaps regretted, making it impossible for him to come home, afraid she would expect more than he could give. He had never been the most reliable of men. When they had first started meeting, he had been engaged to marry Beth Castle. They had spent a couple of weekends in the Grantham hotel in Gorsebank, while Beth still dreamed of marriage. The war was certain to have changed him, but not necessarily made him more trustworthy where women are concerned. Loyalty was something he had lacked before 1939 and it would take a miracle to change him that much. Boxes of his belongings were in a cupboard in her room and, it seemed, there they would stay.

Sam junior didn't see either Lilly or his father over the following few days. He called at the house but there was never any reply. Was his father inside, listening to his knocking and refusing to open the door? After several more disappointments he went to the employment exchange and applied for work in the council offices, where there were vacancies for clerks dealing with housing priorities. When he learned he was successful he put a note through his father's door telling him so, and went back to Mrs Denver's.

Sam picked up the note and tore it through. Then he set the table for tea and went to the library. Reading was his only solace since Lilly had ruined his life.

Matthew had been home for two weeks when he knew that the hero's welcome was not for him. He went to visit other men, people he had served with and envied them. Several of them he had met in hospital and, injured or whole, they all seemed to be secure, safe back home, wrapped around in pride and love.

His wife had tried, he knew that, but there was something holding her back. He wondered if the 'something' was a 'someone', a man she had met while he had been away, but there had been no sign of him. And the children made no mention of another man visiting their house.

The summer season ended, the rides and stalls were packed away for the winter and the nights began to draw in. For the first time since war began, the streets were no longer hazardous, fewer pedestrians tripped over unseen objects. Winter was no longer to be dreaded, except for the shortages of fuel and the continuing food rationing. And Matthew Proudfoot had still not found a job.

Before the war he had worked in the showroom of a garage, selling cars, but the scars on his once handsome face had made it impossible for his employers to take him back. Offices, shops and even the timber yard, where there was a vacancy for a sawyer, out of sight, measuring and cutting up wood needed by builders, had all refused to employ him, the excuses vague and sometimes abrupt.

He knew this was partly his own fault as, with the passing time he was less and less polite to prospective bosses and his surliness discouraged anyone from giving him a chance.

His wife still worked in the factory, which had reverted back from munitions to saucepans and other, less offensive, products and every week made him more frustrated than the last as he had to face the fact that without her wages they would be in what the locals called 'Queer Street'.

One afternoon, he walked several miles, calling at every likely looking place where he might find work. Surely there was some place where he could work where he wouldn't offend anyone, he thought bitterly. His feet ached, his heart was heavy with despair. What more could he do? He stopped in Audrey's cafe, which had become a regular haunt in his frustrating days. She automatically asked whether he'd had any luck, and frowned in sympathy when he told her he had not.

She placed a cup of tea at his elbow and he looked at the list he had made the previous evening of places to apply. All crossed out. Unless the employment exchange had something, or there was an advertisement in the evening paper, there was nothing more he could do that day. Hidden by a large-leafed plant, he overheard someone criticizing someone, accusing them of being lazy, and realized with horror that they were referring to him.

'Some of them need a nudge, mind,' an unseen woman was saying. 'There's that Matthew Proudfoot. He's been home for weeks and is there a sign of him getting a job? No there isn't!

His poor wife has worked all through the war and she should be taking it easy now. You'd think he'd be glad to look after her, wouldn't you?'

He stood up and stumbled from the cafe and out into the gloomy evening. It was raining and as he walked along the pavement, a car drove past and soaked his trouser legs as it sped through a deep puddle. He looked at the car and saw the passenger laughing at him.

A few moments later he caught up with the car, which had parked outside a tobacconist shop. There was no one inside but the engine was running. Without thinking, Matthew jumped in and drove off. He had no idea where he was going, he just had to put a few miles between himself and this town.

He hit the pedestrian as he walked out of the small park in the centre of the town and felt the horrifying bump as he ran over him. He drove on, hardly able to see through his tears, until the town was a long way behind him; then, weeping like a child he abandoned the car and began to walk home.

In the ambulance the severely injured man managed to tell them his name, but he died before he reached the hospital. Lilly Edwards, née Castle, was a widow.

Nine

It was as Sam junior stood outside the house in which his father and Lilly lived that the police called. Unable to decide whether or not he should knock, he watched as the constable arrived and the front door was opened by Lilly. She was dressed in a bright-orange dress that seemed to light the evening as no street lamp could. The glow from the inside surrounding her gave her an aura of gold and he had never seen anything so desirable. He was shaken by a surge of love for her. Illicit love it might be and love he must continue to deny, but desire was making it impossible to think clearly.

Then he heard her scream and she disappeared inside with the constable following. Frantically he knocked on the door until it was opened, and he pushed past the policeman and went to where Lilly was sitting, staring at him as though unable to see him.

'Lilly? What on earth has happened? Is Phyllis all right?'

'Phyllis? She's fine. She's with Mrs Denver.' Her eyes gradually focused and she saw him for the first time. 'It's Sam. He's been killed.'

Sam junior stayed with her and the constable while a neighbour was sent to find Marged and Huw. Within an hour all the family had been told and Beth had agreed to stay with her at least for the night. Mrs Denver brought Phyllis back and was distressed to hear the news.

'First losing my son, dear little Phyllis's father, and now your husband. Oh, you poor dear,' she sobbed. Lilly hugged the child as though she had been in danger of losing her too.

'She could have been with him,' she murmured. 'He loved taking her out.'

171

Audrey and Keith came and squeezed into the small room. No one knew what to do but none of them wanted to leave.

Lilly went with the policeman to identify the body, and Sam junior went with her. They both waited with hands and arms shaking with shock, until he had been made ready. Then they went back to the sad little rooms where the relatives sat talking in whispers.

Audrey had brought the makings of tea and cups were handed around and accepted with automatic indifference. Lilly had never been an easy person to talk to and now, everyone seemed struck dumb. People whispered among themselves. No one offered more than a few clichéd words of comfort. Gradually people drifted away, glad to be free from the stifling grief. Only Marged, Huw and Beth stayed.

Sam junior sat up with them for most of the night while Lilly tried to sleep. He was shocked and tearful, filled with a sense of loss. Guilt made it impossible for him to believe his father's death was an accident and at three o'clock in the morning he couldn't keep quiet any longer. He told them about his affair with Lilly.

'Dad must have found out,' he said. 'He found out and couldn't live with it. All this –' he waved his arms around the small over-crowded room – 'the loss of the house, Dad's death, everything, it's my fault.'

Beth went upstairs to where her sister was sitting on the bed, covered in Sam's dressing gown and hugging Phyllis.

'Have you slept?' Beth asked.

Lilly shook her head. 'Is Sam junior still there?'

'Yes, he's there. Mam and Dad have stayed too. We don't know why, it's just impossible to go. This is a terrible situation. We'll all do what we can, but you'll have to be brave because of Phyllis. She loved him, didn't she?'

'Will you ask Sam to come up?'

'Is that wise?'

'What d'you mean? He's lost his father! I've lost my husband! We need to comfort each other, don't we?'

Beth hesitated, then said, 'He told us. About you and he having, well, you know. He thinks Sam found out and couldn't cope with it. He's afraid Sam's death wasn't an accident. He believes his father was so distressed he stepped in front of that car deliberately.'

'Beth! How can you talk about such a thing now? Can't you see that's what I've been thinking too? How can you be so cruel only hours after my husband died?'

'If it is true, then you and Sam had better meet only in company. If this gets out, you and he would face an embarrassing enquiry.'

'Thinking of me, are you? Or yourself and Mam and Dad?'

'All of us. Particularly you. And little Phyllis.'

'Go away, Beth. You've never been on my side. Too perfect, that's your trouble.'

Beth kissed the sleeping child and left the room.

It was true, she and Lilly had never been close. She had loved the family business and had worked hard while Lilly had been very good at avoiding things she didn't want to do. They had both harboured dislike and even jealousy towards each other all their lives. But this was different. She wanted to help her sister cope with this traumatic situation.

Lilly was lazy but perhaps she couldn't help being weak and easily tempted. This was a time to forget past resentments and do all she could. And, she told herself, with a certain cynicism, I'll do it without expecting thanks. That was the only way to deal with someone like her sister. 'I think she might like another cup of tea,' she announced when she went back to the others.

'I'll take it up,' Sam said, and she shrugged. Who was she to disagree?

'He'd better not stay here with Lilly,' Marged said, her mouth tight with disapproval.

'I think she should come home where we can look after her and Phyllis,' Huw added. 'She'll need a lot of looking after now.'

Marged sighed sadly. 'Poor Lilly. She always has.'

Alice was in Cassie's second shop during her lunch-hour, when Beth came to tell her the following day and she went at once to Marged and Huw's house, where Lilly was ensconced on a couch, wrapped in blankets and being attended by an anxious Marged. Huw was on the floor building castles of coloured bricks with Phyllis.

Lilly pleaded to be allowed to bring the body to her parents' home. Seeing Alice she immediately tried to get her on her side. 'You understand, don't you, Alice? I want the funeral to leave from here. That awful house with us cramped into two rooms, that wasn't his home,' she sobbed. 'I want my Sam to have a proper send-off. He'll have left enough money for me to buy a decent house, he was so good to us, me and Phyllis. I don't want his funeral to leave from that place. Please, Mam. Please, our Dad.'

'But Lilly, your brother lives next door with Olive and their little Rhiannon. She's only four, and I don't think it would be right. In and out of this house all the time she is. I don't think they'd like knowing Sam's—' she corrected hastily, 'Sam, was here. You'll have to leave him at the funeral home.'

'I can't do that! What would people think? The Castles not caring about their daughter's husband, leaving him up there all alone. Mam, you can't want that?'

'Then it's going to be your rooms,' Marged decided. 'Phyllis can stay with us. That was his home, remember. Whether you like it or not, it was where he chose to live.'

Lilly drooped her head and gave a deep shuddering sigh. 'I don't even know how I'll pay for it. I can't get any money until the will's been read and there isn't much cash in the house.'

'We'll lend it to you, Lilly, but it is a loan. Right?' Huw said firmly. 'Tell us how much you need and we'll see you have it, for a loan,' he repeated, ignoring a frown of disapproval from Marged.

'Of course a loan. Sam had the money from the sale of the house, remember. I'll be all right.'

The funeral was not a large one but, to Alice's dismay, Netta and her children were there, standing beside Lilly, Marged and Huw as though they were a part of the family. Alice walked with Beth and Peter, Hannah and her two girls, but looked across at Eynon's parents and wondered if they no longer cared. Back at the house Huw nursed Netta's little girl, Dolly's fat arms hugging him, and her brother kneeling near Huw's knees, possessively.

'What's she doing here, Mam?' Alice asked as she and Marged took used dishes into the kitchen and began to wash them.

'Our Lilly asked her. It seems they're good friends and Lilly doesn't have too many of them,' Marged whispered. 'You don't like her, do you?'

'There's something sly about her. I have the feeling she's watching us and half smiling, as though waiting for something awful to happen.'

'She can't help the way she looks, Alice, love. And we were glad of her last summer.'

Yes, Alice thought, you gave her preference over me. But the words remained unsaid.

'She's nice enough,' Marged went on. 'And those two children are darlings.'

'I know you don't believe me, but she *was* following me, before she started meeting Lilly. I believe she was spying on us, learning about us, but I've no idea why.'

'Come on, Alice, why would she do that?' Marged's tone made it clear she wasn't convinced. 'It must have been coincidence, she just happened to be going to the same places as you.'

'Once or twice maybe, but not the number of times I saw her.'

'Forget it, you're making a mystery out of nothing.'

'I wasn't making it up, she was following me, watching my every move.'

Ending the futile conversation, Marged handed her a plate of sandwiches. 'Take those in, Alice, love. I hope they start leaving soon, I'm running out of food!'

Alice went in and said, loudly, 'Just another bite before you go.' She was pleased to see several people stand up and reach for their coats. She was even better pleased to see one of them was Netta.

When only the family were left, the will was read. Lilly tried in vain to hide her excitement. She would be a rich woman. Sam had money invested and the money for the house had been added to this. She would buy a house, and after a decent interval, she and Sam junior would be together and she'd never have to work.

At first she didn't take in the words as they were read out. She asked for them to be repeated but the result was the same. There was practically nothing for her. Just a hundred pounds and whatever furniture she required. The bulk of Sam's money had already been given to a children's charity, the remaining money was in trust for Phyllis when she reached the age of twenty-five.

'Mam,' Lilly pleaded dully, 'can I come home?'

On the day after the funeral and the shock of the will, both Alice and Hannah received letters telling them their husbands were being demobbed. Alice ran to tell her boss she would be late, then hurried to tell Marged and Huw. At the door she met Hannah on a similar errand.

'Mam, they're coming home,' Alice shouted through the letter box, too excited to wait as Marged came to open the door. 'Johnny and Eynon,' both young women chorused. 'They're both coming home.'

'I'm on my way to tell Johnny's parents,' Hannah said but Marged stopped her. 'No need, Hannah, love. They're both here.' They went inside waving their letters and Alice saw to her dismay that, sitting beside the fire was Netta.

'Damn me, that's wonderful news,' Huw said, hiding the letters they had received, also telling them the wonderful news.

'Tell me what they said,' Bleddyn asked, joining in Huw's deception. 'When are they coming? What you want us to do?'

'Two weeks and they'll be home,' Alice told them.

'What a Christmas we'll have this year!' Hannah said.

Marged, then Hetty hugged them both and they chattered happily about the Welcome Home banners and the party the Castle family had been planning for so long.

'I got a tin of salmon, Johnny's favourite,' Marged told them.

'And I've been hoarding fruit to make a proper cake,' Hetty added. 'Currants, sultanas, the lot!'

When the excitement had eased, and Bleddyn and Huw left to go to the wholesalers for potatoes, and Marged and Hetty were in the kitchen, looking for a bottle of sherry, Netta said, 'You're excited, of course you are, but I bet you're worried too, aren't you? Specially you, Hannah.'

'Worried?' Hannah stared at the girl. 'I'm dizzy with excitement at seeing Johnny again. And so are the girls.'

'Best not to bank on happy endings, though, eh? All this time away, he must have had doubts, you being old.'

She said 'old' not 'older', Hannah realized with a shock. Old had been said harshly, with the intention to hurt. Netta was half smiling as though to take the sting out of her words but the intention to offend was clearly visible in her eyes.

'He'll have changed after all this time,' Netta went on. 'He's seen other men's pin-ups, young, slim, lovely girls – he must be wondering if he made a mistake marrying a woman older than himself and with two children. It's only human nature.'

Hannah stared at her, feeling older than her years, and fat and foolish. Is this how people saw her?

'Get out!' Marged burst into the room, having heard Netta's gently spoken insults. 'Get out and I don't want to see you, ever again. D'you hear me? Wicked you are. Get out.' She grabbed Netta's coat and pushing it against her, shepherded her, none too gently, to the door, which she slammed hard behind her.

But the seeds of doubt were sown. Hannah was white-faced, trembling, being hugged by Alice.

'What a lot of old nonsense,' Marged said angrily.

'Here,' Hetty said. 'Read this if you need any convincing after than idiotic tirade, read Johnny's letter.'

'I don't need to,' Hannah said, trying to smile. 'I know he's coming home to me.'

'That's all he ever writes about. You, Josie and Marie and the home you'll have.'

'And getting back to working on the sands,' Hannah added, forcing a smile. 'He can't wait to be home again. I know that.'

'That girl had better keep out of my way. I never want to look at her again,' Marged said.

'Somehow I don't think we've seen the last of her,' Alice said.

There was a loud knock on the door and when Marged opened it, Netta stood there.

'I wondered when to tell you, but you might as well know now,' she almost shouted.

'If this is more of your wicked remarks I don't want to hear.'

'Alice won't either but I'm not keeping it to myself any longer.' Netta pointed a finger at Alice. 'Your Eynon, he's not the devoted husband you think. He's Dolly's father. He's the man who ran away from me knowing I was carrying his child!'

'Rubbish! More of your rubbish!' Marged shouted as Netta walked away. She turned to Alice. 'Forget it, the girl is full of spite, although I can't imagine why. What have we ever done to her?'

'Only encouraged her, helped her by inviting her into the family and telling her all she needed to know,' Alice said bitterly. 'I knew that was what she wanted. Now I know why.'

'I don't,' Hetty said, hugging the distressed girl. 'What has she got to gain by telling lies?'

'What if they aren't lies?'

'Of course they're lies,' Hannah said. 'There's truth in what she said about me, mind. I am older than Johnny and I do have two children. But there's never been anyone else but you for Eynon.'

Marged held her by the shoulders and stared into her eyes forcing her to believe as she said, 'It's rubbish, Alice. You only have to ask him. He'll tell you it's rubbish.'

'I hope so,' Alice said. Refusing to stay and talk about it any longer, she headed back to the office.

Although it had been her intention when she left Sidney Street, she didn't go straight to the office. She went home to the two rooms in which she had waited for Eynon. Taking out the new cushion covers and the fresh bedding, she dampened them ready for ironing. She wanted everything perfect. The fire would be ready to light; there would be flowers in every vase. She had been saving her meat ration and the few ounces of bacon she was allowed. Mr Gregory would surely find her a few off-ration eggs. Everything would be perfect for Eynon's homecoming.

She passed Cassie's shop when she left for the office and called to tell her friend the news of Eynon's imminent arrival and Lilly's disappointment. A fresh delivery of bedding and towels had arrived overnight, filling the storeroom beyond the shop as well as every space behind the counter. She was easily persuaded to stay and help; she was glad of something to keep her busy, to drive away the black cloud that had settled over her. Eynon and Netta. His child, and born to another woman. The words kept repeated themselves, hammering their message into her brain. It must be true, it explained so much. Netta had ingratiated herself into the Castle family, encouraged them to take an interest in Dolly in preparation for her announcement. It all made cruel sense.

When she went to get out the book to check that the new stock had been entered, she found a couple of large envelopes tucked almost out of sight below the invoices and delivery notes. Curiously she opened them and found dozens of books of clothing coupons.

So this was how Cassie managed to find so-called damaged, off-ration stock. She and Joseph had access to stolen clothing coupons to make up the deficiency when checks were made. She replaced the incriminating envelopes and looked around her at the bales of curtain material, with the price and coupon value clearly marked, and in the back room the sheets, pillowcases and household items, the boxes squashed and torn, some showing signs of fire and smoke damage, some labelled 'damaged by fire', others marked 'damaged by flood', and she wondered. Stolen goods as well as stolen coupons? Was that what Cassie had become involved in?

Was what she long suspected really true? If so, she was implicated. Besides conspiring to sell illegally obtained rationed goods, a supporter of the black market, she herself had several boxes of the goods she had bought from Cassie for her own use.

Coming on top of Netta's accusations about Eynon, this was too much to cope with. Her world was collapsing around her. She apologized to a customer who had walked in looking hopeful and locked the shop.

She found Cassie in the main shop serving a small queue of customers with creased and dusty sheets for which she refused to take coupons. From Cassie's expression she had not had a very good day either. But her concerns were not for Cassie; today they were for herself.

'Here are the keys, I won't be helping you again,' she said, putting the keys on the counter as the last customer left the shop.

Cassie stared at the keys and nodded. 'Stay and have a cup of tea, will you, Alice? If I don't talk to someone soon, I'll burst.'

'Eynon is coming home in fourteen days,' Alice said as she watched Cassie set out cups and saucers.

'But that isn't why you're abandoning me, is it?'

'No, I'm keeping away because what you're doing is illegal and I could be fined or even imprisoned if someone reported you.'

'I wouldn't let that happen, I'd never let you take the blame for what Joseph is doing.'

'Joseph and you,' Alice reminded her. 'You must have known there was something odd about getting all this stock without coupons. You'd have to be stupid not to realize and you're not stupid.'

'Oh but I am, Alice. I've been very stupid. But not any more.'

'What d'you mean?'

'Joseph wrote to me. He wrote, mind, he couldn't tell me to my face. He wrote and said he's leaving me. He's found someone else.'

'At your age?' Alice put a hand over her mouth, regretting the words as soon as they were uttered. They were so similar to Netta's remarks to Hannah. 'Sorry, I didn't mean that to come out as it sounded.'

'At our age, yes. Sixty we are, old enough to be settled, feel safe and secure. This new woman isn't our age though. She's young and pretty, and Joseph wants me to leave.' She laughed harshly. 'Won't the gossips have a great time?'

'What will you do?'

'I don't know. I'm sixty, and besides the humiliation, the prospect of being alone is frightening. I won't have much of a pension, and everything is in Joseph's name.' She looked at Alice and asked, 'I don't suppose I can persuade you to leave your job and help me for a little while, can I?'

'But what you're doing could lead to serious trouble.'

'I know I'm asking a lot. But it'll give me a chance to decide what I'm going to do.'

'Eynon's coming home in two weeks.'

'Two weeks, that might be long enough.'

Eirlys watched as Ralph became proficient at the job she had made her own. Without spite but filled with painful disappointment she gave him all the assistance he needed, making lists of the various people he might need to contact, advising on various ways of dealing with problems. It was October: the visitors no longer came and she knew her time there was almost done.

When a typist came to ask her to go and see Mr Johnston, she knew he would tell her that Ralph no longer needed her. She walked through the corridor and knocked on the familiar door, and stepped into the office in which she and Mr Johnston and Mr Gifford had discussed many ideas for the town's summers.

'Mrs Ward, Eirlys, please sit down,' Mr Johnston said. 'Firstly, Mr Gifford and I want to thank you for your wonderful support during the years of the conflict.'

Eirlys tried to hide a smile. This sounded like a well-rehearsed speech. 'I loved every minute,' she told him.

'But now, with Ralph Proudfoot back and coping well, it's time for us to find you something else.'

'He's a quick learner,' she said, pointing out obliquely that she had been teaching him all she knew.

'There's a vacancy for a secretary which you'd easily fill; would you like me to recommend you?'

'Which of you will I work for?' she asked, presuming it would be either Mr Johnston or Mr Gifford. She liked both men, stuffy and formal though they might be, and her heart lightened a little.

'Not here, I'm afraid. There's a secretary needed in Pillar Place, the wholesale grocery there. Your friend Alice Castle has let them down and left unexpectedly.'

'Leave the council offices? But I thought you were pleased with my work?'

'We are, and I hate to let you go, but with the men coming home and expecting work, we can't keep you, I'm afraid.' He handed her a typed page. 'I've given you an excellent reference and, as I say, Mr Gifford and I want you to know how much we appreciate your wonderful assistance –'

'– during the years of the conflict,' she finished for him.

'Yes. Well, if there's nothing more?'

'I won't be needing the job in the wholesale grocery.' She stood up, accepted the reference, and walked out. At the door, she looked back and with clear sarcasm, added, 'Thank you . . .' the extra words – 'for nothing' – were unspoken but they seemed to echoed around the office. Opening a connecting door, Mr Johnston said, 'That, Mr Gifford, is the worst thing I've ever had to do. What a waste of talent.'

'I agree, Mr Johnston, I agree.'

Eirlys went home and sat fuming, wondering what to do. So far as she could see there were few choices. London with Ken was not a consideration. There was the gift shop, but that wouldn't be enough for her. After so much to fill her life, her work leaving little time for anything else, hours and days stretched before her, ominously empty.

She automatically picked up the sewing basket and began to repair the boys' clothes. No one sat with idle hands, whatever problems they faced. Thank goodness she had Anthony. And there were the three boys too. Anthony, Stanley, Harold and Percival. How would she have coped without them?

Anthony was with Hannah and Beth at the shop and she finished sewing on a few buttons, sighing at the state of the well-worn garments, and went to fetch him.

'I've been virtually sacked,' she told her friends, after hugging her small son. 'So, what shall I do now?'

'What does Ken think?' was Hannah's first question.

'He'll be pleased. He hated my involvement. He'd prefer me to do something less time-consuming.'

'London?' Beth asked.

'No, I don't want to leave St David's Well.' There was a stubborn look on her face, as though she had expected the question and had been ready to field it straight back.

'Have you seen Alice?' Hannah asked then.

Beth told her about Netta's accusation and Eirlys laughed. 'What a nonsense. She's trying it on, looking for a comfortable family to take her on. There are plenty of girls in her situation, trying to find a gullible man to marry her.'

'What if it's true?' Beth said worriedly. 'He'd be obligated to do something to help her.'

'Forget it. She's a chancer. Alice saw through her straight away. Remember how she told us she was being followed? The girl was picking up clues, ingratiating herself, planning to tell us she'd learned all she knew during passionate moments with Eynon.'

'How do we prove it?'

'We can't and that's the point. Neither can Netta! Laugh it off. It's the only way.'

'We'll have to convince Alice before Eynon gets home, or their reunion won't be as perfect as it should be.'

When Alice closed Cassie's shop and joined them for the lunch hour, they told her what Eirlys had said.

'I was going to write and tell him, but I changed my mind,' Alice told them. 'Perhaps we won't hear anything more from her. Marged made it clear she didn't believe her.'

'That's right, plan the welcome home, that's all you need to think about.' Hannah laughed. 'That's all I *can* think about. Look, I've put this zip on the outside!' She held up a half-finished purse and waggled it in the air. 'How can I work when Johnny is on his way back to me and the girls? How can you worry about a spiteful girl like Netta, when your Eynon is coming home to you in a matter of days?'

Eirlys jumped up. 'Come on, let's forget the shop for an

hour and go to the cafe for a sticky bun. I feel like celebrating with you.'

'With champagne or stale tea?'

'Oh, tea. I'm told the bubbles in champagne can make you sneeze!' The three girls went out, taking Beth's baby and Anthony with them. All appeared cheerful but all were hiding fears behind the smiling faces: Eirlys wondering how she could earn enough to keep herself and Anthony if she and Ken finally parted, Hannah and Alice fearful that the reunion with their husbands, dreamed of for so long, would be a disaster.

Lilly came back to her parents' home and seemed to settle for a life of continuing ease. Sympathy for her lasted a while but, knowing Lilly of old, people soon began to realize this was a situation she was beginning to enjoy. The grieving widow was a role that suited her to perfection.

She saw very little of Sam junior. Marged made it clear that he was not welcome and her belief that he was as much to blame for Lilly's lack of a home was something she didn't keep to herself.

'How much longer are you planning to sit there like a wet week, our Lilly?' she asked on several occasions, steeling herself for the wailing and the tears that followed her attempts to persuade her daughter to find herself a job.

Marged didn't work in the winter, but Huw usually found a job to help finance them through the months when, apart from the fish and chip shop-cum-restaurant, everything closed down.

'It isn't good for you to sit there doing nothing day after day,' Huw grumbled one morning, when Lilly came down, draped in a dressing gown, leading a similarly attired Phyllis, to look for breakfast.

'And if you want breakfast you can get it yourself and make sure you clear up after you. I'm not your slave,' an angry Marged said. 'I asked you to get up early and go to the shops for me, remember? Well, I've been, it's done, you're safe from being disturbed from your idleness!'

'Audrey could do with a hand in the cafe,' Huw said. 'I don't think you'd be her first choice, mind, but you might ask her to give you a week's trial; see if you can get your head around putting in a day's work. You owe me money from Sam's funeral, remember,' he added sharply.

'What's the matter with you two today? Can't you see I'm broken-hearted?'

'No, we can't, 'Marged replied. 'All we can see is a lazy, useless woman who's had it easy for too long. Now, we're giving you two weeks to get yourself sorted, or out you go. Right?'

Lilly turned around and went back to bed.

'That went well,' Huw sighed.

'What did you expect? I gave up expecting miracles where our Lilly's concerned years ago.'

When the house was empty, Lilly came down, made some toast for herself and Phyllis then went to see Mrs Denver, Phyllis's grandmother. The house in Queen Street was also where Sam junior was living.

By letter, Ken sometimes arranged to telephone Eirlys at the box on the corner. When she spoke to him a few days after losing her job, she told him what had happened.

'So you'll come to London?' he asked.

'I can't, Ken. You know how hopeless Dadda is, and I can't leave the boys.'

'You're being ridiculous, Eirlys. If you left, your father would have to manage, wouldn't he? It isn't as if we'd be in some far-off country, we could visit every month or so. It's only about five hours away. Please, Eirlys, I'm missing you. There are hours when I sit on my own wishing I had a home to go to.'

'You have, Ken. As you say, London isn't that far away and if we had a telephone installed, you'd be able to keep in touch.'

'I need to be here.'

'And I need to be here, can't you understand that? You'd be the one inconvenienced, I know that, but the alternative is to mess up six lives. Anthony is settled, and has lots of friends. The boys are dug in so deep they consider themselves locals and have the accent to prove it. And I don't think you'd want them to come with me, would you? And there's Dadda. He couldn't cope with having the family split up.'

'I want you with me, Eirlys. I'm your husband and I love you.'

Hearing his voice, she wanted him home so badly. The irony was cruel. At a time when half the town were either celebrating the return of their men or planning for imminent reunions, like Hannah and Alice, her man had gone away.

The pips went and Ken put in his last coin.

'I love you, Eirlys,' he said and her voice broke as she replied, telling him that she thought of him every minute of every day and she and Anthony were counting the days until his next visit.

'Next visit? It sounds as though one of us in in prison,' he said. 'I wonder which one it is?' The pips went again giving her no chance to reply.

Cassie had heard nothing more from Joseph since the letter telling her he wanted her to move out. She sat through a sleepless night wondering what she could do, what would become of her. She would have no home, no money and she would be all alone. Gone were the dreams of a retirement to a bungalow in the Vale of Glamorgan. She would have to settle for a small room with only bitter memories for company.

There had never been time for friendships. She was sixty years old and had no one. The chill night seemed endless and at 5 a.m. she was no nearer sorting out her future. At ten minutes to six, after thinking about Lilly's predicament, the idea came. Over the hours before she opened the shop it was honed to perfection. She would need help and was sure she could rely on Alice. With Alice to help her, everything would work out just as she planned.

The day both Johnny and Eynon were due home began with heavy rain. Alice polished the furniture unnecessarily and put the clean cushion covers and chair backs on the two fireside chairs she had bought. Flowers were expensive but she went to Chapel's Flowers and bought a bowl of daffodil bulbs that were just peeping through the soil, and two bunches of rather boring, bronze chrysanthemums. Still the room looked uninviting. She sat in a chair and looked around her. So many days had passed since she had come here as a bride and then said goodbye to Eynon. She wasn't the same person and she hadn't even left the town.

How different for Eynon, travelling the world, meeting so many people with different backgrounds and knowledge and attitudes. Some of it must have rubbed off on him. He couldn't be the same man she had seen boarding the train that last time.

What would his first reaction be on seeing her? She knew she would be watching his face, searching for a hint of disappointment. And then there was this accusation from Netta. She was certain Netta would reappear soon after Eynon came home and again, she would be watching Eynon's face for some recognition. How could the reunion be anything but uneasy with all that had happened?

Straightening the curtains for the fourth time, she saw Shirley walking past and, pumping up the cushions one last time, she called her in.

'What does it look like?' she asked, waving an arm inviting her to look around the room. 'What's your first impression? Are the curtains all right or would they be better draped? Is the kettle shiny enough or does it need another polish? The tablecloth, what d'you think? Best straight or at an angle?' Then she realized that Shirley was laughing.

'Alice, he won't even notice!'

Smiling ruefully, Alice asked if she would like a cup of tea. 'Best we go out and buy one,' Shirley teased. 'We don't want you to have to clean the room all over again, do we?'

'Have you heard from Freddy?' Alice asked when they sat in a cafe with tea and toast in front of them. Shirley shook her head.

'Not one word. He obviously doesn't want to continue our friendship now his need for letters has ended. But I have some money belonging to him and I need to find him to return it. I don't know where he's gone and I'm worried. Just out of the Army, he'll need it. Remember how vain he was? Always dressed in the smartest suit, his shirt perfectly ironed. He's probably just the same now and where will he get the money for all that?'

187

'Make sure the money's safe, and wait. He's bound to contact you soon.'

Shirley had no idea where Freddy could be. Where else but St David's Well would he go when the Army finished with him? So far as she knew he had no relations. It could only be someone he had met during his service. A woman perhaps, someone he had chosen to stay with. The idea was painful but she was determined not to show it. 'He's probably found himself a woman and doesn't like to tell me. I don't know why though, we were only friends.'

'Isn't there an address for ex-Army personnel?' Alice asked.

'I've tried that but they can't, or won't help. Since he's been demobbed there's been no sign of him. Any letters I've written have been re-addressed back to me, and I can't think of anyone likely to know where he might be. I've asked Maldwyn and Delyth, who live in his parents' house, to pass on any information, explaining I have something belonging to him which I want to return, and I asked their neighbour if he had been in touch, but no one's heard a word.'

'The Gent's Outfitters, where he worked?' Alice suggested.

'They don't know his whereabouts, either.'

Shirley sighed. Andy and Freddy, both home and both hiding from her. What was it about her that two such different men couldn't face her?

She learned from Reggie that his brother had been punished but was now free and working on a farm not far from their parents' home. Shirley no longer cared. His cheating ways had attracted her for a while, in the same way that, as a child, the romantic highway robber appealed, but that had gone back where it belonged, in with memories of childish fancy.

She was increasingly in demand to perform in places further from home, larger towns, bigger audiences and higher fees. She accepted more readily now her legs were stronger and she felt less vulnerable. Then a letter came from a theatre manager in London inviting her to audition for a part in a West End show.

It was only a small part, singing with a small group, but it excited her. This was a dream come true. If only she could tell Freddy. He'd be so thrilled for her. Thoughts of Freddy took some of the excitement away, leaving her less sure that it was what she wanted to do.

As well as the need to tell Freddy, the thrill of appearing on a London stage was also tempered by remembering some of the lonely hours between performances. She had sat in many guest-house rooms, longing to be home between appearances on a stage in some strange town. It had been easier of late, knowing so many of the other performers, but in London she would be completely alone.

'I'm a small-town girl at heart,' she told Hetty and Bleddyn. 'Perhaps that isn't such a bad thing.' It was at night, as she lay unable to sleep, knowing that she wanted to take the part, she wished she and Janet Copp with whom she had begun her singing career was there to share it with her. Doing it alone was not fun any more.

She went to see Ken when he came home for a few days and he offered to act as her agent and negotiate a better deal for her.

'I know this sounds weak, Ken, but I don't think I'm ready yet.' She couldn't tell him she needed to stay in St David's Well in the faint hope of seeing Freddy. Unprofessional bordering on stupid that would sound.

They agreed that, in the New Year of 1946, after which she had only a few more concerts booked, she would go to London and discuss her future with him.

'I don't want to sound ungallant, Shirley,' Ken said, 'but you can't leave it too long, there are young singers coming up all the time and you are no longer a little girl.'

'I'm twenty-two,' she gasped. 'That isn't old!'

'Don't delay. Time passes and so do opportunities.'

She went back home feeling less cheerful than when she set out. She declined the invitation to audition and promised that, once her commitments were cleared, she would write to them, via her agent, Ken Ward.

Beth planned to return to running her market cafe as soon as Hannah agreed to look after her son. She knew she would have to wait until her cousin Johnny was home. Hannah would want to be free to welcome him and they would need time to settle. She didn't mind waiting. She too wanted to enjoy the return of her brother and her cousin after the long absences.

Peter had opened an office and started advertising for both prospective employers and those looking for work, hoping to marry the two lists amicably. To help financially while the business was established, Beth would run the cafe, which was still in the hands of a temporary manageress.

Eirlys offered to help Peter, giving her services free while she considered what she would do. 'I can work for you in the mornings and then go to the shop in the afternoons,' she explained to Peter. 'No wages, I just need to keep busy and Beth is a good friend.'

The arrangement seemed a good idea, and Beth went to the station to see her brother and cousin arrive filled with optimism for the future.

At the station, Hannah and Alice stood watching as the crowded train disgorged its passengers. Many were soldiers and airmen and sailors, still in uniform, carrying hefty bags on their shoulders, their eyes sweeping the crowd searching for loved ones.

Shrieks of delight intermingled with the wails of confused children filled the air, but Alice and Hannah were aware of none of it. They had seen Johnny and Eynon, miraculously jumping from the same carriage. There was no doubt in any mind as the four of them fell into each other's arms. No thought of anything but love, relief and a happiness so intense it was almost a pain.

Arm in arm the two couples walked along the platform, now almost empty, as they had been wrapped in loving arms for so long, and there, at the gate where the porter stood to collect tickets, stood Netta, with Walter and little Dolly.

Alice felt panic squeeze her insides. She wanted to turn away, wait until Netta had gone, but Eynon was hurrying forward, catching up with Johnny and Hannah. He won't know her, Alice told herself. Netta made it up out of malice. She tried not to look at the trio; a smiling Netta and her two children. He won't know her. She made it up, Alice chanted silently as they approached the gate. He won't even notice her.

'Hi there,' Eynon said to her, patting Dolly's head as they walked past.

Ten

Johnny's return was more than Hannah could have wished for. As soon as they were inside Bleddyn and Hetty's house, he opened his arms and enfolded her and Josie and Marie, who jumped about in delight, talking non-stop, asking if he had liked their letters and the pictures they had drawn for him and had he brought them a camel as they had requested.

'No, they wouldn't let him on the plane,' he told them. 'Poor Clarence, he was very disappointed. But I did bring you back some sand, just to show you that it isn't as good as the sand on St David's Well Bay.' He opened a small tin that had once contained tobacco and showed them the coarse grains of desert sand he had carried with him for several weeks.

He hugged his father and stepmother and asked about Shirley and the rest of the family, but all the time he couldn't take his eyes off his quiet, lovely wife.

'I hope you don't think us rude, Johnny, my son,' Bleddyn said, 'but Hetty and I have to go out. We're taking the girls to Audrey's cafe for some tea, a promised treat and we can't disappoint them.'

'We want to stay and talk to Johnny,' the girls protested, but they were coaxed out with the promise of extra cakes.

There was a shyness between them as they sat and unpacked his bag, and he went upstairs to their bedroom to find some civilian clothes neatly washed and pressed ready for him to put on.

'All right if I have a bath?' he called, and she went slowly up the stairs half fearful of rejection but loving him, wanting him so much. Netta's spiteful words were forgotten within moments. His, 'I love you my beautiful girl,' dissolving

191

the barbed words into the air, drifting away never to be feared again.

For Alice there was a tension about Eynon's return that was making her almost tearful. He knew Netta, had greeted her like a friend. The child, Dolly, could possibly be his. Alice had worked out the date of the little girl's conception and it would have been at the time of their marriage. A last fling and the result was the appearance of Netta just when everything was perfect, with Dolly, the child who might one day call him Daddy.

The reason for Netta following her, and her curiosity about members of Eynon's family, was to ingratiate herself into the family circle, knowing Marged and Huw would be unable to ignore a child, sure of her place within it.

'What's the matter, lovely girl?' Eynon asked as she touched the scar on his face, where he had been injured, so long ago, just before he had absconded on a country exercise to escape the Army and a bully, a trainee soldier like himself.

'I can't believe you're really here.'

'I'm here and I'm ready to prove it.' He bent over her and as they were about to kiss, he stopped and asked again, 'Is anything wrong, love? D'you want to wait a while?'

Why was she allowing Netta to ruin this wonderful day? Desire and love for him became stronger than her doubts and she held him tightly. 'Tell me you love me again,' she whispered.

'I love you, Alice Castle, I love you more than before I went away. You are so beautiful, and I've been dreaming of nothing but this moment since the train took me away from you.'

Later, she thought again of the accusations made by Netta and wondered. Perhaps one day, the doubts would be resolved, and it would prove to be just more of Netta's spiteful attempts to spoil the homecomings. Until then she was content to believe that Eynon loved no one but her.

It was October and darkness had fallen but as she closed the curtains on that wonderful day, Eynon said, 'Let's go over to the sands, lovely girl. I've lived with the stuff for years but I want to see our version.'

'It's dark!' Alice said with a laugh.

'All the better, there'll be plenty of chances for kisses and cuddles. Come on, you can wear my army greatcoat if you're cold.'

They caught a bus and walked on the promenade. It was chilly, but with arms around each other and desire building pictures of the night to come, they were unaware of the temperature.

The beach was deserted but the edge of the waves was visible, almost phosphorescent, being picked out by a half moon sailing above. The cafe, high up on the cliff path, was in darkness.

'I can't wait to be back on the swingboats and the helter-skelter, Alice. Not much of an ambition after all that's happened, I know that. Most of the men I served with will be looking for something different, something exciting, but I'll never want anything more. Will you?'

'Life working the sands every summer and finding something to see us through the winter sounds perfect to me.'

Footsteps sounded and they pulled apart and looked around them. An arm waved and they saw to their surprise that Johnny and Hannah were joining them.

'You two!' Hannah said. 'We might have guessed you'd be unable to wait a day before coming here.'

Beth returned to her market cafe in October. Her eighteen-month-old son, Peter, was taken to her mother's house every morning and Marged looked after him until the cafe closed at five o'clock. Marged wasn't busy during the winter months and willingly agreed to look after her grandson until the season began and then, Hannah would take over from her.

Beth knew it would be strange at first. Imagining the days without her infant son made her anxious, and putting in a full day at the busy cafe would be very tiring. Like many of the Castle family, her first thought was to approach Mrs Denver. The kindly, quietly capable lady offered to come in each morning for a week or two, until Beth found an assistant or learned to cope once again, and Beth was grateful.

She knew that being home with her baby, and spending

time with her friends had gone on too long. She had to face rushed mornings, and evenings filled with small routine tasks that she had recently been able to do during the day. The small income she had earned by having a manageress running the cafe had been a help, but now Peter was home and starting to build a business, they needed more. Regretfully she gave notice to the woman who had worked for her for eighteen months and prepared herself for a busier life with little time for friends.

After a week she was enjoying being back. The other stallholders welcomed her and with Ronnie and his wife on a nearby stall, she quickly felt she hadn't been away. Peter spent a lot of time preparing the ground for his agency and they both shared thoughts and ideas on how he should proceed, once the evening meal was over and young Peter was in bed.

'I thought food-rationing would end once the war was over, but there's even talk about cutting the rations further. Would you believe it?' she said to her mother one day, when Marged had brought young Peter in to see her.

'It will be years before we see the end of the shortages,' Marged replied. She looked around her at the women with empty baskets, in the ongoing search for food. Someone said that there were some late apples on Ronnie's stall and like a magnet, the fruit and vegetable stall was quickly surrounded by hopeful women.

'Don't worry,' Marged said. 'Our Ronnie will save some for us, sure to.'

Beth took a tray and collected used dishes from the tables. 'Everyone's so tired, Mam. The victory was an anti-climax in some ways. It's still so hard for us all.'

'But the men are coming home. Your Peter and our Eynon and Johnny are safe. There isn't a day when we don't see a few houses with their Welcome Home banners and hopeful faces.'

'Everyone reunited, except Eirlys. She and Ken have parted. He's in London and she's staying here. Neither will give in and go with the other. Strange isn't it, after all the separations we've all suffered, they choose to live apart?'

'Eirlys put everything into her job and now it's been taken from her. I don't think they'll stay apart much longer. She'll be bored soon enough.'

Beth thought about her mother's words later that evening. At eleven o'clock she was getting ready for bed, Peter was filling in forms and Bernard was standing on the door smoking his final pipe of the day, 'Are you coming up, Peter?' she asked.

'No, dear. Not for a while. I need to complete these forms ready for tomorrow. Thank goodness Eirlys is helping me. I'd never cope without her coming in a couple of times a week. Thank goodness I can afford a decent office.' He looked around the overcrowded room where they sat in the evenings, and where his father's roll-top desk filled a corner with papers spilling out of every space, then at the table on which he struggled to organize his own work. 'Some office this would be, eh? Eirlys will be very impressed!'

Eirlys had agreed to stay in the office for two mornings a week to enable Peter to interview prospective employers. He had found it worthwhile to visit places before sending someone for an interview and he had already turned down several places he didn't consider suitable for clients on his books.

When Ken came home for a visit he was surprised to learn that Eirlys was working for nothing. Eirlys explained what she was doing and he stared at her with such smouldering anger, she was afraid.

'Ken? What is it? I'm helping a friend, that's all.'

'I see. You've lost your job, the work you put before everything else and now you're helping Peter Gregory. For nothing. What about me? I need help, but as usual, I don't count. If you won't come with me to London you could at least be earning money.'

'It was such a shock, Ken. I can't think of another job yet. The truth is, I'd hoped, and almost believed, that Ralph wouldn't be able to manage and they'd ask me to go back.'

'You're assisting Peter to build an agency. I'm in London on my own, trying to do much the same thing. Why aren't you helping *me*?' His voice had risen until he was shouting, glaring at her, and she backed away from his anger.

'Because you're too far away!' she shouted back. 'If you bring work home, or post it to me, I'll gladly help you,' she added defensively. 'We're in an impossible situation, Ken.'

Ken didn't get home very often and when he did, their time together was continuously marred by arguments. Eirlys knew she had been wrong not to follow him to London. She had received no money from him since he went away, and she guessed that, with the rent and advertising and the travelling around involved in starting an agency, it was unlikely that she would.

It was in late October that she determined that his next visit would be a happy one. He would soon tire of coming back if all he had was arguments. Thank goodness Anthony showed none of their confused feelings. He accepted his father's visits with joy and that, she decided, was what she would also do. Choosing her smartest winter coat and a saucy 'Robin Hood' hat with a long pheasant's feather, with Anthony dressed in a suit and coat specially made for him by the talented Hannah, she stood at the station as the train bringing him home steamed noisily alongside the platform.

She greeted him with affection and walked with him arm in arm back home where she had a meal waiting for him. Two weeks' ration of cheese, plus a little extra, some hard, stale pieces given to her by the grocer, had been made into 'cheese boats' by baking potatoes and adding grated cheese to the contents, then browning them with more cheese on top. It was one of Ken's favourite meals and, served with a salad, she knew it would please him. Her father and the three boys had eaten earlier and had gone out: Stanley to meet Myrtle and the others to the pictures.

'Aren't you working today?' he asked, trying to sound civil.

'I only help when I have free time, just manning the office so Peter can interview prospective employers. Most of my spare moments are spent in the gift shop. I've started making rugs again, although it's more difficult to find the material these days.'

'What else is new?'

'Let me see,' she pondered. 'Oh, great excitement. Cassie

Davies is having the most amazing sales. I bought a dozen pillowcases with nothing worse than a bit of dust on the folds. No coupons either, that's the best part. I haven't any coupons left until the new issue.'

'That's absolutely wonderful,' he said and she realized he was laughing. 'What a boring life we lead, Eirlys. The highlight of our week being off-ration pillowcases for you, and a small booking for me, a singer who, incidentally, should be selling newspapers instead of trying to make a living on the stage.'

She shared his laughter and felt an optimism for their future together she hadn't felt for months. Risking a return to their usual wrangling, she put her arms around him, pressed her face against his and said, 'Ken, darling. Come home.' She held her breath waiting for his reply.

'I'll give myself until the New Year and if I'm not at least breaking even by then I'll come home. I'll have to anyway,' he added. 'My savings won't last any longer than January.'

It was a pity he added the last few words. She wanted him to come home to her and Anthony, not give up because he had been defeated by lack of funds. The happy mood she had striven to create was ruined.

Myrtle and Stanley saw a lot of each other that summer and autumn. Stanley would be waiting for her when the cafe closed and Auntie Audrey told her she needn't stay to help clear up. On her day off, they would go out for the day. When the weather was fine they would take food and walk through the fields and woods, just glad to be alone.

Stanley had found work in a second-hand shop where he was gradually learning to help the owner repair furniture ready for resale. He had developed an unexpected skill in the work, patiently sanding and planing, making pieces to replace worn joints and strengthen legs, and was enjoying the new-found talent for working with wood.

Alf Thomas promised that soon he would start taking him on his rounds, examining furniture he was offered and negotiating a price. The scruffy-looking man also visited the council tip on occasions, returning with something that only needed a fresh coat of paint or a polish before ending up in the window with a price ticket on it. With so many difficulties involved in buying new, good-quality second-hand furniture was a thriving business.

'It's magic, Myrtle. The old man can spot a decent piece even though its covered with muck. In a farmer's barn last week he saw this broken old cupboard covered in chicken sh— feathers, it was,' he amended quickly. 'And now it's in the window for sale and he's asking thirty bob. It's a good business to be in and I'm enjoying it.'

'But you'll want to go back to the beach when summer comes?'

'Yeh, I can't see me wanting anything else. Not in summer. Summer's for the beach and larking with the visitors. I'll miss working with Alf, though.'

'He looks a bit rough, wearing old clothes and that greasy cap on his head looks older than Mr Gregory's trilby!'

'That's a ploy. People feel sorry for him, see, and when he offers them less than they'd hoped, they give in and let him take it. No good wearing a suit in his line of work, Myrtle.'

Shirley was still puzzled and hurt by the continuing absence of Freddy Clements. Where had he gone? So far as she could discover, no one else had spoken to him either.

She went to the cemetery one afternoon with Bleddyn and her mother. There was no grave for Bleddyn's son Taff, but he took flowers for him and left them on Taff's mother's grave.

His first wife was buried in a half-hidden corner of the graveyard, where graves of those who had committed the sin of suicide were laid to rest. It was not a place to grieve for his young son, but there was nowhere else and wouldn't be, unless some small plot in a far-off country was dedicated to him, once the confusion had eased.

There were a few figures walking around, some leaving flowers, some tidying their plots ready for the winter. Shirley felt the depressing place lowering her spirits. It was always a sad occasion, trying to understand why a young, happy, innocent man had become a victim of someone else's fight.

On the way home, Shirley said, 'Mam, I want to buy some

flowers, but for you to enjoy in the house. That's where Taff lived,' she said to her stepfather, 'and where you remember him. Not in this solemn place. I didn't know Taff very well but I do know he wasn't solemn.'

They went along the main road and Shirley went into Chapel's Flowers, where Maldwyn Perkins was setting up a display of preserved autumn leaves ready for the window.

'Hello, Shirley. If you want a pretty bunch, I've just had a delivery of little button chrysanths. Lovely they are.'

Shirley selected some bright-yellow blooms and as they were being wrapped in the *South Wales Echo*, owing to the lack of decorative paper, she asked, 'Are you and Delyth happy in the Clementses' old house?'

'Very content,' he replied. 'Funny you should mention the Clementses. We've seen Freddy a few times since you asked about him.'

Shirley's heart leapt. 'Where?' she asked impatiently.

'Outside the house, looking up as though remembering days when it was his home. There's sad it was, losing both mother and father so sudden. Where's he living, d'you know?'

'I was about to ask you,' Shirley replied sadly.

'No idea. Sorry.'

As she handed him the money Shirley asked, 'If you see him again, will you tell him I want to see him? I have some property belonging to him and I'd like to return it.'

'Certainly I will. And I'll make sure Delyth knows too. We called to him one day, mind, and asked if he would like a cup of tea. He looked kind of lost. But he only shook his head and waved as he turned away.'

Instead of being pleased at having news of him, Shirley fell deeper into gloom. He was still around and making it clear that he didn't want to see her.

'Mam,' she said as they turned towards home. 'I'm going to try for a part on the London stage. I need to get away for a while.'

'Good on you!' Bleddyn said. 'If there's an opportunity out there you shouldn't miss it.'

*　　*　　*

199

Freddy didn't know what to do with himself. There were many men who couldn't adjust after the horrors they had experienced; tramps, wandering around the countryside, doing casual work or begging to survive. Perhaps that was how he would end up now he had no base, no place from which to begin again. He hadn't the money to stay in the hotel any longer and the thought of a lonely room sounded worse than existing in fields and barns, depending on the whims of others for food.

He thought then of Maude and Myrtle, whom the Castle family had found living in a derelict stable, surviving on other people's leavings. He couldn't understand at the time but now he knew how easy it would be to slip out of the safety of conventional living if there was no one to care enough to hold you there.

He was walking along the road, his coat collar turned up, his shoulders hunched against the cold. He saw someone approaching, limping slightly, and although the rain had darkened an already dull day and made it impossible to be sure, he knew it was Shirley. His heart leaped and the longing to see her made his feet hurry towards her, but then he stopped and turned into the lane and was soon out of her sight.

Shirley knew it was him although she wasn't close enough to see him clearly. It was the way he had hesitated, then turned away that convinced her. There was no doubt in her mind. Not any more. He was avoiding her. There was no hope of his coming to see her. The time when he might was long past.

Lilly was back home and the few items of furniture she and Sam had squashed into the two rooms were either sold or given to members of the family. Phyllis, now four-and-a-half, had begun school and although her parents tried to encourage her to find work, Lilly ignored their heavy hints, and went out each day and walked to the park, whatever the weather, in the hope of seeing Sam junior.

One morning she saw him coming out of the library and ran after him. He saw her and increased his speed, braking into a run and had disappeared when she followed him around a corner. Like Shirley, she knew, without doubt, that her one-time lover, one-time stepson, Sam junior, was avoiding her.

It was cold and dreary. A cold wind blew through the town but she didn't want to go home. She needed to think about what she was going to do. Her mother wouldn't allow her to stay at home indefinitely without contributing. Even her father, who was more easily persuaded, was telling her of jobs vacant and suggesting other places she might try. The trouble was, none of them appealed. She didn't know what she wanted to do, but office work or selling in the various shops didn't come close. She was born for comfort, she wasn't lazy, just unsuited for a daily session of boring work just to receive a wage packet that wouldn't last until the next one. Handing out money for this bill and that bill, she knew she was intended for better things. She simply wasn't like the rest of them with their boring routine and their boring lives. She was waiting, convinced that something better would turn up.

She sat in the park for a while, wrapped around in her thick winter coat, boots on her feet and fur-lined gloves on her hands. She shivered, her nose felt ready to drop off, but she didn't move for a long time; why move? She had nowhere to go. She didn't even have enough money to go into a cafe and buy something to eat. Her silent misery was accompanied by a pout. Mam could at least have given her a few shillings.

She thought with regret of her kindly, loving husband and was ashamed of the way she had behaved. If only she and Sam junior hadn't been weak, he might not have been in the road when the car had mown him down. And even if he had died, he would have left her comfortably off: she and Phyllis would still be in that dear little house, and happy. What a stupid mistake. And it wasn't that she was keen on what she called 'that side of marriage'. She had submitted to Sam but had found that boring at times, too. The affair with Phillip Denver and then Sam junior had both been wrong and therefore exciting, but she knew that would have faded. The act of love left her unmoved, her emotions untouched. She had enjoyed the power she'd had over the men, the feeling of being needed and loved, but that was all.

Sam junior had been a weakness she wouldn't succumb

to again. No matter how boring it would be, she would have to find herself a job. Meanwhile, she thought, standing up and hurrying towards the park entrance, there was Auntie Audrey's cafe where she wouldn't have to pay.

She was still shivering when she found a table and waited for her aunt to see her and come over.

'Lilly dear. Been job-hunting, have you?' Audrey asked pointedly.

'Oh, Auntie Audrey, not you as well. That's all I hear from morning till night – "When are you going to get yourself a job, Lilly?!" – from Mam and Dad and Uncle Bleddyn. Now you.'

'Beth's husband has set up an agency to help people find jobs that suit them. Why don't you call and talk to him? If you tell him what you'd like to do, he'll look out for something suitable. He interviews clients before sending them to prospective employers and his recommendation helps.'

'Can I have a cup of tea, first?'

'Of course, dear. But don't be too long, it'll be time to meet Phyllis from school in a couple of hours, remember.'

'And a piece of toast?' Lilly asked, ignoring the advice.

It was Maude who brought the snack. 'Where's that awful friend of yours these days, Lilly?' she asked as she placed the toast in front of her. 'What a spiteful girl she is. I don't know how you stood her for so long.'

'I liked her, she made me laugh and I wish Mam hadn't driven her away.'

'Drove herself away, she did, talking like that to the family who'd treated her so well.'

'If I knew where she lived I'd go and see her. I'm fed up being on my own day after day.'

'Then why don't you—'

'Don't say it, Maude. Just don't say it!'

'Funny you being such friends and not knowing where she lives.'

'Ashamed she was. Since her husband died and Dolly's father ran out on her, she's had to manage on very little. She didn't want me to see how dreadful her home was. Nothing wrong with a bit of pride, is there?'

'Not at all.' Maude couldn't resist adding, 'That's why I've always earned my keep. Pride and all that!'

'Oh, shut up!'

Angry, but too hungry and cold to walk out, Lilly took her time finishing the toast and tea, then, calling, 'Cheerio,' to Auntie Audrey, she tensed herself and went out into the cold street. It wouldn't hurt to go and talk to Peter Gregory. As Beth's husband he was her brother-in-law and wouldn't force her to take something she'd hate.

Peter was not in the office and it was to Eirlys she explained her need for something interesting.

'Will it be a temporary job?' Eirlys asked. 'Will you be leaving to go over the beach once the season begins again?'

'No fear! If there's something I don't want, it's sand, sea, chips and hordes of noisy children! Besides, with Eynon and Johnny back, Mam and Dad won't need me.'

'Tell me then, what would you like to do?' Eirys asked, pen poised.

'Nothing, if you want the truth. I want to stay home.'

'Leave it with me,' Eirlys said, hiding a smile. 'I'll let you know if anything suitable for you comes in.'

Lilly went home and truthfully told her parents she had been enquiring about getting a job.

As the winter of 1945 approached, few additional luxuries appeared in the shops, except an occasional and limited supply of oranges, which were sold to children only, the green ration books being marked in a previously unused space at the back of the books, and some tinned fruit offered without points rationing, but allocated one to each family by the grocer.

Shirley took part in a few concerts and also helped with the school choir, while she waited to hear from a London producer. Bleddyn and Huw did their usual winter tasks of maintenance on the house and the cafes, while keeping the fish and chip restaurant open. Marged looked after her grandson, helped Audrey and Keith on some days and on others worked her way through the tedium of mending and making sure everything would be ready for opening up at the beach again in the early summer.

To their delight Marged and Audrey were able to discard many of the worn tablecloths as well as household linens; Cassie Davies's sales of 'under-the-counter' goods without the need for coupons had enabled them to replenish their stocks. If they had guilty thoughts about the legality of the transactions, they put them aside. After six years they were as honest or dishonest as the majority, their minds clear as they reminded themselves that, 'If we don't buy them someone else will.'

As a temporary measure, Freddy had accepted a job in the hotel where he had been staying as a guest. The work involved some cleaning, taking luggage to and from guests' rooms and various errands. It was mindless and he knew he wouldn't be able to stay for long. Just for a while he needed something uninvolving while he tried to make a decision on what to do next.

His ambition had once been to open a shop, a gentleman's outfitters on a rather grand style, but he no longer had the heart for it. In his imaginings he had been working with Shirley beside him and seeing her on stage, realizing just how talented she was, had killed that idea completely. So far, although he had lain awake many nights since, nothing had occurred to him that might replace it.

He didn't want to touch the money Shirley was holding for him. It was safe with her and would be there when he knew what he wanted to do. If only he could see her. He knew he couldn't trust himself: he would give himself away and tell her how much he loved her. He mustn't do that. He mustn't ruin her chances of a brilliant career. While there was a risk of that, he had to avoid seeing her.

Alice and Eynon were house-hunting. While Eynon found himself a job in the local park, tidying the bedraggled flower beds and making sure the swings and rides were safe, Alice had returned to work full-time for Cassie.

The stocks were running down and, to Alice's surprise, large quantities of towels and teacloths were offered, without payment, to the local hospital. Sheets were reduced in price and many houses in St David's Well had better stocks of bed linen than ever before. She didn't question Cassie's generosity, she simply did as she was told.

Whenever they could manage an hour, Alice and Eynon looked at houses for sale. There weren't many vacant and the ones they were offered were either too far from Eynon's parents, or from his beloved beach. Then, on a Saturday lunchtime they found what they immediately thought of as their cottage.

Not far from Sidney Street, it was built of stone and had once been a church hall. The owner had made alterations and inside it had two bedrooms, two living rooms and a kitchen. It lacked the luxury of a bathroom, but Eynon knew one could be added. They spent ages wandering around inside and out, already making plans for when it would be their home.

On the following day, all the family trooped in to admire their choice. They had promises of an army of helpers to redecorate and clean it up. There were also offers of furniture but Alice asked Cassie for a few hours off and on the Monday made enquiries about obtaining dockets to buy new.

A couple of weeks later, Eynon pored excitedly over the book of twenty-four dockets in her Utility Furniture Buying Permit, considering how best to spend them.

Alice blushed as she read out, 'Five dockets needed for a bed.'

'That's for definite,' Eynon agreed.

'And five for a fireside chair. Perhaps we can manage with the ones we've got?'

'Wardrobe?' Eynon suggested.

'That's a whopping twelve dockets! We could go for a dining table, six dockets, and some chairs, one each?'

They mused happily over their choices, content in the knowledge that until they decided, there were sufficient pieces from the generous family to enable them to manage. And with her connection with Cassie's bargains, Alice's linen store was generously filled.

With all the complications of prospective ownership, Alice managed to forget the fear that Netta would appear and spoil everything. Until she saw her again, talking to Eynon across the street from the cottage.

Netta was holding Walter in one hand and Dolly with the other. Eynon was crouched down talking to the little girl and the sight stopped Alice in her tracks.

She and Eynon were going to meet the agents to discuss the contract on their cottage, it seemed the worst possible omen for him to talk to Netta. He appeared to be talking to the little girl but she wondered anxiously what barbed comments were issuing from the mother's lips. She waited until the woman and her children were gone before revealing herself and she said nothing to Eynon about having seen them.

'Did you see that woman with the two children just now?' Eynon asked.

'No,' she lied. 'Someone you know?'

'I think so, but I can't remember where. She seems to know me, that's the puzzling thing. She asked about our Ronnie and Olive, mentioned Johnny, Lilly, Mam and Dad.' He shrugged. 'I was away too long. I can't remember. I'll ask Mam later.'

'Why bother?' Alice tried to sound casual.

Disappointment met them at the estate agent's office. The surveyor had found a serious problem with the front wall and after discussion they withdrew their offer to buy. They went home to discuss their dismay and it was then that Alice made a suggestion that had been hovering around her mind for some time.

'Eynon, how do you feel about buying a larger property?'

'Well, I wouldn't want anything too big to be comfortable, love. I want a couple of children like we've discussed, but there's no point having the extra work of extra rooms we don't need.'

'I was thinking about a really big place, like five or six bedrooms. There'll always be people looking for somewhere decent to stay in the summer months – you've seen how difficult it is sometimes to find accommodation. What if we ran a guest house, taking in summer visitors? Bed and breakfast only, that'll be easy.' She could see the idea didn't immediately horrify him. 'You'd still work on the sands with Johnny and the others, and I'll run it, of course,' she added. 'In the winter we'd still have a few guests, but there'll be time then for maintenance, just like your father and Uncle Bleddyn with the stalls and rides.'

'It will fit in with the Castles' business all right,' he mused. 'Alice, if you think we can do it, I think we should investigate the idea.'

Knowing it would please him, she said, 'First of all, let's talk to your Mam and Dad.'

Hannah and Johnny settled back into civilian life with ease. They continued to live with Bleddyn, Hetty and Shirley but when the excitement of Alice and Eynon's new home was discussed, Hannah wondered if they should be doing the same.

'We can't afford to buy a house,' she said to Johnny, 'but we could apply to the council for a place. These prefabs that are promised for a few years' time sound wonderful. They've even got a fridge, can you believe that? Shall I ask how we get our name on the list?'

'Yes, lovely girl, if that's what you want.'

'Isn't it what you want?' she asked anxiously.

'If you want it, then so do I. We'll talk to Dad and Hetty first, though, shall we?'

'Johnny, I wouldn't want them to think I'm not happy here. Your father has been wonderful to me and the children. I'm more than content to stay, but they might think differently. They might like to have the house to themselves. Shirley has applied for a part in that London show and if she leaves, it would be a chance for them to be on their own – for the first time since they married, remember.'

'We'll leave it for you two to decide,' Bleddyn told them later. 'Either way is fine by us, isn't it, Hetty, love? Just don't move too far away. I need to see those little girls regular or I'll pine right away.'

He spoke light-heartedly but in fact he didn't want them to leave. Besides the need to make up for the years when he hadn't seen his son, and the continuing pain of losing Johnny's brother, he loved Hannah and her girls like his own and he knew Hetty felt the same. He put no pressure on them to stay. He wanted them to be free to decide, but he fervently hoped the assurance that they were free was all they needed.

*   *   *

Myrtle was jealous of her sister, Maude. 'It's not fair, you getting married. I won't be able to marry Stanley for years. He's not seventeen yet.'

'You marrying Stanley? Best you wait till you're asked,' Maude teased.

'He has asked, at least, sort of asked and I've said yes. It's so unfair having to wait until he's considered old enough.'

'Of course it's fair, Myrtle! Stanley needs to make a career for himself, and he'll need some savings too.'

'Some people marry at sixteen, I've seen it in the paper.'

'That's usually because they – you know – have to.'

'Do you and Reggie do that, you know, loving?'

'No, we don't! And you'd better not either!'

'As if we would! But I'm nearly eighteen, our Maude, and two years seems a very long time.'

'Reggie and I won't be marrying before then. It's more than saying, "I do." There's getting your bottom drawer filled, and finding somewhere to live and all sorts of things to arrange.'

'Then I'd better make a start, hadn't I? Who knows, our Maude, Stanley and I might beat you to it!'

Shirley received a reply from the theatre company asking her to attend an interview and audition a week later and she waited several days before replying, to tell them she would be there. It was ridiculous hesitating in the futile hope of seeing Freddy Clements. Too much time had passed and if he intended to see her, he would have arrived on her doorstep a long time ago.

She was at the shop buying bread when a voice she recognized asked for the order for the Seagull Hotel. She turned and stared into Freddy's startled face.

'Shirley!'

'Oh, so you do remember my name,' she remarked coldly. She paid for the bread and walked out of the shop, hurrying to put as much distance as she could between them. She wasn't crying, it was hurt and anger that brought tears to her eyes, she told herself as she turned the corner and walked along the back lane.

When she reached the other end, Freddy was standing there, leaning against a dark green van.

'Shirley, can you spare a minute? Perhaps you deserve an explanation,' he said, frantically trying to invent one.

'Please call and collect the money I'm holding for you. I'll take it out of the bank account I opened, including the interest, and leave it with Mam tomorrow afternoon, will that be all right?'

'No, please look after it a bit longer.' He looked at her, admiration clear in his eyes. 'You're doing well these days, quite a celebrity. It's well deserved, Shirley. You're a star. I always knew that.'

She tried not to respond but asked, 'And you, Freddy? What are you doing, besides hiding from me?'

'Drifting. Trying to make up my mind what I want to do. I've got a job of sorts but only while I decide what to do with myself.'

'The gent's outfitters? What happened to that idea?'

He opened the van door. 'Come and sit down a while, please. Then I'll drive you home.'

She sat in the passenger seat with the delicious smell of fresh bread around her. She knew this would be goodbye and also knew that the memory of this moment would return every time she entered a bakery, for years to come.

She was on the defensive, unwilling to sit there while he told her why he had stayed away, hear his excuses. She couldn't listen to him telling her goodbye: pride insisted she told him first.

'My career is expanding, new openings appearing, offers of work by every post. I haven't any time for much else. No marriage in the foreseeable future, that would be impossible. I wouldn't be able to give the commitment to a loving relationship.'

'That's what I thought. I'm so proud of you, Shirley. The way you coped with that accident and everything. I wish you every success.'

It wasn't what she wanted to hear but she thanked him and asked about his war. 'Tell me the parts you didn't put in your letters,' she asked.

They were sitting without touching, both staring through the windscreen.

'Remember how fastidious I was before the war, Shirley? How I had to have clothes just right, how Mam fussed to get the collar sitting flat and the shirt front smooth and white as white?'

'I remember. All your money went on clothes in those days.'

'That was the hardest part for me, the clothes. Did you know we had to take used underwear, socks, shirts and the rest to the ablutions shed and exchange them for clean ones? Not your own clean ones. Anyone could have worn them last. They'd been used by dozens of strangers. Someone else's clothes and filthy boots. I hated that more than the bullets and bombs and the food.'

They sat for a long time, each talking about themselves more than questioning the other. The talk of strangers, unfamiliar people meeting by accident and sharing a few moments in polite chatter.

When he drove her home, she stepped out of the van, called, 'Goodbye,' and didn't look back.

Eleven

The search for a house, having decided to look for something larger, meant a lot of wandering around for Alice and Eynon. Every spare moment was spent looking at properties. Aware of the importance of good access to the beaches, parks and the shops, they were carefully assessing position as well as size. They had plenty of choice and the prices were comparatively low.

Few women were willing to work for low wages as cleaners and servants now they had learned their true value, and many households no longer having a man at its head after the war had taken its toll. Shortages of materials was another factor and, combined with other considerations, meant that properties were showing neglect. Most owners of large houses were deciding the sensible thing to do was leave their large properties and buy something more manageable.

Alice and Eynon had the support of Eynon's parents and Blethyn and Hetty. When they could, Audrey and Keith also went with them to view one or two properties. Keith was a builder and he added his expertise as each house was considered. They finally chose one about ten minutes' walk away from the beach, near a small park, which they all declared perfect.

Eirlys introduced them to people who helped them examine the viability of their plan, although Alice had already made preliminary enquiries and satisfied herself that the idea was sound. There would be planning approval and fire regulations and a dozen other things, but with careful planning they would have enough money to see them through – just.

Once a decision had been made and the processes of the purchase were underway, there was great activity. The legalities were dealt with rapidly as the owner was anxious to sell, and within three weeks the place was theirs. It was in a row of houses called Rosebay Place and apart from needing cleaning and some redecorating, it was in good condition. This was where the Castle family showed their support for each other.

Huw spent several days stripping wallpaper and, with Bleddyn, painted and papered three rooms. Eynon worked with them and learned. Following their advice he painted the outside of the property. Marged scrubbed floors and repolished the linoleum left by the previous tenant. Even Reggie and Bernard Gregory helped by clearing the garden and promising to set out the borders in the spring. Alice had taken a couple of weeks off from helping in Cassie's second shop and to everyone's surprise, Lilly had accepted the invitation to take her place.

'You'll work in the Davieses' shop?' Alice asked in surprise.

'Yes. Why not? Even I can do something to help you and Eynon,' Lilly pouted.

She didn't explain that her unexpected offer was due to Hannah, who had called to leave some newly hemmed towels for Marged and found her crying.

'Why are you crying?' Hannah had asked, and Lilly showed her a dress which she had been trying to alter to fit. Hannah saw at once that it was too small.

'Can I help?'

'What's the point? I never go anywhere or do anything.'

'Nonsense, it's nearly Christmas and there'll be parties and dances and Beth and Eirlys will invite you. Maude and Myrtle too. They love dancing.'

'They never invite me. They all hate me.'

'Perhaps if you did something really nice, like help Alice and Eynon with their house? Or offer to help Auntie Audrey in the cafe so Myrtle can go out one evening? They don't hate you, Lilly, but you're a difficult person to like sometimes, aren't you?' She held out the dress and added, 'You'll look very nice in this, Lilly. Come on, let's see what we can do.'

Lilly had called to see Cassie and, forcing a smile, offered to take Alice's place while she was preparing to move. 'You'll have to write everything down, mind,' she warned.

Cassie made a list of all the prices and the number of coupons needed for each transaction. She carefully explained the system of the shop, but Lilly looked bored and Cassie wondered if she had heard a word she had spoken. Whenever she looked in after Lilly had started work, it was to see Lilly reading a magazine or just staring idly into space.

'I hope she manages to stay awake,' she said to Alice. 'I'm afraid I might go there and find her asleep and all the stock stolen, she's that idle.'

Alice hadn't mentioned finding the cache of clothing coupon books to Cassie but, aware that Lilly was likely to go snooping, she told her then. Cassie looked at them, gathered them into a carrier bag and without a word, took them home. They were valuable and although she had no idea whose they were or how they got there, she decided they would be safer at home with her. Without fully understanding why, she declined to mention them to Joseph.

The three-storey house in Rosebay Place was quickly cleaned. Floorboards were scrubbed and, in the absence of linoleum, were stained and varnished.

'With what money we have left, I think we should by ourselves some new furniture,' Eynon suggested. It'll be second-hand for the most part, but something special for us. It's our home, as well as a business, isn't it?' Alice happily agreed.

The property had been a guest house, so few changes were necessary. The owner explained the reason for selling, which upset Alice and filled her with superstitious guilt. The woman's husband and two sons had all been killed during the war. She grieved for the sadness the woman had suffered and gave thanks for her own good fortune.

Alice and Eynon discussed their finances and the allowance of their furniture dockets and spent pleasant hours drooling over possibilities before deciding on their purchases. They bought a bed, a small wardrobe and dressing table having chosen to furnish their bedroom with new, utility furniture, and buy second-hand for the rest of the house. The family and friends contributed and the place soon looked welcoming and comfortable.

Hannah made curtains by adjusting some Alice had been given; Eirlys presented them with two beautiful handmade rugs. A brass fender rescued from a shed was polished by Bleddyn to add light to their living room. Alice knew she ought to be happy but she was not. There was a shadow hovering over her that wouldn't go away. Every day brought the fear that Netta Mills would appear, face Eynon with her accusation and ruin everything.

'It's like standing on the edge of a precipice,' she told Marged. 'Just waiting for the touch that will push me over.'

'It's a pity we can't find out where she lives,' Marged replied. 'Huw and Bleddyn would like to have a word with her. Wicked she is, unsettling people with her lies.'

'Is everything all right, lovely girl?' Eynon asked a few days before they were to move in. 'Sorry about the family taking over. Perhaps you'd have preferred to wait and do it ourselves?' he queried.

'They are wonderful. There can't be a happier or luckier girl in the whole town than me.'

'But?' he asked anxiously.

'No "buts". Honestly, I can't wait for us to move into our lovely home and I'll never be able to thank your family enough for what they've done.'

'Be happy, that's all the thanks they'll want.' He kissed her and she responded as affectionately as he could ask, but he was still uneasy. Something was wrong.

Later that day, as he washed and prepared himself for bed, he looked in the mirror and wondered whether his return had been disappointing. With the scar over his left eye, and the thinness of his body, he was hardly the handsome, conquering hero. Although the scar had been there when he'd first met Alice and he'd never been anything but small and skinny. Perhaps he was a disappointing lover? He remembered some of the stories told by men with whom he had served. Had Alice listened to stories too? Had she expected more?

'Vain you are, Eynon Castle. You've been standing there

214

for ages, admiring your handsome self.' Alice came to stand beside him and kissed his wet face.

'Handsome? Me?'

'Handsome, yes. I can't believe how lucky I am, knowing I'll wake up every morning and see your face beside mine.'

'You aren't disappointed?'

Alice looked shocked. 'Do I give you that impression? Eynon, how could you disappoint me? I love you and I'm so proud to be your wife. We're for ever, you and me. Whatever happens, nothing will separate us. Nothing.' She held him so close that instead of reassurance Eynon felt more uneasy. 'What could separate us?' he asked, pressing her face into his neck, loving the warmth of her, the scent of her.

'Nothing and no one.' Her adamant vow only added to his feeling of unease.

Alice had heard nothing of Netta since the day she had seen her talking to Eynon while he had admired her little girl. Was Dolly really Eynon's daughter? Or was the story just Netta's distorted idea of fun? Either way Netta seemed to have given up on any attempt to face Eynon with the story, so Alice decided to put it aside and enjoy this exciting time of her life.

It was sad leaving the two rooms where she had waited for Eynon to come home and, as they packed the last of their belongings into boxes for Huw to take to Rosebay Place, Eynon saw her expression and thought he now understood her slight unhappiness.

'Perfect homecoming it was, coming back to you here, but now we're going to a new home and a new business and everything will be better than before. Don't be sad leaving this behind, lovely girl.'

She hugged him and they stood for a while looking around the now empty hollow-sounding room. A weak winter sun shone and touched Eynon's shoulder and she reached out and put her fingers through the beam. Would their memories of this place fade and would their parting and wonderful reunion be a memory as short lived as the dust motes showing in the slant of sunshine coming through the bare window?

Eirlys continued to help, suggesting the best places to

215

advertise and how to obtain allocations of food. Peter found them a girl willing to help with the cleaning when required. When they moved in, the whole Castle clan helped, then drifted away as though by some prearranged signal, leaving them alone. They slept comfortably in their new bed and awoke with a feeling of excitement. There was only the ongoing fear of Netta's appearance to spoil it, something of which Eynon was blissfully unaware. Dare she hope that the danger was past? If Netta intended to tell Eynon about his daughter, wouldn't she have done so by now?

For Johnny, everything seemed perfect. He had stepped back into his life with his darling Hannah. 'And,' he told his father and stepmother, 'my stepdaughters are a joy.'

'Hannah works too hard, mind,' Bleddyn said.

'She always has, and I hope to take some of the burden of earning money from her now I'm home.'

Johnny had found work in a timber yard, cutting lengths of wood, collecting and delivering orders that, like everything else, were restricted if not actually rationed.

'Not for long, mind,' he told Keith one morning when he called to buy wood. 'As soon as the season starts I'll be on that beach before dawn, shouting for people to ride the swingboats and wearing a funny hat!'

'Audrey tells me you've been enjoying it since before you could walk,' Keith said. 'Lucky the man who earns his money with such enjoyment.'

'Mam used to say my first words were "swingboats", and "helter-skelter",' Johnny joked. 'And the next were "twopence to ride".'

Hannah continued to work at the gift shop and demand for her talent as dress-maker kept her very busy. A second-hand clothing shop in the town was a regular haunt and when some pre-war dance dress came in made from beautiful material, the shop owner would put it on one side for her favourite customer and Hannah would bear it home, planning the garments she would make from its generous skirt.

With Christmas approaching and knowing that, for most young people that meant parties, for a surprise Hannah made

216

Lilly a new dress. She had measured one of Lilly's dresses with the assistance of Marged, planning to give it as a surprise early in December. It hung in her and Johnny's room until then – a pretty diamante design at the waist sparkling at her every time she opened the wardrobe door. She smiled as she imagined the look on Lilly's rather sulky face when it was given to her. Lilly was a difficult person – lazy, unwilling to do anything to help anyone but herself – but Hannah had a soft spot for her. Lilly was not a happy person, and in her own joy at having Johnny safely home, Hannah loved everybody.

When Alice returned to the shop after Lilly's two weeks, it was to find everything in a muddle: piles of towels and pillowcases pulled out of place and left in crumpled heaps. The till roll on which each transaction should have been written was a mass of unreadable scribbles. 'Typical Lilly,' she sighed as she began to sort out the chaos of her two weeks' absence.

She was making progress but the shop was still in a mess when Cassie came at twelve o'clock.

'Do you have to go home for lunch, Alice?' she asked, and Alice saw that Cassie was upset.

'I can pop off a bit early and leave a sandwich for Eynon with a note, if it's urgent?'

'I'd appreciate it, dear.'

It still gave Alice a thrill to open the door of their own home and she went in carrying a pasty still warm from the baker's and quickly made a sandwich to add to it, covered them with muslin and wrote Eynon a loving note explaining her absence. Then she locked up and hurried back to the shop.

At the end of the road Netta watched.

Cassie had made tea and brought food and while they ate, she said nothing important, she just thanked Alice for sorting out the mess left by Eynon's sister and making suggestions about rearranging various displays. When they had eaten, Cassie said, 'Read this,' and handed Alice a letter.

It was private and after getting the gist of it she was afraid she had misunderstood. She had difficulty concentrating on the words, as though she were reading something she had no right to see. It was brief and she read it a second time then a third. 'He's leaving you?' she said at last. 'For this, Joanna Lee-Jones?'

Cassie nodded, her face suddenly much older, lined and grey with shock and misery.

'But he can't do that. He's telling you to go, leave the shops and go! If he's going off with this woman, it's he who should leave, not you.'

'He doesn't want me, just the business.'

'Can he do this? Surely as his wife you have some rights to the business you've run all these years?'

'That's the trouble, Alice, dear. I'm not his wife. We've always intended to marry one day, but somehow we've never got around to it.'

'Oh Cassie,' Alice said sadly. 'He can't do this, he'll change his mind, surely?'

'I had the letter ages ago; I didn't want to talk about it.'

'Ignore it and it'll go away?'

'No, dear. I didn't think like that. No, I didn't ignore it, not at all.'

Netta waited at the end of Roseby Place until Eynon appeared, running, whistling cheerfully as he let himself into the house. 'Come on, Dolly, let's go and meet your father.' She walked purposefully to the recently closed door but once there she stopped. She couldn't knock on the door and blurt out her rehearsed speech. Not today. What she was planning took a lot of nerve and she wasn't quite ready. She turned and walked back the way she had come. 'Tomorrow,' she said to the little girl. 'Tomorrow we'll call and see him. Now I have to get you back home.'

Freddy stayed on at the hotel, still unable to decide what he would do. When Keith Kent walked in with Audrey to book a meal for the weekend to celebrate Audrey's birthday, he recognized them and asked if they had news of Shirley.

'She's still living at home between concerts – you can't have lost touch with her?' Keith said curiously.

'I thought you and Shirley were, well, good friends. You wrote to each other regularly during the war, didn't you? Don't tell me you've lost interest now the danger and excitement have gone?' Audrey looked at him. 'Quarrelled, have you?'

'No, we've never had a cross word.' He hesitated then explained. 'I backed off when I saw how successful she was. A brilliant amateur, that's how I thought of her. Entertaining the troops, a local celebrity. I hadn't realized just how much talent she had. I heard her sing on the day I came home. I was planning to surprise her, you know, turn up after the concert. But I knew then she was in a class of her own. She'd left me behind and she's, well, she's wonderful. She has a voice that convinces a listener into thinking she's singing just for them. She's enchanting. I can't compete with the career she's heading for. I'm pleased for her but I can't expect her to waste time on me. I might hold her back and I'd hate that. Please, don't tell her where I am,' he added.

'Why not, Freddy? I don't understand why you haven't kept in touch. Whatever Shirley does, she'll still need friends.'

'Friends wasn't what I had in mind. No, it's best we don't see each other again. She's on her way up and I don't want to hinder her. My ambition was to open a shop. Not in the same league at all.'

As they were leaving, Keith found him again and said, 'Don't be a fool. Go and see her, at least find out how she feels. What harm can it do? She can only say no, and you're man enough to take a disappointment, aren't you?'

Two days later, Freddy knocked on the door in Brook Lane, where Bleddyn told him Shirley had gone to London.

'She'll be back for a couple of days at Christmas,' he called after Freddy's retreating figure. 'Come and see her, she'll be so pleased.' Freddy waved without turning around or stopping. What was the point, it would only be prolonging the misery.

Reggie and Maude were discussing an engagement. On the way home from the pictures they gazed into jewellery-shop windows and counted their savings. Maude was now twenty and many of her friends and acquaintances were married by that age. She knew she had to tell the family but she hesitated. Although Marged and Huw, and Hetty and Bleddyn weren't related, she suffered the same feelings of shyness when she thought of explaining about Reggie and herself.

'What if we tell my parents first?' Reggie suggested.

'Practise on them?' she said with a nervous giggle. 'I don't know why I don't walk into their house in Sidney Street and come right out with it. But I can't. I'll blush and stutter stupid things and make a fool of myself. And I know Uncle Huw will start teasing me.'

'I think that once you start to explain, they'll help you out. They've probably guessed already.'

'Shall we go together and tell Auntie Audrey?'

'Mam and Dad first,' Reggie decided.

Because of the long hours that Audrey's cafe opened, she was very lenient with Maude and Myrtle regarding time off. When Maude asked if she could take the weekend to visit Reggie's family she agreed at once, but not without the expected teasing.

'Something special, is it? This weekend visiting your boyfriend's parents? Best frock? And a shampoo and set at the hairdresser's?'

'Just another visit. I'll tell you all about it when I get back,' Maude said, making her escape.

Reggie's parents didn't live far away and they went on their bicycles after Reggie finished work on Saturday lunchtime. The first person they saw was his brother, Andy.

'Hi there, Reggie and Maude, nice to see you.'

'What are you doing here? Bringing more trouble to Mam and Dad?'

'What a welcome, eh?' He turned to Maude to share his disapproval. 'You could at least ask how I am. Couldn't he, Maude?'

'What are you doing here?' Reggie repeated.

'Keeping out of jail.' He called to his mother, 'Mam, look who's here, it's our Reggie.' Mrs Probert came bustling in looking anxious.

'Reggie dear, and Maude, I'm so glad to see you both, your room's ready, Maude. Take her bag up, will you, Andy?'

'Not Andy, our Mam. I'm Drew, remember? New name new start?'

Ignoring him, she kissed Maude and Reggie and led them into the living room.

'He just turned up. We knew he was alive, he wrote and told us, but he gave us such a fright when he came here after telling us he'd been arrested again.'

'He shouldn't be here. He'll bring you nothing but trouble.'

'I heard that. Not very brotherly, is it?' Andy called from the doorway. 'I only came to find out where Shirley Downs is. If you tell me where I can find her I'll leave.'

'I don't want you to go. I want you here where I can look after you,' Mrs Probert said.

'No, Mam. Reggie's right. I can't stay. I get restless, see, and when things are ticking along peacefully I'm tempted to do something stupid, just to liven things up. I need risks, danger, and the need for it grows like an itch I have to scratch.'

'Time you grew up,' Reggie snapped.

'I'll be all right. I've lived off the countryside in the past, for weeks at a time. I just want to see Shirley once more, then I'm off to Scotland, I've got a job on a hill farm, assistant to the gamekeeper, would you believe, and me an expert poacher. It'll do, for a while.'

'How d'you cope at night out in the woods and fields?' Maude asked him later when they were finishing their evening meal. 'Myrtle and I lived without a proper home for months one winter and summer but we never slept out in the fields. I'd find that real scary.'

'Making a shelter of sorts isn't difficult,' he explained. 'Food is available once you know where to look. But the first thing to learn is not to be afraid of the dark.' He looked at his parents affectionately and went on, 'Mam and Dad reassured me when I was a kid and afraid of the dark. They would blow out the candle and sit there with me in the blackness then strike a match and relight it to show me that nothing changed. The room or the garden or the woodland was the same whether or not there was light. Reggie and me, we spent hours out in the fields. We walked home from town through the fields and the woods without fear. Easy once you learn that.'

It was as they were leaving that Reggie put an arm around Maude and told his parents that they were planning to marry. At once Mrs Probert hugged them both to show her delight. More formally, Reggie's father shook his son's hand.

'Two down, four to go,' Reggie said as they cycled home after their Sunday lunch of rabbit, caught, no doubt, by Andy. They went straight to Sidney Street where Audrey and Myrtle were talking to Marged and Huw.

Their news was welcomed by all except Myrtle. 'It isn't fair,' she protested, repeating the complaints she had made to Maude earlier. 'Stanley and I want to get married too, but Auntie Marged says we're too young!'

Cassie couldn't sleep. Night after night she lay awake wondering what would become of her. To be abandoned at her age left little time to recover. Where would she go? What would she do for money? She wouldn't need a lot, she had no grand ambitions to own a big house, or have luxury holidays or buy fine clothes. It wasn't the shortage of money she dreaded, it was the loneliness.

Alice offered sympathy. She too felt vulnerable. She tried in vain to put thoughts about Netta's claim on Eynon out of her mind but the fear was a constant threat. Every time she turned a corner she expected to see a smiling Netta walking towards her with Dolly holding her hand. She was still young and she was aware of the greater difficulty faced by Cassie, but they shared the fear of being left alone. Having Eynon's love torn out of her life was a nightmare through which she lived every day.

'I'll do anything I can to help,' she promised Cassie.

'Good, I might need someone to share the final stages of my plan.'

'Plan?' Alice queried.

'Let's get out those illegally obtained clothing coupons, shall we? Then you and I are going to arrange an amazing sale. I want the shops emptied as quickly as possible.' She stared at Alice and there was, as Alice later described to Eynon, the light of battle in her dark brown eyes. 'Are you sure you're willing to help?'

'Just tell me what you want me to do.'

'I want us to go bankrupt. That's what.'

In the loft of her house, Cassie unearthed some Christmas decorations and acquired some gifts from a source she'd discovered by going through Joseph's books. Working without a rest, she filled the shop with everything she could find. Without advertising – there would be no need with goods being so scarce – she allowed rumours to spread about a delivery of off-ration linen that would make wonderful Christmas gifts. It was all very hush-hush, but as soon as the shops opened they were inundated with customers.

The windows of both shops were packed with tray-cloths, dressing-table sets, chair-backs and boxes of handkerchiefs as well as the usual household goods.

'Where did you find all these?' Alice gasped when she went to the shop to open up.

'Oh, they're available here and there, if you know where to look' was the enigmatic reply.

The prices were low, there was no restriction on what people could purchase, and within seven days both shops were left with nothing more than unsaleable oddments. Hints were all that were needed to remind customers of the illegality of the sale and they whispered the news but were careful not to speak to the wrong people.

However, the inspectors did arrive and Cassie looked outraged at the suggestion that she was breaking the law. 'You're mistaken, someone's having a joke,' she protested. Acting the outraged, honest tradeswoman, she showed some of her legitimately acquired coupons added to some of the the carefully cut-out coupons Alice had found.

She took handfuls and threw them into the air. 'Want to count them do you?' She puffed and glared and threw things about, muttered about the difficulties of the past six years and added, 'And all the thanks we get is unfair accusations!'

'No, we don't need to count them, madam,' she was told pompously – that wasn't their job. That tedious occupation was left to others. 'We only investigate.'

'Well, go and investigate somewhere else. I'm busy!'

'If you send us away, madam, others will come. We have to ensure there are no illegalities here.'

No 'others' came. No one else questioned her, and the danger passed.

'Now what?' Alice asked as they swept up and deposited the rubbish in the ash bin.

'Sorry, Alice, I'm afraid you've lost your job.'

Alice laughed. 'You mean you've had me helping to make myself unemployed?'

'I'm afraid so. But if you wait a while, I might be starting all over again, this time with everything in my own name. I'd love to have you back when that happens.'

'No, once we start having bookings for our bed and breakfast, I'd have left anyway. Thanks to Dad we've been able to buy a good property and thanks to you, we'll be starting our business with the best stock of linen in the town.'

'The country more like!' Cassie said with a chuckle. 'There's a couple of wardrobes and two beds at the house if you want them. Either you, or they'll go on a bonfire with the rest.' Then she sighed and her face crumpled into sadness again.

'How did you get into this situation? Why didn't you and Joseph marry?'

Cassie shrugged. 'I was a trusting fool. That's how. Joseph was my mother's lodger and when she died he stayed on. I sold the house to give him a start and we bought the first shop. The silly part was, we were both called Davies and people began to presume we were married, and we let it slide. We intended to marry quietly, not telling anyone, hiding the fact that we'd been living together without the privilege of the clergy. Time passed and it no longer seemed important.'

'Until Joanna Lee-Jones.'

'Exactly.'

'So, what next?'

'Alice, dear, you don't want to know.'

Maude and Myrtle both wrote to Shirley while she was in London and in her letter, Maude told her about Andy's visit to his parents. She called him Drew as Andy had asked, knowing that Shirley would guess.

Thoughts of him unsettled her. She didn't love him, she couldn't love anyone who survived by cheating and stealing. Someone who spent the war years evading the armed forces, then allowed his family to believe he was dead so he could go on doing so. She wondered why she had found him so attractive – he was the worst kind of person to have even as a friend, she told herself; yet there was something about him that touched her. He still found a soft spot in her heart.

If only Freddy were here. She wouldn't think of Andy if Freddy would only get in touch. Her last thoughts at night, before settling to sleep, were of Freddy. He had hurt her so badly by his sudden indifference. She needed at least to understand why.

The show was a success and her role had gained in importance. She now sang two solos, stepping out of the group of girls singing between the various acts.

She had received enquiries and had attended three auditions, which led to offers, but although she gave her best at each performance, aware that people had paid to come and deserved only the best, she was homesick and unutterably lonely. She began turning them down. She would be back in St David's Well for Christmas.

To be a star needed not only talent, but dedication and a real hunger for success. She knew now that she lacked the latter and it was perhaps the most important of all.

Eynon was in the park clearing up the last leaves of autumn when Dolly ran towards him. He looked up and seeing Netta, smiled. 'Hello little girl,' he said, handing his broom to her. 'Come to help me, have you?'

'Are you my daddy?' Dolly asked.

'No such luck. Beautiful you are and I bet your dad is proud of you.' Too late he remembered that such comments were taboo. With so many children having lost their fathers it wasn't a wise remark to make. 'I bet this is your mummy, eh?' He smiled at Netta, still half remembering her but unsure how. 'Lovely little thing, isn't she?'

Netta made up her mind. It was now or never. 'And she's yours, Eynon.'

225

'What?' He laughed and picked the child up. 'Giving her to me, are you? There's a nice Christmas present you'd be.' He glanced at Netta curiously, unable to understand her remark. 'Well, I have to go, little lady, before Mr Wind comes and chases these leaves all over the park again.'

'Dolly is your daughter, Eynon.'

He frowned and stared at her, wondering if her mind was disturbed. Deciding that humouring her was the safest way of dealing with her strangeness, he said, 'I haven't any children, but if I did, I'd like a daughter as beautiful as this one.' He turned away and concentrated on his task.

'Don't pretend you've forgotten.'

Irritated now, he leaned on his broom and glared at her. 'I don't know you and I have work to do, so if you'll go away and let me get on with it, I might not get the sack.' He gestured to where a uniformed man was walking purposefully towards them.

Netta followed him as he began moving away, towards the park keeper. 'The night before your wedding, you and I had a bit of fun. Surely you remember that?'

'Mr Williams, can I have a word?' Eynon walked away with his boss and behind him, Dolly called, 'Goodbye Daddy.' Eynon's ears reddened and he explained to Mr Williams that the woman was obviously deranged.

That evening, he told Alice.

She stared at him, unable to find the words to tell him. Eynon was becoming more and more anxious and she finally told him the full story, about Netta following her, then making friends with Lilly and her insatiable curiosity about the Castle family. 'It's been clear to me that she's planned this. Lilly is gullible and she was so glad to have a friend. She persuaded everyone that I was the one behaving oddly. I didn't know what to do.'

'You should have told me,' Eynon said, hugging her. 'For now, the best thing to do is ignore her. She'll get bored if there's no reaction and probably try her lies on someone else.'

Alice wanted to hear him tell her it couldn't be true, that he had never shared a bed with another woman, but she dared not ask him. To sound as though she needed reassurance would hurt Eynon unnecessarily. The damage Netta was causing would increase. 'Fancy the pictures?' she asked brightly, hoping to disperse their worrying thoughts.

'No, lovely girl. I think we'd better go and talk to Mam and Dad.'

Huw asked the question Alice longed to ask. 'You're sure you didn't see this woman?'

'I can't be sure, no, Dad. That night was a bit of a blur. The wedding was rushed and the night before I might have been a bit drunk, and she does look familiar.' He was holding Alice's hand tightly. 'I am sure of one thing though, I wouldn't have slept with her. I've never wanted anyone but Alice.'

'What are you saying, boy? That you were too drunk to be sure? That she might be right?' Huw looked angry enough to explode.

'No, I'm not!' Eynon looked equally outraged. 'What I'm saying is, she could have been there that night. She could build up a very convincing story, and some might believe her. How can I prove to anyone that Dolly isn't mine, if people saw me talking to her that night and she tells them we spent the night together?'

'No trouble there. Ronnie brought you home here before eleven. I remember that,' Marged said. 'And so will your father when he's calmed down. I remember because we were sitting up waiting for you both. Audrey as well, and it was before eleven when we went to bed.'

'Difficult to prove if she takes me to court,' Eynon replied.

The following morning, with no job to go to, Alice went to see Lilly. 'You must know something about Netta. You've been friends for months. Surely you know where she lives?'

'Sorry, but she never invited me home. Ashamed I expect, living in some untidy place with no money, she didn't want me to know, me being a Castle.'

Alice looked at her sister-in-law sprawled on a couch, with used plates and cups around her amid opened and abandoned magazines. How dare she criticize someone for untidiness and put herself above others? 'And you weren't curious?' she asked.

'We met in the park or in cafes, then she worked for Mam

and Dad and we saw each other there. Then,' she added, rolling her eyes in the hope of sympathy, 'then my dear Sam died and once she realized I had no money she dropped me. Some friend, eh?'

All that day Alice wandered around the shops and the park in the centre of town. She was determined to find the elusive Netta and face her with her lies. Darkness was gripping the town in the chill of a frosty night when she saw her. She was walking through the shops, stopping for the children to look at the gifts on display.

She heard the little girl's high-pitched voice, the mother's laughter, watched her finger pointing and answering questions. It looked just like many other family groups, so innocent, so ordinary that she wondered momentarily if Netta's story could be true.

Why would Netta invent such a thing? She must know Dolly's real father. If that wasn't Eynon, why would she lie? In the hope of money? The Castles were not rich but they weren't exactly poor either. Did she choose Eynon for that reason? Wanting a father for her children she could have selected Eynon because of his position. But the dates fitted and – she gave up trying to sort it out. Her head ached and she was very cold.

She stamped her feet, walked around a bit but didn't approach the three people. She waited and followed their erratic progress, crossing and recrossing the road as one of the children saw a shop window they wanted to investigate. Alice couldn't help thinking that Netta seemed a very patient and caring mother.

She saw Netta straighten Dolly's scarf and fasten her coat around her, and watched as they left the lighted windows and set off down one of the back streets. Protected by the darkness, Alice followed.

It was easy to see through the window of the house into which Netta shepherded the children, as the light shone within and the windows were devoid of curtains. Alice looked around but there was no one about and she knew she wouldn't be seen from inside. There was a broken gate leaning drunkenly against an abandoned pram and she had to step carefully around it. There were many obstacles blocking the path. She had to look away from the window until her eyes adjusted to the darkness for fear of tripping over the rubbish-strewn garden.

The tangled remains of bicycles lay amid empty boxes and the innards of a wireless set and unrecognizable chunks of metal – the carcass of a motor car, she guessed, identifying a bumper gleaming dully in the light from the window.

There were several children inside and she saw Netta go up to a boy aged about five years old and hug him. 'Mam,' she heard him call as Netta left him, '– can we have some chips?' She replied with a shake of her head and left the room, taking off her coat as she went. Alice's heart lurched at the realization that Netta had three children, not two. How could she have lived such a life?

She continued to stare into the room, unable to decide what she should do. Then she heard a sound and turning towards it, saw Netta standing watching her. 'You'd better go away,' she said.

'I'll go, but I'll be back with the police,' Alice replied with a confidence she didn't feel. Two young men came out then, whom Alice presumed to be Netta's brothers. A husband would surely have stood beside her, protecting her. These two stood together, silent, but threatening. It flashed through Alice's mind that if Netta had produced three illegitimate children, their care was seriously inadequate.

'Go, and don't come back,' one of them said, and, backing off, Alice said,

'Well, at least we know where you live.'

She walked with deliberate slowness, her heart racing and her legs like jelly, until she was out of sight, then she bent almost double and ran home.

Twelve

A lice went home after her confrontation with Netta in an uneasy frame of mind. She didn't know how to approach the subject with Eynon. How would he feel about her following the girl and facing her at her home? She would never have acted so boldly before working in the factory. The girls had certainly 'brought her out of herself', she thought with some anxiety. She had become so strong-willed and Eynon might not like the change from the shy, hesitant girl he'd left behind.

Another consideration was that Netta's family were unlikely to know what the girl was attempting to do and she might have caused Netta serious problems. While accepting that the girl deserved whatever happened to her, having caused the problems herself, Alice couldn't forget the children. Netta had Walter and little Dolly, plus the little boy called Danny, apparently with no way of supporting them. Despite her initial anger against the girl, she felt a growing need to help.

When she put her key in her front door she knew that she had to tell Eynon exactly what she had done and also, how she felt. Mentally bracing herself for the story she had to tell, she went in and discovered that Eynon was out. She felt a relief from the tension of explaining all she had learned. Closing the door again, she went to see Hannah.

'I know she was foolish and she shouldn't have had any children without a proper marriage and a home for them, but I don't think she's wicked, just weak. She must have been very young and she hasn't even got a friend to talk things over with, from what I could gather. Just the two aggressive men whom I presumed to be her brothers.'

'Isn't Lilly her friend?'

'I doubt whether Lilly would be much help.'

'Three children! Unbelievable.'

'What can we do? We can't magic up a husband or a home.'

'Right. If her family won't help her, what can we do?'

'Would Johnny's parents, or Eynon's mother give her another chance and offer her some work when the beach opens again? Eynon's Mam is a sucker when it comes to people in trouble, isn't she? A job would be a good beginning for her to start building a life.'

'You'll have to ask her.' Hannah looked doubtful. 'Marged wasn't thrilled at the way Netta tried to ruin my peace of mind when Johnny was coming home. And she deliberately tried to harm your marriage. I doubt that Bleddyn would want her there.'

'We'll keep it in our minds, shall we? If anything turns up we can let her know.'

'You could have a word with Lilly. She and Netta were friends, perhaps a friend is what she needs right now. Although,' Hannah whispered with a grin, 'our Lilly's the last one to advise her about getting a job!'

The houses in St David's Well had all their decorations up by the second week of December and as Alice had no traditional store of trimmings, she made her own. She and Eirlys used a sewing machine and some crêpe paper they had managed to buy and made streamers to criss-cross their rooms. The children contributed by making chains from the packets of paper strips sold for the purpose.

Hannah made yards of bunting from oddments of material, some of which she sold in the shop. She and Hetty added colour and sparkle to the rooms and windows of the house in Brook Lane, knowing Shirley would be home and wanting her to feel the excitement of the joyful season.

'Every year since 1939 they've told us the war would be over by Christmas. This year, at last, they're right,' Audrey said to Keith as they added streamers, and painted branches bought from Chapel's Flowers, to the cafe walls.

'Thank goodness all our children are safe,' Keith added, as Audrey passed up a spray of mistletoe. 'Because it's a special Christmas, we mustn't forget any of the traditions, this year.' He took her in his arms and kissed her. 'Christening the mistletoe is a tradition we must keep.'

'I've never heard of that one,' Audrey said, holding him close so he could feel her smile against his own.

'This is also a good year to begin new ones.'

In the now empty shop, Cassie fixed the latest bills and reminders that had come by that morning's post on to the spike she had used for years to hold her unpaid bills. When they came back with a receipt, they were transferred to another spike and that, basically, was her accounts system. Today there were none at all on the paid spike, the one for those awaiting payment was full.

She had heard very little from Joseph, just a weekly letter asking her to send the totals from the till roll showing the daily totals of the week's takings, which she ignored. The sales details she had written in her book were completely fictitious. She hadn't opened the shops for business since the sale had emptied them. There were still a few of the normal items for sale, and the coupons she had taken for what she had sold were in a couple of carrier bags thrown carelessly in the corner of the now empty stock room

She went to the shops each day to collect the post, idly walking through the town without haste, knowing that all day, every day was now her own. The second post that day had brought more urgent requests for money and during the afternoon, at home where she was sitting idly thumbing through catalogues of previous suppliers, she saw a man carrying a notepad and a leather briefcase knocking furiously at her door, and peering in through the window. She watched but didn't open the door as he scribbled furiously in his notebook before hurrying off.

It was Tuesday, the eighteenth of December, exactly one week before Christmas, when she parcelled up all the bills and sent them to Joseph. In another parcel she sent the remainder of the stolen clothing coupons but these were not addressed to Joseph. They went to the police. She wondered, with little

232

emotion, which of the shocks she had planned would hit him first.

Lilly was surprised to see Hannah when she opened the door to her knock. 'What d'you want? Mam's out,' she said ungraciously.

'Hello, Lilly, it's you I've come to see.' Hannah, carrying a brown-paper-wrapped parcel, pushed past Lilly and into the house.

'Come to remind me that I need a job?'

'I don't think you need reminding, do you?'

'It isn't easy to find something to suit me, you know. Peter said he'd look out for something. I am trying.'

Hannah declined to give the obvious answer to that one. 'Trying' was something Lilly had always been! 'This is for you, Lilly,' she said offering the parcel. 'A little gift from Johnny and me.'

Lilly took the parcel and placed it on the table. 'What is it?' she demanded, unable to smile or show any pleasure. It was sure to be something sensible coming from Hannah. A boring apron or a knitted cardigan – certain to be brown – garments she wouldn't be seen dead in. Who wants sensible? she asked herself silently. She turned back the folds of paper to reveal a pretty velvet sea-green dress. She had to be mistaken. This couldn't be for her. 'Brought it to show me, have you? Clever you are, Hannah, and it's very nice. One of your favourite customers, I'll bet, posh material like that.'

'It's for you, Lilly. I thought you might like it for some of the Christmas parties or a dance.'

Lilly held it against her and burst into tears.

'Lilly, what is it? Have I chosen the wrong colour, I thought—'

'It's lovely, I love it. Thanks, Hannah.'

Hannah stood, wanting to hug her but afraid of offending. Lilly might not accept a hug, she was not a demonstrative person and had never shown any great liking for her cousin Johnny's choice of a wife. She waited while Lilly dried her tears clumsily, like a child, with great rubbing movements accompanied by a few remaining sobs. 'I'll go then.

233

Unless you'd like to try it on, so I can do any adjustments needed?'

'Wait there,' Lilly said, picking up the dress and walking from the room. Hannah folded the brown paper, too valuable to waste, and sat to wait for Lilly to reappear. When she did so, she had washed her face, put on some lipstick and she had combed her long hair. The dress fitted perfectly and, although Lilly didn't possess a perfect figure, the tight waist, the fullness around the flaring skirt and the diamanti decoration on the waist and neckline were flattering.

'Turn around, make the skirt swing out so I can see the effect,' Hannah asked. Then, as a self-conscious Lilly stopped in front of her, head lowered, she said, 'Lilly, you look lovely. You really do.' The dress had been bought from a woman who had become tired of seeing it in her wardrobe, knowing she no longer had the figure, or the opportunities to wear it again, and it had needed very little alteration.

'I'm not too fat for it, am I?'

'You're no bean pole, Lilly, but you're all woman!' she said teasingly.

'It's beautiful,' Lilly muttered and Hannah was amused to see her blush. Perhaps she wasn't as indifferent to admiration as she appeared.

'The next thing we must do is persuade you to accept every invitation that comes your way,' Hannah said softly. 'Whether or not you really want to go, you must accept every one and maybe there'll be a few surprises. Places where you don't expect to enjoy yourself might turn out to be some of the best times of your life.'

'There haven't been many "best times" in my life, not really.'

'Those days are over. This dress will be filled with good memories before the winter is over. So much so that you'll smile every time you look at it. That's a promise.'

Ken came home on the day Lilly was given her beautiful dress. Eirlys didn't know how to greet him. She was glad he had made up his mind to leave London and come back to her permanently, but her delight was tempered by the realization that for Ken, it was failure. If she were too pleased, he might

234

think she was gloating, proved right when she had advised him not to go.

'Dadda,' she called and when Morgan poked his head around the door of the sitting room, where she sat making puppets to sell in the shop, she asked, 'Will you stay in with Anthony and the boys tonight? I want to talk to Ken.'

'I'll take the boys to the pictures if you like, then there'll only be you and Anthony and Ken?'

'No, Dadda, I want us to go out.'

'Fine by me. I don't suppose Stanley will be in though. He spends most evenings sitting in Audrey's cafe waiting for her to tell Myrtle she can leave early. Seriously courting, those two if you ask me, for all he's only sixteen.'

'And Maude and Reggie talking about getting married. Honestly, Dadda, I'm beginning to feel middle-aged!'

'A brother or sister for Anthony would cure you of that!' He darted back out and closed the door before she could respond. It wasn't his business, but she and Ken had been acting the fool for long enough. Separating, arguing about whether or not she should work. Both trying to be strong against the other. Daft, it was. Time they settled down and behaved like responsible parents, he thought, as he took out the family's shoes ready for cleaning.

When Ken walked through the door later that day, Morgan greeted him and disappeared back into the kitchen. Eirlys silently stood up and hugged him. Apart from a whispered, 'I love you, I've missed you,' which he echoed, she didn't know what to say, so she said nothing. Morgan, whistling noisily, banged the back door as he went out.

She felt surprisingly shy, as though he'd been away for years rather than weeks. She eased away from him and went to make tea and bring in the snack she had prepared on a tray.

'Don't eat much, Ken, I've booked a table at the Ship tonight. Don't waste a good appetite on sandwiches.'

'For all of us?' Ken asked. She looked into his eyes, afraid of seeing provocative accusation.

'No, darling, just you and me.'

Making sure Anthony was ready to be left in her father's care, they waited for the boys to come home, and again,

Eirlys watched anxiously for some irritation with them, but he seemed genuinely pleased to see them and had brought his sweets ration for them to share.

The meal was a treat. There was even a generous helping of meat, which was served with roast potatoes that were dry but palatable, and the tinned vegetables were enhanced by a few early sprouts and some fresh carrots that were perhaps a trifle woody and past their best, but welcome just the same.

Ken told her some of the smart, clever, interesting and downright stupid people he had met, and confessed that the boredom and loneliness outweighed the good times. Eirlys admitted that being home with Anthony and working at making things to sell in the shop was enough, for the moment.

'We need extra money, but perhaps I'll find a job that's less demanding, like helping Peter on an official footing once his agency is –' She stopped. Assuming that Peter's agency would succeed while Ken's had failed was the worst possible remark to make. She looked at him anxiously and to her relief, Ken laughed.

'Peter's agency fills a real need in the town. I could do worse than join him. I tried to find a niche for myself among people who had been doing the job for years, established agencies with good reputations. If I'd been fortunate and found one or two new stars and set them on their way I might have managed it, but new stars with ambition wouldn't take a chance on me, and why should they?'

They walked home, ignoring the buses that passed them, relishing the chance to be on their own, a couple, without the ties of Morgan and Stanley, Harold and Percival.

As they went into the house, they could hear the boys arguing about some game they were playing. Ken held her tightly and kissed her before whispering, 'I never thought I'd say this, but darling, darling Eirlys, I'm so very glad to be back and I wouldn't move away from this rowdy rabble again for a fortune.'

Eirlys met Ralph a few days later. To her fury, he told her he had left the job.

'Why now? Why not while I was still employed by the council? I stood a chance of getting it back then!'

'Sorry, Eirlys. I thought I'd enjoy it, but it's too confining. The walls close in on me and I can't stand it. All right, I know it sounds like I'm using the war as an excuse, but it's true. All the years I was away, living in uncomfortable conditions, I dreamed of a quiet office and going home each day to a clean, orderly home. But I can't cope with it, I keep waiting for something to happen and I don't even know what I'm waiting *for*!'

'What will you do?' she asked.'

'Rejoin the army, if they'll have me.'

Forgetting her words to Ken about being satisfied by having no work, she went straight to see her ex-boss.

'Eirlys, how nice to see you.' He called to the typist and asked for some tea.

While it came he asked about Ken and the family, then, when the tray had been brought and the girl had left, she said. 'I'm sure you'll guess why I'm here?'

He tilted his head questioningly.

'I met Ralph and he told me he's leaving. I'd like to apply for my job back, Mr Clifford.' He looked away, busying himself with the milk jug and the packet of saccharine tablets that substituted for the sugar bowl. Her heart plummeted. 'Is there a problem?'

'I'm afraid there is, Mrs Ward. We can't choose who we employ, not any more. While there are rules about employing ex-Army men, we have to comply. A man feeds a family, you see, and for a woman it's only a stopgap until she marries or has a child. I'm so sorry.'

'There aren't any other vacancies, I suppose?'

'Only one, and it wouldn't suit someone with your abilities. We're looking for an office junior, someone to take telephone messages, make tea, run errands, you know the sort of thing.'

Eirlys thanked him and left. She couldn't drink the tea, it would have choked her.

Freddy decided that the only way to get his life back in some kind of order was to see Shirley again, talk to her and find out whether there was any hope of them at least continuing to stay friends. The contact through their letters, in which they had poured out their thoughts and fears, and their plans for the future, was no longer there and every time he saw the postman he remembered the joy of receiving them. He had imagined that the letters would have been replaced by seeing her, talking to her, really talking, not in the stilted comments on a letter to which he could never fully reply. But instead there was nothing.

He went to Brook Lane and asked Hetty if she had an address for her daughter. 'I've got to go to London,' he lied, 'and I thought I'd maybe see her performance and take her out afterwards. If she wants to,' he added hastily. 'She's probably too busy with other friends, mind.'

Hetty smiled and handed him the address written on an envelope. 'Take this, I've just addressed it ready to write to her. I'll write the name and address of the theatre on the back, so if you miss her at one place you'll find her at the other. I'm sure she'd love to see you, Freddy.' Freddy clutched the envelope like a lifeline and went back to the hotel to pack a small bag.

He was unaware of the date and the approach of the Christmas season. The following Tuesday was Christmas Day and on Saturday, three days before, he tramped around the busy streets and found the theatre where Shirley was appearing. It was closed. Notices stuck all over the walls and the entrance explained that the theatre would reopen on Boxing Day with the pantomime *Puss in Boots*.

Shirley's mother must have known. She was letting him know that Shirley didn't want to see him. Angrily, he walked through the excited shoppers, pushing people rudely aside when his way was blocked. Why couldn't Shirley have told him herself? All that was needed was a letter. Then he remembered that although he knew her address, she no longer had his. Perhaps she was about to tell him when they had talked in the van that day but couldn't find the words. Calming down, he knew she would have tried to be kind.

He'd better go back to Brook Lane and stay there until she turned up. She would certainly be home for Christmas now the show had finished. This unresolved affair had to be ended or he would never get his life together.

When he returned to the hotel where he had booked for two nights, he changed his mind and extended his booking through Christmas. Better here among strangers than at home trying to pretend he still belonged.

Alice told Eynon that she had followed Netta home to see if she could learn something and he was shocked at first, not with her temerity but because she could have walked into danger.

'Alice, love, don't do anything like that again. I'll go and confront them when it's necessary, I can handle myself against two protective brothers and you can't. We have to talk about what we know and then decide what should be done.' He held her tightly and laughed. 'Can you imagine what they'd say if I turned up threatening to fight them? Little squirt, that's what they'd think, but they'd be surprised, mind. Eat 'em for breakfast and spit out the pips I would, small as I am.'

He deliberately made light of it but he was worried about the risk she had taken. Now they knew what she looked like, Netta's brothers could threaten her at any time. 'Promise me, Alice, love, if you see any of them again, Netta or her brothers, you'll come straight and tell me.'

'I promise.'

There was a knock at the door then, and they looked at each other in surprise. 'Must be someone important, Alice. None of the family ever knock.'

'D'you think – could it be Netta's brothers come to cause trouble?'

Mentally preparing for confrontation, Eynon opened the door to a couple carrying suitcases. Their guest house had its first visitors.

The arrest of Joseph, charged with illegally supplying restricted goods, came as no shock to Cassie, but she did feel a sadness. It seemed such a waste, for their life together to end like this. The police questioned her for a long time on three occasions, but she was able to convince them that the business was not in her name. The local constable, Charlie Grove, was ill at ease during the interviews, having bought, in innocence, some of Cassie's damaged goods for himself and Madge, the girl he was soon to marry. Cassie was unable to resist embarrassing him further by winking and promising to say nothing, when the other officer was out of hearing range.

She continued to empty the shops and her house until there was very little left. Jumble sales were popular both to buy things a household needed and for raising money for various good causes and it was at these that Cassie disposed of her oddments. The house in which she and Joseph lived was rented and the rentbook was seriously in arrears. Any day now she expected to receive notice or a court order demanding payment. The rent book being in Joseph's name, she waited until the demand came and posted it to him without a letter of explanation. It would be delivered with his and Joanna's Christmas cards – a nice touch.

A few days later Joseph turned up at the house and she opened the door and stared at him as though he were a stranger. 'What d'you want?' she asked coldly.

'To come in of course, woman! What's been happening here? Why haven't the bills been paid, and where's the stock? The shops are empty. Come on, Cassie, what's going on?'

'Going on? Nothing to interest you. You've got a different life now, you and – what's her name – Joanna Lee-Jones? She wouldn't be interested in running your shops for you while you have fun elsewhere, so why should I?'

'Having fun? What's got into you? What have you done with the stock? And how did the police get all those coupons?'

'The stock is sold or given away. I thought the coupons I found hidden were stolen or counterfeit, so I handed them in as a respectable citizen and business woman should. Why? Cause you some trouble, did they?'

'Respectable citizen! That's rot! You deliberately set me up and now I face a prison sentence. Is that what you wanted?'

'Yes, it was! I found out about you and that woman and decided I'd been a fool long enough. Go back to her, Joseph, or is it Joe these days? Go back and leave me be. What's done is done and I hope she's worth it!'

'She's gone.' The bluster, the fizzing anger suddenly left him.

'What d'you mean, gone?'

'When the police came and charged me, I was given bail and when I went back to our – the rooms she rented, she was gone. I owed a month's rent and all I had was a note telling me goodbye.'

For a moment the recent agonizing months floated away, the anger and hurt were gone and instead, the years of companionable partnership returned. He was in trouble and needed her help. He had thrown it all away for a pretty young face but could she do the same now the pretty face was gone? He stood there, still having got no further than the doorway and he looked so forlorn. Shoulders drooped, looking past her with a glazed expression, like a beaten dog. Pity flowed through her. All she had to do was step aside and allow him to pass, to walk back into her life, and all the lonely years stretching before her would be nothing more than a nightmare from which she had awoken.

In the gloomy half-light of the dark passageway she watched his face, undecided whether to be strong and lonely, or stupid but with a future. His head turned towards her but he glanced through the open door of the front room and his eyes blazed. 'Where's the furniture gone?' he demanded angrily.

'Gave most of it to young Alice who worked for me. They've bought a guest house and—'

'Gave it away?' He pushed past her and went from room to room, and in disbelief saw that, except the small kitchen with its table and solitary chair, they were empty. He ran upstairs to find one single bed and little besides. Bedding was piled on the floor in the absence of cupboards, and there were a few clothes thrown across the banisters.

Cassie stood watching his progress with some satisfaction. Now he'd understand just how much he had hurt her. She was softening towards him. Knowing that the woman had let him down, that he was on his own and needing her, she couldn't send him away. They'd pick up the pieces and work together as they always had and put it all right. She followed his progress, his footsteps echoing as he went back to each room as if unable to believe what he saw the first time. She began to regret her enthusiastic house clearance. Fool that

241

she was, she might have known he'd be back. Thirty and more years couldn't be pushed aside all that easily, even for a pretty young face.

She heard him coming along the landing, the footsteps loud, linoleum harsh underfoot. Now he would come down and apologize and after making him suffer just a little longer, she'd tell him to go and collect his things and come home.

There was a half smile on her face as he stamped down the stairs at a run and took hold of her shoulders. Not gently as she'd so often imagined, but tightly, painfully, as he shook her. 'You damned fool! I've got nothing left! You've lost me everything. Are you getting senile?'

Cold anger, rarely seen in Cassie's eyes, glittered. 'Senile is it? I'd be completely crazy, not ill, if I took you back!' With a strength that startled Joseph and surprised herself she pushed him and then, with her foot on his backside, kicked him out of the door, slamming it satisfactorily behind him.

Maude and Reggie planned to marry the following April and Myrtle was not pleased. Having no real family, she and Maude had both dreamed of marriage and children, to start building a family of their own. She loved Stanley and knew they would be happy together. She knew that for Stanley too there was the urgent need to start making a place for himself in a family of his own. His mother had never married and Harold and Percival and he had different fathers, if they could be flattered by calling them fathers, Myrtle thought sadly. 'Father unknown' on the birth certificate was a terrible rejection to live with all your life. That was what was written on hers and Maude's, even though they had known their father for the first years of their lives. He had left his wife to live with their mother but hadn't divorced her.

She waited on the corner of the lane for Stanley and they ran to greet each other affectionately. As usual they started talking immediately – although they met almost every day there was so much to tell each other. The lanes were edged by dripping hedges and they made their way to one of their secret places.

They had found a hay barn on the edge of a farmer's field

where they could sit undisturbed and talk over their future plans. It was there they went on this cold, crisp Christmas Eve. Stanley had finished work and Audrey's cafe had closed until after the holiday. They had set off to do some last-minute shopping but instead had wandered away from the houses and into the misty fields. They made their way over the hard ground, squeezed between strands of barbed wire and snuggled deep into the hay.

Outside the barn the trees of a nearby wood were scarcely visible, an abandoned plough, a fallen tree, some rusty tangled wire, were shrouded in the mist that made the well-known scene unfamiliar.

'I wish we were married and had a place where we could meet in comfort, somewhere cosy and comfortable. I've worked out that we could afford to take a room in Alice and Eynon's guest house. Not a proper start, not what I want for you, but we could save an' save until we have enough for some furniture and, oh, Myrtle, I wish we were old enough to defy them all, don't you? I want to marry you, I want you to be my wife, not have to meet in soggy haylofts and—' She stopped his complaining with a kiss. A kiss that was not like any other, a kiss that did things to her insides and brought on a longing so strong she was breathless when they parted.

'It's not fair,' she said breathlessly. 'Our Maude and Reggie are getting married on the sixth of April and even though it's a Saturday, Auntie Audrey's closing the cafe and having the party there.' Her words were interrupted by his kisses as she went on, 'They've even been promised rooms in Auntie Audrey's house with Ronnie and Olive. The whole family's getting involved and they talk about nothing else. While you and I aren't allowed even to get engaged.'

'We are engaged, Myrtle. You and I know it, so why worry about anyone else, eh?'

'I love you, Stanley Love. I long to be Mrs Love. What a name, eh?'

'There is one way, Myrtle,' Stanley said. 'A certain way of telling them we're old enough. If you had a baby, they'd make us get married, wouldn't they?'

Myrtle laughed. 'Yes. That would make them take notice

of us, eh?' She raised her head to look at him and share the amusing thought, but Stanley wasn't laughing. There was a look on his handsome face she hadn't seen before. He gently pulled her closer and gathered her into his arms, held her so they touched along the whole length of their bodies. He began kissing her more urgently; some were short, teasing kisses and others long, demanding, enveloping every part of her.

'Let's do it, shall we?' His kisses and the passionate urging in his husky voice easily persuaded her.

Shirley came back to St David's Well with a sadness she couldn't shake off. The theatre closing and then being told by her mother that Freddy had called to see her seemed to be the end of everything. She had declined offers of further work, knowing that her heart was no longer in it. A career on the stage, once a dream, was no longer important. On Christmas Eve she walked through the main street, looking at the shops, aware of the effort being made to make the season a joyful one. She bought a few presents for the family, gifts to place under the tree, and on impulse bought a smart shirt for Freddy. If she didn't see him, Johnny would like it and they were about the same size. She wondered where he was staying. He had to be in the town: there was nowhere else for him to go, but where?

Freddy was shopping too, but for himself. He had very little money but he bought a pair of trousers and a jumper with the clothing coupons he'd been allocated. In a second-hand shop there was a brooch that appealed. It was in the shape of a heart set with rubies and, being gold, it took almost all of his money. He took the clothing he'd bought, asked for a refund, and paid for the brooch gladly. Perhaps, one day he'd see Shirley and give it to her. One day, but he didn't know when.

Christmas was another excuse for a party but although the war had ended and most of the men were safely back with their families, austerity still restricted the way it was celebrated. Families gathered, everyone bringing food. Neighbours lent glasses and china and chairs and borrowed for themselves when their get-togethers took place.

The weather was cold but doors stood open: people popped

in to offer season's greetings and stayed for a while. Audrey's house, being the largest and only a few doors up from Marged and Huw's, was the venue on Christmas night for the Castles' gathering.

Shirley was there with her mother and Bleddyn, Morgan came with the three boys and Eirlys, Ken and their son. Stanley winked at Myrtle and said to Audrey, 'You'll be needing a bigger house for parties like this, with the family growing so big.'

Myrtle watched as her sister measured and discussed what she and Reggie would need when they moved in. With luck, now they had 'done it', Maude might not be the first to marry, despite all their plans. She glanced at Stanley and blew a kiss.

Lilly wore the lovely dress Hannah had made for her and accepted the compliments with ease that sounded like boredom. Hannah knew differently. She could see that Lilly was flattered to be admired. She was careful how she sat down and carefully eased the dress smoothly under her so as not to crease it. Her manner had changed: putting on the dress seemed to make her aware of herself as a young woman and she posed rather than stood, joining animatedly in the conversations and even playing a game of draughts with the three boys. Hannah hoped that the dress and the realization that she was too young to give up on life would stay with her. Perhaps she would make her a skirt and bolero for the spring.

Then Eirlys spoilt Lilly's happy mood by saying, 'Oh, by the way, Lilly, there's a job going in the offices where I used to work. Nothing frantic, just someone to man the phone and make tea, you know the sort of thing.'

'Nice for you, Eirlys,' Lilly said off-handedly as she brushed imaginary crumbs from her dress.

'No, not me, I recommended you. If you'll go and see Mr Clifford or Mr Johnston after the holiday, I think the job will be yours.'

Thirteen

Chapel's flower shop was a regular rendezvous for Marged Castle, who bought flowers each week to place on the tables of the beach cafe during the summer, and for Bleddyn and Hetty to add to their tables in the fish and chip shop-cum-restaurant. So when she went there and saw Mrs Chapel making tiny rose buds from crêpe paper, painting them and even touching them with scent, she asked for details.

'Who are they for? A wedding bouquet, I'll bet. Anyone we know?'

'You know Constable Charlie Grove? Getting married he is and his Madge wants roses. Roses being unavailable in February it's the best I can do.'

Marged picked up one of the exquisitely made flowers. 'And this is the best there is, Mrs Chapel. They'll do any bride proud. Such clever fingers you've got.'

'It was Maldwyn who showed me how. Honestly, since he's come here to work, the business has grown and so has my enjoyment of it. Full of ideas, he is.'

'Enthusiasm, that's what makes the difference in what you choose to do, don't you agree?'

'Oh, Maldwyn's enthusiastic all right. He goes out in the fields and brings back branches and ferns, dead wood and even stones, and he transforms them into something beautiful. Glad I am that he'll be here to follow me when I give up. The business is in good hands.' Leaving her work, she stood to serve Marged with some small posies that were mostly ivy with a few grasses and painted berries. She looked up and smiled as the door opened and Charlie Grove walked in. 'Here's the man himself. Don't look at the work table, mind – secrets we've got this morning.'

Charlie turned away and shaded his eyes with a smile. 'I wonder if you know of a place where Madge's family can stay, Mrs Chapel? About eight of them will be staying for two nights. Not pleased that we're being married in St David's Well instead of Madge's home, mind. But Madge and I decided it's where we're going to live and it's here we want to start our married life.'

'Good on you for making your own decisions,' Marged said, then added, 'Mind, if one of mine had wanted to be married anywhere else but here I'd have created hell!'

Mrs Chapel laughed. 'Rules are important, but for other people only, is it?'

'Madge's parents don't really mind, but I have promised to find them somewhere comfortable to stay.'

'What about Eynon and Alice's place? Just starting they are, so they're bound to do their best.' She wrote down the address in Rosebay Place and he promised to go there straight away and make arrangements for Madge's family to stay.

It was as he stood at the door talking to Alice, notebook at the ready to write down details of the rooms available, that Netta saw him. She immediately thought he was there about her threats and she panicked. She watched in dread as Alice stood back to allow him to enter. Her name was on that notebook, she was certain of that, and Alice knew her address. Any moment she could have the police knocking at her door and what would happen then, she dreaded to think. Would she be locked up while they made investigations? What would happen to Dolly and Walter? And even Danny needed her there when he came home from school. She couldn't rely on her mam.

With Dolly in her pushchair and Walter standing on the front and holding on to the sides, she hurried away, but with no destination in mind. With two small children, where could she go except back home?

Alice proudly showed Charlie around the house with its simply furnished but attractive rooms. They decided on which rooms would be needed and Alice wrote the bookings in her big diary. This would be something to tell Eynon when he came home from work! Two nights for eight people.

'I like the top rooms with their sloping ceilings,' Charlie said as he was leaving. 'I bet there's a view of the beach from the window up in the eaves. Pity it's too high to look out.'

When he had gone, Alice went back up to the smallest room and climbed on to a chair. Charlie was right. There, between the chimneys opposite, was the sparkling sea. A room with a view! Just wait till Eynon heard about that! Her happiness lasted until she came downstairs and saw, through a landing window, the scurrying figure of Netta with her children, and felt again the threat of imminent disaster.

As Netta reached the park in the centre of the town, she almost bumped into Lilly, who was walking through on her way to the council offices.

'Hey, Netta! Where are you off to in such a rush? Nearly knocked me off my feet you did. And where have you been? Ashamed are you of what you've been saying about my brother?'

'Come to a cafe where I can tell you what's happened?' Netta asked and, seeing some interesting gossip on offer, Lilly readily agreed.

'Can't stop long, mind. You'll never believe where I'm going. Only after a job! Yes,' she said, laughing at Netta's surprised expression. 'I won't get it, but Eirlys recommended me, see, and I'll at least have an interview. What a laugh, eh?'

They went into the cafe from which they had once been asked to leave, but the woman serving didn't recognize them and they found a corner table, ordered tea and some drinks for the children and Netta told Lilly all that had happened.

'Go and own up,' Lilly advised, when Netta admitted her deceit. 'Go and face our Eynon and Alice and tell them you're sorry, that you were a bit off your head or something. You'll have to put up with a good telling off, mind, but if you take it and show how ashamed you are, I don't think they'll go to the police.'

'They already have. I saw Constable Groves talking to Alice.'

'Look, I'll come with you now this minute.' Lilly loved a

drama and she would come out of it looking good, having tried to help a friend. 'If you leave it you'll find it even harder to do, and you'll have to face it sometime. I'll come with you and talk to Alice. Then you can come with me to my interview and help me celebrate when I'm told I'm not suitable, right?' They were laughing as they left the cafe but Netta's laughter was forced. What if Alice had reported her threats? What would she do? It was easy for Lilly to be light-hearted about it, she had family to support her.

Seeing her serious expression, Lilly said, 'Mam and Dad will forgive you once they know the truth. They might give you a job again in the summer, if you want one. Better be re-e-eal sorry, mind. Then explain that it was for the children, and you were desperate. They'll understand. Love children they do.'

Feeling noble and generous-hearted, she went to Rosebay Place and knocked on Alice and Eynon's door. She tried the latch and, finding it unlocked, she walked in, helping Netta with Dolly's pushchair. Netta was shaking with nervousness when Alice appeared, pushing back her long hair in an attempt to tidy it.

'Lilly, this is a surprise. And, what do *you* want, to tell me more lies?' she said as she glared at Netta.

'She's come to say it was all a dreadful mistake and she's sorry,' Lilly said, smiling as though the matter was so simply settled. 'Aren't you, Netta?' she coaxed as Netta stood silently staring at Alice. 'Go on, tell her what you told me.'

'No. It's almost half past twelve,' Alice said. 'Eynon will be home for his dinner, you'll have to wait and tell both of us.'

'Half past twelve?' Lilly gasped, and took out a comb and lipstick. 'I've got to see a Mr Johnston at quarter to one! Terrible it'll be if I'm late, I might not get the job!' She winked at Netta, who was too nervous to respond. She quickly explained to Alice about the interview for a dogsbody in the council offices then turned to Netta. 'Look, I'll come back here and meet you, right? Now, don't be afraid to tell Alice everything. It's the only way.' In her new role as comforter and adviser to those in trouble, Lilly went to the council offices, head held high, and demanded rather haughtily to see Mr Johnston.

*   *   *

When Eynon came home, he started with shock at seeing Netta there. 'I thought we'd seen the last of you.'

'Netta has come to apologize,' Alice said calmly. 'I told her she must wait until she can talk to both of us.'

'Well?' Eynon demanded.

'I'm sorry,' Netta sobbed, jumping up to grab Dolly, who was beginning to wander.

'No tears, they won't help!' Eynon said.

'All right, I lied about you being Dolly's father. I was tempted simply because of the coincidence of the dates, nothing more. I fell for her around the time of your wedding and I began to see a way out of my struggles.'

'So you followed me, and then made friends with Lilly so you could glean enough information to convince us?' Alice asked.

'I'd thought of it before that. It was talking to your parents over the beach one day that gave me the idea, the dates and . . .' She stood then and glared at Alice. 'It's all right for people like you! Everything comes easy.'

'You don't think you've created your own troubles, having three children and no husband?' Eynon asked, tight-lipped.

'Three children? Me?' She looked surprised. 'Oh, you mean Danny? No, neither Danny nor Walter is mine. I only have Dolly.'

'If they aren't yours, then whose are they?'

'I look after Walter because Mam works and he's too young to go to school.'

'Then what about Danny? What happened that you're responsible for three children?'

'I'd been thrown out of the room in my auntie's house, Mam's house was packed full with soldiers billeted on her, and I didn't know how I was going to manage. I went home the night of Eynon's stag do, and there was this soldier, and he comforted me, promised that everything would be all right. I'd had too many free drinks and I had a great need for sympathy and well, I took the only comfort I could find.'

'What about Walter and Danny?' Alice persisted.

'Danny and Walter's mother died and their father couldn't cope. I took them in, Mam didn't mind, she's casual about such things, having three children of her own and widowed at twenty-one. It's been difficult to work since but I was determined to look after the boys. Pitiful to see them it was; frightened and having no one who cared for them in the whole world. The alternative to us taking them in was for them to go into a home, probably be separated. They knew us, see, spent most of their days in our house they did. Best all round, I thought, for them to stay permanent with us.'

'Couldn't your mother look after them?'

'Mam couldn't help, working herself, see. But she packed us in, and once the soldiers were gone, she set to, filling every inch of the place, mostly with junk, making sure the house is an over-crowded mess, in the hope that I'll be given one of these new prefabs when they come.'

Eynon and Alice were silent listening to the girl's story and imagining how much she'd had to struggle to look after three children, two of whom weren't even hers.

Eynon glanced at the clock. 'Look, I've got to go back to work. Pack my food, will you, Alice love? I've no time to eat now, but,' he went on, looking at the still tearful Netta, 'well, thanks for being so honest with us, eh, Alice?' He looked at Alice for approval and she nodded.

'Yes, thanks,' she said but she spoke grudgingly, without sincerity. 'Netta, can you imagine what you did to me? I've been very distressed and I can't say I forgive you. What you did was cruel. But, all right, we'll say no more about it.'

'And you'll tell the police to forget it?'

'Police? We haven't told the police.' Alice frowned. 'Oh, you saw the constable here did you? He was looking for rooms for wedding guests. His bride's family are staying with us for two nights, that's all.'

'I don't suppose I can ask a favour?'

Alice frowned and waited for her to explain.

'Will you tell Mr and Mrs Castle what I've told you? They were so kind to us, and I'm so ashamed.'

'We'll explain to Mam and Dad, so they know what drove you to do such a terrible thing.'

'I'm sorry.' Netta stood to go. 'I'll wait outside for Lilly. It was she who persuaded me to face you.'

'Our Lilly?' Eynon said in surprise. 'That doesn't sound like her!'

'She's gone for an interview for a job,' Alice said.

'Blimey! That doesn't sound like our Lilly either. Is the world going mad?'

Lilly was shown around the dark, rather dreary offices where the typists worked and shown what her tasks would be. There was a notepad on which she would write down telephone messages, which she would then pass to the person concerned. Lilly at once decided that the person would have to come to her, she wasn't going to run around after typists. Who did they think she was?

She would make tea during the morning and afternoon breaks, and run any messages required, including going to the baker's for cakes each morning. It didn't sound too strenuous. She wasn't excited at the prospect but decided that she wouldn't mind giving it a try. Better than the boring beach or waitressing! So she smiled and promised to do her very best, and the job was offered to her. With a feeling of triumph, she accepted.

When she returned to Rosebay Place, the two children were playing with utensils from Alice's kitchen cupboard and Netta and Alice were sitting at the table, talking like friends.

'Everything all right?' Lilly asked, peering around the kitchen door. 'No bloodshed?'

'No blood,' Alice said. 'How did you get on?'

'I got the job! And d'you know, I think I'm going to like it.'

She was still smiling happily as she set off to tell her parents, leaving Netta with Alice. She was hurrying, something she didn't often do and, turning a corner, she bumped straight into Sam junior. They stood and stared at each other.

Lilly had often wondered how she would feel on seeing him again and for a moment her heart leapt uncomfortably, but then, as she looked at him, staring into his eyes, shifty eyes, wondering anxiously how she would react, she felt shock leaving her and knew he no longer had any attraction for her. She was seeing only the man who had ended her comfortable marriage. 'Excuse me, you're in my way,' she said and, pushing past him, walked on with no feeling of loss. She was over him and no matter how many times they met in the future, she would feel nothing.

She went into the house with a light-headed euphoria like she'd never known before. 'Mam! Dad! I've got a job. What d'you think of that then, eh?'

Myrtle and Stanley found it easier to find places where they could be alone once they had made love in the haystack. There were plenty of places like old barns and once in a while they were alone in the flat above Audrey's cafe and lay in utter comfort on Myrtle's bed. When the date she had been waiting for had passed and she knew she was likely to be carrying a child, she clung to Stanley and cried. 'I'm scared,' she wailed.

'What is it? You aren't afraid I'll leave you, are you, Myrtle? Never. I want us to grow old together surrounded by our family. Our family, Myrtle, just what we dreamed about, eh?'

'I'm not scared you'll let me down, Stanley, I know you'd never do that. I'm scared because I've got to face the family and tell them. Can you imagine what Auntie Audrey will say? And as for Auntie Marged and Uncle Huw. Oh, Stanley, I want to run away!'

He held her tightly and murmured soothingly. 'I'll be with you when you tell them and I think we should start right now, with Auntie Audrey.'

They stood sheepishly while the words were stuttered out painfully. They held hands and avoided looking at Audrey or Keith.

'You what? You think you might be carrying a baby? You can stand there and tell me such a thing so casually, and without shame?'

'We wanted to get married, Auntie Audrey, and you kept telling us that we were too young.'

'I was clearly correct. This is a childish way to get your own way! Misbehaving, letting yourselves down. Children you are, for all you're eighteen years old, Myrtle!'

'Can we? Get married?' Stanley asked, his voice trembling. 'I will look after her and we'll be happy together, no doubt about that.'

253

'Where will you live? How will you afford a baby? And what—'

'What does Morgan say?' Keith intervened.

'Nobody else knows, you're the first ones we've told,' Myrtle said, hoping the hint of flattery would soften Audrey's anger.

'Then we'll go straight away and tell the others. Right?'

There were mixed reactions although everyone expressed their disappointment in the young couple. In public, and when each member of the family was told, Myrtle was contrite and tearful, but in private, when she and Stanley were alone, she was ecstatically happy.

In haste, arrangements were made for them to marry on the 15th of February, which made Maude cry floods of tears. 'That's before Reggie and me.' she wailed. 'I'm the oldest! I've been engaged all proper and you're spoiling it by getting married first! Auntie Audrey, tell her she can't. It isn't fair!'

'What about a double wedding?' Keith suggested, but this brought more wails.

'No! I don't want Myrtle muscling in on my wedding day!'

'Myrtle's wedding will be a small affair, yours will be different, properly planned,' Marged comforted.

'But she'll be married first!'

There seemed no amicable solution and Myrtle just smiled and allowed the arguments to roll around her. She had her own way and the rest was not her problem. When her period began, almost two weeks late, she hid her discomfort as griping pains tormented her, and said nothing.

Myrtle's supposed pregnancy and hasty marriage had one result besides allowing Myrtle and Stanley to marry. It made Eirlys consider having another child. Testing Ken's reaction, she told him she believed a child was happier with a sibling reasonably close in age. They were in the house alone. Morgan was taking part in a darts match, the boys visiting friends. Eirlys and Ken were playing with their son, and Ken stared at her and said, 'Eirlys, darling, are you saying what I hope you're saying? You want us to have another child?'

His eyes were shining and there was hardly need for her to ask if he agreed. 'I want that more than anything,' he said.

They hugged Anthony, and that was the tableau Morgan saw as he came through the door, having forgotten to take his 'lucky' darts.

When Ken took Anthony up to bed, Morgan asked Eirlys if she were happy. 'Yes, Dadda. Fears of Ken leaving me for Janet, or someone else, are gone.'

'You still argue a lot, mind.'

'Yes, but the rows are over small irritations, they don't threaten our marriage.'

Ken came in, having overheard, and said, 'If I hurt Eirlys, I hurt myself more. I've too much to lose for the sake of brief, illicit fun.'

Morgan remembered how he had damaged his own marriage with a foolish affair with Bleddyn's wife, and was sad. He hugged Eirlys and wished them both luck.

Talk of weddings and the increasing number of pregnant women walking around the shops depressed Shirley. She was almost twenty-three years old and with no hope of marriage or, since she had turned down every London offer, of expanding her career either. She constantly wondered where Freddy was. She couldn't seek him out. It had to be up to him to come to her. She hadn't moved. He knew exactly where to find her.

The days passing without him making contact, or even calling to collect his money, showed clearly that he had no intention of doing that. The money she still held for him was a thin thread of hope to which she clung. While that was there, she knew he had to come and see her one day, even though it was only to ask for the return of what was his.

There were still concerts planned locally and she was always a popular choice. Every time she stood in the wings, waiting to step on to the stage, she would look into the audience and wonder whether Freddy was out there, waiting to see her perform. No one knew of her misery except her mother. Like many others, she hid her unhappiness under false gaiety. She laughed a lot, cracked jokes and was the centre of attention at parties, but inside she ached with loneliness and regrets.

'Why don't you go and see him?' Hetty asked her one day. 'After all, you do have the excuse of wanting to return his money.'

'Where would I find him?'

'You know perfectly well where he works. The name of the hotel was on the side of the van, wasn't it?' Hetty reminded her.

'Perhaps, one day.'

Hetty opened the window on the warm spring day and said, 'Today looks like a perfect day for going for a walk, to visit friends, or something.'

Shirley shook her head.

Cassie took possession of the terraced house she had secretly rented, on the day of Myrtle and Stanley's wedding. She saw the few pieces of furniture into her new abode, thanked the van driver and went to Audrey's cafe to see the bride and groom. All the Castle family were there and she went to sit beside Alice.

'You've moved into the house?' Alice asked.

'Now just,' Cassie replied. 'I hope I can afford to stay there. The bills are pouring in and I can't see an end to them! I'll have to get work of some kind, but at my age, what can I do?'

'The same as Eynon and me. Take a lodger or two.'

While the few guests at the low-key ceremony chattered and wished the young couple well, and Maude seethed with anger in a corner, Cassie mulled over Alice's suggestion. A lodger was a good idea, it would solve two problems: beside the extra money, she would have someone to look after, no more loneliness. Not a man, a couple of young girls would be nice. Perhaps nurses from the local hospital, she mused.

Shirley walked to the hotel where Freddy worked and went to the small reception desk. A girl was behind the counter, typing. When she saw Shirley she stood up and removed her glasses and smiled. 'Miss Downs, isn't it? Shirley Downs? Oh, Miss Downs, what a pleasure. I've seen nearly all your local concerts, and a friend and I once went all the way to Newport to see you.' She stopped and with a smile asked how she could help.

'Thank you for your kind words,' Shirley said with a smile. 'I'm flattered by your interest. I'd like to leave a message for Freddy Clements, who works here, driving the van and other things.'

Regretfully the girl shook her head. 'Sorry, Miss Downs, he's left us. At Christmas he went up to London and when he came back he seemed very unsettled. Then a couple of weeks ago he left.'

'You have an address?' Shirley was surprised at how calm she sounded.

'Sorry again. He lived here, so when he left he vacated his room and I've no forwarding address for him. If you wish you can leave your address and if we hear from him, I'll let you know.'

'Thank you, but he knows where to find me.' Shirley turned to leave but was called back.

'Miss Downs, d'you think I could have your autograph?'

Smiling, Shirley went back and signed her name in the book the girl offered. Fame, of a sort, was gratifying, but she'd give it all up to see Freddy looking at her with love.

That wouldn't happen now and it would be best if she made up her mind, now this minute, to forget him. She didn't know where he'd gone and there were no leads to guide her in a search for him. Perhaps London had called him if he'd been there at Christmas. She had been leaving as he had arrived: that must mean they were destined not to live in the same town.

She sometimes wondered about Andy, although not with any regrets. He would never be important to her. Fun for a while but she would never trust him with her heart. It was likely they would meet again, at his brother's wedding, but she had no fears of being tempted. It was Freddy for whom she grieved and he didn't want to know her.

Freddy called at the hotel later that day and when he was told that Shirley had called, he thanked the receptionist, listened to her description of Shirley's visit, that had delighted the girl, then put it out of his mind. Shirley was in a different league from him, he didn't even have a job any more, and was living in a single room with a gas ring and a small sink.

To everyone's surprise, including her own, Lilly settled into the job at the council offices. She took messages efficiently and when she had written them out, called for the person nearest to deliver them, insisting she needed to stay with the phone. The authority in her voice made it impossible for anyone to argue.

Once or twice, she was allowed to use the typewriter and soon became interested. Sometimes over the weeks, she was invited to type an occasional letter and although she was slow, she was accurate and this led to others using her skills. The feeling of superiority grew: Lilly had found her place. The lowliest position but with the greatest sense of importance.

Preparations for the wedding of Reggie and Maude increased as the day approached, with Marged and Audrey vying for the greater role. Maude had chosen to have the wedding breakfast in the cafe overlooking the beach, and to hold the evening party in Audrey's cafe, when as many as could possibly get in were invited.

At the Gregorys' smallholding ploughing was a priority, with an extra field added to land already tamed. Reggie worked long hours ploughing the new ground. Bernard went around with his loads of firewood; chopping and sawing in the mornings and delivering each afternoon and evening. It was Beth's job to prepare the evening meal and when Peter came home from his office, he helped feed the hens and ducks and walked up to Sally Gough's field to feed the donkeys. Life was busy, and just a few days before his wedding, Reggie made up his mind to finish the new field before stopping for the day. He was tired, but carried on even when the sun went in and a cold mist drifted across the hills. Darkness came early and shadows filled corners of the field and sneaked out of the wood.

The field had been a place where he had often stood to watch rabbits feed and he saw one out of the corner of his eye, hopping out of the wood. He imagined the creature frowning as he wondered what had happened to his feeding ground and he smiled, the whimsical idea amusing him.

It was probably one of the entrances to the rabbits' burrow that caused the tractor to falter. But whatever it was, the wheel slipped as he drove up a steep slope. He knew the danger of falling under a tractor with no protection above him and he leapt wildly away as the vehicle fell and rolled on to its side. Reggie felt excruciating pain as his leg was caught beneath it. He called but, so far away from either Sally or Bernard, he knew it was unlikely for help to arrive for a long time. The pain increased as shock left him and he slipped in and out of consciousness, the evening mist wrapping him in its chilly blanket.

Freddy had returned to a childhood hobby and taken up fishing. He was glad of the hobby to fill the time between his new job driving the van for the wholesale grocery firm and sleeping, and he was reasonably successful. The rivers offered good sport and a rainbow trout made a tasty supper and one easily cooked. He hated making his own meals, although he was more proficient at looking after himself since his time in the Army. A freshly caught fish placed between two buttered plates placed over a pan of boiling water, as he had seen his mother do many times, was a foolproof supper.

He was walking through the wood with his rod and reel plus a few sandwiches stuffed into his pocket when he heard the tractor. It was passing near then fading and slowly returning as the driver went up and down the field, but the sound changed and it seemed to be on one place for a long time. Perhaps the driver was taking a break. He might like a chat about the state of the river. He often picked up a few tips talking to the local farmers.

He pushed his way through the low, tangled bushes at the edge of the wood and looked out. He saw the tractor on its side and heard it stutter to a stop. He ran, shouting, as he saw a figure lying on the ground beneath its side. He spoke to Reggie, assuring him he'd soon be out of there and tried in vain to lift the tractor to free Reggie's leg.

'Look, mate, I'm only making things worse. I'm going to

fetch Mr Gregory and a few others, they'll soon get the thing shifted. Right? Now don't worry, I'll be no more than ten minutes. Here –' he handed him his watch. 'Time me. Ten minutes, right?' Throwing his rod and reel beside the silent man, Freddy ran like he'd never run before, and burst into the Gregorys' house without waiting to knock.

'Come quick, Reggie's hurt, the tractor's on top of him.'

Bernard and Peter followed him back to the field but Bernard stopped before they reached the edge of the wood. 'Best I go back for the horse,' he said.

After telephoning for an ambulance, Beth picked up the baby and hurried to the next farm, where three men came at once to do what they could.

Peter and Freddy were afraid they might make things worse by lifting the heavy vehicle just a fraction then having to put it down again, so it wasn't until Bernard came with the horse and the three men came from the neighbouring farm that Reggie was released. To their relief they saw Reggie, conscious but in pain, being carried on a stretcher down to the waiting ambulance.

It wasn't until the following day that Freddy remembered he had left his fishing rod in the field near the damaged tractor. And he didn't go to collect it until the following Saturday afternoon when he had finished work for the day.

The rod and the reel were where he had left them and the tractor still stood where it had been righted, with the assistance of Bernard's horse and the neighbouring farmers. He gathered up his possessions and made his way to the river, gently chuckling along near the banks, almost silent further out where it flowed towards the sea. He sat with his line slowly moving downstream, waiting idly for the float to tell him a fish might be interested in his bait, and marvelled at the tranquil scene. Did the smooth river water slip without fuss below the turbulence of the waves? he wondered. Or joyfully join the excited turbulence on the surface of the sea? He fixed a peg on the rod with a bell to warn him of untoward movement and sat, relaxed, to eat a sandwich.

Shirley had been asked to call on Bernard Gregory to check that the order for chickens to cook for Maude's wedding had been cancelled. Bernard took off his hat and handed her his notebook with the order struck out. He assured her the chickens were alive and well. He gave her three off-ration eggs but suggested she went for a walk first, calling for them on the way back.

'It's a perfect day for a walk,' he said, puffing on his pipe. 'Go up through the wood and see how everything is starting into life. If you can, walk down by the river, the swans are nesting and the small birds are pairing up and searching for nest sites. Plenty to see with those who have eyes.'

Shirley didn't often walk in the countryside. She had enjoyed it as a child but since her career had grown there had been little time. Something in the man's words reminded her of what she had been missing.

The walk through the wood was far from silent. Birds were busy searching and testing out nesting sites and there were a few noisy quarrels as two made the same choice. Squirrels ran ahead of her chattering in irritation, their undulating run a joy to watch.

It was muddy in places but by taking care she managed to make her way through to the far side, where, below her, the river flowed. She couldn't see the swans and she hesitated to walk down the sloping field to the river bank. Her legs felt strong, but it would be quite a pull coming back up. In the distance she saw a car, then a bus travelling along the road and decided that she need only walk a bit further to get a bus back to town. Slowly, cautiously, she made her way down the sloping field to the river.

She saw the swans, elegantly cruising in a backwater, where a small island had offered a safe nest site. Smiling at the thought of reporting their position to Bernard, she walked on. A man sat near the edge, a rod stretching up at his side. She approached, hoping for a chat to glean more about them to tell Bernard. He had been right about recommending this walk, she felt relaxed and was enjoying the peaceable sound of the river.

'Hello, Shirley, looking for a fish supper?'

'Freddy? What are you doing here?'

'Fishing!' he said with a grin.

'I mean, I didn't know you did such a thing.'

'It was Bernard's idea. He lent me a rod, came with me a few times, and I revived a childhood interest. Sit down,' he invited. 'There's a sandwich or two left if you're hungry.'

'No, thanks. I'm going to walk on towards the main road and get a bus back to town.'

The bell on the top of the rod rang then, and he jumped up and began to play the fish caught on his hook. The glistening creature was lifted out of the water as Freddy reeled in. 'Less than half a pound, I'll throw him back,' he said. He carefully released it and they watched it slide back under the water. 'Silly fool,' Freddy said. 'Risking his life for a mangled bit of worm.'

He added fresh bait to the hook, set up the rod and sat down near Shirley. Was it her imagination or did he sit closer than before?

'Where are you living now?' she asked. 'Or is it a secret?'

'I've got a room in Main Street, just a room with a bed and a gas ring, nothing more. It'll do until I decide what I'm going to do.'

'And a job?'

Delivering groceries for a wholesaler.'

'Why, Freddy?'

'I have to earn money,' he replied, adjusting the reel slightly to allow the line to move further downstream.

'Why are you accepting such low standards for yourself?' she asked softly. 'Remember what dreams you had? A top-class gent's clothing shop selling only the best to the best?'

'It all sounded so easy then. But coming back I found everything had moved on. Mam and Dad gone and not even the house to come back to. I realized I didn't have roots here any more, they'd all been pulled up and discarded.'

'And your friends? They were still here, but *they* were discarded by *you*. What was the reason for that? I was still here.'

'What was the point in trying to find a place for myself? You've reached the heights and still climbing. I'm so proud of you, Shirley, but like everyone else, you've left me behind.'

'I'm still here,' she repeated. 'Still waiting for you to start building your dreams.'

'I don't want to hold you to any promises, not now. I'd hold you back and you deserve more than that.'

'Oh, I've done with climbing. I turned down the offers I had in London, I lack the determination and what an agent called "fire in my belly", and I'm content to be a small fish, like that one you've just caught and reprieved, a small fish in a small pool, that's me.'

Freddy packed up his gear and together they walked along the river bank towards the sloping field leading to the wood. He looked at the steep climb and turned away. She would find it a struggle to walk home. 'Let's catch the bus, eh? I think we have some talking to do.' When he helped her over the stile at the road bridge, she didn't move away from him. Their eyes met and he threw down his encumbrances and kissed her, holding her close as though he would never let her go.

Cassie opened the door to an impatient knock. She had received a typed letter from a Mr Davy, asking if she had a vacancy for a lodger, and whether he might see the room. She had replied telling him the room was offered to women only, but their letters must have crossed as a second letter arrived telling her he would call on Sunday afternoon to view the room.

Standing on her doorstep was Joseph. Her heart leapt but she said, 'Sorry, but you can't come in, I'm expecting someone.'

'A Mr Davy?' he asked with a crooked grin. 'Sorry for the deception but I thought it was the only way to be sure you'd open the door.'

'What d'you want?' she demanded.

'Please, Cassie, I want to come home.'

'No chance of that!'

'You make the rules. Just as a lodger if that's what you want, but please let me come home. I've been a fool and I don't blame you for not trusting me, but I nearly got sent to prison and there's nothing more sobering than that, believe me. That brings everything into clear focus. Please, Cassie. Let me at least come in and talk about it.'

With relief in her heart disguised by the stony expression on her face, she opened the door wide. He darted around the corner and came back with two suitcases and staggered in to drop them in the hall.

'No further,' she said. 'And it's only temporary, until you find something else, right?'

Joseph smiled abjectly, humility and shame showing in his eyes when she looked at him. A foot in the door, that was the hardest part; persuading her to take him back was going to be easy.

When Cassie told Alice later, Alice said, 'This time, make sure he marries you!'

To Maude's dismay, her marriage to Reggie had to be postponed. He was still in hospital on the day they were to have walked down the aisle, with a grieving Maude sitting at his bedside.

'Everybody's getting married except us,' she said with a sigh.

'First for fussy, last for lucky,' he said. 'Ours will be the best. You'll be the most beautiful bride and me the luckiest man.'

'You're right. Being first isn't important; it's marrying the right one.'

When Shirley and Freddy told Hetty and Bleddyn they were going to marry, there seemed to be only one way to celebrate.

'We'll have a street party,' Hetty said. 'No more scrimpy meals and economy wedding cakes. The street will enjoy the third and last celebration.'

Rations had been cut again, the large loaf had been cut by four ounces and there was talk of bread being rationed later in the year. Most of the precious food luxuries women had kept for special occasions had been used up on V.E. and V.J. celebrations; there was little to create a party atmosphere, but they did it.

Out came the old piano and a wind-up gramophone with a pile of records. A bonfire was lit on the field opposite the house and potatoes were scrubbed ready for baked potatoes.

'Although why we scrub them before putting them in the ashes, and then eat them, charcoal, soot an' all, I'll never know,' Marged complained.

A happy Eirlys was there with Ken, and her father with the three boys. The newly wed Constable Charlie Grove and his wife, Madge, came, and Mrs Chapel from the flower shop, with Maldwyn and Delyth. Bernard came on the horse and cart with Peter, Beth and their son, plus old Sally Gough, who wore a frivolous hat that hadn't seen daylight since 1903, and nearly caught fire when she went to retrieve a potato from the fire.

Shirley had received an anonymous gift of twelve cups and saucers. Each one different, every one beautiful. She knew they were from Andy but said nothing. Wherever he was, she hoped he was happy.

Unseen in the street filled with the Castle family and all their friends and a number of strangers attracted to the noise and made welcome, Andy stood in the shadows and watched the others having fun. The singing as always began with humorous songs from the music hall but as the evening ended they became more and more sentimental. Couples sat close together as they sang romantic melodies, the words having special meanings with the long separations still fresh in their minds: 'Let Me Call You Sweetheart, I'm In Love With You' and 'You Made Me Love You' being among the perennial favourites.

A cloud of melancholy settled over Andy as the mood of the evening changed. In the shadows was where he belonged and he couldn't foresee that ever changing. That's where he would spend his life; watching from dark corners. His uncontrollable need for excitement, for taking a risk, created a life that was impossible to share. He slipped away as the mood again changed and enthusiastic dancers began to dance to 'Knees up, Mother Brown' and ended with the now traditional conga.

Shirley smiled at Freddy and asked, 'Remember you saying everyone had moved on and there was no place for you? Look around. This is your town. All these people are friends, tomorrow is going to be a wonderful day, for us both.'

Happily, Freddy agreed.

*　　*　　*

The season began just as it always had. Marged looked down at the families covering the sand, making the scene a colourful patchwork with discarded clothes and bright towels, and buckets and spades, and windmills and sunhats. The mothers trying to keep all their belongings within a small circle, fussing over the children, making a tiny part of the beach their own for the afternoon.

Children slipped into bathing costumes – still called 'dippers' by the locals – and shrieked as they danced down to where the waves touched their toes.

Many families were complete now, Marged noticed, with fathers and brothers as well as grandfathers sharing the pleasures of the sunny sandy bay, although, for some there would always be an empty place, like Bleddyn, who had lost his son, Taff.

Behind her Huw, Hetty and Myrtle, plus a newly re-appointed Netta, were preparing for afternoon teas. Down below her on the sands, she saw a couple of young men setting out deckchairs for hire. Bleddyn had left them to get the chip shop ready for opening; Johnny and Eynon were brushing sand off the signs advertising rides. One day soon, Bleddyn would get out his boat and offer trips around the bay. In spite of the continuing shortages, things were getting back to normal.

On the glass door of the cafe, the faded verse which had been painted there so long ago by her grandparents, Joseph and Harriet Piper, had been rewritten by the sign-writer, Will Bowler. It told visitors all that St David's Well Bay had to offer. Only the name had changed. The names and memories of Molly and Joseph Piper had faded and been replaced by the Castles.

> *Teas for trippers, donkeys and dippers*
> *Sunhats, hoopla and tides*
> *Castle's kingdom, cloths of fresh gingham*
> *Fortunes, windmills and rides.*